D1464327

PRIMAL CUT

PRIMAL CUT

ED O'CONNOR

Allison & Busby Limited
13 Charlotte Mews
London W1T 4EJ
www.allisonandbusby.com

Hardcover published in Great Britain in 2007
This paperback edition published in 2008

A CIP catalogue record for this book is available from
the British Library.

10 9 8 7 6 5 4 3 2 1

ISBN 978-0-7490-8024-2

Typeset in 10.5/14 pt Sabon by
Terry Shannon

Printed and bound in the UK by
CPI Bookmarque, Croydon, CR0 4TD

ED O'CONNOR studied History at Cambridge University before moving over to Oxford University to take an MPhil in International Relations. He then worked in London and New York as an investment banker but left to concentrate on his writing. In 2002 his first novel, *The Yeare's Midnight*, was published by Constable and Robinson and was followed in 2003 by *Acid Lullaby*, both of which were shortlisted for awards. Now working as the Head of the History department at a local school, Ed lives in Maidstone, Kent, with his wife and two young daughters.

Also by Ed O'Connor

The Yeare's Midnight
Acid Lullaby

For Esme & Isabel
with love

Contents

PITUITARY PUREE

1.

Leyton, East London
December 1995

Common wisdom remembered brain paste. The old
ladies of Silvertown would tell you. The porters at
Smithfield market would tell you. No doctor would
tell you, but what do they know? Any idiot can read
a book. And knowledge is not the same as wisdom.

Cockney women used to mash up the pituitary
glands of cows and smear the paste on toast. They
said it helped people with mental illness, that it
made their minds more alert. In the days before the
National Health Service and the pick and mix drug
cocktails of modern psychiatric healthcare, such
remedies were commonplace in the East End. Ideas
spread by chatter in the doorways of terraced
houses and the corners of gloomy pubs, through
anecdotes and recipes: mother to daughter, father to
son.

Science had failed the Garrods. To Bartholomew,
the brain paste was a desperate measure. Although
it had its compensations: when mashed up with

boiled potatoes, milk and oil it tasted vaguely of corned beef. He hoped the strange pituitary chemistry would help his brother's screaming fits, his lapses of memory and behaviour. Raymond's outbursts were making him a liability and his prescription pills were useless. Bartholomew knew that his brother needed full time care but refused to have him committed. Besides, the government were closing psychiatric hospitals across the country – he had researched the subject. Ray would have to be cared for in the community.

Bartholomew tried to be optimistic. This new mash was stronger, more concentrated than his previous efforts. And the pituitary glands it contained were not only taken from cows.

'Put your bib on Ray. I don't want no mess today.'

'Yes Bollamew,' said Raymond Garrod, unable to enunciate the complexities of his brother's name. 'Ah ate some bit of this mash before I think.'

'This is better mash – stronger mash.'

Bartholomew Garrod used a serving spoon to scoop a large serving of mash for his brother. Ray's eyes glowed with excitement as the grey pile of food slapped onto the plate in front of him. Ray ate happily, oil running down his chin.

'Delicious Bollamew,' Ray grinned between mouthfuls.

Watching his brother eat made Bartholomew hungry himself. He felt a sudden desire for steak. He left his brother at the table and headed down the narrow staircase to the rear of his butcher's shop. He pulled back the handle on the door of the freezer and turned on the light.

An hour previously, he had placed some unsold beefsteaks on a shelf at the back of the freezer. They were still soft. He picked the largest he could find and licked the cold surface of the meat. The tang of beef blood was unmistakeable. Beef was his favourite. Beef was noble. He drew strength from it. Chicken flesh gave him speed and flexibility. Pork gave him cunning. Beef gave him power.

Lying against the wall of the freezer was the decapitated body of the woman he had killed. Most of her blood had ebbed down the drainage duct at the centre of the freezer room although some had frozen around her. Bartholomew looked at the body wondering what to do. He had always been surrounded by death. She was just another carcass, albeit a headless one. He realised that her continued presence in his freezer was becoming problematic. The council often did spot checks on butcher's shops. Their inspectors could close down disreputable establishments and he did not want to sully the good name of 'Garrods Family Butchers'. Besides, it was probably unhygienic.

He slammed the freezer door shut and returned upstairs.

Common wisdom remembered brain paste and other horrors too. It also recalled saucy Jack cutting the whores of Whitechapel and the murder of Jack the Hat. Common wisdom remembered the firestorm of September 1940 that incinerated hundreds on the Silvertown Way. It recounted the 'Bermondsey Horror' and the crimes of John Christie.

Now there was another story to tell.

The Leyton Ripper was murdering people for their meat.

DOGFIGHT

2.

Wednesday, 9th October 2002
Balehurst, Cambridgeshire

It had been a brutal fight. For nearly thirty minutes the two Staffordshire bull terriers had snarled and torn into each other. Now Rampage was dead and the gathering was breaking up. Keith Gwynne climbed over the makeshift wooden boarding into the fighting ring. The area was about twenty feet in diameter and divided into two halves by a scratch line made from silver masking tape. The floor of the fight ring was covered in rotting carpet. This gave the dogs extra grip.

Gwynne knelt on the carpet next to the dead body of his dog. Rampage had fought poorly to begin with. The large ring and the screaming audience had unsettled the dog. It had backed away from the line, uncertain and angry. Gwynne had wondered for a moment if his new fighter would be 'up to scratch'. However, once their handlers had left the ring, the two dogs had fought with unbridled ferocity. Its money-making potential aside, Gwynne believed there was something fundamentally beautiful about dogfighting. In his sterile world of supermarkets and televisions, carrier bags and speed cameras, the bloody savagery of his hobby reminded him he was still alive.

Rampage had acquitted himself well. Eventually, the superior fitness of Bob Woollard's pit bull had proved to be the difference between the two animals. Woollard's dogs had a well-deserved reputation as 'stayers': they were better trained and better fed than most of their competitors. Gwynne lifted the heavy carcass of his dog into a black dustbin bag.

'He was a game little bastard in the end then?' Bob Woollard observed from the other side of the fence. 'Thought he was going to piss himself to start with.'

Gwynne tied the bag and looked up. 'The lights freaked him out. All these people. This was his first fight in the ring. He's done a few small contests but nothing in a ring as big as this one.'

'He was game though,' Woollard conceded. 'Gave old Gizmo a good scrap.' Gizmo was Woollard's favourite dog: a prize fighter worth over a thousand pounds.

'Win some, lose some.' Gwynne tried not to let his disappointment show. 'I suppose you want paying then?'

'You're a gentleman, Keith.' Woollard clambered

over the wooden boarding to collect his 'purse'.

'Four hundred right?'

'That'll do nicely.'

Gwynne pulled a roll of banknotes from his jacket pocket and peeled off the requisite amount. 'If we carry on like this I might have to get a proper job.'

'Now that would be a first!' Woollard grinned. 'Times are hard for all of us Keith. How much income tax did you and your pikey pals pay last year? Sometimes I feel that I'm funding the whole British Government on my own.'

'Don't make me laugh. You bloody farmers are raking it in,' Gwynne grunted.

'You reckon?'

'Of course. The bloody EEC pays you not to farm these days. Whatever genetically modified crap that you do manage to produce, it buys off you!'

Woollard shrugged. 'It's the "European Union", Einstein, and do you think I'd be buggering around with the likes of you if I was creaming it in from the Common Agricultural Policy? I've got significant overheads.'

'Haven't we all?' Gwynne finished counting out his money and slapped the wad into Woollard's extended hand. 'I've lost my best dog and four hundred quid.'

Woollard looked at Gwynne for a second, feeling

an unexpected pang of sympathy. 'The problem with you pikeys is that you haven't got no system.'

'System?'

Woollard lit a cigarette. 'Take old Rampage there. He was a mean little sod when he got going. He showed courage. He had potential.'

'Not anymore.'

'And that's because you didn't bring him on right. There was a stage in that fight when he was getting on top but he faded. That's your fault not the dog's.'

'How come?'

'What do you train him on?'

'You mean other animals?'

'Yeah.'

'He's fought some other dogs.'

'Let me guess. You warmed him up on a couple of poodles and a cocker-fucking-spaniel. I bet you nicked some asthmatic domestic pet that was so fat it couldn't even clean its own arsehole.'

Gwynne shifted uneasily. Woollard was uncannily close to the truth. 'What does it matter how you bring them on?'

'A professional boxer doesn't spar against hairdressers, mate. They train. You got to work your dog. Build his stamina. Train him at fight intensity. It's the only way to make money in this game.'

'I suppose so.'

'Come with me, leave that thing here.' Woollard left the ring and gestured for Gwynne to follow. The two men made their way through the chattering crowd of drinkers – Woollard's friends and farm employees – that had watched the fight. They left the barn then crossed the stable yard to the main farm building. In the hallway was a large wooden cupboard leaning awkwardly against the side of the staircase. Gwynne assumed it was some tasteless family heirloom. However, as always Woollard was full of surprises. The farmer heaved the cupboard to one side revealing a door in the panelling behind it. Woollard unlocked it and took Gwynne inside, leading him downstairs to the basement.

'Here you are mate,' Woollard said as he turned on the light. 'Perfect preparation prevents piss-poor performance.'

Inside were five cages. Two contained Staffordshire bull terriers, next to them were two American pit bulls. The final cage held a large, menacing Tosa. The dogs began to bark furiously. Gwynne looked around the room. There was a long shelf along the back wall that held a number of video boxes, marked with dates and locations. He picked up one that was annotated 'Gizmo, Essex June 2002'.

'I try to video the fights,' Woollard observed. 'It's

a good training resource. Sometimes people like to buy them as a souvenir.'

'Did you video tonight?'

'One of my boys did. Want to buy a copy?'

'No thanks.' Gwynne moved to the centre of the room. 'Is this a treadmill?'

'Yep. It's for training the dogs. Stamina building. Stick them on that for two hours a day. Makes them hard as nails.'

Gwynne shook his head. He realised that Woollard was right. The man had a 'system'. Rampage and Gwynne's other contenders had been fighting beyond their class. 'Is that why the fighting ring is so big then? Is that because you know your dogs have better stamina?'

'Partly.' Woollard thought for a moment, wondering how far to admit Gwynne into his confidence. 'I don't just fight dogs there though.'

'What? You mean you run some bare knuckle too?'

'Sometimes. You fancy yourself as a welterweight then, Gwynne?'

'Do me a favour. I couldn't punch a bus ticket.'

'As I thought. Shall we depart then?' Woollard showed Gwynne the open door. 'The lesson has ended. By the way, tell anyone what you've seen in here and your remains will end up fertilising my crops.'

Gwynne was thoughtful as they returned to the barn. He had a fertile, creative mind, particularly where money was concerned.

'Do you fight the Tosa very often?' he asked Woollard, referring to the Japanese fighting dog he had seen in the basement.

'Rarely. Conspicuous breed. If you've got American pit bulls you can pass them off as Irish bull terriers or some other bollocks. A Tosa is distinctive. There's not many of them about.'

'I suppose there'd be good money in staging that. Unusual fight, eh?'

Woollard smiled. 'Don't tell me you've got a Tosa?'

'No, but I might know someone. He's got a Tosa just like yours. It's an older dog but it could still do a job. I'm thinking maybe I could organise something for you.'

'Out of the kindness of your heart?'

'Obviously not.'

Woollard frowned. 'I don't know. I'm not big on getting strangers involved.'

'What if I could spice it up for you? Maybe do it as a double header?'

'You've lost me.'

'This guy I know. He's an ex-fighter himself. Big, hard bastard. Maybe we could fight the Tosas then have a bare knuckle afterwards.'

Woollard suddenly showed a flicker of interest. 'How heavy is he, this mate of yours?'

'Eighteen stone – maybe more.'

Woollard cupped his hands to his mouth and called over to one of the group of drinkers standing at the entrance to the barn. 'Oi! Lefty! Get over here.'

A huge farm labourer looked up and wandered over. Lefty Shaw was a notorious local hard man. Gwynne knew him by reputation. Shaw revelled in his title as 'the hardest man in Balehurst'.

'What's up boss?' he asked Woollard, towering over the two men.

'We might have a fight for you, Lefty. Gwynney here reckons he knows a contender.'

'That right?' Shaw stared down at Gwynne. 'I hope he's bigger than you mate.'

Gwynne tried not to be intimidated. 'He's not as tall as you but I'd say he's heavier. Got a neck like a fucking tree trunk. He's got some form. He told me he used to do pub fights in London.'

'How old is he?' Woollard asked.

'Mid-fifties.'

Shaw laughed a heavy, humourless laugh. 'Old age pensioner!'

'He's a mean bastard. Trust me. It'd be worth your while.'

Woollard had heard enough. 'All right. Speak to your mate. Let's say a purse of five hundred for the dogs and a grand for the bare knuckle.'

'What's my cut for organising it?'

'How about I give you back a ton from tonight's purse?'

Gwynne nodded his agreement.

'I'll expect to hear from you then,' Woollard said. 'Don't forget to take your dog with you.'

Gwynne retrieved Rampage and slung the remains into the back of his car. He checked his watch. It was just after 10 p.m. If he hustled, he could be in Heydon before closing time. He had a proposition to put to George Norlington, the bed and breakfast tenant at the Dog and Feathers. His old Fiat threw shaky beams of light onto the farm trackway and turned out onto the main road.

From a concealed position behind a hedgerow, DI Mike Bevan watched the car leave the farm and noted down its licence plate. He had been forced to move from his observation point opposite the farm courtyard about an hour previously. Bob Woollard didn't just own fighting dogs. He also owned a Rottweiler guard dog. This formidable animal caught his scent on the wind and had begun barking furiously in his direction. Fortunately, the dog was chained up and its owner engaged inside the barn. Nonetheless, the unwelcome attention had forced Bevan to relocate. Unable to gain photographs of the activities taking place within the barn, he contented himself with taking the licence plates of all those in attendance. The clock was ticking on Bob Woollard. Bevan was building a case that he hoped would put the farmer away for a long time.

3.

The Dog and Feathers was busy for a Wednesday night. The pub was trying hard to attract a wealthier clientele: young couples and families that bought dinner and bottles of wine rather than just pints. Some of the old locals found the pub's change of character disconcerting. As a new arrival, George Norlington couldn't care less. He sat in a corner of the pub quietly studying the *Cambridge Evening News* and the *New Bolden Gazette*. Keith Gwynne saw him immediately.

'George! My old mate. How are you?'

The man he knew as George Norlington looked at him. 'What do you want?'

'What are you reading?'

'I'm reading about a psychiatric hospital as it happens. Which is where I should be put after buying that miserable, broken down excuse for a van off your mate.'

Gwynne sensed hatred in Norlington. He

desperately didn't want to upset the man. 'Let me buy you a drink. I've got a business proposition.'

'I've got a pint. Say what you have to say then piss off.'

Nervous, Gwynne outlined the details of the double header. Norlington listened quietly.

'I don't like to fight the dog no more. He's getting old,' Norlington observed.

'It's big money, George. You don't want to live in a grotty flat behind a pub forever, do you?'

Norlington stared at Gwynne blankly. 'It's a temporary arrangement. I won't be up here for long.'

'You can make fifteen hundred quid for a night's work. That has got to be worth your time.'

'I'll think about it.'

Gwynne noticed Norlington's massive, rough hands resting on the newspapers. His fingertips were stained red, dark lines of dried blood had collected under his nails. Norlington was a huge man. A shade under six feet tall with short greying hair but still powerfully built with heavy arms and a bull neck.

'I think you'd win the bare knuckle,' Gwynne continued. 'Lefty Shaw is a big lad but he's thicker than pig shit. You'd have the edge of experience.'

Norlington downed the remains of his pint and stood up. 'Saturday suits me. You arrange the details. I'm in here Friday night. Come find me then.'

'Understood.' Gwynne watched Norlington push his way out of the pub. A few bumped drinkers turned angrily but bit their lips when they saw the size of the man barging past them. Smiling, Gwynne made his own way to the bar and ordered a pint of Stella Artois lager.

George Norlington walked across the pub garden to the door of the small flat he was renting. His Tosa dog barked and leapt at him as he entered the hallway. It scurried excitedly around his feet. Norlington made his way into the little bed-sitting room. The room was crowded and dirty, piled high with old newspapers and dirty clothes. He ordered the dog to sit down in the cardboard box it slept in and fell back on to his uncomfortable bed. George chewed over the offer Gwynne had made. It was risky. He had tried to remain as inconspicuous as possible since arriving in Cambridgeshire a few months previously. A prize fight with an audience could be problematic. However, fifteen hundred pounds was a great deal of money. It was enough to pay for a false passport when his actions made such a thing necessary. He reached into the back pocket of his trousers and withdrew a folded piece of newspaper. Carefully, in the dim yellow light of his claustrophobic little room, George Norlington unfurled the page. It was a newspaper cutting from the *East London Advertiser*. He stared at the words for some time, unable to go to sleep.

4.

Thursday, 10th October 2002

At 4 p.m. the following afternoon, DI Alison Dexter emerged from Peterborough Crown Court, blinking into the sunlight. The trial had been an arduous process: the culmination of five months of intensive police work. She had been the fulcrum of the investigation and it had drained her stamina. Dexter wondered for a moment if this was how the future would be: with each case more demanding and exhausting than its predecessor. She buried the thought before it had a chance to infect her.

At the foot of the steps was a small group of journalists and a local television news camera crew. Dexter disliked the public exposure that sometimes accompanied her job. She usually shunned press conferences, preferring to delegate to more junior officers. Seeing her image on TV or in the newspapers embarrassed her. More importantly, it made her vulnerable. Dexter always tried to resist the opportunity to raise her head above the parapet. However, on this occasion, contact was unavoidable. George Gardiner from the *New Bolden Echo* recognised her first.

'Sergeant Dexter!' he barked. 'Can we have a quick word?'

Dexter stopped opposite him and tried to smile. 'It's Inspector now, George. Maybe you'd get promoted too if you got your facts right.'

Gardiner grinned. 'Could you give us a comment on the case please? You must be happy with the outcome.'

Dexter shifted uneasily as a local BBC news crew swung their camera towards her. 'I can read you our official statement. "New Bolden CID is delighted with this verdict. Nicholas Braun, of Gorton Row, Peterborough, is a danger to women and we hope that tomorrow's sentencing will reflect the gravity of his offences".' Dexter had been planning her statement as she left the courtroom – she was rather pleased with its fluency.

'Could you comment on the nature of Mr Braun's offences,' Gardiner continued, 'and perhaps explain how you caught him?'

'I won't comment on the assaults specifically other than to say that they were brutal attacks carried out on women in their own homes. Explaining how we identified Mr Braun is a little complicated. Read the court transcripts. It's all in there.' Dexter tried to move through the group but her path was blocked. Still the TV camera bore into the side of her face.

'Inspector Dexter,' asked a female journalist with a microphone, 'Suzy James from BBC East. Is it true that you took DNA samples from an entire factory in New Bolden?'

'It's certainly true that we confirmed Mr Braun was the rapist using DNA sampling,' Dexter nodded.

'What would you say was the turning point in the investigation?' Suzy James continued.

Dexter took a deep breath. 'Two women raped by Braun had been shopping on the afternoons they were attacked at the Hypermarket on Argyll Street, New Bolden. Both were followed as they drove home. Braun attacked them as they unlocked the doors to their homes and pushed them inside.'

'You said in court that the timing of the two attacks was a vital clue?'

Dexter winced at the corny expression, recognising suddenly that Suzy James was never likely to win a Pulitzer Prize. 'Both attacks took place between 1 and 2 p.m. on weekdays. That led us to believe that the perpetrator worked nearby and was opportunistically attacking women during his lunch break.'

'Why couldn't any of the victims identify him?' Gardiner interjected.

'If you were in court, George, you'd know he wore a mask.'

'Yeah,' Gardiner sniffed, 'you said he wore the mask of a cartoon character. Can you tell us which one?'

Dexter shook her head. 'No. It's an unnecessary detail that you will sensationalise.'

'How did you identify the killer's place of work?' James asked.

'Our forensic analysis showed tiny fragments of copper on the victims. Microscopic amounts. Research showed us that it was the type used in complex electronic components. That led us to look for engineering companies in the immediate vicinity of Argyll Street. As you probably know, there's only one. We took a chance and DNA tested all the employees of that company.'

'Was the company Meredian Components?' asked Gardiner.

'Yes.'

'Did Braun give his sample voluntarily?' another journalist asked.

'Eventually.'

Dexter noticed that Nicholas Braun's brother Henry was staring at her from the other side of the road, unseen by the journalists. She had seen him in court glaring at her when she had given evidence. His neatly pressed white shirt seemed incongruous with his savagely shaved head.

'Are you linking Braun with any other unsolved sexual offences in the area?' James asked.

Dexter looked directly at her. 'Braun's been found guilty of three rapes and nine indecent assaults. At the moment we have no reason to link him with any other cases.'

'Did you interview Nicholas Braun's wife during your investigation?' queried Gardiner.

'We did.'

'Did she know about her husband's behaviour?' he continued.

'No, she didn't,' Dexter lied. 'I have to go now. New Bolden CID will make a formal statement after sentencing tomorrow.'

Dexter finally pushed through the pack of reporters. A TV camera followed her across the main road to her car, which was parked in Draper Street – a narrow side road. As she sank gratefully into the driver's seat of her Mondeo, feeling the weariness rising behind her eyes, Dexter saw that the news pack had now surrounded Henry Braun. He seemed to be enjoying his new celebrity status. Dexter had suspected him of involvement in his brother's crimes but had been unable to prove it. She tried not to feel frustrated: putting Nicholas

Braun away had been a satisfactory result.

The car roared to life as Dexter accelerated out of Peterborough and headed south towards New Bolden and she realised that for the first time in months she was free of cases: that she had a second to reflect. She opened the driver's side window and allowed the bitterly cold East Anglian air to wash over her. It served a purpose. As she drove into the outskirts of New Bolden twenty minutes later, Dexter felt as if the brutalities of Nicholas Braun and the stresses of the trial had been, for the most part, blown out of the back of her head.

She decided not to return to the police station. A free evening was an increasingly rare commodity for Alison Dexter and she resolved to make the most of it. First she would go to the gym, then buy a bottle of red wine and crash in front of her video of 'Guns 'N Roses Live at Wembley'.

5.

Fifteen miles away, Keith Gwynne finalised the arrangements for Saturday's double-header with Bob Woollard. The Tosas would fight at 9.30 p.m. The main event would follow shortly afterwards.

'I don't want your boy crying off,' Woollard stressed over the phone. 'If he does, then you are responsible for covering the purse.'

The thought made Gwynne's heart flutter briefly. 'He'll be there, Bob.'

'Good. He better be as good as you say he is. I have a very select audience coming to this one. If Lefty flattens him in the first ten seconds we might have to put you in the ring to kill some time.'

'I'm telling you, Bob, this bloke will be a handful. He's fucking enormous. You should see the size of his hands.'

'Doesn't mean he's got a good chin though – just because he's a monster. I've seen a lot of fat lads peg out the first time they ride a proper punch.'

'This bloke isn't fat. Trust me, Bob.'

Woollard laughed at the thought. 'That will be the day, Gwynney.'

Gwynne paused for a moment, choosing his next words carefully. 'Bob, you know that hundred notes you promised me for sorting this one for you?'

'I do but don't think you're getting any more.'

'I know. I know. I was wondering if you're interested in wagering it.'

'You never learn do you, Keith? Go on then, what are you after?'

'A simple bet. I'll stick the hundred on my boy to beat Lefty. You offer me some odds. If I win, you pay me the stake plus the odds. If I lose, you don't have to pay me at all.'

'How can I offer odds on a fighter I've never seen?' Woollard asked.

'You're confident old Lefty can do the business, aren't you?'

'He's never let me down before,' Woollard mused. 'OK. I'll offer you evens on your boy knocking out Lefty.'

'That's not very generous. You just said he's never been beaten!'

'Take it or fucking leave it.'

'I'll take it.'

Gwynne put the phone down and wondered if he had done the right thing. In some ways Woollard was right: he was a mug punter, betting had gripped him like an infectious disease. He could never resist an opportunity to chuck away his money. On the other hand, two weeks previously he had seen George Norlington labouring at a local farm; throwing 100kg sacks of cattle feed and scarcely breaking sweat. That sight had awed him at the time. Now it gave him great confidence.

6.

At 5.45 p.m. an exhausted Alison Dexter gave up on the cycling machine that she had occupied for the previous twenty minutes. The gym was crowded and, tiredness apart, she was beginning to find the drifting, invasive eyes of men tiresome. Furthermore, the machines were starting to bore her. She decided to give up.

After a quick shower, Dexter walked into the lobby of the sports centre and bought herself a Lucozade from a drinks dispenser. As she drank from the cold bottle, she became aware of shouting from the main sports hall. Interested, she climbed a flight of stairs to the main viewing gallery and took a seat. A five-a-side football match was taking place between two female teams. Dexter quickly realised that it was actually a five versus four match as one of the teams seemed to be missing a striker. Dexter loved football. A refugee from East London she had the game – and West Ham United Football Club – in her blood. That was only one of the reasons she found her attention fixed on a particular player: a blonde woman wearing the latest West Ham shirt.

The match was of a reasonable standard. Dexter began to think that this might be a better form of exercise than pounding away at a cycling machine in front of MTV. She glugged at her Lucozade and wondered if her motives were appropriate.

As the game scuttled to a close at 6 p.m. and the players began to head for the changing rooms, Dexter tossed her empty bottle away and walked down from the viewing gallery. The girl in the West Ham shirt was waiting for her at the foot of the stairs.

'Don't suppose you play do you?' she asked in a strong London accent.

'I'm sorry?' Dexter replied uncertainly.

'We're always a player short. I saw you watching. I thought you might be interested.'

Dexter's eyes drifted and evaded. 'I haven't played for a while.'

'Don't matter. It's about having a laugh.'

Dexter nodded. 'I see you're a Hammers fan.'

'Born and bred. Yourself?'

'The same.'

'No way!'

'I'm from Walthamstow originally,' Dexter said, warming to her theme. 'Then I lived in Leyton.'

'Whereabouts?'

'Wilmot Road.'

'You are joking me?'

'No.'

'I grew up on Dawlish Road.'

'By the primary school?'

'I went there as a kid. I'm Kelsi, by the way. Kelsi Hensy.'

'Alison Dexter.'

There was an awkward moment as the two women considered the peculiar coincidences. Kelsi broke the silence.

'So can we expect you next week? We can have a

drink afterwards. Talk West Ham and stuff.'

Dexter thought for a second. 'Yeah. I'd like that.'

'5 p.m. meet here. We play on Mondays and Thursdays,' Kelsi smiled. 'Bring your shin pads. It gets a bit tasty sometimes.'

'See you then.'

'I look forward to it,' said Kelsi Hensy as she pushed open the door of the women's changing room.

Dexter left the sports centre hurriedly, afraid that she had exposed some terrible vulnerability, afraid that logic might suddenly catch up with her in the car park.

7.

DI John Underwood sat in a meeting room on the first floor of New Bolden police station. He looked out at the scrap of lawn and the forlorn-looking hedgerow that enclosed the station perimeter. A group of birds dropped and twisted across his field of vision, playing in the air, illuminated by electric light. The image made him smile: it was reassuring that a pointless universe could still permit pointless enjoyment. However, that same universe had given him a lump on the underside of his ribcage – a lump that he feared was far from pointless.

The door opened and DI Mike Bevan from Scotland Yard's Special Operations Executive stepped inside.

'John! I'm so sorry to keep you waiting.'

'No problem. I've been bird watching.'

Maybe it was just gristle.

'Your photocopier must have been designed by Fred Flintstone. It's taken twenty minutes to copy ten pages.'

Underwood gestured for Bevan to join him at the table. 'So how was your night in the undergrowth? Make any new friends?'

'Just a Rottweiler the size of a pit pony.'

Bevan handed over the folder he had spent the previous half hour trying to copy. Underwood opened it. Inside were a handful of gloomy photographs and Bevan's typed report of his activities. Underwood considered one of the photographs: it showed a group of men in discussion outside a barn.

'Recognise any of them?' Bevan asked.

'Bob Woollard obviously,' Underwood commented, 'but you knew that already.' He turned to another image that showed a slightly built man dropping a dustbin bag into the boot of his car. 'This could be a little twat called Keith Gwynne. I can't make out any of the others.'

'I ran a DVLA check on the car. It does belong to

a Keith Gwynne. Address 3 Simpson Road, Balehurst. That's an old council property. I checked and Gwynne doesn't live there any more.'

'I know Gwynne. He's a pikey. A slippery customer. Always on the make. He sells, he thieves, he gambles. We arrested him two years ago for selling hooky video recorders. Got a fine and a suspended sentence if memory serves me. Frankly, I'm not surprised to see his ugly mug there. Dog fighting is right up his grotty little alley. Try the gypsy site on the other side of Balehurst. I bet he's living there with all the other detritus.'

'Will do. What do you know about Woollard?'

Underwood sat back in his chair. 'He is a different animal altogether. I checked his file after our initial conversations. He was arrested at a cockfight outside Cambridge in 1992. He got a warning and a fine. There was no suggestion that he had either organised the event or that he owned either of the birds. Next time he crossed our radar screen was for drunk driving last year. He's divorced which doesn't surprise me. We heard rumours that he beat up on his missus but she wouldn't support an investigation.'

Bevan nodded. 'We first heard about him in connection with a different case. We were looking at a syndicate based in Ireland that was exporting horses illegally to the UK. In 2001, the RSPCA had complaints that Woollard was mistreating his horses. Tying them up, not feeding them properly. Problem was that whenever they turned up, there was no sign of anything. It's like he knew they were coming.'

'There is a diabolical cunning about the bloke, that's for sure,' Underwood nodded. 'He acts the dumb innocent but he's bloody clued up about his rights. Why did the RSPCA contact you?'

'Two reasons. Firstly, they are constrained legally. They have limited powers under legislation. My group has a bit more latitude. Secondly, one of their inspectors visited his farm randomly six months ago. There was no one about. She had a snoop in his barn and found a big square of carpet on the floor. She thought she could see blood on the carpet but before she could check it out, Woollard turned up. He was abusive, pushed her around a bit, scared the shit out of her by the sounds of it. She claims he shoved her up against a wall and stuffed his hand down the front of her trousers. Nothing came of it though. Anyway, I made a connection between the Irish syndicate and Woollard. Once I started looking, I saw that he isn't just into maltreating horses.'

'Why is the carpet significant?'

'Experienced dog fighters sometimes use carpet in their fighting rings. It gives the dogs extra grip so that they can inflict more damage on the opponent. It makes it a more exciting spectacle.'

'And you can throw the carpet away after a fight,' Underwood added. 'Dispose of the blood evidence.'

'Absolutely,' Bevan agreed. 'Except it seems on this occasion Woollard got sloppy. That's when we got involved.'

'Have you got enough for us to go in with a warrant and strip the place?' Underwood asked.

'Not yet. These photos don't prove anything. I couldn't get any closer because of his sodding great Rottweiler shouting the place down.'

Underwood thought for a moment, then looked again at the picture of Keith Gwynne. 'He's the weak link. Gwynne is small time and not that intelligent. He is not a proper crook. We could pull him in and put the frighteners on him.'

'We'd have nothing concrete to work with. As soon as we let him out he'd be on the phone to Woollard and we'd have no chance of a result.' Bevan thought for a second. 'What other pies does Gwynne have his fingers in?'

Underwood shrugged. 'You name it. He does up old cars and flogs them. He used to drive around in a beaten up 1950s ambulance. Like I said, he's a chancer.'

'You said he was a gypsy?'

'That's right.'

Bevan scratched his head. 'Does he have ponies? Most of them do.'

'I'm not sure.'

'Let's check. If he does, I might have a way to get closer to him. I might need you to let me have a couple of plods for the day though.'

'Shouldn't be a problem. Now we've put this Braun character away, there should be some uniforms about who'd fancy hassling a pikey.'

'Good. I will drive up to Balehurst and have a look around. I'll try to become a familiar face.'

'Fine. I'll sort you two uniformed officers. How much can I tell them?'

'Bare minimum.'

'Understood.'

Bevan got up from the table and shook Underwood's hand. 'I appreciate your help, John.'

'To be honest, Mike, I'm happy to be involved. They don't give me anything substantial to work with these days.'

'The famous Inspector Dexter?'

'I'm flapping in her slipstream.'

'I've heard a bit about her. She was at the Met before? A bit of a ball breaker.'

Underwood smiled at the description, imagining Dexter's volcanic reaction if she had heard Bevan's comment. 'A victim of her own success,' he observed.

'I'll tread carefully,' Bevan winked at Underwood as he left the room.

Underwood suddenly felt bad for bantering about Dexter. She was too obvious a target for his frustration. That his protégée had outstripped him was disconcerting but, like Twain's self-made man, he had no one but himself to blame for his own lack of success. He looked out of the window at the scrappy station garden: a pool of light in the darkness.

The birds had gone.

8.

Alison Dexter's interview with Suzy James was screened on the BBC local news that night. Kelsi Hensy started with surprise as the image of her new football recruit appeared in front of her. She stopped eating her tea and listened much more carefully to the news than was her custom. Dexter looked uneasy in front of the camera, she thought; pretty though. Kelsi watched intently as the camera trailed Dexter's footsteps to her car. The screen then filled with the grim visage of Henry Braun whose large yellow teeth certainly weren't pretty.

'*This is a miscarriage of justice,*' Henry Braun snarled into the camera. '*My brother has been the victim of a witch-hunt by New Bolden CID. The behaviour of Inspector Dexter and her team has been a disgrace. They are arrogant bullies. An innocent man has been convicted today.'*

In a different part of Cambridgeshire, in his squalid room piled high with newspapers and smelling of dog food, George Norlington watched the news too.

9.

Friday, 11th October 2002

At 11.15 a.m. the following morning, Nicholas Braun was sentenced to twelve years imprisonment for three rapes and a string of indecent assaults. In the back of the crowded courtroom, Dexter clenched her right hand in triumph. The sentence had justified her efforts. After a moment's thought, she felt a terrible twist of guilt. Twelve years would mean little to Braun's victims: the women whose lives he had ruined. Dexter wondered how she had become so de-sensitised. Previously, she might have blamed her own brutal, lonely upbringing but over time had become bored with self-pity. Perhaps the job itself was hammering her emotions out of shape. She remembered how it had almost destroyed John Underwood. Maybe now her own personality was being re-fashioned. Dexter was uncertain of what she was changing into. The idea disturbed her.

She drove back to New Bolden police station in a curious mental state, for once forgetting her plans for the day. Her mind was focused on Kelsi Hensy and on the confusion of emotions that she engendered. Dexter was sliding. She had always tried to channel emotion, to dam it and draw intellectual energy from its controlled flow. And yet, that strategy had not worked: she was alone. Her appetite for information was her greatest strength and her greatest weakness. She needed it like some addictive drug. All her decisions were based on a cold evaluation of information. Dexter decided that she needed to know more about Kelsi Hensy.

Returning to New Bolden CID, Dexter nodded at John Underwood through the glass wall that separated their offices. She found the transparency intrusive and angled her computer screen away from Underwood's gaze. She logged in and, after a moment's delay while her system rebooted, accessed the Cambridgeshire police online records. Within a couple of minutes she had ascertained that no one called Kelsi Hensy possessed a criminal record.

Ashamed of herself, but driven on, Dexter tried an alternative but more obvious source of information. She ran an Internet search using 'Kelsi Hensy' as a search descriptor.

It produced twenty-seven search results. Dexter scanned through the list, her eyes eventually coming to rest on a headline from a computer trade magazine: 'ComBold appoints new Head of Communications'. Dexter double-clicked on the article and read carefully as it appeared on her screen.

'Cambridgeshire-based Internet security firm ComBold have appointed Kelsi Hensy, 34, as Director of Communications. This is an internal appointment. Ms Hensy previously worked in a junior capacity within the Communications Department.'

Dexter scrolled down the page. There was a small photograph of Kelsi Hensy sitting in her new office at ComBold next to her contact details. Dexter wrote them down on her blotter. There was a knock at her door; without looking up she quickly closed down her Internet connection and Kelsi Hensy's smiling face disappeared from her screen. When she looked up, Underwood was already in her office.

'Good result today then,' he ventured.

'Very. Good riddance to that toerag,' Dexter smiled back.

Underwood sensed guilt. Dexter never smiled. He

decided to let it go. 'I met with Mike Bevan yesterday.'

'Is he making progress?'

'Of sorts. He's asked for some resources.'

'Fine.'

Now Underwood was convinced that something was wrong. Dexter was fiercely protective of her departmental resources and yet she hadn't even queried his statement. He had been observing Dexter's personal life from a distance. He liked to think of it as taking an invisible responsibility for her. The bitter truth was he had nothing else to fill his dark imagination. Something had clearly upset her: he would endeavour to find out more.

10.

Leyton, East London
December 1995

To his surprise, Alan Moran found that he was still alive. He was aware of the cold first, his right side felt like stone. Then he remembered the pain. He was standing in the dark; leaning against what felt like a refrigerator wall. His unusual circumstances disorientated him. He tried to move but found that the pressure around his neck was being caused by some kind of leather strap – like a collar.

His eyes gradually adjusted to the darkness. A rope led from his collar upwards, disappearing into blackness. His hands were tied behind him. Alan resisted the urge to panic. He was ex-army. He tried to keep a cool head. His memories of the previous evening were scattered in the jumble of his semi-conscious brain. The nightclub had shut at two. He'd had a quick drink with a few of the other bouncers then walked down Church Road to the junction with Leyton High Road. He'd turned left up towards Midland Road Station. He remembered going under the rail bridge and smelling the stale piss of Leyton's tramps; he recalled the sound of a car door slamming. He had crossed the High Road and headed towards his flat in Abbots Park Road. There the trail of memories ended.

He wondered if he had offended someone important. Smashed up some little wanker outside the club without realising his importance. The East End had changed beyond recognition in his lifetime but there were still some toes you didn't tread on. Had he battered some relative of the Cowans'? Or the Moules'? Was this payback time? Alan strained against his bindings.

Suddenly, a terrible high-pitched screaming started outside the room. The noise intensified and was punctuated by the sound of a fist crashing against a steel door. Then Alan heard another voice: a man, remonstrative, half-threatening. The screaming suddenly stopped. A bolt slid back on the refrigerator door. The room was suddenly filled with electric light.

Ray Garrod ran straight up to Moran, jumping up and down in excitement.

'Give me the pen, Bollamew. Lemmee do the pen. You promised me.'

Alan Moran looked at the huge figure of Bartholomew Garrod standing in the doorway.

'Listen, mate,' he gasped against his collar, 'there's been some misunderstanding.'

Bartholomew stepped towards him. In close up, Alan half-recognised the huge, rutted face as it stared impassively back at him.

'I don't know who you work for but I've done nothing.' Alan now saw that he was in a huge refrigerator. Sides of beef and pork hung in neat lines next to him. There were sausages, chops and steaks on shelves around him.

Bartholomew Garrod didn't say anything. He handed his brother a permanent marker pen, taking care to remove the cap because he knew it posed problems for Ray. Scarcely able to contain his excitement, Ray Garrod grabbed Alan's head with his left hand. With his right he drew two diagonal lines across Alan's forehead. They intersected directly in the centre. Bartholomew watched his brother's careful artwork. Moran's crossed forehead now reminded him of the Scottish flag.

'What are you doing?' Moran spluttered in surprise and fear. He had done a tour in Northern Ireland. He had heard stories about what IRA snatch squads had done to Squaddies. He didn't want to lose an eye or his kneecaps or his bollocks.

Bartholomew Garrod brought up the poleaxe that he held in his right hand. It had a steel head fixed on a wooden shaft. The steel had been sharpened to a point. Bartholomew rested the point of the axe head on the intersection made by the lines on Moran's forehead.

'This won't hurt much. There are no nerves in your brain.'

With that, he drove the sharpened axe head straight through Moran's forehead. He held it in position for a few seconds, maybe ten, until the body eventually relaxed. Ray Garrod clapped happily as blood plopped gratifyingly onto the stone floor.

'That was an old-fashioned "stunning", Ray. We used a poleaxe but they have bolt guns for that now.' Bartholomew felt the impressive muscle bulk of Alan Moran's twitching body.

'A bolt gun?'

'That's right. They make a hole with the gun. But sometimes they have to pith it.'

'Pith it?'

'Yep. They feed a metal stick into the hole and scratch up the brains a bit. To make sure the animal is dead.' Bartholomew looked around for one of his meat knives. 'Now we have to bleed it you see. Blood has bad stuff in it so we drain that out then the meat will keep longer.'

Bartholomew Garrod made a vicious incision across the front of Moran's neck below his collar. The body was hanging forward in its harness and it began to haemorrhage impressively. Bartholomew slid a steel bucket under the blood flow to collect it.

'Blood's not all bad though, is it Ray?'

Ray was staring at the filling bucket. 'Why's that, Bollamew?'

'Well, we can make bread with it, can't we?'

'Blood bread.'

'That's right,' Bartholomew said. 'Seven parts rye flour, three parts blood. Very tasty it is too.'

'And black pudding, Bollamew, don't forget that.'

'We could make some blood sausage if you like.'

Bartholomew knew that the organs had to be removed in a specific order before he could remove the primal cuts. He would need to consult his 'Handbook of Meat' for that information. He had

decided to use the procedure for cattle: swine
slaughter was altogether more complicated.

He checked his watch. He had two hours
before he had to collect the day's stock from
Smithfield. They could dump the remains on the
way there.

Just beyond Bow Industrial Park is a deserted scrap
of land where the River Lea narrows. There's a
bridge that crosses the river, leading out onto Dace
Road. The Garrods parked their butcher's van on
that bridge at 5.30 a.m. It was a desolate spot,
bitterly exposed to the winds raking across
Stratford Marsh. A council notice fluttered on a
broken streetlight. The noise was unsettling to
Bartholomew Garrod. While Ray slept in the
passenger seat of the van, exhausted by the night's
excitement and weighed down with a heavy meal,
Bartholomew hauled two dustbin bags full of Alan
Moran from the back of his van. With an effort he
heaved them, one by one, off the edge of the bridge.
They splashed and sank without trace into the filthy
water.

Bartholomew paused to regain his composure.
His hot breath twisted in front of him. The notice
still fluttered. He ignored its irritating rattle and
climbed back inside his van. He would be a little bit
late for his Smithfield pick up; perhaps if he gunned

the engine and got lucky with the traffic, he could make up time.

Apparently meaningless moments can have disproportionate effects. An extra ten minutes in bed might make you run over the child you would otherwise have missed; reading your partner's emails might make you want to murder someone you've never met; watching a television programme might save your life.

Bartholomew Garrod made a mistake at 5.31 a.m. on the morning of 7ᵗʰ December 1995. He didn't read a council notice. The notice said that, as part of an urban regeneration project, the River Lea was to be cleaned from Walthamstow Marshes to Bow. Old oil drums, supermarket trolleys and other rubbish would all be hauled from the river's murky depths in an attempt to revitalise it. Work was to start on the Leyton stretch at 9.00 a.m. on the 10ᵗʰ December.

It was a tiny mistake that was to have disproportionate consequences for the Garrods and for the then Detective Sergeant Alison Dexter.

11.

Saturday, 12th October 2002

The ring was set up. Woollard had put down a new circle of old carpet. There was a smaller group of punters than normal. Woollard had marketed the evening as something of a special event. He didn't want anyone there that he didn't trust.

Norlington led in his Tosa from the car. It was a large animal, about 150 pounds, well fed and powerful. The dog stayed close to him, uncertain at the strange faces and unfamiliar smells.

'He looks like a game animal,' Woollard said with a smile, 'good bones.'

'He's a strong dog,' Norlington replied.

'You've fought him a lot before?'

'A couple of times. Essex.'

Keith Gwynne had joined them. 'I see you've been introduced. Fuck me! That's a big dog!'

The dog stared blackly at Gwynne. Norlington gently massaged the dog's muscular neck to keep him calm.

'Hard to find Tosa fights these days,' Woollard observed. 'Does he have a name?'

'I call him Tyndall.'

'Weird name. Where'd you get him?' Woollard asked. 'You can't import them now.'

way from the dogs. Thirdly, my decision
is my decision to suspend the fight.
need to postpone the contest for any
he kind of reasons that smell of pork and
anda cars – the match will take place at
ive venue in three days' time. You will all
d of the details.'

he pit!' shouted the timekeeper, starting
tch. The tension and noise levels in the
denly ratcheted up. Woollard climbed
rrier, leaving just the two dogs and their
the fighting zone.

seconds,' shouted the timekeeper.

ur dogs!' boomed Woollard.

o Tosas turned to face each other,
against their handlers' grips. To
the next ten seconds seemed like an

!' screamed the timekeeper. The two
ted their hands clear in accordance with
d clambered out of the ring.

econd later the two dogs flew into each
ss the scratch line. Watching from the
st the screams and shouts of empty-
n, Keith Gwynne gasped at the spectacle
t animals tearing at each other. Standing
, Norlington quickly saw that the only
uld be time. The gulf in size between the

'I won him in a fight out at Clacton about two years ago. I put his owner in hospital,' Norlington replied.

'If you fought him in Essex you must have come across Jack Whiteside. He fought Tosas out of Maldon.'

'I don't think I've met him.'

'He was a top man Jack. He died just after millennium night. Some toerag cut his throat. Can you believe that?'

'I haven't heard of him. I would have remembered that. When are we weighing the dogs?'

Woollard exchanged a glance with Gwynne. 'Didn't Keith tell you? We're not bothering with a weigh-in?'

'Then we don't fight. The rules say there has to be a weigh-in.' Norlington was unhappy at the flouting of this convention.

'Look, my dog's a little heavier than yours. So what? I'm not daft. Your dog is more experienced. He's got scars and white fur all over his face. That means he's seen a lot of action. My dog is a first timer. It all evens out,' Woollard insisted. 'It'll be like a "game test" to see if he's got a future in the pit.'

'I don't like it,' said Norlington angrily, 'I've been fucking set up.'

'Look,' Woollard responded, 'I'll up the purse for

the bare knuckle by two hundred notes. Seventeen hundred quid! It's easy money. These people have paid good money. Tosa fights are a special attraction. Don't let me down, George, I was told you were a man of your word.'

Norlington thought for a second. 'Seventeen hundred then. Don't bend any other rules either.'

Woollard nodded. He looked Norlington over, studying his fearsome hands and battered face. 'We'll do the bare knuckle straight after. Big Lefty fancies his chances.'

Norlington nodded. 'Shall we get on with this then?'

'Take him into the ring now, Kev!' Woollard boomed to one of his farm lads. 'Go and fetch Karl in.'

Norlington took Tyndall into the arena. The dog's claws scratched against the carpet. In one or two places, Norlington noticed that the carpets had been torn up: through the gaps he could see the exposed and unforgiving concrete floor. Tyndall was beginning to get agitated, sensing what was about to come. Norlington whispered quietly into the dog's ear as they waited.

A moment or two later, Kev returned with Tyndall's opposition. Immediately, Norlington knew that the fight was lost. Woollard's Tosa was enormous: at least thirty pounds heavier than

Tyndall. It was a no-c[...] huge, unnatural muscle [...] was mean too. Norling[...] in its eyes. The two ani[...] began to snarl aggressi[...] hold his dog steady [...] brought into the ring.

'Arthur over there is [...] counting down the fig[...] the contestants and au[...] second. George Norlin[...] "Tyndall". The owner [...] weigh-in. I have been [...] is final.'

Norlington quietly [...] faced the wooden w[...] opposite side of the r[...] Karl.

'Normal English [...] continued. 'First, neit[...] dog or behave unfai[...] second once the fight [...] must not be thrown [...] dog constitutes a fou[...] the fight. I am oblige[...] once they have turne[...] their hands in front o[...] "release" command, [...]

vertically[...] is final. Should v[...] reason – [...] arrive in [...] an altern[...] be inform[...]

'Clear [...] his stopw[...] room su[...] over the l[...] seconds i[...]

'Twent[...] 'Face y[...] The tv[...] straining [...] Norlingto[...] eternity.

'Releas[...] handlers l[...] the rules a[...] A split [...] other acro[...] side, ami[...] minded m[...] of two gia[...] to his rig[...] variable w[...]

two animals was instantly telling. He had walked into a mismatch. He hoped that, for Tyndall's sake, Woollard would suspend the fight quickly.

Despite his physical disadvantages, Tyndall was the first animal to draw blood from his opponent, clawing an ugly gash in Karl's ribcage. However, the larger dog did not recoil at the wound.

'Hardy animal your dog!' Woollard shouted above the din, 'cunning fighter.'

Norlington ignored the comment, his eyes focusing on the spectacle. He knew Woollard was trying to persuade him that the fight was an even contest. Norlington watched Karl closely. The giant animal had taken a serious hit and was bleeding profusely, yet its enthusiasm and ferocity were undiminished. He began to wonder if Karl was drugged up on some amphetamine or other. The animal was clearly unaware of the damage it had sustained. The two animals clashed again, each frantically struggling for domination of its opponent. They tumbled and collided across the floor of the ring, unable to secure a telling grip. Tyndall crashed into the wooden slats encircling the ring, his head taking the force of the impact. Karl broke clear, then turned into the centre of the ring, before launching at Tyndall in what proved to be a devastating assault. Karl finally seized the smaller dog's neck between its jaws and hauled it to the ground, clawing furiously as it did so.

Tyndall eventually tore free but at the price of a terrible neck wound; blood gushed from the opening as the dog staggered backwards in the ring. For the first time in an otherwise mute contest, Tyndall began to growl.

'Bad sign,' said Gwynne to Norlington, 'he's had enough.'

Norlington knew Gwynne was right. When pit dogs were confident and enjoying the contest they fought silently. Tyndall was backing into a threat display; growling and snapping at his opponent defensively; trying to discourage his opponent from further attacks.

'Call the fight!' Norlington shouted at Woollard, 'suspend the fucking fight!'

On the other side of the arena Woollard feigned deafness, placing a hand to his ear, mouthing, 'I can't hear you.'

Furious, Norlington looked back into the arena as Tyndall, now disorientated and backed up against the wooden wall, wet himself in confusion and terror.

Sensing victory, Karl flew into his weakened competitor, viciously tearing at the wound on his neck. Tyndall yelped in pain and fell to the floor. Surprised by the high-pitched shriek, Karl stepped back for a second. Norlington jumped into the ring, ignoring Karl's aggressive circling, and made directly for his dying dog. Finally, a bell rang indicating the end of the fight.

Norlington stared at the mess in the centre of the ring. People around him were exchanging money. Some said that the fight was the best they had ever seen. Others bemoaned the fact that it was over so quickly. There was agreement, however, that Tyndall had been a 'game' contender. Two of Woollard's farm workers harnessed Karl and hauled the barking, excited animal from the ring. Norlington knew that the fight was a mismatch: that Karl was extremely large, even for a Tosa, and that his apparent ignorance of his wounds was unnatural. Still, that was the risk that you took. Woollard had bought his agreement to forgo the weigh-in. Norlington had the dog's death on his own conscience and someone would now pay a price for that. He climbed over the wooden boards into the arena and carried Tyndall out of the barn. Then he noticed the monstrous frame of Lefty Shaw looming in front of him.

'I hope you fight better than your fucking mongrel, fat man!' Lefty observed.

Norlington placed Tyndall on the ground next to his car and returned to the barn.

Woollard gestured the two men towards the centre of the ring. It was a formidable sight. Shaw was well over six feet with huge shoulders and powerful arms. He had a tattoo of an eagle on his right forearm. His opponent was no less formidable. Norlington was shorter, about five eleven, but weighed over three hundred pounds.

Woollard had placed two upturned steel buckets on either side on the arena. Lefty Shaw sat down on his bucket sizing up the opposition. Norlington was older and heavier than him; he figured that he would go for an early knockout before his energy ran out. Lefty had fought the type before. He would let him come on to him, use his reach to keep him away, then eventually wear the fat bastard down.

Norlington stared at the bloodstains on the carpet left by his Tosa five minutes previously.

'Come up to the scratch please, gentlemen,' Woollard ordered, pointing to the line of masking tape that divided the centre of the ring. The two men obliged. Lefty Shaw grinned a toothless grin at Norlington.

'Let's go, fat man,' Shaw said.

Norlington, making no reply, lifted his eyes from the carpet and stared intently at Shaw's tattoo.

'Normal bare knuckle rules apply,' Woollard announced to the fighters and to the gathered onlookers. 'There is only one round. It is not timed. It finishes when one of the fighters is knocked out. If a fighter is knocked down, he has thirty seconds to come up to the scratch in the centre of the ring. If he is unable to do so, the fight is over. Fighters may not rest during the contest. If one falls from exhaustion, the other is declared the winner.'

Lefty Shaw was pumped. Sweat was pouring in rivulets down his back like a racehorse on Derby Day. 'Let's get this started, Bob,' he grunted.

Woollard climbed awkwardly out of the ring. At his signal, Gwynne rang an old cowbell and the fight began.

Shaw immediately stepped back, expecting Norlington to come at him hard, looking for the quick knockdown. However, Norlington didn't move and just stood on the scratch line looking at his opponent. Annoyed that his assessment had been wrong, Shaw lumbered forward, slamming a haymaker punch into Norlington's midriff. His opponent stayed quite still. Again, Shaw's left arm connected with Norlington's stomach, then with his face, then with his kidneys. Blood dripped across the floor from a cut under Norlington's eye. And yet, he remained quite still, apparently oblivious to the pain Shaw was inflicting.

Sitting in a plastic garden chair outside the ring, Woollard turned to Gwynne in disgust. 'What's all this about? I paid to see a fighter not a punch bag. You told me this idiot was notorious.'

Gwynne shrugged, 'I don't know what he's up

to. C'mon, George! Sort it out!'

Norlington tasted the blood in his mouth. He liked the taste. Always had. He was vaguely aware of Lefty Shaw approaching him again, more confident now, sensing victory. He was coming right at him, no fancy approach, he was walking straight towards him. As Shaw drew back his left hand, Norlington launched himself forward. He seized Shaw's right arm and then bit down furiously onto his eagle tattoo. Blood spurted. Shaw screamed in pain, falling to the ground under the weight of Norlington's body. Norlington bit down harder, feeling his teeth cut into Shaw's flesh, blood drooling over his tongue. Frantically, Shaw punched the back of Norlington's head with his free hand; the pain was absolutely excruciating. Norlington began to pull his head back, tearing a sizeable chunk of flesh from Shaw's bicep. Woollard stood up in shock at what he had just seen. Gwynne sank into his seat – this was going horribly wrong.

Free at least of Norlington's ferocious bite, Shaw reeled backwards in agony clutching the torn flesh of his right arm. He looked on in horror as Norlington chewed and swallowed the meat he had ripped free. Norlington wiped the blood from his face. He moved quickly across the ring, hearing for the first time the anxious cries of support for Lefty in the crowd. Approaching his wounded opponent,

'I won him in a fight out at Clacton about two years ago. I put his owner in hospital,' Norlington replied.

'If you fought him in Essex you must have come across Jack Whiteside. He fought Tosas out of Maldon.'

'I don't think I've met him.'

'He was a top man Jack. He died just after millennium night. Some toerag cut his throat. Can you believe that?'

'I haven't heard of him. I would have remembered that. When are we weighing the dogs?'

Woollard exchanged a glance with Gwynne. 'Didn't Keith tell you? We're not bothering with a weigh-in?'

'Then we don't fight. The rules say there has to be a weigh-in.' Norlington was unhappy at the flouting of this convention.

'Look, my dog's a little heavier than yours. So what? I'm not daft. Your dog is more experienced. He's got scars and white fur all over his face. That means he's seen a lot of action. My dog is a first timer. It all evens out,' Woollard insisted. 'It'll be like a "game test" to see if he's got a future in the pit.'

'I don't like it,' said Norlington angrily, 'I've been fucking set up.'

'Look,' Woollard responded, 'I'll up the purse for

the bare knuckle by two hundred notes. Seventeen hundred quid! It's easy money. These people have paid good money. Tosa fights are a special attraction. Don't let me down, George, I was told you were a man of your word.'

Norlington thought for a second. 'Seventeen hundred then. Don't bend any other rules either.'

Woollard nodded. He looked Norlington over, studying his fearsome hands and battered face. 'We'll do the bare knuckle straight after. Big Lefty fancies his chances.'

Norlington nodded. 'Shall we get on with this then?'

'Take him into the ring now, Kev!' Woollard boomed to one of his farm lads. 'Go and fetch Karl in.'

Norlington took Tyndall into the arena. The dog's claws scratched against the carpet. In one or two places, Norlington noticed that the carpets had been torn up: through the gaps he could see the exposed and unforgiving concrete floor. Tyndall was beginning to get agitated, sensing what was about to come. Norlington whispered quietly into the dog's ear as they waited.

A moment or two later, Kev returned with Tyndall's opposition. Immediately, Norlington knew that the fight was lost. Woollard's Tosa was enormous: at least thirty pounds heavier than

Tyndall. It was a no-contest. The other dog had huge, unnatural muscle bulk about its shoulders. It was mean too. Norlington recognised the hard fury in its eyes. The two animals clocked each other and began to snarl aggressively. Norlington struggled to hold his dog steady as Woollard's animal was brought into the ring.

'Arthur over there is timekeeping. Listen for him counting down the fight,' Woollard announced to the contestants and audience. 'Kev here is "Karl's" second. George Norlington is handling his own dog "Tyndall". The owners have waived the right to a weigh-in. I have been selected as referee. My word is final.'

Norlington quietly turned his dog around so it faced the wooden wall of the arena. On the opposite side of the ring, Kev did the same with Karl.

'Normal English rules apply,' Woollard continued. 'First, neither second can touch either dog or behave unfairly to the opposing dog or second once the fight is underway. Secondly, dogs must not be thrown across the ring. Throwing a dog constitutes a foul punishable by forfeiture of the fight. I am obliged to remind the handlers that once they have turned their dogs, they must keep their hands in front of the dogs' shoulders. On the "release" command, they must lift their hands vertically away from the dogs. Thirdly, my decision is final. It is my decision to suspend the fight. Should we need to postpone the contest for any reason – the kind of reasons that smell of pork and arrive in panda cars – the match will take place at an alternative venue in three days' time. You will all be informed of the details.'

'Clear the pit!' shouted the timekeeper, starting his stopwatch. The tension and noise levels in the room suddenly ratcheted up. Woollard climbed over the barrier, leaving just the two dogs and their seconds in the fighting zone.

'Twenty seconds,' shouted the timekeeper.

'Face your dogs!' boomed Woollard.

The two Tosas turned to face each other, straining against their handlers' grips. To Norlington the next ten seconds seemed like an eternity.

'Release!' screamed the timekeeper. The two handlers lifted their hands clear in accordance with the rules and clambered out of the ring.

A split second later the two dogs flew into each other across the scratch line. Watching from the side, amidst the screams and shouts of empty-minded men, Keith Gwynne gasped at the spectacle of two giant animals tearing at each other. Standing to his right, Norlington quickly saw that the only variable would be time. The gulf in size between the

two animals was instantly telling. He had walked into a mismatch. He hoped that, for Tyndall's sake, Woollard would suspend the fight quickly.

Despite his physical disadvantages, Tyndall was the first animal to draw blood from his opponent, clawing an ugly gash in Karl's ribcage. However, the larger dog did not recoil at the wound.

'Hardy animal your dog!' Woollard shouted above the din, 'cunning fighter.'

Norlington ignored the comment, his eyes focusing on the spectacle. He knew Woollard was trying to persuade him that the fight was an even contest. Norlington watched Karl closely. The giant animal had taken a serious hit and was bleeding profusely, yet its enthusiasm and ferocity were undiminished. He began to wonder if Karl was drugged up on some amphetamine or other. The animal was clearly unaware of the damage it had sustained. The two animals clashed again, each frantically struggling for domination of its opponent. They tumbled and collided across the floor of the ring, unable to secure a telling grip. Tyndall crashed into the wooden slats encircling the ring, his head taking the force of the impact. Karl broke clear, then turned into the centre of the ring, before launching at Tyndall in what proved to be a devastating assault. Karl finally seized the smaller dog's neck between its jaws and hauled it to the

ground, clawing furiously as it did so.

Tyndall eventually tore free but at the price of a terrible neck wound; blood gushed from the opening as the dog staggered backwards in the ring. For the first time in an otherwise mute contest, Tyndall began to growl.

'Bad sign,' said Gwynne to Norlington, 'he's had enough.'

Norlington knew Gwynne was right. When pit dogs were confident and enjoying the contest they fought silently. Tyndall was backing into a threat display; growling and snapping at his opponent defensively; trying to discourage his opponent from further attacks.

'Call the fight!' Norlington shouted at Woollard, 'suspend the fucking fight!'

On the other side of the arena Woollard feigned deafness, placing a hand to his ear, mouthing, 'I can't hear you.'

Furious, Norlington looked back into the arena as Tyndall, now disorientated and backed up against the wooden wall, wet himself in confusion and terror.

Sensing victory, Karl flew into his weakened competitor, viciously tearing at the wound on his neck. Tyndall yelped in pain and fell to the floor. Surprised by the high-pitched shriek, Karl stepped back for a second. Norlington jumped into the ring,

ignoring Karl's aggressive circling, and made directly for his dying dog. Finally, a bell rang indicating the end of the fight.

Norlington stared at the mess in the centre of the ring. People around him were exchanging money. Some said that the fight was the best they had ever seen. Others bemoaned the fact that it was over so quickly. There was agreement, however, that Tyndall had been a 'game' contender. Two of Woollard's farm workers harnessed Karl and hauled the barking, excited animal from the ring. Norlington knew that the fight was a mismatch: that Karl was extremely large, even for a Tosa, and that his apparent ignorance of his wounds was unnatural. Still, that was the risk that you took. Woollard had bought his agreement to forgo the weigh-in. Norlington had the dog's death on his own conscience and someone would now pay a price for that. He climbed over the wooden boards into the arena and carried Tyndall out of the barn. Then he noticed the monstrous frame of Lefty Shaw looming in front of him.

'I hope you fight better than your fucking mongrel, fat man!' Lefty observed.

Norlington placed Tyndall on the ground next to his car and returned to the barn.

Woollard gestured the two men towards the centre of the ring. It was a formidable sight. Shaw

was well over six feet with huge shoulders and powerful arms. He had a tattoo of an eagle on his right forearm. His opponent was no less formidable. Norlington was shorter, about five eleven, but weighed over three hundred pounds.

Woollard had placed two upturned steel buckets on either side on the arena. Lefty Shaw sat down on his bucket sizing up the opposition. Norlington was older and heavier than him; he figured that he would go for an early knockout before his energy ran out. Lefty had fought the type before. He would let him come on to him, use his reach to keep him away, then eventually wear the fat bastard down.

Norlington stared at the bloodstains on the carpet left by his Tosa five minutes previously.

'Come up to the scratch please, gentlemen,' Woollard ordered, pointing to the line of masking tape that divided the centre of the ring. The two men obliged. Lefty Shaw grinned a toothless grin at Norlington.

'Let's go, fat man,' Shaw said.

Norlington, making no reply, lifted his eyes from the carpet and stared intently at Shaw's tattoo.

'Normal bare knuckle rules apply,' Woollard announced to the fighters and to the gathered onlookers. 'There is only one round. It is not timed. It finishes when one of the fighters is knocked out. If a fighter is knocked down, he has thirty seconds

to come up to the scratch in the centre of the ring. If he is unable to do so, the fight is over. Fighters may not rest during the contest. If one falls from exhaustion, the other is declared the winner.'

Lefty Shaw was pumped. Sweat was pouring in rivulets down his back like a racehorse on Derby Day. 'Let's get this started, Bob,' he grunted.

Woollard climbed awkwardly out of the ring. At his signal, Gwynne rang an old cowbell and the fight began.

Shaw immediately stepped back, expecting Norlington to come at him hard, looking for the quick knockdown. However, Norlington didn't move and just stood on the scratch line looking at his opponent. Annoyed that his assessment had been wrong, Shaw lumbered forward, slamming a haymaker punch into Norlington's midriff. His opponent stayed quite still. Again, Shaw's left arm connected with Norlington's stomach, then with his face, then with his kidneys. Blood dripped across the floor from a cut under Norlington's eye. And yet, he remained quite still, apparently oblivious to the pain Shaw was inflicting.

Sitting in a plastic garden chair outside the ring, Woollard turned to Gwynne in disgust. 'What's all this about? I paid to see a fighter not a punch bag. You told me this idiot was notorious.'

Gwynne shrugged, 'I don't know what he's up

to. C'mon, George! Sort it out!'

Norlington tasted the blood in his mouth. He liked the taste. Always had. He was vaguely aware of Lefty Shaw approaching him again, more confident now, sensing victory. He was coming right at him, no fancy approach, he was walking straight towards him. As Shaw drew back his left hand, Norlington launched himself forward. He seized Shaw's right arm and then bit down furiously onto his eagle tattoo. Blood spurted. Shaw screamed in pain, falling to the ground under the weight of Norlington's body. Norlington bit down harder, feeling his teeth cut into Shaw's flesh, blood drooling over his tongue. Frantically, Shaw punched the back of Norlington's head with his free hand; the pain was absolutely excruciating. Norlington began to pull his head back, tearing a sizeable chunk of flesh from Shaw's bicep. Woollard stood up in shock at what he had just seen. Gwynne sank into his seat – this was going horribly wrong.

Free at least of Norlington's ferocious bite, Shaw reeled backwards in agony clutching the torn flesh of his right arm. He looked on in horror as Norlington chewed and swallowed the meat he had ripped free. Norlington wiped the blood from his face. He moved quickly across the ring, hearing for the first time the anxious cries of support for Lefty in the crowd. Approaching his wounded opponent,

Norlington smiled a bloody smile.

'I didn't like that tattoo,' he said to Lefty. 'A man shouldn't decorate himself.'

With that, Norlington engulfed Shaw in a terrible bear hug. He squeezed hard, locking his hands behind Shaw's back, forcing the air from his lungs. Again, Shaw fired rabbit punches against Norlington's huge frame but to no avail. Then, just as Shaw felt himself losing consciousness, Norlington dropped him to the ground. Falling on all fours, Shaw frantically gasped for breath as his assailant walked around the ring waiting for him.

Across the ring, Norlington savoured the taste of blood. He wondered what Alison Dexter would taste like when he went to work on her. That time was coming. But first things first. Norlington picked up the steel bucket from the floor of the ring, advanced on the wheezing form of his opponent and smashed the bucket down onto the back of Shaw's head. Then he did it again as Shaw slumped forward. And again as the back of Shaw's head split open to reveal a white panel of bone. Confident that Shaw wasn't going to get up, Norlington turned to face the shocked audience and Woollard in particular. Breathless with the exertion, Norlington pointed at the farmer and grunted, 'Give me my fucking money.'

* * *

Ten minutes later, with most of the invited guests gone, and with Lefty Shaw still unconscious on the floor of the barn, Norlington placed his dead dog in the boot of his car. Woollard was standing near by, but keeping a distance nonetheless.

'It's all in there.' Woollard handed over an envelope as Norlington slammed his boot shut.

'It better be,' Norlington muttered. 'I don't want to come looking for you.'

Woollard almost laughed. 'Do you honestly think I'd short change you? After what I've just seen? No, mate, it's all there.'

Norlington nodded and climbed into the driver's seat. 'I'll be seeing you then.' The door slammed.

'I sincerely fucking hope not,' Woollard replied as the car roared to life.

'Boss! You better get in here!' one of Woollard's farm hands shouted from the barn.

Woollard followed him back into the barn. Keith Gwynne was kneeling over Lefty Shaw. He looked up.

'We've got a big problem, Bob. He's dead.'

'Oh, Christ!' Woollard exclaimed, 'you're sure?'

'Pretty fucking sure. His heart's not beating.'

'Can't we give him mouth to mouth or something?'

'Bob, he's gone mate,' Gwynne said grimly, 'I ain't kissing a corpse.'

'Shit.'

'What are we going to do then?'

Woollard thought for a moment, his mind exploring the possibilities. 'Only got one option, haven't we?'

'And that is?'

'We got to get shot of the body.'

Gwynne stood up. 'What's all this "we"? I'm not going anywhere. It's nothing to do with me.'

'Perhaps you won't mind me giving your name to the old Bill then,' Woollard snarled, 'if it's nothing to do with you. And if I remember rightly, it was your maniac mate who did this.'

'He's not my mate, Bob. Just someone I know.'

'Well, you keep some curious company, Keith,' said Woollard angrily.

Three of Bob's employees were still in the room. Woollard knew that he had to act fast. He picked out one he knew that he could trust.

'Ben, you stay and clean this shit up. I want this spotless. The rest of you help me get him out of here.'

'Where are we going to put him?' Ben asked uncertainly.

'To begin with, in the back of the transit van. After that, I'm open to suggestions,' Woollard replied.

'We could take him down to the Cam. Weight

him and chuck him in,' Gwynne volunteered.

'Too far,' Woollard shook his head. 'We need something less risky. I don't want to be driving him around Cambridgeshire all night.'

They thought for a moment, temporarily flummoxed. In the distance, a train rattled northwards towards Ely. Woollard looked up suddenly. 'I've got an idea.'

Norlington drove for about ten minutes; he gunned his aged car through the sprawling Cambridgeshire darkness. He was beginning to be aware of discomfort; his chest was aching after bearing the brunt of Shaw's assault. Shaw had been strong but he wasn't an intelligent fighter. Back in London, Norlington had fought much shrewder men: men that didn't bother battering your midriff or your kidneys, men who went straight for your windpipe, your solar plexus, or the balls or your eyes. Shaw had tried to knock him over; they had tried to kill him.

He pulled over onto a farm track and turned off the engine. He was sorry to have lost his dog. Norlington was not an affectionate man but the dog had kept him company. It had fought a lost cause with bravery and ferocity. It deserved his respect. Norlington reached into the glove compartment and withdrew the pocket knife he kept for emergencies. He climbed out of the car and lifted the dead Tosa from the boot.

The dog was still warm although the blood had dried, matting its fur. Norlington placed the dog on the hard earth and withdrew a Tupperware box from amongst the rubbish on the back seat of his car. Returning, he felt the dog's muscle bulk around its shoulders and hips. Then, with care and expertise, he sliced two significant cuts of meat from the dog: the first from its left shoulder, the second from its left thigh muscle. One by one, he laid each piece into his Tupperware box and sealed the lid.

Norlington placed the carcass in a roadside ditch and covered it with as much rubbish and foliage as he could find. Driving back to his digs, Norlington occupied his mind with the taste of Alison Dexter. He found his mind wandering through forests of herbs and garnishes. He remembered a chapter from the Imperial history book that had belonged to his father. It had been about a British sailing ship called the Boyd. In 1809, it had visited Whangarei Harbour in New Zealand. The British had affronted the local Maori. So, in retribution, Maori warriors had overrun the ship, killing most of its crew. Norlington couldn't remember all the details but he did recall, with some excitement, what the tribesmen had done with the bodies. It had given him an idea.

The fight had cost him a dog but bought him some time. He now had the time to locate and isolate her, and the money to equip himself properly. The problem would be accommodation. He needed a new place to stay: somewhere remote and private. Finding the ideal spot could prove awkward but his mind was fertile with ideas.

12.

Sunday, 13th October 2002

The mail train rattled through Balehurst station without stopping. It was 2.27 a.m. In the driver's cabin, Duncan Capel was fighting off sleep. He had only recently been switched on to night work and his system still hadn't adjusted. He had finished his thermos of coffee as the train was loaded with mail sacks at Cambridge; now he was struggling. Once clear of Balehurst, Capel accelerated the locomotive through 90 mph on the long, straight run through the fens to Ely.

Capel yawned with exhaustion, then frowned out into the onrushing darkness. The earlier showers had receded. He could see something moving above the track. There was a footbridge about a mile ahead with figures moving on it, silhouetted against the recently revealed moon. Instinctively, Capel eased off on the accelerator, the train slipping back through eighty then seventy miles an hour. He suspected kids. This stretch was notorious for vandals chucking stones at trains and leaving debris on the track. He didn't want to risk a shattered windscreen or a derailment. The train eased back to 60 mph. When he was fifty yards short of the bridge, Capel saw a body drop down and go under the wheels of the locomotive: a sight that would haunt him. He slammed on the brakes, sending squealing metal shock waves out into the still Fens. His heart pounding, Capel radioed Cambridge station for assistance, then, afraid of what he might find, headed nervously out of the driver's cabin and jumped down onto the track.

DI John Underwood's mobile phone shrieked at him through the darkness. It was just before 4.00 a.m. Sleep clung on agonisingly to his eyes.

'Underwood,' he muttered.

'Sorry to wake you, sir. Harrison here.'

'What's up?'

'Accident down on the railway.'

'For fuck's sake.'

'Victim hit by a mail train under the Fen Combe footbridge. Right spaghetti bolognese.'

'Suicide,' Underwood decided. 'Body to the

hospital, uniform supervise the clean up, week off for the driver.'

'It's a bit more complicated than that, sir. The driver says he saw people on the bridge before the body fell. Could be foul play.'

Underwood hung in the last moment of comfort before he inevitably crawled out of bed into another freezing night.

'OK. I'm on my way. You want picking up?'

'I'm already here, thanks Guv.'

He felt a dull ache on his left hand side, radiating from his hip up to and around his ribs.

An hour later, Underwood peered under the wheels of the locomotive and concluded that Harrison's 'spaghetti bolognese' reference was well made.

'What a mess,' he muttered.

'I know, sir. I can think of better ways to start the day,' Harrison replied grimly.

Marty Farrell, New Bolden's most senior scene of crime officer, crawled out gingerly from under the engine section holding an evidence bag of remains.

'Nice work if you can get it,' Underwood observed.

'With the greatest respect, sir,' Farrell replied as he got to his feet, 'up yours.'

Underwood smiled through his tiredness. 'I suppose I asked for that.'

'I was in bed with a woman half an hour ago, a very nice one, now I'm here in the perishing fucking cold picking up organs.'

'Anything unusual?'

'Not really. The body's in four main sections; the head's pretty messed up but recognisable I suppose. Guts dragged halfway down the track. And I think I've got a kidney here.' He held up the bag for Underwood's inspection.

'Any ID on the body?'

'Nothing yet.'

'No suicide note?'

'Not a sausage.'

'Assume foul play then. Bag and tag everything. Ultra careful.'

'Always, boss.'

'Thanks, Marty. You work with him, Harrison. Get him whatever he needs. Where's the driver?'

'In the plod car with uniform. He's pretty wobbly,' Harrison cautioned.

Underwood left Farrell to his grim pickings. Capel was sitting in the front seat of a squad car. A female police sergeant stood at his side, she looked about fifteen years old to Underwood. The force was changing. He didn't recognise half the uniformed officers at New Bolden. Feeling time breathing down his neck was unsettling. He showed his warrant card.

'I'm DI Underwood.' He turned to Capel. 'How are you, son?'

'Pretty freaked out.'

'I'm sure. Stupid question. What did you see?'

Capel looked back down the track. 'I was about a mile out from the bridge. I'm pretty sure I saw people on the bridge. I decelerated. I thought it could be vandals. Just before I got to the bridge, I saw something fall onto the track. I didn't have time to stop. It just went under the engine.'

'How many people?'

'Eh?'

'On the bridge.'

'Oh. Two, maybe three.'

'You're sure?'

'Fairly sure. Why would anyone want to do that? Chuck someone on a track I mean? That's a terrible way to kill someone.'

'Terrible and clumsy.' Underwood looked back down the track. 'Maybe he was dead already.'

'I don't understand.'

'Let's wait for the post-mortem. Have you made a written statement yet?'

'I gave it to the black copper over there,' he pointed out towards Harrison.

'Get yourself home then.'

Underwood turned towards the footbridge.

FIRST TOUCH

13.

Monday, 14th October 2002

DI Alison Dexter found herself sitting in the car park of ComBold Ltd on the outskirts of New Bolden. She felt a frisson of excitement: the electric thrill of a voyeur. She hadn't tried to justify her actions to herself. Dexter had used her ruthless logic against herself too often before. She had argued herself into the ground. You can destroy any emotion with logic; undermine any initiative; magnify any risk. She was here. Simple as that. She wanted to have another look at Kelsi Hensy, the person she had allowed to occupy her thoughts. Was she obsessed? Dexter refused to analyse the possibility. In any case, it had to be healthy to be obsessed with something other than dead bodies and bad memories.

Cars drew into the yard. ComBold employees stepped out into the cold October morning in not-yet crumpled suits and skirts. From a distant corner, in the relative anonymity of her Mondeo, Dexter observed their faces carefully. Perhaps it was 'control freakery'. Alison Dexter liked to be in control of situations. She liked to think that her rational mind could manage any incident or emotion life hurled up at her. She had admitted to herself that she found Kelsi Hensy attractive. Dexter had buried any similar feeling in the past under a mountain of logic and pretence: she had preferred to consider them as slips of concentration rather than indications of something altogether more profound.

And yet, here she was. Kelsi Hensy was different. What was so special about a person that she didn't know? A common knowledge of the topography of Leyton was hardly the most solid or stimulating basis for a relationship. Nor was their shared love of West Ham United: an association that had given Dexter little other than grief since she had adopted the club in 1980. There was nothing concrete at all for her to work with and that knowledge was destabilising DI Alison Dexter to the point that she couldn't concentrate on much else. Maybe, she told herself, there was nothing special about Kelsi Hensy at all. Perhaps something had changed in her: she had slipped an emotional gear and was now shuddering to a standstill. It was also possible that she was finally being honest with herself.

Her self-indulgence was ruptured by the sight of Kelsi Hensy driving into the car park in a new

Peugeot 206. Dexter sank into her seat when, for a single horrible intestine-twisting second, she thought that Kelsi was about to park in the space alongside her. Once the moment of crisis had passed, Dexter cursed her idiocy: next time she would park between two cars to eliminate that risk.

Next time?

The voice in her head had a point.

Dexter leaned forward as Kelsi slammed her car door shut, remote-locked the car and walked across the car park.

Kelsi Hensy wore a black skirt and smart white blouse. She wore black business heels that accentuated the firm lines of her calf muscles through her stockings. She had very short blonde hair that she had wet-gelled back away from her face. Dexter thought of Kelsi's face between her legs, the cold wet touch of that hair against her inner thigh. The thought jack-in-the-boxed up out of nowhere; Dexter found the surprise stimulating. She wondered where her mind would take her next.

So far, she was enjoying the ride.

14.

Leyton, East London
December 1995

'Two dustbin bags full of body parts,' said DCI Patrick McInally of Leyton CID, 'all messed up. Council contractors pulled them out of the river this morning. One victim according to the pathologist. Male about forty years old. Someone has carved him up. Frenzied attack. Uncertain about time of death at the moment but less than a week.'

Detective Sergeant Alison Dexter shivered on the bleak riverbank.

'ID on the victim?' she asked through chattering teeth.

'Nothing. No personal effects at all.' McInally paused, smiling at his protégée. 'You a bit chilly there, Dexy?'

'My knickers are icing over,' she said bitterly.

McInally laughed.

'And not for the first time!'

'Not funny.'

Dexter had endured a bad year. A few months previously, McInally had wondered if she'd survive in the force. But she was tough, he knew that, tough *like flint. The riverbank was alive with SOCOs and uniformed police. A white forensic tent had been erected a few yards away. McInally was an experienced and conscientious officer: Dexter respected him above anybody. She read his mind.*

'Not much for me to do here, Guv,' she observed. 'How can I help?'

McInally looked around him. There were journalists already camped at the end of Dace Road. He put his right arm round Dexter and led her around the side of the forensic tent.

'Dexy, I've got a funny feeling about this. Someone has really hacked this guy up. That's unusual. I've worked this patch for fifteen years. In that time we've only had one other case like this.'

Dexter saw where he was going. 'The Smithfield Porter? What was his name?'

'Patterson, Brian Patterson.'

Dexter hadn't worked the case. The body of Smithfield market worker Brian Patterson had been found in a shallow grave on Wanstead Flats. Patterson had been a resident of Francis Road, Leyton in a house no more than two hundred yards away from Leyton police station. Dexter had been on emotional leave after a personal relationship with a fellow officer had become public in unpleasant circumstances. Trapped in her flat while the investigation took place, she had cursed her misfortune at missing out on the excitement.

'*Patterson was found with the front of his head smashed in and flesh missing from his right arm and leg. This body also has the front of his head smashed in. Now, DS Horton and DS Payne drew a blank when they looked into the Patterson murder.*'

'*Surprise, surprise.*'

'*I'll pretend I didn't hear that Detective Sergeant,*' *McInally remonstrated softly.* '*Listen. I want you to discreetly have a look at the Patterson case. See if they missed anything. Get yourself down to Smithfield. Speak to some of the bloke's mates. You know the drill.*'

Dexter nodded. '*Horton and Payne?*'

'*Keep them out of it for the moment,*' *McInally advised.* '*I want a fresh approach. They'll be resentful if they know I've got you checking up on their work.*'

'*Understood.*'

'*I want this kept quiet, Dexy. The press are sniffing around here. Once they twig the connection with Patterson there'll be serial killer stories everywhere and we'll find ourselves doing interviews instead of investigating.*'

'*Mum's the word.*'

That afternoon, Dexter visited Brian Patterson's widow in her house on Francis Road. Jessie

Patterson told Dexter the same story she had told DS Horton. That Brian had left for work as normal on the day he had disappeared. He travelled to work by bus from Leyton High Road. That his colleagues said he completed his shift at Smithfield Market at 7 a.m. and had a beer with his friends in the pub under the market before leaving. After that, no one saw him alive again.

Dexter left the sad little house at 5 p.m. none the wiser.

That night she stayed late at Leyton CID sifting through the Patterson case file. Horton and Payne had been fairly methodical. They had taken witness statements from Jessie Patterson and two porters at Smithfield who had worked that final shift with Brian on the day he vanished. They both had corroborated alibis. Dexter scribbled their names in her notebook. The paperwork was complete but uninspiring; that didn't surprise her. Horton and Payne were 'jobsworth' coppers: nine to fivers going through the motions. They had done precisely enough to avoid criticism without making any progress or identifying any relevant leads. Dexter found that contemptible. She had virtually nothing to work with. Dexter read and reread the Patterson case file, lingering for as long as she felt appropriate over the post-mortem photos. Lumps of flesh had been removed from Patterson's arm *and leg, a hole punched in his forehead.*

At midnight, she left a message on the management office answer phone at Smithfield Market telling them to expect her the following morning.

Dexter got up at 3.45 a.m. It took her about twenty minutes to drive from the East End down to Smithfield. She parked in Charterhouse Street and walked down the side of the vast nineteenth-century complex of buildings. She had never seen the market before, a fact that surprised her. The sprawling construction reminded her of a huge London railway station, St Pancras or King's Cross. Grey stone arches ornamented the front wall of the main building. A St George's flag fluttered above the vast vaulted entrance. Dexter tried to ignore the ribald shouts of the porters and meat cutters as she entered the market. The stench of meat was overpowering. Dexter immediately wanted to puke.

'Fancy some fucking sausage, darling?' A cutter held up an unpleasantly shaped piece of meat.

Dexter made her way through the noisy chaos to the management office. Gavin Doyle was waiting for her.

'You found us then,' he said unnecessarily.

'Some of your staff need to learn some manners,' Dexter replied. 'I don't like sexual innuendo being shouted at me. I am not a piece of meat.'

'I apologise. Needless to say this is pretty much an all male environment. They can be rather brusque.'

'I want to talk to the men who worked with Patterson on the day that he disappeared.' She checked her notebook. 'Dew and McCain.'

'I'll walk you down there.'

'I don't need a chaperone.'

'Nevertheless, I suspect the men will be less aggressive if I'm with you.'

'Let's get on with it then.'

Doyle led her back through the market explaining as he went.

'We have twenty-three units here in the East building and another twenty-one in the West. The units themselves are then divided into temperature controlled areas.'

Dexter looked at the meat stalls lining the central avenue. 'What kind of businesses buy from Smithfield?' she asked.

'All sorts. Butchers, of course, caterers, restaurants and hotels. We don't just sell meat, some of the stalls sell cheese, pies, all sorts really.'

'Could you get me a list of all the stall holders?'

'I suppose so. Is it essential?'

'Yes it is.'

Doyle sighed a sigh of irritation. 'Very well. I'll arrange it. This is where Dew and McCain work.

I'm afraid you can't go into the stall without the relevant protective clothing. Hygiene issues you see. Wait there and I'll send them out.' With that Doyle disappeared behind the stall, returning a moment later with two enormous Smithfield porters.

'Who's Dew and who's McCain?' Dexter asked. They duly identified themselves.

'Tell me about Patterson's last day,' Dexter asked loudly. The stall was next to the main entrance. Vans were being loaded a few feet away. The shouting and clattering made it almost impossible to concentrate.

'There's not much to tell really,' Dew replied. 'Worked his shift no problems. He was a musical cunt. Always whistling. Molly-fucking-Malone, Land of Hope and Glory, Blaydon Races. You name it. We had a pint with him at The Old Red Cow and a bite to eat. He seemed happy as Larry.'

'Talked about his missus all the bleedin' time,' McCain added. 'They were saving to go on holiday. Spain somewhere I think. Proper couple they were.'

Alison Dexter didn't notice the vast bulk of Bartholomew Garrod loom behind her. She was making notes and did not look up.

Dew noticed him. 'Morning, Bart. Bring the van up. The order's ready.'

'Thank you, Marcus, much appreciated.' Garrod returned to his van outside the building.

'Do you mind if I do this order, Sergeant?' asked Dew. 'It's our busiest time of day.'

Dexter half-looked up from her notes. 'Go ahead.'

'Will that be all then, Detective Sergeant?' Doyle asked.

'Not quite.' Dexter turned to McCain, 'How did Patterson get home usually? Bus or tube?'

'Not sure to be honest. Bus I think. I know he came in on the bus. I suppose he had a pass.'

Dexter nodded. She had briefly entertained the idea that there might have been security video footage of Patterson at the nearest tube station. She discounted the idea as unlikely: in any case, she doubted whether London Transport kept archived surveillance camera footage for more than a few days. She had drawn a blank.

A van drew up beside her. Bartholomew and Ray Garrod climbed out. Along with Marcus Dew, they began to load the van with meat. The Garrods heaved pig carcasses effortlessly.

'I think I'm done,' Dexter said to Doyle. 'If you could fax me that list of stall holders to this number, I'd appreciate it.'

'We certainly will.'

Dexter became aware of a man staring at her: an unnerving, flesh-stripping gaze.

'Wake up, Ray. Haven't you seen a lady police

officer before?' Marcus Dew said to the man.

Broken from his reverie, Ray Garrod wrenched his eyes from Alison Dexter. 'Ah have seen some bit of one I think,' he said before moving away to the rear of the van.

'Don't worry about old Ray, Sergeant,' Dew said, noticing her interest. 'He's harmless enough but he'll never win Mastermind.'

Dexter felt an inexplicable sense of uncertainty for a second. She looked at the old-fashioned butcher's van then back at Ray Garrod. Bartholomew lumbered past carrying a pig carcass under each arm. He stared through her. Something seemed to flicker in his black eyes. For a millisecond, Dexter thought it was fear.

It was an odd moment: one that she couldn't rationalise. Suddenly, she wanted to be somewhere else. Dexter thanked Gavin Doyle and hurriedly left the building, glancing over her shoulder as she walked out under the high stone arch of the exit. Ray and Bartholomew Garrod were standing completely still watching her leave.

Dexter returned to her car in Charterhouse Street. Something had unsettled her: maybe it was the smell of meat and death that pervaded the place, maybe it was the strange staring eyes of the Garrods. Maybe it was something else. Something subliminal: a connection that the conscious mind *hadn't quite made. Something she had seen.*

Dexter climbed into her car and locked the door. She sat looking towards Smithfield, uncertain how to proceed. After a minute, she saw the Garrods' van turn down Hayne Street: she watched the strange, ancient vehicle trundle down the incline. It stopped directly in front of her car as it indicated right to make the turn into Charterhouse Street. Ray Garrod sat in the passenger seat, he seemed to be shouting something excitedly to his brother. He hadn't noticed her. Dexter stared in fascination at the odd pair then allowed her eyes to drift along the side of the van to the text printed there:

'Garrod and Sons, Family Butchers, Norlington Road, Leyton, E10.'

Dexter felt a sudden shock of excitement.

Brian Patterson worked at Smithfield. Brian Patterson lived in Francis Road Leyton. Francis Road runs parallel to Norlington Road. The Garrods' shop is on Norlington Road.

Dexter immediately started the engine and swung out into the traffic behind the Garrods' van. She felt detached from the moment, unsure of where her thoughts were pushing her.

The Garrods buy meat from the stall at Smithfield where Patterson worked. At least one of the Garrods is fucking peculiar. Jesus Christ. Had they driven Patterson back to Leyton after work on the day he vanished? But who were the Garrods and what motive could they have for killing him?

Detective Sergeant Alison Dexter's thought process was accelerating. Her mental curiosity demanded satisfaction. She trailed the van all the way back to Leyton then parked up at the end of Norlington Road and watched the brothers unload their new stock.

15.

Pathologist Roger Leach watched John Underwood eating a lunchtime sausage roll with obvious disdain.

'How can you eat that muck?' he asked. 'It's all ground up bone and fat. It'll go straight to your heart.'

'Thank you Doctor Leach,' Underwood replied spraying pastry across his desk. 'Your professional opinion is duly noted and duly ignored. Now, tell me about this Shaw character. How did you ID him?'

Leach opened his file. 'We fingerprinted his remains after we'd brought them in from the railway. Farrell got a match. Leonard Shaw of Balehurst, Cambridgeshire. Farm worker. Convicted of ABH in 1992 after a punch up in a boozer.'

'Interesting,' Underwood observed. 'A bit of

violent previous. Cause of death?'

'Not the train,' Leach replied, knowing that was the critical fact that Underwood was awaiting. 'He was dead when the train hit him.'

'How do you know?'

'Pattern of decay to brain tissue and heart muscles. Once you die and those areas are deprived of oxygenated blood they start to degenerate. My guess is that Shaw was dead at least an hour before he was mashed up by the train.'

'Roger, you are a genius,' Underwood said between mouthfuls. 'How did he die then?'

'The back of his head had been bashed in. Repeated blows with a heavy metal object. We found splinters of steel in his hair.'

'Murder then?'

'Absolutely.'

'Someone beat this bloke's head in and dropped him onto a railway track.' Underwood looked up; DI Mike Bevan was at the door. He waved him in. 'Mike have a seat, I'm just finishing off with Roger.'

'Anything interesting?' Bevan asked, nodding a hello at the pathologist.

'Murder. Farm worker with his head bashed in,' Underwood explained.

'Charming!' said Bevan with a smile. 'It's like Dodge City up here. I had no idea that New Bolden was such a nest of evil.'

Underwood grinned and turned to Leach. 'Good stuff, Roger. Anything else?'

'Just one thing.' Leach turned a page in his notes. 'A portion of flesh was missing from the victim's right arm.'

'The train?'

'I don't think so. It looks more like a bite wound. A pretty savage one at that.'

'What? From a dog?' Underwood frowned in confusion.

'Possibly. It's hard to say at the moment. We'll run some more checks. It looks like someone's tried to rip off his tattoo. There's half an eagle tattoo left on his upper arm.'

'It's an identifying mark,' Bevan interjected. 'Maybe whoever killed him didn't want us to find out his name.'

Underwood checked his notes. 'Good idea, mate, but we know his name already: Leonard Shaw.'

Bevan started slightly. 'Leonard Shaw from Balehurst?'

Underwood and Leach exchanged surprised expressions. 'The very same,' Underwood replied. 'Something you want to tell us, Mike?'

Bevan reached into his briefcase and pulled out a sheet of typed paper. 'Remember I scoped out Woollard's farm last week? I've been running DVLA checks on all the car licence plates I got that night. One belongs to a Mr Leonard Shaw of 3 Old Lane, Balehurst.'

'Well, well!' Underwood exclaimed, 'what we have here gentlemen is a curious coincidence. Leonard Shaw, a convicted violent offender, attends an illegal dogfight at Woollard's farm, then turns up murdered less than a week later. I suggest that we go and have a word with Bob Woollard.'

Bevan raised an admonishing hand. 'John, if you'll bear with me, I might have a better alternative.'

'Let's hear it then,' Underwood instructed.

16.

At 5 p.m. that evening, DI Alison Dexter drove her Mondeo into the car park of New Bolden leisure centre. She was wearing an old West Ham shirt that she'd owned since 1988 and a pair of black shorts that she'd bought in town earlier that afternoon. She felt vaguely ridiculous but sensed an undeniable rush of excitement.

Kelsi was waiting in the Sports Hall, tying her laces at the side of the football pitch. She smiled at Dexter's outfit.

'I thought you were the ghost of Bobby Moore for a minute!'

'More like Bobby Blunder,' Dexter replied. 'I just hope I don't make a complete fool of myself.'

'You'll be all right,' Kelsi assured her. 'Come and meet the others.'

Eight other players were kicking a ball between them on the five-a-side pitch. Some saw Dexter's arrival and turned away from the warm up.

'I'm Bev,' said one.

'Alison,' Dexter replied.

'Not another Hammer?' Bev exclaimed in mock exasperation.

'You leave her alone,' Kelsi remonstrated. 'Remember who scored a hat trick in the World Cup final in 1966. West Ham is the home of football.'

Bev shook her head. 'If I hear another bloody Geoff Hurst story, I swear I'll whack you.'

Kelsi quickly introduced the other players, first names only. Dexter, her mind flying, could only remember a couple of them. Once the match had started, Dexter realised that this was a serious drawback.

The game was fast and of a standard that surprised Alison Dexter. She hadn't played for years, a fact that was very quickly exposed. Her mind wandered between extremes. She found it impossible to control the ball, her first touch was embarrassingly clumsy. Although there were no complaints from her team, Dexter sensed their frustration as she repeatedly squandered possession and misplaced passes. At half time, her heart pounding against her ribcage and sweat streaming down her back, she collapsed onto a wooden bench next to Kelsi.

'God, I'm fucking useless,' Dexter gasped.

'Don't be daft,' Kelsi replied, 'you're just out of practice.'

'I couldn't trap a bag of cement.'

'You're not concentrating on the ball,' Kelsi advised. 'Watch the ball right onto your foot. Keep your eye on it as you kick it away again. You are looking up all the time, trying to see the pass before you've made it.'

Dexter nodded, realising the comments were valid. 'Eye on the ball,' she said.

'Eye on the ball,' Kelsi confirmed.

In the second half, Dexter played much more effectively, following Kelsi's advice to the letter. She started to receive congratulations and encouragement from her team. Now thoroughly warmed up, she found it easier to move about the pitch and even scored with a neat six-yard shot. Her team won 3–2. Kelsi put an arm around her shoulder at the end.

'There you go, Ali. You did great.'

Dexter enjoyed the touch and the compliment.

Her second half performance had at least been respectable; a vast improvement on the previous catastrophic effort.

Ten minutes later, Alison Dexter stood next to Kelsi Hensy in the women's changing room. She had already showered in her usual quick and efficient manner: perhaps even more quickly and efficiently than usual. Now as she clambered into her grey tracksuit trousers and police sweatshirt she found her eyes drawn inexorably across Kelsi Hensy's naked body, lingering with the thrill of the voyeur. Was that all she was? Was she just a thrill seeker without the courage to act on her instincts? She found the idea pathetic. However, the alternative frightened her even more.

Dexter suddenly looked up, her hungry eyes locking onto Kelsi's. Dexter tore her gaze away, dying of embarrassment inside. How long had Kelsi been watching her?

'Are you coming upstairs for a drink then?' Kelsi asked, standing naked directly in front of her and vigorously towelling herself dry.

'I don't know.' Dexter found it hard to look her in the eye. 'Busy at work.'

'I saw your interview on TV the other day.' Kelsi reached into her bag and pulled on a pair of white knickers. 'I didn't realise that you were a copper.'

'The flat feet are a giveaway.'

'You haven't got flat feet,' Kelsi said through a smile.

'It felt like it during the match.'

'You did fine. Come up for a drink. You can tell me what you were doing in my company car park the other morning.'

Dexter froze in horror, her mind frantically tearing itself apart in search of an excuse. Kelsi turned away and finished getting dressed. Shortly thereafter, Dexter found herself sitting in the leisure centre bar with Kelsi, Bev and Sue. The conversation washed over and around her. She drank Budweiser from a bottle, twisted with shame inside.

'It must be interesting,' Sue was saying, 'more interesting than being a legal secretary anyway.'

There was a silence. Dexter realised Sue was talking to her.

'I'm sorry?'

'Being a policewoman. It must be so interesting.'

'It has its moments,' Dexter conceded, Kelsi's smiling gaze burning into the side of her head. 'It's good when we put one inside, like that arsehole Braun for example. I was happy to see him put away.'

'Do the male coppers give you shit?' Kelsi asked.

'They used to,' Dexter replied. 'Not anymore though.'

The conversation went on. Kelsi stared at Dexter over the top of her beer bottle. It made Dexter feel uncomfortable. *She had been seen in the car park of Kelsi's company. What did Kelsi think she was doing there? Stalking her probably. But, Dexter reasoned, that's exactly what I was doing. Half of her wanted to run away, the other half felt an overwhelming urge to stay.*

At 9.30 p.m., the party broke up as Bev and Sue left together. Dexter and Kelsi followed them downstairs. At the exit to the leisure centre Kelsi turned to face Dexter.

'Ali, would you mind driving me home. Getting cabs from here is a nightmare.'

Dexter floundered; she could see Kelsi's Peugeot 206 parked a few yards away. What did the question mean?

'I've had a few beers tonight,' Kelsi explained as if reading her mind. 'I don't want you to arrest me if I drive into a lamp post.'

'No problem.' Dexter pressed her remote control car lock and the Mondeo clicked open.

'That's really sweet of you.'

The drive took about ten minutes. Kelsi Hensy lived in a small mews development: six small houses arranged neatly around a central courtyard. Dexter pulled up and parked as directed.

'Nice place,' she observed through the windscreen.

'It's a bit pokey but I like it,' Kelsi replied. 'Come in for a coffee?' Dexter's mind swam.

'Just five minutes,' Kelsi compromised.

Dexter turned off the engine and followed Kelsi out into the biting night air. On the doorstep of her house, Kelsi turned, put a hand either side of Dexter's face and kissed her. Stunned, Dexter felt Kelsi's tongue push into her mouth, insistent and confident. Dexter felt a hot rush of sexuality tinged with a sudden panic. It was an intoxicating mixture that she had never previously experienced.

'I saw you looking at me,' Kelsi breathed as they broke off the kiss. 'I want you too.'

'This is a bad idea,' was all Dexter could muster in response.

Kelsi unlocked her front door and drew Dexter inside. The warmth was comforting. They kissed again. Now Kelsi's hand toyed with the drawstring at the top of Dexter's tracksuit trousers. Dexter was panicking, awash with desire and confusion, her ability to control was disintegrating. Her tracksuit trousers fell around her ankles.

'We can't do this, Kelsi,' Dexter gasped, the elastic of her knickers tugging at her skin as Kelsi's hand pushed further.

'You don't mean that. You came to my office to look at me. You want me.' Kelsi kissed her again this time with reassuring delicacy. Alison Dexter felt herself weakening. She was surrendering to the moment with an intensity that was overwhelming.

She allowed Kelsi to push her back into an armchair.

Rain began to patter at the windows of the house. Sitting in his car outside, a figure, indistinguishable in the dark, watched the rain speckle on his windscreen.

17.

Leyton, East London
December 1995

The shop bell tinkled as DS Alison Dexter entered 'Garrod and Sons, Family Butchers'. It was an old-fashioned shop: ancient grinding machines along the far wall, black and white ceramic tiles on the floor. Bartholomew Garrod was sitting behind the counter reading a book and eating a sandwich.

'Mr Garrod? Can I talk with you?'

He didn't look up. 'What about?'

'I'm Detective Sergeant Dexter from Leyton CID. I saw you at Smithfield this morning. I'm investigating the death of a man called Brian Patterson.' She watched him carefully. His expression didn't change.

'That's nice for you,' he said continuing to read his book. As Garrod chewed, a piece of pig intestine fell from his sandwich onto the floor. Dexter wanted to retch. She saw that Garrod was eating 'pig's fry', a dish once popular amongst the poor of the East End: fried pig entrails wrapped in bread.

Dexter noticed the dirty mincing machine behind the counter. 'When was your last council inspection?' she asked hoping to get a rise out of Garrod. She was pleased to see he suddenly stopped eating.

'Eighteen months ago. The paperwork is in order. Do you want to see it?'

'No.'

'Why ask then?'

'Did you know Brian Patterson?' Dexter asked.

'Never heard of him.'

Dexter eyeballed Garrod. 'That surprises me. He worked at Smithfield.'

'Lots of people work at Smithfield.' Garrod smiled through his yellow-stained teeth.

'He worked at the wholesale stall that you use. Are you absolutely sure that you don't remember him?'

Bartholomew considered for a moment, weighing his options. 'Hold on. Was he a big, tall bloke? Very muscular?'

'Yes, he was.'

'Black straggly hair?'

'Yes.'

'The guy that got murdered?'

Dexter was tiring of Garrod's ponderous questions. 'So you did know him then?'

'I have heard the name. I might have seen him at the market. It's possible.'

'Did you know that he lived near here?'

'I didn't.'

'Are you sure about that? It seems odd to me that a butcher who buys from Smithfield, and a Smithfield meat porter, two men that lived one hundred yards away from each other, never properly met.'

'Life's full of little coincidences, isn't it?'

'Not in my experience.'

'Maybe you're not very experienced. I could help you there. We could go out back. I'll make your knees tremble.'

'Don't forget who I am, Mr Garrod,' Dexter snarled, 'or I'll have the council down here in an hour to close you down.'

Garrod eyed her with quiet hate. There wasn't much meat on her.

'Am I a suspect then?'

'Why would you think that?'

'You're here aren't you?'

Dexter was running out of steam. Garrod was

right in some ways; she did lack the experience of a proper copper: the wisdom of a McInally. However, she had other advantages.

'*What's that book you're reading?*' *She pointed to the blue bound manual resting under Garrod's monstrous left hand.*

'*It's called* A Handbook of Meat. *It was published by the Meat Trades Journal in 1929. It's about the craft of butchering. My Dad swore by it.*'

'*I thought you just hacked things up.*'

'*Then you are showing your ignorance. Maybe you should read it.*' *Garrod held the book out to her.* '*Bone up, so to speak.*'

'*No thanks.*' *Dexter could feel the interview losing momentum. She decided to lob a hand grenade into the conversation. She had picked her moment: wound up Garrod, made him angry and aggressive. Now she would watch him squirm.* '*Is your brother about?*'

Bartholomew tensed visibly, his hand clenching around the book. '*I don't think he's in.*'

'*He is. I saw him out in your back yard before I came in. In fact, I'm pretty sure I can hear him singing now. If you can call that singing,*' *Dexter said tartly, trying to spike Garrod into saying something he'd regret.*

Garrod turned his head towards the noise: a half-shouted rendition of a familiar tune that was emanating from the back of his shop:

'Oh me lads, you should've seen us gannin'
Passin' folk along the road
And all of them was standin'

'That's him,' Bartholomew Garrod said
eventually. 'I'll fetch him in.' He turned and
lumbered heavily out of the shop.

Dexter leant over the counter but couldn't see
past the bottom of the Garrods' staircase. She
picked up 'A Handbook of Meat' and flicked
through. It was a manual for butchers. There were
pictures of different kinds of cattle, pigs and sheep.
There were pages of advice on equipment, slaughter
methods, knives and grinding devices. On p317 was
a diagram of a side of beef. It was entitled 'Home
Killed Beef – Primal Cuts'. The picture showed the
most important meat areas on a beef carcass: the
sirloin, silverside, tenderloin, chucks and others.
The areas were marked with dotted lines: sirloin on
the forelimbs, tenderloin on the hind legs, and
silverside down the back.

Voices floated down the hallway; she closed the
book and replaced it on the counter. The Garrods
had returned.

'Here's the police lady, Ray,' Bartholomew said,
suddenly overcome with nervous politeness, 'Miss
Dexter. You answer her questions. Be a good lad
now.' Ray blinked uncertainly at Dexter.

'Ray, did you know Brian Patterson?' she asked.
'He was a porter at Smithfield.'

Unsure, Ray turned to his brother. 'Honnable
lady, I didn't know Mister Brian Patterson, the
porter.'

'What did he call me?' Dexter asked.

Bartholomew put his hand on Ray's shoulder.
'He called you the honourable lady. Ray's not very
good with names. When he forgets them he gets
himself angry, don't you, mate? Our Dad had the
idea of using terms like they use in Parliament. You
know, honourable lady, honourable gentleman, and
all that stuff. That way he doesn't make himself
upset or annoy anyone else.'

'Has he got a mental problem?' Dexter asked
with deliberate tactlessness.

Bartholomew was struggling to keep calm. 'He
hasn't got a mental problem. Our Dad used to keep
motorbikes. He stripped the engines, refitted them
and then flogged 'em. He'd do it in the house when
it was raining. When Ray was a baby, our mum was
carrying him down the stairs. She slipped on the
carpet and Ray fell. He smashed his head on the
engine casing of an old Triumph.'

'Ah fell ten feet apparently,' Ray nodded.

'So he hasn't got any mental problem, it just
takes him a bit longer to get things.'

'Ah ain't got no mental problem,' Ray shouted

angrily. 'Ah ain't mental. Tell her, Bollamew.'

Dexter felt a mixture of fear and pity. She also felt something else: a bell was jangling in the back of her mind. She felt excited.

'What was that song you were singing, Ray?' she asked quietly.

'What?'

'The song you were singing just now. You were really good.'

'Do you think so? Bollamew hates my singing. Don't you, Bollamew?'

Bartholomew Garrod forced a smile. He didn't take his eyes off Dexter. Her question had unsettled him: he couldn't decipher its purpose. His fingers clenched around the handle of his favourite cutting knife behind the counter. 'I wouldn't say that, Ray.'

'The honnable lady liked my singing, she said so.'

'It was great, Ray. What was the song?' Dexter pressed.

'"Blaydon Races",' Ray said excitedly. 'Shall I sing it again?'

Dexter's heart raced as she realised that Ray Garrod might have inadvertently incriminated himself. She looked Bartholomew Garrod directly in the eye and smiled, 'I don't think so. But thank you very much. Thank you both for being so helpful. We'll be in touch if we need anything else.'

The two brothers stood in silence as she left the

shop. Bartholomew had been unnerved by Dexter's strange line of questioning. Had he underestimated her? Why had she asked Ray about the song? Twice? She had really wanted to know. Garrod wracked his brains for an answer.

'Where did you learn that song, Ray?' he asked.

'What song?'

'The fucking "Blaydon Races". The fucking song she was just asking you about.'

'Don't shout at me!' Ray screamed covering his ears. 'The honnable gennelman mustn't shout at me. Dad said you mustn't never shout at me.'

'Was it Brian? You've got to tell.' Bartholomew shook his brother violently. 'Brian the porter, did he teach you the song?'

Ray nodded, tears running down his face.

Bartholomew Garrod smashed his fist on the meat counter. 'Fuck! Fucking hell, Ray! What have you done? You fucking stupid bastard.' Shaking with rage, Bartholomew Garrod frantically tried to arrange his thoughts. Dexter had made the connection. He had seen that in her eyes. They had lied to her about not knowing Brian Patterson and she had clearly recognised that. The bitch would return with a search warrant. Bartholomew Garrod felt time slipping away from him.

They had to move quickly. 'Ray, listen to me. We have got to go away now. We're going up to the *caravan. Remember the old caravan up by the sea?'*

'On holiday?' Ray had stopped crying.

'That's right, mate. Holiday. Listen, I have to go out now. I have to go out and get some money. Do you understand me, Ray?'

'Yes, Bollamew,' Ray nodded.

'Lock up the shop after me. Don't let anyone in. No one comes through that door except me.' Bartholomew pulled his overcoat off its hook at the bottom of the stairs. 'I'm going up to the bank in the High Road. I'll be half an hour. Wait here for me, Ray. Don't let anyone in.'

'Yes, Bollamew.'

Bartholomew Garrod slammed the door shut behind him and waited for Ray to fix the bolt after him. It was starting to rain. He walked as quickly as his heavy frame would allow.

18.

Tuesday, 15th October 2002

Underwood sat glumly in his glass-walled office, trying to read the full post-mortem report on Leonard 'Lefty' Shaw. In his vainer moments, he had once liked to think of himself as a tragic hero: an essentially noble but flawed character. True he had endured his moments of catharsis; his marriage had foundered and his sanity had nearly slipped away from him. Now he felt a curious sense of nothing: nothing except the dull ache that was growing inside him. It was a strange form of redemption: to salvage hope and sanity only to be consumed from within by some evil malignancy. Heroes didn't get cancer. Ordinary people got cancer: it was an ordinary little disease; an ordinary little lump. It was mundane, tragic in its predictability. Underwood didn't know whether to fight. Perhaps redemption would come for him in death. Or, he reasoned, perhaps it would come in a noble struggle against it. He wondered if the rest really was silence, and if so, whether silence was such a bad thing.

He turned his attention to the matter of Lefty Shaw's inauspicious death.

Name: Leonard Arthur Shaw. Age: 38 years 2 months. Weight: 134 Kilos.

Underwood passed over Shaw's other personal details with the recklessness of the jaded copper.

Time of death: Sunday 12th October at approx 2 a.m. Cause of death: Damage to rear of head resulting in fractured skull and brain damage.

'Foul play,' thought Underwood. There was a time, earlier in his career and long before the arrival of Alison Dexter, when the prospect of a murder investigation would have excited him. Now it was just something to do. He had lost his sense of revulsion, his sense of justice even. Underwood wondered when this transition had taken place; when this emotional shell had hardened around him. Perhaps there hadn't been a moment of transition. Maybe time had ground him down like waves grind rocks into sand. That was a more frightening thought.

The surface of Shaw's body was caked in dried sweat. Obviously, this suggests he undertook serious physical exertion before death. It should be noted that Shaw's blood group was O negative. However, traces of AB negative blood were found on his hands, arms and face. My supposition is that Shaw was involved in some kind of fight before he died. This hypothesis is supported by the severe bruising to the victim's ribcage.

Underwood sipped his coffee, drowning his anxiety in hot, brown water. He tried to focus his mind. His thought processes, always erratic, were at their most unreliable in the morning.

The victim's right arm also shows an extremely unusual pattern of damage. A portion of flesh has been torn away and is missing. The victim appears to have had a tattoo of an eagle in the upper arm area. It is a common design. It appears that there was some crude attempt to remove it by force.

Underwood looked out of the grey window at the grey skies above his grey world. Why try to remove the tattoo? Did it reveal something about the killer's identity? He looked up as Alison Dexter arrived in the next office to his. Underwood looked up at the office clock. It said 8.02. He wrote that piece of information down in the notebook in which he noted such details. Dexter sat down and flicked on her computer. Underwood studied her black hair and elegant neck intensely, with the hunger of desolation.

He continued to read Leach's report: *The wound to the upper arm is, in itself, peculiar. The flesh is torn and ragged resembling the kind of damage inflicted by dangerous dogs. However, an enzyme analysis of the area revealed traces of human saliva on the flesh. This matched the AB negative blood traces found on the victim's hands. The obvious conclusion is that Shaw's assailant removed the flesh with his teeth.*

A warning bell jangled in Underwood's head. In the gloomy recesses of his mind, something was screaming at him. Edgy now, he read on:

The actual killing blows were struck with tremendous ferocity. Splinters of steel were lodged in the victim's skin and hair. The cranium was fractured an inch above the nuchal crest, fatally piercing the brain itself in two places.

Something vague and indistinct bothered Underwood. A memory frantically gasping for life: like some prehistoric creature crawling out of the primordial soup.

*The post-mortem evidence points to a rather obvious conclusion: Shaw was engaged in some form of physical violence immediately prior to his death. His assailant is of the AB negative blood group and, in addition to administering the fatal blows to Shaw with some kind of heavy steel instrument (hammer?), he bit a sizeable chunk of flesh from Shaw's right arm. Without question, Shaw was dead **before** his body was dumped onto the railway track.*

Underwood sat back in his chair and for a moment or two watched Alison Dexter stare into space in the office next to him.

The computer screen glowed in front of her, waiting for her to log in. Alison Dexter was aware of the faint musky aroma on her face and her fingers. She thought that she liked it. However, everything else was uncertain: her feelings ricocheted between shame, pride and excitement. The thrill and terror of losing control electrified her. She now knew that she was alive but had no idea what she was becoming. She groaned inwardly as Underwood came to her door.

'Got a minute?' he asked.

'Of course.' Dexter waved him in.

'Everything OK?'

'Fine.'

'You seem…'

'Fine,' Dexter crashed the sarcophagus lid shut on that twitching corpse of a conversation. 'What can I do for you?'

Underwood handed her the post-mortem report on Lefty Shaw. 'This is Leach's PM analysis of the railway body, Leonard Shaw.'

'Foul play?'

'So it seems. It also appears that there's an overlap with the work Bevan's been doing.'

'The dog-fighting thing?'

'That's right. Shaw attended one of the fights at Woollard's farm. Bevan got his car number. Bevan's helping out on this. I hope that's OK with you.'

'How did he die?' Dexter didn't feel alert enough to tackle a full post-mortem report.

'Back of his head was bashed in. Chunk of flesh was torn off his arm too. I'm wondering if it was a prize fight.'

'Are you happy to run with it?' Dexter offered the report back to Underwood without opening it.

He didn't accept it. 'Delighted to but you should read it.'

'Why?'

'I'm not sure. It doesn't feel right. I'm afraid I might have missed something important.'

'Leave it on the desk then. I'll look at it.'

Conversation over. Underwood tried to find a spark of interest in Dexter's stone green eyes; the spark that usually ignited his day. For once, he saw nothing and, deflated, left the room without another word. Dexter felt a wrench of guilt: professional guilt this time. She tapped her password into her computer and opened Microsoft Outlook. Kelsi had written her mobile number and email address in Dexter's notebook. Dexter dangled over a precipice of uncertainty. She felt like a cartoon character who had run off the edge of a cliff and stopped dead in the air; its legs still running uselessly. Was it bad form to send an email message so soon? Was it bad form not to? She didn't want Kelsi to think that she was an obsessive maniac: the poor girl had, after all, already spotted Dexter lurking in her company car park. Perhaps, Dexter reasoned, that was precisely why she should send a message; to reassure Kelsi that she was not a basket case.

Irritated at the impossibility of sexual diplomacy, Dexter cursed herself. This was exactly the kind of distraction that she had battled studiously for years to avoid. Her normal lattice of logical thought was fragmenting by the second; like a child tearing down a spider's web. And yet, she felt impelled to write to Kelsi. The simple truth was, she wanted more.

To: *HensyAK@ComBoldUK.Net*
From: *Adex@CamCpol.Org*
Hello, just a quick note to say thanks for a great evening. Sorry about the car park thing: coppers are naturally suspicious. Legs ache like mad: football is not a forgiving game especially for us flat-foots. Would love to have a drink sometime. Drop me a line when you get a moment. Alison.

Satisfied, Dexter sent the message. She liked the mixture of sensitivity and assertiveness. She had expressed interest without cloying; terse but friendly. That was the balance that she had wanted to strike. Instantly bored once the message had disappeared, Dexter opened Leach's post-mortem report on Leonard Shaw.

Ten minutes later, her mood had suddenly changed. In a mild panic exacerbated by her fragile emotional state, she called Roger Leach and requested a full DNA profile of the AB negative blood found on Leonard Shaw's body. Then she called Leyton CID and requested that a copy of the Primal Cut case file be immediately couriered up to her. A demon had stepped from the shadows at the back of her tired mind.

19.

Leyton, East London
December 1995

DS Dexter ran up two flights of stone stairs, brushing past cleaning ladies and uniformed officers on the way. She burst through the double doors of Leyton CID and headed straight for McInally's office. The DCI was staring at crime scene photographs of the body hauled from the Lea and of the remains of Brian Patterson. He looked up in surprise as Dexter crashed through his door without knocking.

'Is the building on fire?' he asked.

'Guv?'

'It's polite to knock.'

'Sir, it's important. I think I've found something. Something about the Patterson case. There are these two brothers. They're butchers on Norlington and they...'

McInally sat back in his chair and raised a heavy hand. 'Dexy, sit down, count to ten and talk me through it slowly.'

Annoyed, breathless but compliant, Dexter took a grip of her emotions and walked McInally through her two meetings with the Garrods. Her boss was thoughtful.

'It's all circumstantial of course,' he observed. 'How certain are you it's them? If we go charging in with a search warrant, we need to be confident.'

Dexter bit her thumb, the pain sometimes helped her concentrate. Then she saw the photographs spread out across McInally's desk. She focused on the bloodied torso and arms.

'Sir, in both cases pieces of flesh were removed from the victims. We thought the attacks were frenzied. I'm telling you that they were thought out. Look at the damage to the River Lea body: sections of flesh removed from the shoulders and ribcage. Patterson was cut up in a similar way. These are not accidental, sir, they are butchers' cuts of meat: the primal cuts. I fucking saw them in a book in the Garrods' shop.'

McInally looked at her. 'Show me these primal cuts then.'

Dexter sensed she was winning. 'Can I use your computer?'

'Go ahead.'

Dexter sat behind McInally's PC and logged onto the Internet. She ran a search for 'Primal Cut'. Eventually she found a picture of a beef carcass annotated with the various cuts. McInally leaned forward. Dexter picked up a photograph of the River Lea torso.

'OK. Look at the shoulder's missing portion of

flesh. Look at the diagram; that area is called the "chuck tender". Look at the back of the victim. Missing flesh here. Look at the diagram; that area is called "striploin". On the Patterson body flesh was removed from the back of his upper right thigh. On the diagram that cut is called "silverside". Guv, only a butcher would know the primal cuts.'

She sensed that McInally was on the point of being persuaded. He needed a final shove in the direction of her thought process.

'There's something else, sir,' she continued. 'The Garrods knew Patterson. I'm sure of it. When I asked them they claimed they'd never met him. Brian Patterson's mates told me that he used to sing the "Blaydon Races" while he worked. Ray Garrod was singing the same song today. They knew Patterson, sir. They knew him and they lied about it. Why would they do that?'

'Go on,' McInally encouraged.

Dexter hesitated. There wasn't much else to add. Her assumption of the Garrods' guilt had been based on some fairly flimsy ideas. There had to be something else they could use.

'The River Lea corpse was a large man, right? Muscular, heavy set.'

'Yes.'

'He could defend himself. You'd need two people

to take him down. The Garrods are both powerful men.'

'Dexy...'

'Then there's the head wound,' she continued. 'Didn't the PM report say that the fatal wound was a massive blow to the centre of the forehead? Like a poleaxe?'

'Yes.'

'That's a way of stunning cattle, Guv, before you slaughter them. A butcher would know that.'

'Alison, I trust you,' McInally said quietly. 'And you are a fucking good copper. But you do realise that if we go marching in there and find nothing there'll be hell to pay. Someone will swing and I don't dangle alone.'

'I know I'm right, sir,' Dexter said with quiet conviction.

'OK. We'll get a team down to the shop and check it out.'

'We'll need some muscle, sir. The Garrods are fucking enormous.'

'We can probably get a firearms unit out of City Police. I could pull in a favour. It might take an hour. Did they twig you'd rumbled them?'

'I don't think so,' Dexter replied. 'Firearms would be sensible, sir. Bartholomew Garrod is an ox.'

'Right.' McInally picked up his phone. 'You sort

out a SOCO unit and commandeer some uniformed plods from downstairs. I'll see about this shooter team.'

Dexter felt a rush of pride and excitement; she hovered for a second, enjoying the moment of triumph.

'Well stop pissing about,' McInally barked. 'We've got work to do!'

He smiled as he watched her leave.

Bartholomew Garrod withdrew just over four thousand pounds from his bank on Leyton High Road, leaving five hundred pounds in his account. He stuffed the money into his inside jacket pocket. The look in DS Dexter's eyes had told him enough: she had somehow sensed they had murdered Brian Patterson. Bartholomew hurried back down Leyton High Road. It was pouring with rain now; water streamed across the pavement. The money would buy them some time at least. His father had owned an old caravan on a communal site: a scrap of wasteland near a seaside resort. He had taken Ray to the caravan regularly since their father's death. Ray liked the water, the smell of the air and the fish and chips in polystyrene trays. The caravan would be an ideal place to lie low.

Bartholomew crossed into Norlington Road. Then he stopped dead in his tracks. Two police squad cars were parked outside his shop. He quickly ducked behind a car and watched. He counted five uniformed police officers and two more in black combat fatigues who appeared to be armed. Bartholomew cursed his stupidity: he should have taken Ray with him to the bank. Now, his brother was trapped.

One hundred yards away, DS Dexter banged on the locked door of the Garrods' shop. No one came to open it. She tried again and called out this time: 'Mr Garrod. This is Leyton Police. Open the door please.'

'Perhaps they've done a runner,' McInally said as he joined her.

'No. They're here. The van's still parked down the side alley,' Dexter replied. She crashed on the door again.

'What's our strength?' he asked.

'The two of us, five plods and two from the City Police ARU. One more squad car on the way.' Dexter banged furiously at the door again.

'Pack it in, Dexy!' McInally found the noise irritating; he turned and gestured to a uniformed police sergeant crouching next to a squad car. 'Brown! Get the ram up here.'

A moment later PC Brown carried the black battering ram up to the door.

'You want me to bosh it, sir?' he asked.

McInally nodded, pulling Dexter out of the way. 'Go ahead, son.'

The door smashed open at the second attempt. Dexter and McInally were first in, stepping over the carpet of broken glass. The firearms officers they had seconded from City Police followed close behind, fanning right and left across the shop floor. Dexter pointed through the door towards the living quarters. McInally nodded and waved the armed policemen past him. Two uniformed officers now blocked the entrance to the shop.

Through the commotion, Dexter heard a man crying. Ahead of her, one of the armed response officers called out, 'We got one!'

Ray Garrod was sitting sobbing at the bottom of the stairs, his knees drawn up to his body, his giant arms wrapped tightly around them.

'Ray, it's me, DS Dexter. Remember the "honourable lady" you called me?'

Ray looked at her, then at the two guns pointing at him. 'Bollamew's gonna be so angry with me. I promised not to let you in. I promised.'

'It's not your fault, Ray,' Dexter said. 'Where's your brother?'

'He went out. He shouldn't have gone out and left me.'

McInally sent an armed officer to each of the front and back doors. 'Listen to me, Ray,' he said, returning to the staircase, 'you need to tell us about Brian Patterson now. It's the only way to get Bartholomew out of trouble.'

Dexter shot him a concerned look. McInally shrugged apologetically.

'Brian taught me some songs. Brian liked my singing too.'

'What happened to him, Ray?' Dexter pressed.

'Ah ate some bit of him,' Ray replied. 'Bollamew cooked some kidney and ah ate it.'

McInally produced a pair of handcuffs from his jacket pocket. 'Ray, I'm going to put these on you now. We need to take you away from here for a while. Could you stand up for me and face the wall?'

'Yes. Ah'll face the wall for the honnable gennelman.' Ray clambered to his feet. For the first time, McInally became aware of the sheer size of Ray Garrod. He had to have a size twenty collar. He took hold of Ray's right wrist and snapped a cuff onto it. The metal cut into the skin and Ray wheeled around in pained surprise.

'What are you fucking doing to me?' he shouted, lashing out at McInally. Caught off guard, the DCI crashed into the wall with blood pouring from his nose. Dexter screamed for assistance as Ray Garrod pushed past her and ran out into the shop. DS Morgan, the armed response officer at the front *door, turned a split second too late. As he lifted his gun, three hundred pounds of Ray Garrod crashed into him. The deafening bang of a gunshot rang out, the bullet smashing into the glass of the meat counter. Ray, screaming in panic, barged past the two terrified uniformed policemen at the door, sending them flying out onto the pavement.*

Dexter sprinted after Ray Garrod, uncertain of what she would do if she caught up with him.

Bartholomew Garrod watched in horror as his brother ran out onto Norlington Road, lumbering in his direction.

'Bollamew! Bollamew!' Ray shouted, unaware that his brother was hiding behind an old brown Ford Sierra only eighty yards ahead of him. He staggered on, lurching across the junction of Norlington and Albert Road. Dexter ran out onto the road. Bartholomew watched her running his brother down, powerless to act. A siren wailed somewhere ahead of him. Bartholomew knew that he would have to act; either intervene or run away. At that moment Ray ran out onto Morley Road and was hit by the source of the siren, the reserve squad car that Dexter had requested. Bartholomew watched in horror as his brother was thrown up into the air before crashing head first into the windscreen of the police vehicle. Ray didn't move. Alison Dexter arrived at the scene a few seconds later. Bartholomew

could hear her shouting 'Call a fucking ambulance' at the bemused driver of the police car.

Bartholomew wanted to rip her into pieces and chew on her gristle. He had to contain his fury, his agony. Blood roared into his head. He struggled desperately to remain calm. His tears stung. More policemen were running out onto the street. It was time to move on or risk capture. Unnoticed in the midst of the chaos, Bartholomew Garrod eventually turned his back on his dead brother and his family home. He walked hurriedly to Leyton Underground and took a Central Line train to Liverpool Street. An hour later he sat down in the smoking compartment of a train destined for Harwich.

Late that night, as Bartholomew Garrod unlocked the padlock to his family caravan near the North Sea coast, Scene of Crime Officers in Leyton found a stockpile of human remains secreted at the back of the Garrods' refrigerator.

20.

DI Mike Bevan drew up at the edge of the gypsy site. The two uniformed officers he had seconded from Underwood were parked out of sight a few hundred yards behind him. He hoped he would not need them. Bevan counted about twenty caravans.

Children played on an area of open grass next to the vehicles. He had decided to tackle Keith Gwynne on his own: in his experience, going mob-handed into pikey sites was a recipe for unnecessary grief.

As soon as he slammed his car door shut he was confronted by two shaven-headed men.

'Wha' d'ya want?' one asked.

'I'm from Cambridgeshire Council,' Bevan replied. 'I need to speak to someone called er...Keith Gwynne.' He tried to appear vague; coppers were always aggressively specific.

'Never heard of him.'

'Look, go and get him,' said Bevan with a smile he hoped was disarming. 'Tell him I'm from the council. It's about the ponies he's got tethered on the other side of Balehurst. There's a council issue. It will save him money if he talks to me.'

One of the men turned and walked back into the site. As he disappeared from view, Bevan tried to be friendly with the figure barring his entry to the site. 'So how many of you live on this site?'

'If you're from the council, you should know,' came the reply.

'They don't tell us everything,' Bevan observed.

'They told you Gwynney lived here though.'

Bevan shrugged and said nothing: he'd been clumsy there. He was getting sloppy in his old age.

A minute later, Keith Gwynne emerged from a caravan and approached Bevan suspiciously.

'Who the fuck are you then?' Gwynne asked.

'Mike Bevan from the council. I need to talk to you about your ponies.'

'I sold them ponies last week.'

'Why don't we talk in private?' Bevan replied as a group of youths began to gather, interested in the strange confrontation.

'You're a copper!' Gwynne snorted. 'Good fucking disguise!'

Bevan leaned forward and whispered menacingly in Gwynne's ear, 'Now you listen to me, dickhead. I've got a dead body on a railway line and I've got your fucking car number plate at a crime scene. I am trying to be delicate. I respect the sensibilities and privacy of your friends here. So here's a deal for you. Come with me now or I'll come back here with a squad and rip this shithole apart. Who knows what we'll find. Your mate over there stinks of pot, for example.'

Gwynne took a step back, surprised and frightened. 'Danny,' he said eventually to the lad who had originally intercepted Bevan, 'I can handle this. You and the boys take off now.'

Alone with his target at last, Bevan relaxed a little. 'We need to have a serious chat Keith.'

'You're wasting your time. I've done nothing.'

'Look, sonny. You are in deep shite. Be straight, be useful and you've got a chance. Otherwise you are looking at a stretch. We are going to drive down to New Bolden nick and you are going to sing like Maria Callas.'

'If I don't come?'

'Accessory to murder, perverting the course of justice, resisting arrest, violation of the Dangerous Dogs Act – I'm guessing eight, maybe nine years.'

'That's bollocks. I didn't murder anyone.'

'Get in the car.'

21.

Alison Dexter was too agitated to sit down. Instead, she stood staring out of the window of John Underwood's office at the square scrap of grass that constituted his horizon.

'Tell me what you know about this Woollard character,' she asked Underwood after he had briefly explained the circumstances surrounding the death of Lefty Shaw.

'He's a farmer. Wealthy. Mike Bevan has been watching him for weeks. He suspects that Woollard is importing and fighting illegal breeds of dog: pit bulls, that kind of thing. Bevan photographed some faces coming out of Woollard's a couple of weeks ago. He suspects they were paying customers for a dog fight.'

'What about bare knuckle fighting?' Dexter asked.

'No idea.' Underwood considered the notion. 'Although given the nature of Shaw's injuries it's plausible I suppose. Very smart of you. What made you think of that?'

Dexter turned to face him. 'The bite wound.'

'What about it?'

'Remind you of anything?'

'No.' Underwood hesitated; something about the wound had unsettled him. 'Maybe. I don't know.'

'I've asked Leach to run a full DNA profile on the saliva sample.'

Underwood caught an edge in Dexter's voice. 'Do you know who did this?'

'Does "Bartholomew Garrod" ring any bells?'

Underwood frowned for a moment before he remembered, 'The "Primal Cut" thing? Are you sure?'

'Of course I'm not fucking sure, John,' Dexter hissed, 'but I do know that Bartholomew Garrod fought bare knuckle contests across London for twenty years.'

'That's tenuous, Alison. Garrod's been missing for what? Seven or eight years now? He could be dead. He could be out of the country. The chances of him turning up on your patch are remote.'

'Maybe.' Dexter sat down in a chair opposite Underwood. She tried to rub the acid of exhaustion from her eyes. 'After Ray Garrod was killed, we interviewed a bunch of locals and people that knew them. Two blokes, toerags the both of them, said they'd seen Bartholomew Garrod fight bare knuckle. It used to be quite a big deal in London. Loads of pubs would arrange after hours contests in their cellars and back yards. One of the guys I questioned said he'd seen Garrod take a bite out of someone during a fight and swallow it.'

Underwood tried to allay Dexter's concern. 'Look, Garrod isn't going to come up here, is he? If he's still alive, he'll be hiding in a big city. He'd be too conspicuous in a tinpot place like this.' He had added the derogatory reference to New Bolden to appeal to Dexter's cockney snobbery about Cambridgeshire. It didn't work. 'Why would he come up here?'

'Me,' said Dexter quietly. 'Maybe he's come for me.'

'Don't be daft. He's not an idiot. I can't believe he'd risk a life sentence to come looking for you on some revenge trip.'

'I disagree. In any case, I've requisitioned Ray Garrod's post-mortem file and medical records along with a copy of the Primal Cut case file. I'm going to get Leach to do a DNA comparison with the saliva found on Shaw.'

'That's your prerogative,' Underwood replied, 'but I think it's a waste of time.'

There was a knock at the office door. DS Harrison stood in the doorway.

'Guv, Bevan is in interview room 3 with someone called Keith Gwynne. He wants you down there.'

Underwood walked around his desk, pulling on his jacket and collecting his notebook as he did so. 'This guy was at Woollard's the night Shaw was killed.'

'I'm coming with you,' Dexter replied.

'You're jumping to conclusions, Alison,' Underwood said as they headed down the stone stairway to the ground floor. 'Nothing that you've said proves that Garrod killed Shaw.'

'We'll do the interview together,' Dexter conceded as she opened the door to interview room 3.

Keith Gwynne sat opposite Mike Bevan, hunched unhappily in his chair. He shifted uncomfortably as Dexter and Underwood entered the room. Bevan leaned towards the obligatory recording equipment. 'Inspectors Dexter and Underwood have joined the interview,' he announced into the microphone.

Dexter didn't waste any time; she stared hard at Gwynne. 'Tell me what happened at Woollard's.

Tell me what happened to Leonard Shaw. Tell me everything. Tell me now.'

Bevan looked up at Underwood, their toes trodden on. Underwood shrugged; he was used to Dexter's dynamism.

'Fuck me!' Gwynne exclaimed. 'What have I done to deserve you lot? You'd think I was a great bleeding train robber.'

'Answer the question,' Dexter snapped.

'I suppose a lawyer is out of the question?' Gwynne asked.

'You haven't been arrested, Keith,' Bevan said gently. 'You are helping us out. You haven't been charged with anything so why do you need a lawyer?'

Dexter was getting increasingly impatient. 'You were there. Tell us what happened. Or I'll make sure you will be charged, convicted and eating porridge from a different cock every day for the next ten years.'

Gwynne took a deep breath. 'All right, all right. Enough already. There were two fights at Bob Woollard's: a dog fight and a prize fight.' He looked up at Dexter. 'That's a bare knuckle fight,' he explained.

'I know what a prize fight is,' Dexter shouted, ignoring the restraining hand Underwood had placed on her shoulder, 'just tell me what you saw.'

'Lefty took a bad beating. The other guy battered him with a steel bucket. I've never seen anything like it.'

'What happened after the fight?' Underwood asked.

'I went home.'

'You're lying,' said Dexter, 'tell me about the other man. The guy who killed Shaw. Do you know his name?'

Gwynne hesitated; he did not want to incur the wrath of George Norlington. 'No,' he replied, his eyes darting left and downwards.

'Liar. Describe him then,' Dexter instructed.

Gwynne was sweating now. 'I don't know. Maybe three hundred pounds...about six feet tall...fat around his middle but strong as an ox.'

'Eye colour?' Underwood asked.

'God knows, brown maybe.'

'This is not enough, Keith,' Bevan said firmly. 'It's not enough to help you. You are an accessory to murder looking at eight years in prison. If you don't start being cooperative, we'll have no option but to turn over your camp site.'

Dexter found Bevan's quiet, insistent manner half-irritating, half-impressive. It seemed to work on Gwynne too.

'The guy's name is George. He rents a room behind the pub in Heydon; the Dog and Feathers.'

'That's better,' Bevan said with a smile, 'keep going.'

'He's a big, scary bastard,' Gwynne continued. 'He had a Tosa dog. One of Woollard's animals killed it. Maybe he was pissed off by that and wanted revenge on Lefty.'

'Surname?' Underwood asked. 'What's his surname Keith?'

Gwynne scratched his head as if in admission of defeat. 'Norlington. George Norlington.'

Dexter's heart jumped, stopped then jumped again. She turned to Underwood.

'It's him,' she said quietly.

Alison Dexter tried to banish all thoughts of Kelsi Hensy from her mind. Now she had to concentrate.

22.

Leyton, East London
December 1995

The first parcel arrived a week after the newspaper story. Dexter and McInally were plastered all over the Evening Standard *and one or two of the East End local papers. 'Cannibalism in the East End' was the most tasteful of the headlines. The articles* told the story of the Garrods; of how the brothers had abducted, murdered then eaten parts of their victims; of how Alison Dexter had been promoted to Detective Sergeant; of how Ray Garrod had been hit by a police car; of how Bartholomew Garrod was still at large and a danger to the public.

The parcel was enclosed neatly in brown paper, postmarked 'Edmonton' and addressed to Detective Sergeant Dexter at Leyton CID. She opened it at 10.00 a.m. on Christmas Eve. Inside, wrapped in cling film, was a kidney. Dexter dropped the parcel in shock. A pathologist subsequently identified it as a human organ but not one belonging to one of the Garrods' known victims.

A week later, a letter arrived, postmarked 'Watford'. More alert this time, Dexter put on a pair of white plastic evidence-handling gloves before opening it. She read it carefully.

'Dear Detective Sergeant, You must be proud of yourself. Killing an innocent man that was no more than a child in his head. You must be proud of your promotion you fucking bitch. I think about you all the time. Your time is coming, bitch. The clock is running down on you. Don't think I can't find you before you find me. I know where you work. When I get you, and I will get you, let me tell you what I plan to do. You have small breasts that are hardly worth my effort but I noticed that you have nice hard nipples. I *am going to eat them first, probably dipped in olive oil. Thinking about it, there's not much meat on you at all. I saw in the newspapers that you recognised the butcher's cuts on Patterson and Moran. Well consider this then. After I've had your tits off, I'm going to take a silverside and a chuck from you. You'll still be alive of course, in fact, I might let you join in. You are a stringy little bitch and probably taste like a dried up bit of turkey left over from Christmas. I've got some piccalilli here to moisten you up a bit. I'm working on getting your home address. Expect a visit. BG.'*

In the first week of January 1996, what turned out to be a human pancreas arrived at Dexter's flat in Leyton. Panicking, she drove immediately to the police station.

'He knows where I live, Guv!' she shouted at McInally. 'How the hell did he find that out?'

'My guess is that he's made some heavy-duty London mob connections through this bare knuckle business. I hate to admit it, but big chunks of the East End are still run by some pretty unpleasant faces. If you know who and how to ask, they can find practically anybody.'

Dexter slumped in a chair. 'What am I going to do then?'

McInally thought for a moment. 'Well, you can't go home. Not alone anyway. Take a squad car back with you. Get what you need and move in with

Janice and me for a while. At least till we catch this arsehole.'

'I appreciate that, Guv, but what if we don't catch him? I mean, we've got nothing so far. He could be anywhere. Watford, Edmonton, he could be sitting out in the car park waiting for me.' Dexter was arguing herself into a position from which there was only one escape. 'Maybe I should move on.'

'Move on?'

'Transfer. Piss off out of it.'

'Where to?'

'I haven't got a clue. It'll have to be out of London.'

'I agree. I don't want to lose you Dexy,' McInally said sadly, 'you are the best copper on the station.'

'Second best,' Dexter replied politely although she suspected McInally was probably right.

McInally sat back in his chair, thoughtful. 'I might have an idea. Have you ever been to Cambridgeshire?'

'Not that I remember.'

'You probably wouldn't. It's not very memorable. Flat, cold, wet, students.'

'You aren't selling it very well.'

'I know the DI that runs CID in a place called New Bolden.'

'Never heard of it.'

'Commuter town. Reminds me of Milton Keynes.

Few drug problems but it's fairly quiet.'

'What's this bloke's name?'

'John Underwood. He's a good lad. How would you describe him? Intense, I suppose, but his heart's in the right place.'

'Why are you telling me his life story?'

'There was an accident a couple of months ago. His DS got killed in a car on the M11. Spun it into the central reservation chasing some armed robber.'

'So they are short of a Detective Sergeant?'

'Enter the upwardly mobile DS Dexter of the Met.'

'I don't know, Guv. I'm not really a small town girl. Messing about with farmers and shoplifters isn't really my cup of tea. It all sounds a bit bleeding anonymous to be honest.'

'Exactly,' McInally put his feet up on his desk, 'anonymous is what you need. You want me to roll the dice with this Underwood geezer? You could handle him with your eyes shut.'

DS Dexter realised that she was out of options.

23.

Bartholomew Garrod drove to Sawtry in west Cambridgeshire. With his right hand he steered his van through the centre of the village, with his left he withdrew a fillet of raw meat from the Tupperware tray that rested on the passenger seat. He felt no guilt in eating the remains of his dead Tosa: consumption was a mark of respect. His dad had taught him that; told him how the Japanese had eaten vanquished Allied soldiers in the jungles of Burma.

Garrod drove slowly out of the village and followed a winding B-road for a mile or so due west. His body ached. His fight with Lefty Shaw had left him bruised and uncomfortable. Garrod regretted smashing in Shaw's head: he knew that his opponent had probably died. There were no rules in prize fighting but killing someone could draw unwanted attention: the heat and glare of a police investigation. There were at least a dozen people, Gwynne and Woollard included, who could give accurate descriptions of him if the police tracked them down. He realised that and was not taking any chances. He had a rough growth of beard on his face to disguise his features. Garrod had also bought and used a small bottle of black hair dye the previous day: he liked the result.

Garrod realised that he could no longer make a living through fighting. For a start, it made him conspicuous. Secondly, Garrod knew that a beard and hair dye couldn't disguise the fact that his power was fading. His strength, whilst still formidable, was ebbing away from him. It would only be a matter of time until some young thug took him down; that was an outcome Garrod could not allow. It was a harsh realisation. However, the pains in his chest and back, still lingering days after his last fight, were a grim reminder that time was now an enemy that he could not consume.

Garrod had become an avid reader of the *Cambridge Evening News* and the *New Bolden Gazette*. He watched the local news carefully, seeking stories about DI Alison Dexter. The television report that he had seen about Nicholas Braun had been a rare joy. He had seen her interviewed, sensed the little bitch's discomfort as the camera beamed her face across the region. The newspapers had talked little about Dexter, mentioning her by name only once. They had preferred to discuss Braun's crimes and the terrible revelations that had emerged in court. Garrod had found the details energising. He had developed an interest in Braun. Once he had found a new place to live, Garrod had resolved to drop him a line at HM Prison Bunden. Or perhaps try something more imaginative.

On the advertising board of a newsagent's shop near Heydon, Garrod had seen a promising notice. It was an advert for a labouring job at an abattoir near Sawtry. It was a chance for him to sink into industrious anonymity until he had completed his preparations for Alison Dexter. To enact his plan fully he needed space, some money and maybe even some help. He had already driven to New Bolden Police Station, he even knew that Dexter drove a dark blue Ford Mondeo. Garrod knew where his target was; and he knew how to isolate her.

The abattoir was roughly three miles outside the village of Sawtry; a tiny cluster of retirement houses, a post office and an overpriced mini-supermarket. It was a larger abattoir than Garrod had anticipated; a featureless long low grey stone building. The site office was located in a Portakabin at the front of the car parking area. Garrod knocked politely before entering; the floor of the little office seemed to sag under his weight. Robert Sandway, the abattoir manager, looked up from the glowing screen of his laptop computer. He was in his early thirties with an open, friendly countenance that Garrod felt instantly drawn to.

'You must be George Francis?' he asked.

'That's right,' Garrod replied without blinking. 'I'm here about the labouring job.'

Sandway opened his desk drawer and withdrew a sheet of paper. He scanned through the notes that he had made during his phone call with George Francis the previous evening.

'Ah yes,' he said eventually extending a hand, 'nice to meet you George.' He shook Garrod's huge hand. 'Look, I'll be honest with you. You seem a bit over-qualified for this job.'

'How do you mean?' Garrod responded.

'Well, you say you have thirty years' experience of butchery; that you once ran your own shop in Essex and so forth. This job is really just lifting and loading. It seems a waste of your talent.'

'I've had some bad luck recently,' Garrod stated. 'I lost my shop you see: problems with the taxman. I'd be happy to work cash in hand. No national insurance. You're a businessman and I'm a bankrupt. I don't want the Inland Revenue taking my hard-earned.'

'This could get me into trouble of course. Would you sign an injury waiver form? As you know, this can be dangerous work.'

'No problem. I'd be happy to fill in if any of your cutters are absent. I wouldn't expect any extra pay.'

'That would be helpful,' Sandway nodded. 'OK George, here's the deal. It's a fifty-hour week starting at seven each morning. You get three hundred quid a week cash. You collect it from me after work on Friday. You will also sign an injury waiver clearing the firm of any liability if you hurt yourself on the job, so to speak. As far as the Inland Revenue are concerned, you don't work here. If we get a visit from anyone looking like a copper, the taxman or the Ministry you make yourself scarce.'

'Don't worry about that,' said Garrod with a smile, 'I know the score.'

Sandway smiled the smile of a businessman who knows he has engineered a good deal. 'Welcome on board then. We'll see you at seven o'clock sharp tomorrow morning. Report in here and I'll take you down to meet the boys. I'll need an address and phone number off you tomorrow though. There might be opportunities for work at the weekends or after hours. I need a way to contact you.'

'No problem,' Garrod lied.

Half an hour later, he sat parked in his van on Sawtry High Street. Garrod considered his alternatives. He needed a base quickly. It would be impossible to return to the Dog and Feathers in Heydon. The police were now undoubtedly on his trail. He needed to lie low. Also, to satisfy his imaginative plans for Alison Dexter, he would need space, privacy and ideally a garden. He considered murdering some forgotten old-age pensioner and commandeering their bungalow. Sawtry seemed to be over-furnished with old ladies driving electric buggies and the occasional shuffling war hero. However, it was too dangerous: even the most useless anonymous old bastard would be missed eventually.

He wasn't afraid of roughing it. As long as he was dry and secure he could cope with the most basic living quarters. The caravan that had concealed him for seven years was too far away to be practicable while he worked in Sawtry. Bed and breakfast was high risk. Sleeping in the van didn't really appeal either. Perhaps there was an alternative. Garrod began to think about occupying some derelict accommodation. Maybe he could locate some deserted factory or some disused RAF base. Somewhere away from the main roads where fences and condemned building notices deterred unwanted visitors.

Then he remembered a night spent reading newspapers in the Dog and Feathers: the same night that Gwynne had first suggested the prize fight to him. He remembered reading about some local psychiatric hospital that had been closed down in 1993. The *Cambridge Evening News* had bemoaned the waste of a listed, historic building and demanded that the site be renovated or the hospital demolished. The article criticised the County Council for doing nothing with the building for nine years. What was it called? Garrod rubbed his eyes and tried hard to remember.

'Callington…Caxington…Caxford…'

Craxten. Craxten Fen Psychiatric Hospital.

Garrod opened his Cambridgeshire Street Atlas and located Craxten Fen. It was about ten miles away. He started up his van and headed out of Sawtry.

* * *

In 1898, the Health Committee of Cambridge Council visited a number of possible sites in the county for a new lunatic asylum. They eventually decided upon two hundred acres of land on the edge of Craxten Fen, north-east of Cambridge. The quiet rural location and unpolluted air were expected to assist the rehabilitation of those committed to the asylum. The buildings were designed in the neo-gothic style by a local architect called Richard Steadman. The project cost thirteen thousand pounds to complete. Patients were first admitted to the asylum in 1902. At its peak, the hospital accommodated over two hundred men and women.

From the early 1960s, Craxten Fen Psychiatric Hospital (as it had become) gradually fell into disrepair. Its functions were steadily transferred elsewhere over time. By 1989, when the first psychiatric ward opened at Addenbrookes Hospital in Cambridge, the number of patients at Craxten Fen had fallen below twenty. By 1992, with the addition of a new Psychotherapy Unit and other facilities at the Addenbrookes site, Craxten Fen was empty. Formally closed in March 1993, the sprawling complex of buildings had sat vacant ever since. In 1999, after stories that the site had become a haven for drug users, the County Council erected a temporary steel fence around the hospital and forgot about it.

Bartholomew Garrod initially drove past the entrance to the overgrown track that led down to the hospital, rattling on through the featureless fenland for ten minutes until he realised his mistake. Once he had finally located the crumbling buildings, which were obscured from the main road to Cambridge by unkempt hedgerow and conifer trees, he felt encouraged. He drove up the main drive, weeds and branches slapping at the sides of his van, and parked on a grass verge. For the most part, the hospital seemed in reasonable condition: glass remained in most of the windows and the main entrance was padlocked shut. There was some graffiti on the wall of an outhouse but Garrod sensed that the site had been untouched for some time.

He was able to kick open a gap between two panels of the temporary steel fencing and force his way through. Garrod walked along the side of the east wing of the hospital looking for an access point. He found himself walking through an elephants' graveyard of mangled machinery: rusting metal bedsteads, old fridges and washing machines. There was a water tower overlooking what had once been staff parking spaces and a huge pile of refuse sacks containing what Garrod discovered to be rotting bed linen.

Now, at the rear of the facility, Garrod realised

the hospital must look like a capital 'E' from the air, its east and west wings sandwiching what appeared to be a central utility and office area. He forced his way inside by tearing back a flimsy piece of wooden boarding that had been used to nail shut an open doorway. The wood was rotten and splintered easily. He found himself in a gloomy corridor cluttered with boxes and ancient pieces of medical equipment. It was treacherous going and Garrod had to watch his step. Eventually, after picking his way past a number of storage cupboards and the hospital administrator's office, he found a sign pointing to the hospital kitchen.

The facility was not ideal. There was no electricity or running water. Garrod could find neither cooking implements nor knives. However, it was dry, relatively free of rubbish and there were large work surfaces on either side of the room. Most encouragingly, there was a huge wooden table that Garrod felt was ideally suited to the carving of Alison Dexter and a grubby fireplace that he thought could be easily adapted for spit roasting. He kicked down a side door and found that it opened onto a rectangle of grass in front of the dark bulk of the east wing. This was promising too.

Garrod had seen enough. Over the next hour he unloaded his two gas camping stoves, shovel, sleeping bag, paraffin lamps and other more personal items from the van and set up a base in the hospital kitchen. By late afternoon, he had a reasonable fire burning in the kitchen grate and a half-light in which to work. Then, after cleaning down the table, Garrod went outside onto the grassed area beyond the kitchen door.

With steady, heavy strikes of his shovel, he began to dig a hole. He wanted it to resemble an upended cylinder: about one yard across by a yard and a half deep. He knew it would become more difficult to shape once the hole got beyond three feet deep. However, it was necessary work: the bitch was about five feet six inches tall.

24.

Cambridgeshire
January 1996

DS Alison Dexter roared through the speed limit on the northbound M11. She regularly checked her mirror for fear of monsters. Dexter was uncertain about her impending meeting with DI John Underwood. Patrick McInally had described Underwood in unsettling terms. The last thing she needed was a basket case for a boss. McInally was highly regarded throughout the Met. Dexter knew that she had been fortunate to crash land at Leyton CID. He had taught her to be self-reliant, disciplined and clinical to the point of ruthlessness. Her instincts were sharp and her procedural knowledge rock solid. McInally had forged her into a decent copper: now she was preparing to leave him behind.

She left the M11 at Cambridge, skirting the ancient city on its ring road before accelerating towards New Bolden. The new town came up on her more quickly than she had expected: within fifteen minutes she found herself slowing through its southern suburbs. She immediately understood McInally's association of the place with Milton Keynes: roads had numbers as well as names; there were roundabouts where none was necessary; avenues of skimpy looking trees. It didn't inspire or repulse her. It had no defining character. Like so many of Britain's 1960s new towns, it was just there.

New Bolden police station was a featureless concrete rectangle behind a miserable lawn. That came as no surprise. Police stations were always grim in their architectural functionality.

DI Underwood met her at reception. Dexter studied his appearance carefully, looking for warning signs. He was slim, tall. Perhaps he was younger than McInally – early forties maybe.

Dexter had expected him to be fat: the stereotypical regional copper gone to seed. That was the only thing that surprised her: in his grey eyes she sensed an intelligence to match her own. Something else lurked in there too; maybe a flicker of desperation.

'Sergeant Dexter, it's a pleasure to meet you.' Underwood shook her hand gently, but with no hint of lasciviousness.

'You too, sir.' For once she found holding a man's stare difficult.

'Patrick speaks very highly of you.'

Dexter wondered how to respond. She decided to lie.

'Of you too.'

Underwood laughed. 'That surprises me. We did some work together about eight years ago. One of my villains – an armed robber – turned up on his "Manor". That's what he calls it right?'

'"Manor", "Shit tip", "Beirut" – take your pick.' Dexter smiled. There was something endearing about Underwood.

'We met once. Spoke a few times. He took me to that pub on the Mile End Road. The one where "Jack the Hat" was murdered.'

'The Blind Beggar,' Dexter said. 'Let me guess. He had a pint of London Pride and a pork pie.'

'I take it he's a regular then?'

'He likes to think he's a proper cockney. I've told

him he's an Irish bastard but he won't have any of it.' Dexter noticed a slight change in Underwood's demeanour. Perhaps she shouldn't have sworn about her old boss. 'We have lunch there sometimes,' she added diplomatically.

Underwood showed her around the cluttered CID offices.

'We are a little stretched,' Underwood said eventually, sensing Dexter's disapproval of the shambolic scene. 'My old detective sergeant was the organisational force. I'm more "big picture". I'm afraid I'm hopeless with paperwork. I find it terrifying. I suppose, to put it more positively, there's a big opportunity here for someone to impose their own personality. How would you feel about handling the day to day running of the department?'

'No problem. To be quite honest, sir, I'd insist on it.' Dexter wasn't lying. McInally ran a much tighter ship than Underwood, whose office was buried under an avalanche of paper. She could see that there was an opportunity for a fixer. 'What kind of cases are you running at the moment?' she asked, deciding to take control of the interview.

Underwood's eyes rolled left, as if accessing some cumbersome memory in the back of his brain. 'A wife beater, some burglaries – drug-related, most likely. We've got a murder case in Cottenham. Some bloke had his face taken off with a twelve bore shotgun.'

'Any leads on that one?' Dexter asked.

'Not much. The body hasn't been identified yet.'

'What forensic support do you have here?' Dexter sensed a weak link.

'Pretty good. We have a decent SOCO team downstairs: it's small but very high quality. Our forensic pathologist is a guy called Roger Leach. He's a minor legend in the community.'

'I think I've heard of him.'

'He wrote some famous pieces on the classification of gun shot wounds and on scene of crime recording procedures. Most CID departments have got copies I think.'

'I didn't realise he was up here.'

'He's our greatest asset,' Underwood confided. 'McInally was vague about why you wanted to transfer. Some "local trouble" was all I could get out of him.'

'Did you follow the coverage of the "Primal Cut" case?' Dexter asked.

'The cannibal thing? Were you involved in that?'

'I caught the Garrods.' Dexter instantly rethought her statement. 'Well, I caught one of them. The other escaped.'

'How did you identify them?' Underwood seemed impressed.

Dexter shrugged. 'Long story. Something about them unsettled me. They lived very close to one of the victims but claimed they'd never met him. I knew they were lying. The victims had butcher's cuts of meat removed from them and one was killed with a poleaxe: the way you might stun cattle at a slaughterhouse. It was intuition really. The problem is that when we raided the Garrods' shop, one of them was killed trying to get away.'

'What about the other one?'

'At large. Presumably looking for me.'

Underwood was beginning to understand her predicament.

'Alison, there's no guarantee that he won't find you up here.'

'True. The problem I have is that in London this guy has some heavy-duty connections. He has some previous for bare knuckle fighting. McInally reckons that he has some nasty contacts. In London, I'm conspicuous.'

'So you're hoping that those contacts don't extend up here?'

'That's the idea. This could buy me some time until London can track this guy and arrest him.'

Underwood thought for a moment. 'If you decide to come here, I'd need a commitment from you. Two years minimum. Otherwise, it will be *hard to run this place efficiently. We need some continuity.'*

Dexter hesitated: two years in New Bolden could feel like an eternity. 'I was hoping for something more flexible, sir.'

'That's the deal. Take it or leave it.'

Dexter was surprised by Underwood's inflexibility. She realised that she had underestimated him. She looked around the chaotic little department, as if trying to extract the essence of the place with her eyes. In terms of her career, it would be a retrograde step; unless she made it otherwise.

'If I do two years, there are a couple of conditions.'

'Go on.'

'I manage the department. I sort out the paperwork. I establish the procedures. I organise and assign cases. I do the shift timetabling and staff reviews. I also want to be the main liaison with Leach and the SOCO team.'

Underwood suppressed the urge to cheer. He had wanted to offload most of those tasks for a couple of years. He had a profound horror of mundane organisation. 'I think that's possible,' he said eventually. 'Anything else?'

'I want my own office.'

'No problem.'

With these matters resolved, Alison Dexter turned to shake Underwood's hand. 'Do I call you "Guv" then?' she asked.

'Fine,' Underwood replied, although he had an uneasy feeling she wouldn't need to call him that for very long.

25.

Five hours after interrogating Keith Gwynne, Alison Dexter sat in her office trying to decide whether she was going mad. Her treatment of Gwynne in the interview room had been embarrassingly slapdash. She had always prided herself on her professionalism and yet her screeching had made her sound amateurish.

Bevan had worked Gwynne much more effectively than she had and he'd hardly raised his voice. Worse, Dexter had felt waves of disapproval rolling over her from Bevan and Underwood. Her mind had been derailed. Dexter had a terrible sinking feeling that wasn't only due to lack of sleep. She opened her email account to see if Kelsi Hensy had replied: she hadn't. Dexter tried to focus on the job in hand.

On her desk sat the 'Primal Cut' case file that a motorcycle courier had delivered an hour previously. The Garrods' crimes had been christened the 'Primal Cut Murders' by one of the tabloid newspapers at the time. The killers had removed the primal cuts of meat from their victims. Dexter recalled the press feeding frenzy at the story with a shudder. In the appendices to the files were Ray Garrod's post-mortem report and DNA profile. Dexter looked up from her desk.

'Alex!' she called across from her office to Detective Sergeant Sauerwine, 'I need a favour.'

Dexter managed a faint smile as he appeared in her office doorway. 'Can you do something for me?'

'Of course, Guv,' he replied.

'Take this PM report and DNA information down to Leach. I've asked him to compare this profile with the blood and saliva found on Shaw.'

Sauerwine took the files. 'Inspector Underwood told us about this in the briefing. Do you really think it's the same guy?'

Dexter nodded. 'Pretty certain. The bite wound to Shaw is similar to the kind of wound Garrod was notorious for inflicting when he participated in prize fights back in London. Also there's the name.'

'I don't understand,' Sauerwine frowned.

Dexter took a deep breath; she was in no mood for protracted explanations. However, he had potential and she remembered what it felt like to be trodden on.

'Gwynne said that the guy who killed Leonard Shaw was called George Norlington. Well, Norlington Road is a street in Leyton. As it happens, Bartholomew and Ray Garrod had a butcher's shop on Norlington Road. It's too much of a coincidence.'

'I understand. I'll get these over to forensic.'

Underwood entered the office as Sauerwine hurried off. 'Alison, we've got the warrant to search the Dog and Feathers.'

'About bloody time,' Dexter snorted as she stood and pulled on her jacket. 'These fucking magistrates need a rocket.'

'I've got a couple of plain clothes coppers stationed outside the pub,' Underwood replied. 'They've been there for two hours. They haven't seen anything suspicious. Nobody matching the description of Norlington, Garrod or whoever the bloke is. I was about to go over there and serve the warrant on the landlord.'

Dexter nodded. 'Take as many spare bodies as you can muster. This guy is strong and downright evil. There's no chance of a firearms team I suppose?'

Underwood laughed humourlessly.

'Stupid question,' Dexter admitted. 'Let's go.'

'You're coming?'

'Of course. Problem?'

Underwood scratched the back of his neck. 'I think it's a bad idea. I can handle it. This is an emotional issue for you. Let's say you're right and this is Garrod. If he sees you, he might freak out. That's the last thing we need.'

'Bollocks. I'm coming. Nobody else here can identify the bloke. Besides, I want to be there when this arsehole is put down.'

Dexter picked up the 'Primal Cut' file as she left the office. 'I'll talk you through what I know in the car. How long is the drive?'

'Twenty minutes.' Underwood followed Dexter down the stairs of New Bolden police station. Dexter was wearing a black suit from Marks and Spencer. He knew that she had three very similar black suits; that she sometimes interchanged the jackets. He knew that they were from M&S because he had seen her there. He buried his madness.

Underwood drove them out of New Bolden. Dexter silently read through the file.

'So talk to me then,' he said eventually. 'Tell me about this Garrod guy then.'

Dexter looked out of the window as Cambridgeshire raced past. 'I'm sure you recall the basics. When I worked back in Leyton, McInally and I were investigating a murder case. Someone hauled a dismembered body out of the river Lea. There was a connection with another case, a

Smithfield porter who'd also been dismembered. I made a link to the Garrods. They ran a butcher's shop in Leyton. We took a squad to raid the place. Ray Garrod did a runner and was hit by a car. Bartholomew Garrod wasn't there. He's been missing ever since. Bartholomew was the "brains" of the outfit: although that's a very generous description. Ray was slow. He had some form of mental disability. The post-mortem showed he had a metal plate in his head. He was brain damaged as a child. They were a weird pair, both of them. I think that's why I caught them: I knew that there was something odd about them.'

'Had they always lived in London?' Underwood asked, wondering where Bartholomew Garrod could have hidden for nearly seven years.

Dexter nodded. 'Yes. The father was from Leyton, the mother from Dalston. Both died in 1975.'

'How?'

'Natural causes apparently. He had a heart attack in January. She had a massive stroke in March. Slightly odd coincidence, I suppose.'

'Not really,' Underwood replied. 'Often happens. One partner dies and the stress of burying them kills the other one.'

'The father had bought the butcher's shop after he left the army in 1947. They ran it as a family business. "Garrod and Sons, Family Butchers". Can you believe that?'

'An unfortunate name, given what happened,' Underwood agreed.

'We turned up and found a bunch of human remains in their refrigerator.'

'How many victims?'

'Uncertain.' Dexter flicked through the report trying to jog her memory. 'We only positively identified three: the porter, a librarian and a night club bouncer. There were more though. Forensic showed remains from at least four other bodies; bits of brain, kidney and stuff. Completely disgusting: like tapas night at Sweeney Todd's.'

'Strange choice of targets,' Underwood mused. 'The porter and the bouncer could have been awkward. They must have been big men. They must have wanted them for a reason.'

'To be honest,' Dexter replied, 'I always found the librarian the weird one. The other two were people that they would have seen about: either at Smithfield or amongst the boozers on Leyton High Road. I always thought that the librarian must have been killed for a particular reason,' Dexter said only half-registering Underwood's attempt at humour. 'She was the only female victim.'

'She must have had something specific that they wanted,' Underwood mused.

His mind tried to explain the anomaly. He loved these engagements with Dexter. He likened conversations with her to plugging a lava lamp into a power socket: the melting lights came on in his mind. Did she experience similar feelings? Unlikely, he decided. Dexter was different: she was just an electrical current, unaware of the light that she created.

'Garrod blamed me for killing his brother. He sent me body parts and threatening notes. It was like Jack the Ripper sending kidneys to the Whitechapel Vigilance Committee. It must be an East End thing. When the stuff started arriving at my house, I decided to get out. McInally told me about you and here I am.'

Underwood considered Dexter's words. 'A silver lining for me, in any case,' he said.

They arrived in Balehurst within fifteen minutes. Three squad cars were already at the scene, parked around the corner from the Dog and Feathers; invisible to the pub's occupants.

'Let's go then.' Dexter unbuckled her seat belt and climbed out of the car.

'You're coming in?' Underwood looked concerned.

'I'll be all right.'

Underwood took the lead, sending police officers to the front and rear of the pub. He pushed open the front door and stepped inside. The Dog and Feathers was almost empty. Dexter followed him in, tense, carefully scanning the quiet pub for cannibals.

'Can I help?' asked the landlord.

'New Bolden CID,' said Underwood flashing his warrant card, 'we have a court order enabling us to search these premises.'

The landlord looked surprised. 'Why? We haven't done anything.'

'Do you have a George Norlington staying here?' Dexter asked.

'We did,' the landlord replied, 'but he's left. I was about to go and clean his flat out. I've a new guest coming in tomorrow.'

'Show us the flat,' Underwood replied.

James Bull stepped out from behind the bar.

'OK. Come with me. It's out on the back yard.'

Opening the back door, Bull was surprised to see four uniformed policemen waiting there. 'God! What's this guy done to deserve all these idiots?'

Underwood and Dexter did not reply. Bull crossed the small courtyard behind the pub and, after what seemed an age, managed to find the correct key from a huge jangling bundle. Dexter was first into the room; it took her eyes a split second to adjust to the dark. Underwood was a second behind her.

'Jesus Christ,' he said quietly, looking about the room in shock.

Hearing the oath, Bull looked in from the doorway. 'Fuck me! What's he been doing in here?'

Dexter turned to him. 'Go back into the pub please, Mr Bull. We'll be in shortly.'

Gingerly, Underwood stepped into the room.

The floor was covered in dozens of discarded local newspapers. Lying on the filthy bed sheet were various lumps of meat. Flies buzzed grimly from piece to piece.

'He knew we were coming,' Underwood said. 'He must have guessed that we'd find out from Gwynne or Woollard after Shaw's death. He's not daft is he?'

'He's lasted seven years on the run without being spotted,' Dexter conceded. 'He's no mug.'

She was frightened now. Her worst fears confirmed.

'We need to get a forensic team in here to do a proper search,' Underwood said, aware now that Dexter had not taken her eyes from the terrible writing on the wall. 'Let's go and talk to the landlord. We'll get a description from him then compare it with Garrod's old photofit. Then I suggest we print a few thousand and run a full search for this arsehole. In the meantime, I think that it's a bad idea for you to go home.'

'You're kidding me?' Dexter gasped. 'John, if he knew where I lived I'd be dead already. I'm not running away anymore.'

'Even so,' Underwood urged, 'he found you once before. Is there a friend or someone you could stay with for a few days?'

Dexter wondered if there was.

26.

In the musty shell of Craxten Fen Psychiatric Hospital, Bartholomew Garrod was enjoying an evening of relative comfort.

Once he had finished digging, Garrod sat down at the table in his new kitchen and, by the light of a paraffin lamp, began to compose a letter to Nicholas Braun at HM Prison Bunden. He was certain that in Braun he would find something of a kindred spirit and a possible means of advancing his enterprise. Garrod chose his words carefully:

Dear Nick, you don't know me. I followed your trial on TV and in the newspapers. You don't deserve prison. I imagine the police trumped up the charges to grab some headlines. That little fucking bitch hurt me too. Now I'm back. Do they read your mail? I imagine so. I have marked this envelope as a communication from your lawyer so

I'm hoping you will receive it unopened. I have seen your brother on TV. We have a mutual interest. I'll be in contact. Yours sincerely, George Francis.

Garrod folded the paper over and slid it inside an envelope. He wrote Braun's prison address out as neatly as he possibly could, then on the top left hand edge of the envelope he printed: 'Prison Rule 37A'. This denoted a communication from a prisoner's legal adviser: in theory, the prison authorities would not be able to open it. He had used the same trick ten years previously when sending money to some of his old associates in Wormwood Scrubs. It had worked then. Garrod hoped that the rules hadn't changed.

27.

Alison Dexter drove nervously around the New Bolden ring road. She regularly checked her mirrors and even left the dual carriageway an exit early to see if she was being followed. Confident that she was in the clear, Dexter pulled up at the bottom end of her road. She turned the car engine off and peered out into the darkness for a few minutes. Nothing seemed unusual: the same cars were parked in front of her small block of flats. There were no figures skulking about in the shadows that she could see. Dexter bit her lip thoughtfully and decided to risk it. She started her engine and drew up outside her flat.

She checked up and down the street again; satisfied, she unlocked the outside door to the block and then that of her ground floor flat. The burglar alarm system beeped reassuringly at her. Dexter felt her heart rate slowing as she decoded it. She slammed the door behind her and drew the safety chain across.

The day's events had drained her. She selected a small bottle of Stella Artois from her fridge and flopped into the new armchair that she had recently bought herself. Dexter tried to push Bartholomew Garrod from her mind: it was possible that he had left the area after the death of Lefty Shaw. He certainly seemed to have quit his digs in Balehurst in a hurry.

Her phone blasted at her; the noise made her jump in shock.

'Hello?' she asked warily.

'Is that Ali?' asked a female voice that Dexter half-recognised.

'Yes. Who's that?'

'Kelsi.'

Dexter felt a surge of relief and excitement. 'Hello. This is a nice surprise.'

'You sound tired,' Kelsi said with an audible smile.

'Long day,' Dexter confirmed.

'And a late night.'

Dexter smiled a guilty smile. 'Yeah. It was.'

'Fun though,' Kelsi observed.

'Are you eating an apple?' Dexter asked. 'I can hear scrunching.'

'It's a pear actually.'

'I'm glad I've got your full attention.'

'Of course you have! Look, I'm sorry I didn't reply to your email. We have to be careful at ComBold. The company screen all of our personal messages.'

'I understand,' Dexter replied, remembering with a shudder that Cambridgeshire Constabulary did the same thing.

'If we'd got into an email conversation, I'd have said something filthy to you and I'd have been sacked.'

Dexter felt a charge of excitement building in her stomach. 'Like what?'

There was a pause. 'Just the things that I'd like to do to you. That kind of stuff.'

'Yeah, that could be tricky.'

Kelsi paused for a moment. 'Would you like me to come over?' she asked eventually.

'Why don't I come over to you?'

'Why's that? Is your husband in?'

'Don't be ridiculous!'

'Come over then. Have you eaten?'

'Not that I remember.'

'I'll sort us something out.'

'I'll be a while. I need to have a shower and get changed.'

'You can do that here,' said Kelsi quietly.

Dexter found the idea enticing. She wanted to get out of the flat as quickly as possible: its emptiness was grimly apparent.

'I'm on my way,' she said.

With an excitement that surprised her, Dexter filled an overnight bag with a few basic items. She locked up and alarmed her flat, then drove across town. By the time she arrived at Kelsi's house it was almost 9.30 p.m. The living room was warm and comfortable.

'Go and have a shower,' Kelsi instructed, after kissing her firmly on the lips. 'Help yourself, I'm cooking pasta.'

'Thank you.' Dexter placed her car keys on the living room table and wearily climbed the stairs to the shower room she had used that morning. The water was refreshing but the dull ache behind her eyes lingered on as she towelled herself dry ten minutes later. She pulled on a pair of shorts and a T-shirt. There was a bottle of moisturiser on the top windowsill. Dexter decided to purloin some, staring out into the darkness as she applied the cool fluid to her face.

The window overlooked Kelsi's back garden. It was small but tidy. Dexter could see a tiny flowerbed, a couple of stone statues and something else. Something unusual. She quickly turned off the bathroom light; having equalised the darkness within and without, she could see more clearly. At the back of the garden, almost obscured by shadows, was a man.

Dexter's blood ran cold. She hurried downstairs; Kelsi heard her running and came out of her kitchen in surprise.

'There's someone in your garden,' Dexter gasped.

'Are you sure?'

'Completely,' Dexter nodded. She looked out through the kitchen window. 'There, can you see? Against the back fence?'

Kelsi peered out into the gloom. 'Oh my God! I can see him. Shall I call the police?'

'I am the police.' Dexter could see the figure more clearly now. It wasn't Bartholomew Garrod, she was sure of that. Garrod was broader and heavier than the man that she could make out. At least, she hoped that was the case. She relaxed a little.

'I'm going out there. I think you've got a peeping tom.'

'You can't go outside,' Kelsi protested.

'I'll be OK. Close and lock the back door once I'm outside.'

'I'll come with you.'

'Just do as I say. Do you have a torch?'

'In the cupboard under the sink.'

Dexter withdrew the torch and unlocked the back door. As she threw a powerful beam of light onto the back lawn, she saw the man clamber awkwardly over the back fence. Dexter ran across the lawn and shone her torch down the adjoining street in time to see the fugitive disappear around a nearby corner. Kelsi joined her at the fence.

'I told you to wait inside,' Dexter remonstrated.

'Did you see him?'

'No. Just the back of his head. He was about six feet tall wearing black clothes. Beyond that, I couldn't see anything.'

'You're not thinking of chasing him?' Kelsi asked.

'I haven't got any shoes on,' Dexter said. 'Can you think who it might be? You haven't got any weird neighbours or a demented ex-boyfriend?'

'That's not funny, Ali.'

'I only ask because I used to have a mad ex. I wasn't trying to be funny.'

'OK.'

'I mean, nobody in the world knows I'm here tonight,' Dexter explained. 'I just came here straight from home.'

'Can we go inside?' Kelsi asked. 'I'm getting

cold.' She turned and walked back to the house, her arms folded with cold and frustration.

Dexter shone her torch onto the ground where the man had been hiding. Its beam illuminated a small patch of ground. Something glinted in the artificial light. Dexter crouched down, balancing herself by placing her left hand on the cold ground. Lying on the patchy grass were two tiny silver keys on a ring. They looked like the padlock keys used for locking suitcases, Dexter mused, or maybe keys to a gate or a safe. She put down her torch and picked the tiny keys up.

'Are you coming in, Ali?' Kelsi called from the kitchen door.

'On my way.' Dexter headed back towards the light. 'I don't suppose these are yours?' she asked, holding up her discovery for inspection.

Kelsi looked the keys over. 'No. Did he drop them?'

'It looks that way.' Dexter walked through the kitchen to the dining room. 'Make sure you bolt the door behind you,' she called out.

Dexter sat at the dining room table and looked at the keys again. Kelsi sat next to her.

'What kind of keys are they?' Kelsi asked.

'It's weird,' Dexter replied. 'They're unusual but they look vaguely familiar. My guess is that they open a padlock or a safe. The design is odd though.'

Kelsi took the keys from Dexter. 'I think they look more like keys that open a filing cabinet. We have those at work, I'm always losing the bloody things.'

'Me too,' Dexter agreed. 'We have secure evidence lockers in CID. We keep case materials in them.'

A horrible realisation began to fall on Dexter's mind like a shadow thrown by the rising sun. She reached across the table for her own key chain. Fumbling through the various different shaped keys she eventually found two silver keys to the CID evidence lockers. 'There, they look like these don't they?'

Kelsi looked at Dexter's keys closely, comparing them with the ones from her garden. 'Ali, they're identical.'

'They can't be!' Dexter looked again, her mind already seeking an explanation.

'Your keys are marked with serial numbers.' Kelsi squinted at the tiny digits. '2495 and 2496.' She put down Dexter's key chain and picked up the discovered keys. 'These are numbered 2480 and 2481. They are from the same series. The same batch of keys.'

Dexter understood the significance of Kelsi's comment: someone from New Bolden CID had been lurking in Kelsi Hensy's back garden.

'I'd better go,' Dexter said without enthusiasm. 'I need to check this out.'

'Should I report this?'

'Call the local plods. Tell them you saw someone in your garden. They'll have a squad car do a drive by. I'd appreciate it if you didn't mention me or the keys.'

'I understand.'

Ten minutes later, dressed again in her work suit, Alison Dexter left Kelsi Hensy and wearily drove the short distance to New Bolden police station. CID was deserted when she entered and switched on the lights. The evidence lockers were kept in a small storage room on the far side of the floor. They were large, black metal cabinets numbered according to the key numbers. Dexter found 2480 and 2481 immediately. She unlocked 2480 with the keys that she had found. She withdrew the case summary sheet from the first folder: it referred to a burglary at Mount Pleasant retirement home. Dexter looked down to the bottom of the page: 'Officer in Charge: J Underwood'. Horrified, Dexter then opened 2481 and repeated the exercise. It was the case file on the murder of Leonard Shaw: 'Officer in Charge: J Underwood'.

Dexter tried frantically to seek an alternative explanation. She needed confirmation. A brief check of the key register that was stored upstairs in the central administration office proved the point: CID Cabinet keys 2470–2490 were assigned to DI J Underwood.

Dexter returned to CID resolved to search Underwood's desk and locker. He kept his office locked, but Dexter as the Senior CID Officer kept a master in her safe. At 11.15 p.m., frustrated and betrayed, she started to root through Underwood's files and possessions.

28.

At roughly the same moment, Underwood crashed back into his own flat on the east side of New Bolden. Exercise did not come easily to him; his chest burned with pain as he gasped for oxygen. It had been a close call. Thank God that he had seen the kitchen light flick on as Dexter opened the back door or else she would have had him. As it was, he was extremely fortunate that she had not decided to chase after him: his progress after the first adrenalin-driven hundred yards had been painful. He splashed water onto his face from the bathroom taps. He was confident that Dexter could not have recognised him given the lack of light and the distance between them. It had been a profoundly uncomfortable moment. Still, at the same time, it had exhilarated him.

Calming down, Underwood sat on a sofa in his living room. On his coffee table was the large file of material he had been compiling on Alison Dexter. Underwood didn't like to think of himself as a stalker, though he realised that was how unkind souls might perceive him. He had begun by collecting information, rather as a child collects shells or models. Then, other motivations had taken over.

He had photocopied Dexter's personnel file. This contained details of her record within the police service, listed her various commendations and promotions. It even contained an old passport-sized photo of her from her days at Hendon Police College. Underwood liked the picture: she was younger, of slightly fuller face and a softer complexion. A few weeks previously he had sent the small photo to a local artist who had used it as the base for an oil painting. It had cost Underwood one hundred and fifty pounds. The finished product now hung opposite his bed: his own oil portrait of Alison Dexter. He would often lie in bed, as the new light of morning reminded him of the lump growing in his chest, unable to face another day. The picture comforted him; more perhaps than its subject could have.

The file also contained the four manager reports he had written about her before she had replaced him as the Senior Officer of New Bolden CID. Underwood liked to read them. He had described her in glowing terms: 'a model police officer', 'highly intelligent', 'a gifted organiser', 'a courageous and intuitive detective'. He had even managed to purloin copies of the two reviews that Dexter had written about him since returning from his breakdown: 'a popular officer' was about as gushing as she had been about him. Underwood didn't mind that.

Also in the file were photographs of Alison Dexter off duty. Underwood had initially been rather ashamed of following her about town on Saturday afternoons. He had pictures of her drinking a coffee alone at a table outside Starbucks in the market square; a picture of her in her gym kit outside New Bolden leisure centre; a Polaroid picture of her dropping off a blonde woman at a mews house the previous day. Underwood knew that Dexter had stayed over that night. He had no idea who the mystery blonde was. He had rather built his hopes on the notion that Dexter did not really have any friends outside of work. His mind had raced to all sorts of conclusions. Wriggling on a hook of his own creation, Underwood had returned to the same mews house that evening seeking clarification. What he had received instead was near arrest and public humiliation.

He turned a page in his file. Here there were news cuttings; records of cases that he and Dexter had worked on together. There was also a photograph clipped from the *New Bolden Echo* of Dexter standing outside Peterborough Crown Court. Underwood remembered Bartholomew Garrod's deserted flat with old newspapers strewn all over the floor. The SOCO team had shown that Garrod had also clipped stories relating to DI Alison Dexter. Underwood wondered if there was a moral difference between their respective obsessions. He didn't want to kill Dexter. He wanted to feel close to her. It was a form of love; he knew that.

However, Underwood was not delusional. He was not some tragic erotomaniac convinced that the object of his affection was also in love with him. It was precisely the opposite. It was precisely because Dexter patently did not love him that he had felt the desperate urge to cling onto whatever aspects of her that he could. If possessing a file of information about Alison Dexter was the closest he could get to possessing the real thing, then so be it.

It was harmless. It made him happy. Besides, he told himself, don't proud parents keep photo albums and birth certificates and mementos once their children have left home? Or died? Underwood had obtained a photocopy of Dexter's birth certificate from the Public Record Office in London two months previously. He had felt more guilt in obtaining that than in following Dexter about New Bolden on her days off; or than in photographing her kissing another woman. If the hope of loving Alison Dexter had gone, at least he could read about her life, touch her photograph and invent memories and a future. He could share those memories too.

Garrod was different. Garrod wanted to kill her and consume her. Consumption was a form of possession too.

And yet, Underwood sensed that the man would torment her first.

APPETISER

29.

Wednesday, 16th October 2002

It dawned a bright, crisp morning. Robert Sandway led Bartholomew Garrod out of his office down to the abattoir unloading area. A farm lorry was emptying cattle from its tailgate onto a ramp; the cattle moved on into the lairage area.

'We are governed by very strict hygiene and welfare regulations now,' Sandway said above the din of clattering hooves. 'The ramp for example needs to be of a certain height. Apparently, animals don't like sudden drops.'

'They get skittish after long journeys too,' Garrod replied. 'Wobbly on their feet. Pigs scream too.'

'Quite.' Sandway pointed at the surface of the ramp. 'This has to be a "non-slip" surface now, by law. So the cattle don't fall down. However, hygiene rules say that we have to hose the urine and faeces off it regularly. Slipping can still be a problem.'

Garrod noticed that the unloading bay was covered by corrugated iron.

'I'm surprised this is undercover.'

'Welfare rules again. That is to protect animals from adverse weather. How ridiculous can you get? We'll be made to provide psychiatrists for them next. Are fields covered?'

Sandway walked Garrod around to the side entrance to the lairage room, a bleak box of concrete and steel. It was filled with patient and uncertain cattle divided up into pens. After the chaos of the unloading area, Garrod found the room calming.

'Again,' Sandway was saying, 'the floor is cross-ridged to reduce slippage. The whole lairage is drained and kept very clean. No animal waste or blood is allowed to stay in here. If you look at the far end you can see the passageways that lead the animals up to the stunning pens.'

They edged along the side of the pens. Garrod peered down one of the concrete passages. 'Why are the tunnels curved? I can't see the end.'

Sandway smiled. 'That's the point really. If they were straight the animals might be nervous if they could see the stunning process take place. Also we find that cattle are naturally curious: if the races are curved they want to walk down them to see what's at the other end. I suppose it's a kind of abattoir psychology. You'll notice they are narrow enough to prevent cattle turning around.'

'Yes. Once they go in, they ain't coming out again,' Garrod nodded.

'Not in one piece anyway.' Sandway led Garrod out of the lairage room and into the stunning area. Here the cattle emerged from their curved concrete races to be secured one at a time in the stunning pens.

'The animals can't be stunned in sight of each other.' Sandway peered into the nearest pen where a large Friesian cow was about to encounter a bolt gun. 'Here you are, George. You can watch. The guy with the gun is Rick. That's Lee over there.'

Garrod knew the procedure. He had used a similar method on Alan Moran seven years ago. A slaughterman leaned over the cow and pressed a captive bolt pistol against the centre of an imaginary cross on the animal's forehead. There was a sharp 'crack' as the steel bolt fired into the front of the cow's brain.

'You use the penetrative bolts then?' Garrod asked Rick the slaughterman.

'That's right mate. More effective.'

Garrod looked as the cow fell down onto its knees, its jaw dropping open allowing a huge pink roll to fall out on one side. Rick pulled down on a lever. The side of the pen opened and the stunned animal slid onto a conveyer belt. Immediately, Lee locked a shackle around one of the cow's rear legs.

The animal was quickly hoisted into the air and, as it dangled above the floor of the stunning area, Lee cut into its throat, blood streaming into a drainage duct. The whole process had taken less than a minute.

'You stick them in the jugular furrow?' Garrod asked Lee.

'Yeah mate. Just at the base of the neck. You get all the fucking big veins and arteries in one go. Using the penetrative bolt gun, I've got 60 seconds to get the big bastard up and bled before we start breaking the law.'

Next, Sandway showed Garrod the slaughter hall. Here the dead animals were gutted, sawn and carved into meat cuts. It was an impressive operation.

'I want you in here today, George,' Sandway added. 'As I said, hygiene is our major watchword. I want you to ensure the slaughter hall is kept immaculate today. Our normal hall cleaner is away today. The hoses and brushes are in the cupboard over there – I'll get you a key – clean waterproofs are hanging in that little room on the right.'

Garrod was disappointed: he wanted to be cutting.

'Maybe we can find you something more interesting tomorrow,' said Sandway remembering his new employee was a trained butcher.

Garrod kitted up and worked efficiently through the morning. He kept himself to himself, not wanting to attract attention. He ensured that the drainage channels were kept clear and flowing red, he continually mopped the slaughter hall floor with disinfectant; he brushed splinters of bone from the electric sawing area into his pan. He managed to work up a good sweat. By mid-morning one of the team of cutters had attracted his attention: he was young, perhaps not much older than twenty. The other workers called him 'Damo'.

Garrod watched him closely. Damo was a clumsy cutter. He was third in line. Damo's job was to gut the carcasses. Unfortunately, he was a careless worker. Even from a distance Garrod could see him swinging his knife with the misplaced confidence of youth, gouging a savage incision from the udder of the upended cow to the heart of its ribcage. Garrod had watched in fascination as the four stomachs and intestines spilled out of the dead animals. Then he saw that Damo was cutting too deep. His knife was actually tearing open the digestive organs. Garrod knew that the reticulum contained a high density of bacteria and gas. Sometimes, usually due to exuberance or lack of concentration, Damo was piercing the reticulum. This sent a high-pressure spurt of stomach contents onto the conveyer belt, often directly onto the primal cuts of meat. This was a serious disease risk. At lunchtime Garrod explained his concerns to Sandway.

'Thank you, George,' his new boss said. 'I'll pop by this afternoon and have a look myself. Let's keep this between ourselves for the moment.'

At 2 p.m. Garrod noticed Sandway ghost in through the rear entrance to the slaughter hall. Damo and the others worked on, oblivious to the presence of their boss. Garrod watched carefully, hoping that Damo would repeat his error to an audience. After about five minutes, Damo cut too deeply into a cow. Brown liquid spat down the forelimb of the dead animal. Sandway had seen enough. He crossed the hall and activated the speaker system: 'Stop cutting please!' he ordered, his electronically enhanced voice echoing around the hall.

Sandway crossed the floor to Damo.

'Do you know what you just did, Lewin?' he asked.

'What do you mean?'

'You just sprayed stomach acid, fungi, protozoa and probably E. coli all over a cut of meat. That meat is about to be packed and sent to a supermarket. What you've done could kill someone. That would put me out of business.'

'I didn't do nothing,' Damo said confused by his boss's aggression.

'I just saw you,' Sandway asserted. 'You were talking to Callum there. You weren't looking at what you were doing.'

There was an uneasy silence amongst the slaughtermen. Most felt that Sandway was being excessively harsh. However, after salmonella, foot-and-mouth and CJD had entered the human food chain and decimated the industry, they all knew that their work was more tightly regulated than ever. Nobody spoke. They awaited Sandway's judgement.

Sandway was unrepentant: 'I want you off the cutting floor. Clean yourself up and tell Ozzie in packaging to swap positions for the rest of the day. Come to my office after work.'

Garrod watched impassively.

30.

She had ignored him all morning. Underwood worked quietly in his office, oblivious to the fact that Dexter had checked through all his files until one-thirty the previous morning. Alison Dexter hadn't found much during that time. However, she had discovered a notebook that listed times when she had arrived and left the office, even when she had used the toilet. Another notebook contained information about her movements out of work; it even had Kelsi Hensy's address scrawled on the inside back cover.

Underwood had been keeping a record of her life. Information given on previous pages suggested that he had been following her for months. The front page contained a peculiar list of dates stretching back about six months, each date approximately four weeks after the preceding one. Dexter had stared at them for a moment in confusion. The first date was her birthday; 1st May. The others seemed to have no meaning. Then she remembered. She had had her period on her birthday. She had made an ill-judged joke about it to Underwood. She checked the dates again. They roughly corresponded to her menstrual cycle. The revelation spiralled in Dexter's brain. She knew that Underwood was something of a 'fruit loop' as McInally had called him. However, she had never expected him to derail completely. What on earth was he trying to do? Her mind had tried to sustain its defining logical momentum through the cloud of his betrayal. Now, the morning after a night of hideous surprises, Dexter watched her former boss through the glass wall that separated them, wondering what on earth she would do with him.

Her meeting with Roger Leach began at 9.30 a.m. Underwood and Mike Bevan joined them. Leach was characteristically to the point.

'The DNA profiles match. I compared the DNA sample taken from the AB negative blood splashes on Shaw with the profile of Raymond Garrod from the "Primal Cut" case file. We inherit half of our chromosomes from each of our parents.' Leach handed a photocopy of the two DNA profiles across to Dexter. 'Now those charts might not mean much to you. In cases like this we look for similarities at certain key points in the DNA sequence.'

'DNA markers?' Underwood asked.

'That's right.' Leach handed out three copies of another sheet of paper on which he had printed the following table:

DNA marker	DNA Profile 1 AB- Blood found on Leonard Shaw	DNA Profile 2 Raymond Garrod
D3	15, 16	16, 17
VWA	16, 16	16, 16
FGA	19, 24	19, 21
AMEL	X, Y	X, Y
D5	11, 11	11, 13
D7	8, 10	10, 10
D8	12, 13	12, 13
D13	9, 11	11, 12
D18	12, 15	12, 13
D21	10, 10	10, 10

'Now,' Leach continued, 'you'll see that there is at least one match at each of the ten genetic markers. It's incontrovertible proof. The man who killed Leonard Shaw was Raymond Garrod's brother.'

So that was it. Bartholomew Garrod's reappearance was now a verifiable scientific fact: one quantifiable in a series of black bars and numbers printed on two sheets of A4 paper. Alison Dexter was prepared for this realisation. Her instincts were rarely wrong. However, seeing the stark numbers in front of her was an unsettling experience. The middle column of numbers was the genetic blueprint of the man who wanted to destroy her.

Underwood struggled to find a crumb of comfort. 'At least we now know it's him. We can put up posters and photofits; do a proper manhunt. That's if he's still here of course. I wouldn't be surprised if he's done a bunk.'

Bevan nodded. 'He's survived for years on the run. He obviously knows that he's vulnerable after the Leonard Shaw killing. John might be right. This guy hasn't evaded capture for all this time by staying in one place.'

Dexter wanted to agree but her intuition told her otherwise. She was finding it hard to keep a lid on her anger at Underwood. He was apparently oblivious to the fact that she had unearthed his seedy little hobby. Dexter decided to be malicious.

'John, could you go and get the case file on Leonard Shaw? I want to re-read it.'

Underwood frowned. 'Now?'

'Yes please.'

Trodden on, confused by the edge in Dexter's voice, Underwood left the office fumbling in his pocket for the cabinet keys that Dexter knew were not there.

'There is something else that you should know,' Leach continued. 'This blood sample – we can now safely assume that it's Bartholomew Garrod's – is HIV positive.'

Now it was Dexter's turn to look surprised. 'You're kidding me?'

'No. He is carrying the virus. It does not seem to have become activated. He probably doesn't even know he's got it. I doubt he visits a GP regularly.'

Dexter sat back in her chair. At the other end of the department, she could see Underwood groping uselessly in his pockets for the missing keys. She felt great pleasure in observing his discomfort. A moment later he was back in her office.

'Alison, could I borrow your master key? I've left my set at home.'

Dexter reached into her drawer and withdrew her key chain. She tossed it across to him. 'You've got to be careful, John. Those case files are confidential. You lose your keys and any Tom,

Dick or Harry could mess with them.'

Embarrassed at his humiliation in front of Leach and Bevan, Underwood restricted his response to a guilty nod.

Leach watched him go. 'How's he doing these days?' he asked Dexter.

'Don't ask. So Garrod's at large carrying HIV?'

'That's right.'

Dexter could hardly imagine a more terrifying scenario. 'Mind you, thinking about it, we shouldn't be surprised. Is there a chance the disease could be activated? Is nature likely to help us out?'

Leach shrugged. 'There's no certainty of that. Some people carry it for years.'

'So we need a plan.' Dexter looked up as Underwood returned bearing the Shaw case file.

'Here we are,' he said, slightly breathlessly, 'as requested.'

'Put it on the desk,' Dexter instructed, avoiding Underwood's eye. He began to sense something was wrong.

Bevan leaned forward. 'Can I suggest we pull in Bob Woollard for questioning? I've deliberately held off until now. I was hoping we could sort the Shaw case independently and I could continue my investigation into Woollard. I don't think that's possible anymore so we might as well give him a going over. He might know where this Garrod character went. He may know if he's working somewhere else. Woollard is very well connected.'

'Good idea,' Dexter agreed. 'John, I want you to coordinate the efforts at ground level. This is a full scale manhunt now and you are the most experienced officer in that area.'

'What area exactly?' Underwood asked suspiciously; the sparks that he loved in Dexter's eyes seemed to have become flames.

'Poster campaign, distribution of the photofit to uniform, coordinating press strategy. That kind of area.'

Underwood resisted the urge to argue: such tasks hardly inspired his imagination.

'One idea,' Bevan added, 'Gwynne told me that this Norlington/Garrod character drove a van. Given that he is unlikely to have a permanent address, I'll bet that the van isn't taxed or insured. It might be worth telling traffic to keep their eyes open for untaxed transit vans.' Bevan addressed his comments mainly to Underwood who seemed to have been put in charge of such things.

'I'll do that,' said Underwood grimly.

'We should think about what this guy is doing for money and accommodation,' Dexter asserted. 'I'll handle that. Given that he used the name Norlington, I'll also compile a list of other street names from Leyton. It seems Bartholomew has a fairly limited imagination when it comes to false identities. We can circulate the names locally: we might get lucky.'

'What precautions are you taking?' Underwood asked. 'You want me to book you a hotel room until this is over?'

Dexter stared coldly through him. 'You just do what I've asked you to do.'

Her acidic comment chilled the silent room. Leach was the first to break.

'I'll let you know when the SOCO report on Garrod's room at the Dog and Feathers is complete. Marty Farrell tells me that they've found nothing of any specific use yet though.'

'Thank you, Roger.' Dexter stood. The meeting was over. Only Underwood remained in the office.

'Can I have a minute?' he asked.

'One minute,' Dexter nodded.

'You trampled me a bit then. Was there any particular reason?'

Dexter wanted to scream and shout abuse into Underwood's pathetic, crumpled face: bellow his betrayal, his madness straight back into his wounded eyes. Instead, she settled for ice.

'I'm annoyed you lost your case file keys. That is sloppy.'

'And you've never lost anything?' Underwood asked, irritated.

'Nothing as important as that. John, I've gone out on a limb for you.'

'I realise that.'

'After what you did to that bloke back in 2000, frankly you should have been booted out of the force.'

Underwood said nothing: his attack on his ex-wife's lover was ancient history to him now.

'One of the reasons that you weren't,' Dexter continued, 'is that I stood up for you. I offered you another chance. Not many people would have done that.'

'I know Alison. You have no idea how much I appreciate that. I just feel that your criticism is disproportionate to the offence.'

'Go and do your job then. Prove me wrong.'

Dexter sat at her desk and dug out the London street atlas that she kept in her bottom drawer. Underwood left her to it.

The street map of Leyton was on page 51. It covered an area from the southern edge of Walthamstow down to Stratford and Hackney Wick at the bottom of the page. Dexter traced some of the familiar roads with her finger. There was Wilmot Street, just north of Leyton Orient Football Ground, where she had lived for two years; across and to the right was Dawlish Road where Kelsi Hensy had once gone to school. Her index finger moved past Francis Road, the location of Leyton CID, and eventually came to rest on Norlington Road, the former home of Bartholomew and Raymond Garrod.

Dexter took a pen and began to note the names of the closest streets: Belgrave, Morley, Claude, Murchison, Albert, Newport, Tyndall, Francis and Cavendish. She discounted Pretoria Road and Rhodesia Road as too exotic to attract Bartholomew Garrod. Next to Francis Road she saw St. George's Road. Was that where the George of George Norlington had come from? Alison Dexter sat back and wondered how to present the information. The combinations were endless.

Or were they? Some of the road names could only really be surnames. Likewise, others could only be Christian names. It took her about fifteen minutes on her computer to create a working table of potential names:

	Claude	Albert	Francis	George
George	George	George	George	NO
Morley	Morley	Morley	Morley	Morley
Claude	NO	Claude	Claude	Claude
Murchison	Murchison	Murchison	Murchison	Murchison
Albert	Albert	NO	Albert	Albert
Tyndall	Tyndall	Tyndall	Tyndall	Tyndall
Francis	Francis	Francis	NO	Francis
Cavendish	Cavendish	Cavendish	Cavendish	Cavendish
Norlington	Norlington	Norlington	Norlington	Norlington

Dexter read through the list trying to find the strongest candidates. She paid little attention to the last row and column of her table. Surely Garrod wouldn't use the same name again? She wondered if the list was useful. Garrod was no fool. Still, they didn't have much to work with. Maybe a name would spark someone's memory. She printed it and created a photocopy for Underwood to distribute to uniform.

Then, bored with her life and most of the people in it, she decided to write an email.

31.

Kelsi Hensy had endured a difficult morning. ComBold was about to undergo a corporate restructuring and her department had been charged with the responsibility of explaining the changes to the workforce. Kelsi had written most of the draft internal communications herself the previous week and so she was especially annoyed when her proofs came back to her covered in mark-ups and deletions. Perhaps she had taken her eye off the ball. Her two nights with Alison Dexter had been intense; disruptive almost. The first had been an energy-sapping explosion of sexuality; the second had been an anxiety-brewing disaster.

Intense. That was a good word to describe Alison Dexter. Kelsi had sensed the fierce intelligence behind Dexter's jade green eyes when they had first met. Jade seemed appropriate. Hard, green and precious. Kelsi owned a jade statuette that she had bought on holiday in Thailand. She loved jade. The stone contained sodium and aluminium; salt and metal. That seemed appropriate for Dexter too.

Intense. The word kept rebounding inside her mind. Was intensity what she wanted? Kelsi's outlook and attitude was relentlessly positive. Even now, as she agonisingly retyped the restructuring notice that she had sweated blood over a few days previously, Kelsi tried to focus on the positives: clearer language meant better explanations, better explanations promoted understanding. Her job was to create understanding. Alison Dexter played football in an intense fury of semi-competence. Kelsi had not been embarrassed by Dexter's mistakes, but by her self-deprecating reaction to them. She found Dexter interesting company and sexually exciting but, in a funny way, Dexter was hard work. Kelsi's job was well paid but extremely demanding. She needed relief and stimulation in her social life: Alison Dexter was stimulating, but in no way a relief.

Kelsi's computer beeped, signifying an incoming message. Wearily, she turned and checked the

inbox. It was from Alison Dexter. Kelsi clicked the
message open.

'To: *HensyAK@ComBoldUK.Net*
From: *Adex@CamCpol.Org*
*Just a quick one to apologise for last night. Did
you report the guy in the garden? There's nothing in
our call log. I am making some enquiries here.
Nothing yet. Would like to meet up. Are you free
tonight? I'll buy you dinner. Marco's in town is
good. Let me know. X'*

Intense. Kelsi considered her options for a moment
before writing a terse reply.

'To: *Adex@CamCpol.Org*
From: *HensyAK@ComBoldUK.Net*
*Dinner difficult but let's have a drink in the bar
at Marco's as want to talk to you. Say eight o'clock.
Kelsi.'*

She sent the message and returned immediately to
her rewrites.

32.

Barthlomew Garrod finished work at 7 p.m. and drove directly from Sawtry into New Bolden. There was a pub on Huntingdon Road that looked out onto the car park of New Bolden police station. Garrod knew he was taking a risk. However, he was confident that, other than his size, he looked very different to the last time Alison Dexter saw him in his butcher's shop in Leyton. He nursed a pint and watched.

Alison Dexter left the main building shortly before eight o'clock. Garrod tensed as he saw her. He quickly finished his pint and hurried out the back of the pub to his van. His plan was to follow her home. As yet, he did not have her home address: that would open up all sorts of possibilities. The actual killing would take place elsewhere, most likely in his new kitchen at Craxten Fen Psychiatric Hospital, but Garrod had other ideas too.

He followed Dexter for about five minutes, keeping well back from her dark blue Mondeo. To his surprise and disappointment, she did not head home but instead parked in a town centre 'Pay and Display' car park. Garrod pulled up on a double yellow line briefly and watched the distant Dexter jog across Market Street and into the reception of a restaurant. She was a butterfly in his net. Not wanting to attract attention, Garrod waited until she was safely inside, then drove his van around a corner into a road called Maltings where he found a parking space. He locked his van and headed back towards the car park in search of cover.

33.

Kelsi Hensy was already waiting at the bar of Marco's when Dexter came through the front door.

'Hello,' Dexter said, slightly out of breath, 'sorry I'm a bit late. We've been buried all day today. Manhunt. Murder investigation. Complete nightmare.'

'Drink?'

'I'll have a gin and tonic, I think,' Dexter announced. 'Let's go crazy, eh?'

Kelsi ordered a Martini for herself. 'I'm sorry to blow you out for dinner. It's just that I'm exhausted. Last night was the final straw really; I couldn't sleep after you'd gone.'

'I'm sorry about that. I think I know what's going on.'

'What?'

Dexter paused, unsure how much she should reveal. 'One of the guys in CID had a nervous breakdown a couple of years ago. He's never been the same. He's harmless enough but he has, well, lapses.'

'You think that last night was a "lapse"?' Kelsi asked unhappily. 'What if he'd tried to break in? Or was taking photos of me getting changed?'

Dexter was anxious to reassure Kelsi that the matter was in hand. 'Look, trust me. I will sort this out. I'm a much better copper than I am a footballer.'

The drinks arrived and Kelsi took a comforting draught. 'Ali, I wanted to talk to you about things.'

Dexter felt a flash of panic. 'Oh,' she said sadly, '"things". "Things" generally mean trouble.'

'We've gone a long way very quickly, Ali,' Kelsi explained, 'maybe too quickly. That was my fault. I forced the issue. I couldn't help myself.'

'And now you've had enough?' Dexter thought that she had got the message; her gin tasted especially sour.

'Don't say that. That's not what I said. You are twisting my words. Listen, I like you. I like you a lot. From the first moment I saw you, I fancied you rotten.

'And you're a good laugh, Ali, when you want to be,' Kelsi continued.

'What is that supposed to mean?'

'It's just too intense for me: at the moment anyway.'

'Intense,' Dexter said, mainly to herself. 'That's original at least.'

'Can't we just cool things down for a week or two? I'll call you in a fortnight.'

Dexter stood up and walked out of the bar without replying. Kelsi ran out into the street after her.

'Ali, wait!'

Dexter kept walking.

Across the square, on the other side of the car park, Garrod watched from a safe distance.

'Ali, listen,' Kelsi said as she caught up with her, 'I just want a little break that's all. This is a busy time for me. I still want you.'

Dexter stopped walking and turned. She was crying.

'Honestly?' she asked.

'Honestly,' Kelsi replied, kissing Dexter softly on the lips.

Bartholomew Garrod watched dumbfounded. He had never seen two women kiss each other. It was a thrilling experience.

'And you will call me?' Dexter asked.

'Two weeks today. I promise. I'll have more free time by then.'

'OK.'

Kelsi kissed Dexter again, less passionately this time. 'I need to go home and get some sleep now.'

Dexter laughed despite her tears. 'I understand.'

'There,' said Kelsi, 'you've got a great laugh. You look better when you laugh. Do it more often.'

Dexter nodded. 'I'll speak to you soon,' was the last thing she said before Kelsi Hensy climbed into her car.

Garrod had seen enough. Excitement was making his mouth water. He hurried back into the Maltings and fired up his transit van. As he pulled back onto the market square, two cars drove across in front of him. The first was Alison Dexter's Mondeo, the second was Kelsi Hensy's new Peugeot 206. He rolled out behind them. At the first junction, the Mondeo turned left and the Peugeot turned right.

Garrod hesitated for a moment. He held a butterfly in his hands. First he would pull its wings off.

He turned right.

34.

Thursday, 17th October 2002

Bob Woollard rose at 6 a.m. the following morning. As was his habit, he ate two fried eggs and a hunk of ham for his breakfast. Since his wife's departure four years previously, he always ate alone. At 7 a.m.

he toured the farm to make sure that all his employees were going about their tasks in the correct fashion. Then at 8 a.m. he unlocked the door to his cellar and fed his dogs. He kept their food out of sight inside the cellar itself. The animals barked furiously as he approached, sensing the arrival of their morning feed. He currently owned four fighting dogs: 'Karl', the huge Tosa that had destroyed George Norlington's dog, and three American pit bulls: 'Buster Boots', 'Pitt the Elder' and 'Pitt the Younger'. Woollard still smiled whenever he thought of the last two.

Buster Boots was his favourite: a powerful, experienced animal that had won him a small fortune over the years. Buster was so named as he had white patches around each of his feet. There were also small patches of white hair around the dog's face and shoulders that contrasted starkly with his otherwise tan-coloured coat. The patches weren't caused by old age. They were the sites of old wounds over which hair had eventually re-grown. It was a tell-tale sign of an experienced fighting dog.

Woollard fed them on a consistent diet of dry food. This he kept in sacks in his cellar. He varied their diet very little. Despite their tough exterior, his pit bulls had sensitive stomachs. Besides, it paid to keep them lean and hungry. Fat dogs rarely won fights. He slid their food trays through the feeding flap in the side of their steel cages. Although the animals were generally affectionate towards him, it was best to be wary with fighting dogs. After breakfast he would watch his stable lad Kev working the dogs on the 'turntable': a type of treadmill with a flat surface that moved under the dogs as they ran. It was an old-fashioned training device but Woollard preferred traditional methods.

He left the dogs to their breakfast and returned upstairs, locking the padlock on the cellar door behind him. The door itself was contained within a false cupboard. This rendered it invisible from inside the house. As he stepped out, Woollard replaced the false panel at the back of the cupboard. It was a cumbersome precaution but he was acutely aware of the laws against training and fighting dangerous dogs in the UK. He resolved to send Kev down immediately: the dogs got restless until they had been thoroughly exercised. As he left the main house again in search of his dog trainer, a police squad car and van drove into the courtyard of his farm. Woollard had been half-expecting this moment since the death of Lefty Shaw. He wondered if Gwynne had squealed on him: if so, the pit bulls might have a new toy to play with very soon.

DI Mike Bevan got out of the squad car and

headed directly for Woollard. Outwardly unperturbed, Woollard lit his first cigarette of the morning.

'Mr Woollard?'

'Of course.'

'I'm DI Mike Bevan. We have a warrant for your arrest and one to search your premises.'

'Why may I ask?'

'We are investigating the murder of Lefty Shaw. He was an associate of yours.'

'I knew him,' Woollard nodded. 'I had no reason to kill him though. He was a friend.'

'I should warn you that anything you say will be recorded,' Bevan said through a helpful smile.

'You're charging me then?'

'No. We have information that Shaw was killed on these premises and moved elsewhere.' Bevan handed over his paperwork. 'That's the search warrant.'

Woollard read it carefully. It seemed in order. He was not particularly nervous. The barn where Lefty Shaw had fought George Norlington had been thoroughly cleaned and rearranged. 'OK. You boys go and look around.'

'We'll need to check the house as well,' Bevan added, watching Woollard's face carefully.

'Go right ahead. There's nothing of interest there though.'

Bevan waved to the Scene of Crime team and a few minutes later an intensive search of the farm's outbuildings began. Marty Farrell called Bevan over to join him at the entrance to the main barn.

'Mike, you reckon this is where the fight took place?' Farrell asked.

'Certain of it. I photographed a bunch of people coming in here,' Bevan replied.

'In which case,' Farrell led Bevan inside the barn, 'someone's done a serious job on this place over the last couple of days.'

Bevan instantly saw what Farrell meant. The barn was packed full of animal feed sacks and agricultural equipment. There was hardly any exposed floor visible. There was no sign of a fighting ring.

'Fuck.' Bevan clenched his fist in fury. 'That bastard knew we were coming. We're too slow.'

Farrell tried to be positive. 'Don't despair. We might find something. Even if he's cleaned the floor, we have chemicals that can reveal bloodstains.'

'Problem is that the ring would almost certainly have been carpeted. It helps the dogs grip better.'

'Look, we'll clear this place and do a full SOC check on it. If he had a ring here he must have disposed of the wood and the carpet somewhere. Have a look around for waste sacks, a skip, the remains of a bonfire. Anything that looks like he was trying to make some rapid disposals.'

Bevan nodded. Out in the courtyard, he could see Woollard puffing thoughtfully on a cigarette.

It took Farrell's SOCO team almost an hour to shift the heavy feed sacks from the barn into the courtyard. Next they lifted the selection of heavy metal chains, harnesses and broken milking equipment, that Woollard's men had helpfully deposited in the barn, onto white plastic sheets spread and secured in the yard. Powerful halogen lamps were fixed in the barn, powered by a portable petrol generator. Then, Farrell and two fellow SOCO officers, Regis and Rashid, began the painstaking task of checking the floor of the barn, inch by inch. It was uncomfortable work. Farrell felt sweat streaming down his back inside his protective plastic clothing. On the first run, they found nothing.

'It's too fucking dingy in here,' Rashid said in irritation.

'You're right. Let's get the other halo lamp in.' Farrell called out to one of his team checking the grain sacks to bring in the third lamp. Once it had been fitted up, the third lamp made a huge difference eliminating some of the shadows that had hampered their progress.

'Now we go back again,' Farrell instructed his team, 'anything remotely odd, you shout.'

Rashid and Regis sank to their knees again and started to repeat the process. After ten minutes, Regis called out.

'What have you got?' Farrell asked, joining him.

Regis shone his pocket torch onto a tiny lump in the concrete. 'There. Can you see? There's a dark spot of some-thing on the side of this bump.'

Farrell looked at the tiny black mark. 'OK, we'll do a Kastle-Meyer test on it.'

Rashid withdrew a piece of filter paper from his kit bag and, returning to the centre of the barn, rubbed it gently against the minuscule stain that Regis had located. Satisfied that a small amount had been smeared onto his paper, Rashid returned to his bag. Using a pipette, he added a drop of alcohol followed by phenolphthalein, then finally hydrogen peroxide.

The stain turned pink.

'Bingo,' said Farrell quietly.

'Looks promising,' Rashid confirmed.

'It's good enough for me. Right, we spray this fucking place: the whole barn. Use orthotolidine. Keep it quiet. No one comes into the barn now except us. I want photographs of everything. Let's go.'

Outside, Bevan skirted the perimeter of the farm buildings in search of the remains of Woollard's fighting ring. To his immense frustration, he found nothing. Maybe one of Farrell's hawk-eyed SOCOs would have more success. Woollard had most probably transferred the carpet and any other material from the premises completely. Perhaps there were other ways to nail the guy. Bevan returned to the squad car in the courtyard; his leather documents pouch was on the front seat.

Woollard joined him, still smoking. 'I told you there's nothing here.'

'We haven't finished yet. We haven't started on the house yet,' Bevan added. 'Actually, I wanted to ask you about the farmhouse. It's seventeenth century isn't it?'

'You a historian now then?' Woollard sniffed.

Bevan smiled and opened up a piece of A3 paper from his document case. 'There you go,' he said, '1640. These old buildings have all sorts of nooks and crannies. Turbulent times weren't they? The civil war and all that. This area was Cromwell country, wasn't it? Old houses like this had secret rooms. Priestholes, that kind of thing.'

Suspicious, Woollard looked more closely at the document in Bevan's hand. 'What's that?'

'This? When I found out that you lived in a historic building I did some checking. It's listed.'

'I could have told you that.'

'At the town hall in Cambridge they keep records of all the listed buildings in the area. Some even have plans. This document is a Victorian room plan of your farm. Apparently in 1863 the owner did some renovation work on the south wall. He had an architect do a plan of the whole house. This is a copy.'

Woollard said nothing.

'Why don't we go for a look around?' Bevan asked. 'Let's start at the top and work down shall we?'

Marty Farrell waited impatiently for his team to finish spraying the floor and walls of the barn with re-agent. Eventually the call he had been waiting for came.

'Marty,' Regis shouted from the centre of the barn, 'we're done.'

Farrell stepped forward. 'OK magic man, what have you got?'

'Two patches. Here and here,' Regis pointed.

Farrell saw them immediately. Othotolidine showed up old bloodstains in an ugly, luminous green: and there they were.

'The left one looks like the remains of a spurt,' he observed.

'I agree,' Regis said. 'There are four spots – each about a half inch apart. If you look closely each spot is slightly above the preceding one.'

'Conclusion?' Farrell asked.

'It's from a wound on a living subject. Spurting means the heart was beating.'

'It's a small sample,' Farrell mused, 'only four spots.'

'True but I'm thinking, if this floor was carpeted, maybe the carpet soaked up most of it. Chances are that if Woollard was fighting dogs on it, we're not talking about his best Wilton here. I'm guessing there were holes in the carpet. There must have been tears in it. Blood spatter through a gap in the material is my best guess.'

'What about the other one?' Farrell pointed at the second glowing green area. It was roughly circular and about nine inches in diameter.

'That's pooling,' Regis replied. 'No sign of splashing though so the blood didn't fall very far. Injured person – or dog I suppose – lying on the ground. Blood drips through hole in the carpet.'

'How have they tried to clean it off?' Farrell asked.

'Cold water. Some disinfectant too maybe,' Regis said. 'I can probably be more specific given time. I'm not sure we'll be able to tell whether the blood stains were caused by human or animal victims though.'

'True. Let Leach see the photographs. He might have some ideas. We also have the fragment of dried blood that you found and Rashid tested.

We'll be able to identify that.'

'True enough,' Regis nodded.

'Nice job magic man,' Farrell grinned.

'Learned from the master, didn't I?'

After a fruitless search of the upper floor of Woollard's house, Bevan followed his room plan down to the main hall.

'Where's the entrance to your cellar?'

Woollard's cigarette tip glowed orange. 'Don't know,' he replied, 'it's sealed off I think. We don't use it.'

'We? I thought you were alone now, Bob?' Bevan replied, hoping to provoke a response. He was unsuccessful.

'Force of habit,' Woollard said without expression.

Bevan looked closely at the room plan that he had photocopied at Cambridge Town Hall the previous afternoon. 'According to this, the stairs to the cellar should come up into the hall. But there's no sign of them.'

Woollard blew smoke up into the air. 'That plan is old. It could be wrong.'

'It's been right so far.' Woollard traced his finger along the two lines on the plan that represented the stairs to the cellar. As he did so, he tried to match sketched points of reference to features in the house. Eventually his eyes came to rest on a large wooden cupboard near to the kitchen door.

'What do you keep in there, Mr Woollard?' he asked.

'Nothing much, I was planning to get rid of it.'

Bevan opened the double doors of the cupboard. It had a wooden panel at the back. He pushed it hard and felt it clonk against a wooden surface behind it. Downstairs, directly underneath them in the cellar, Buster Boots heard the noise. In anticipation of his morning work-out, he began to bark excitedly.

Hearing the noise, Bevan turned to Woollard, unable to resist smiling in triumph. 'Well, well,' he said, 'why don't you show me how to open this, Bob?'

35.

Underwood stood before the assembled members of Leyton CID and the eight seconded uniformed officers that their Superintendent had assigned for the Bartholomew Garrod manhunt. Alison Dexter hovered at the back of the room. He wanted to impress. He was determined not to let her down. Her words had stung him. Underwood was resolved to use the pain constructively.

'OK everyone. Settle down.' He moved in front of the computerised white board that had been installed a month previously. It had cost the department four thousand pounds. Underwood was uncertain how to use it – his computer skills were not very sophisticated – but he was eager to show Dexter that he could change; grow even. He clicked on the remote handset and, to his immense relief, a photofit picture of Bartholomew Garrod appeared on the screen.

'This is our suspect, Bartholomew Garrod. The older ones amongst you might remember him. Garrod and his brother Ray perpetrated a series of murders in East London in 1995. There was a lot of publicity about the case. One of the national newspapers, the *Mirror*, I think, christened the case the "Primal Cut" murders.'

'It was the *Daily Star*,' said Dexter from the back of the room. 'It gave the murders a glamorous cachet that they didn't deserve.'

Underwood acknowledged his error with a small nod. Continuing unabashed, he pointed his remote control at the white screen. This time a diagram of a cow appeared. 'The primal cuts are the best cuts of meat on an animal: sirloin, tenderloin and so on. Bartholomew Garrod was a master butcher. He removed the primal cuts of meat from his human victims and, we suspect, ate them.'

That caused a nervous flash of chatter in the room.

DC Sauerwine, recently promoted from the uniform division, raised a hand. 'Sir, how do we know that Garrod is the man we are looking for? And why is he in Cambridgeshire?'

Underwood sipped water from a white plastic beaker. 'DNA samples taken from Leonard Shaw have been matched with the profile of Raymond Garrod: the sample had to come from a close relative. Also we have an eye witness – Keith Gwynne – who has positively identified Bartholomew Garrod from a photofit impression. As to why he is up here,' Underwood paused, he looked at Dexter who shook her head admonishingly, 'we are not sure of that yet. He may have left the area already but we have to assume that he's here.'

Detective Sergeant Harrison who had studiously been making notes throughout Underwood's speech now raised a hand. 'Guv, I have a question. How public is this investigation going to be? Given the notoriety of Garrod, if we start putting his picture about the press will be all over it like a shot. I don't just mean the local idiots either: we'll have national newspaper journalists about too. That can inflame and complicate a situation.'

Dexter answered that one. 'That is an excellent

point. Unfortunately we don't have much choice. We don't know where this guy lives. We know he drives a van but we don't have a licence plate. He may have changed his appearance. Given those problems, we as a group need help. The public can be our eyes and ears. If we get his picture on the front pages of a few newspapers then so much the better. It might provoke him into making a mistake.'

'We'll be under the spotlight like never before,' Harrison observed thoughtfully.

'True but we can handle it. We are going to try and control the press strategy. Normally we ignore them, this time our approach to journalists is going to be more coordinated.' Dexter looked Harrison directly in the eye. 'Joe, how would you feel about being the press liaison?'

Harrison smiled a slow smile. 'I knew I was in trouble when you called me Joe.' Sitting next to him, Sauerwine laughed: Dexter called him Alex when she wanted a coffee.

'You've done press liaison before,' Dexter explained. 'When you were with the Met in Tottenham. I remember seeing on your file that you'd been the point man on a couple of high-profile cases.'

Harrison nodded. 'Fine by me. It's better than knocking on doors in the pouring rain.'

'Thank you,' Dexter acknowledged. Her opinion of Harrison had rocketed in the last few months. Previously, she had clashed with him over his romantic involvement with a junior female officer. Harrison had matured in recent months. *Maybe she had too.* Dexter regretted her former harshness towards him. Harrison was potentially a kindred spirit but she had probably alienated him already. She focused out of her self-indulgence and tried to concentrate on what Underwood was saying.

'There are one or two lines of inquiry open to us,' he said pressing a button on his remote control. This time the screen went black. Underwood frowned in confusion. Dexter groaned to herself and bit the nail of her right index finger.

'Hang on,' he flustered, frantically pressing buttons.

'Sir, you've turned the screen off,' Sauerwine said helpfully. 'Press the green standby button. Top right of the remote.'

Underwood did so and the screen glowed white again. This time a photograph of a white transit van appeared. He could feel Dexter's eyes burning like lasers into the back of his head. He wondered what she would see in there: confusion, paranoia and an oil painting of herself perhaps.

'Here we are,' he said eventually, 'we know that Garrod is driving a white Bedford transit like this one. Keith Gwynne confirmed that to us. It is highly likely that it is not taxed or has a stolen tax disc. We have told traffic to stop any vehicle they see which matches this one. You should do the same.

'Secondly, it is possible that Garrod is using false names. He called himself George Norlington when he fought Leonard Shaw. Norlington is a street in Leyton. It is conceivable that Garrod might use another name based on a street that was close to where he lived. On page three of your handout you will see a table of possible names based on streets in that area. Use it when you do house-to-house enquiries. If you have any questions on that, please address them to Inspector Dexter.

'Thirdly, we want ideas on how this guy is living. He was staying in a bedsit at the Dog and Feathers in Heydon. We should check other pubs and boarding houses in the area. Remember, it's unlikely that he has much money so focus on the bottom end of the market. Anything else, Inspector Dexter?'

'Yes.' Dexter came to the front of the room. 'Bartholomew Garrod is extremely dangerous. He is a powerful man and fought professional prize fights in London for twenty years. He killed Leonard Shaw who was a fighter himself. Leach also believes that Garrod is HIV positive. If you find this man, if you even think you are getting close, you must not, repeat *not* attempt to arrest him. He is a formidable individual and will not hesitate to kill you if he's cornered.'

'Do you know him then, boss?' Harrison asked, hearing an edge in Dexter's voice that was unfamiliar to him.

'I identified the Garrods when I worked in Leyton,' she confirmed. 'Listen to me people: a word of warning. The things I saw in the Garrods' freezer are still giving me nightmares. If you make contact, call in immediately. We will send significant backup. Huntingdon, have a shooter team on standby. This man is not to be trifled with. I don't want any of you getting hurt.'

There was an uneasy exchange of charged conversation as the meeting began to break up. Dexter crouched down next to Harrison.

'Joe, I want you to do a press conference at four this afternoon. Give them the bare minimum: the name, the photograph. Keep my name out of it. If they ask, Underwood is the officer in charge. I don't want them to make the connection with me for as long as possible.'

'I understand.' Harrison scribbled his instructions in his notebook as Dexter walked away.

Underwood watched her walk past with a heavy heart. Was it possible that she had seen him hiding in the darkness of her friend's garden? He could not see how: he was away before she was within twenty yards of him. It had been pitch black. He had worn a woollen hat. It could not be possible. Perhaps Dexter's mind was elsewhere.

Underwood had watched her kissing another woman with a mixture of horror, profound sexual excitement and despair. He wondered if her emotions had been similar. It was likely that Dexter's mind was in turmoil, he reasoned. A monster from her past had reappeared at the same time that she seemed to be starting a new and volatile period in her emotional life. He wanted to help her. However, he decided that it might be expedient to suspend his hobby for a week or so.

As the meeting broke up, Underwood felt empty. For him emptiness was the precursor to desperation: his darkest lapses had usually been preceded by what he called 'hollow mind'. He needed to occupy his brain. With his analysis of Dexter suspended, he had to find some other conundrum to blot out his demons.

In her glass office, Alison Dexter stared at the photofit of Bartholomew Garrod. As was her habit, she tried to imagine him with different coloured hair, glasses or a beard. In every articulation of her imagination, the man was still monstrous. Dexter felt very alone. There was a message on her desk that Mike Bevan was bringing in Bob Woollard for questioning in half an hour or so. Dexter felt a powerful urge to write an email to Kelsi Hensy. However, remembering their discussion of the previous evening, she resisted the temptation, turning instead to the 'Primal Cut' case file that she had compiled with Paddy McInally seven years before. She was not entirely convinced that unleashing the whirlwind of publicity on Garrod was sensible but, tactically, there was no other realistic option. Dexter was concerned: she did not know the man well enough to predict how he would react. Would she reap the whirlwind?

Alison Dexter was a positive, logical thinking personality, not one prone to fatalism. However, sitting in the glass box of her office, staring into the dark eyes of Bartholomew Garrod, she had a profound sense that she was making a terrible mistake.

36.

Bob Woollard sat in interview room 2 at New Bolden police station.

'So exactly what laws am I supposed to have broken?' he asked DI Mike Bevan.

'It might be easier to list the ones that you haven't broken,' Bevan replied. 'How about the

Dangerous Dogs Act and the Protection of Animals Act for starters? That's to say nothing of the fact that you have been implicated for illegally disposing of a dead body. We could probably add perverting the course of justice to that list.'

'I never take those dogs out in public. They are always muzzled on the farm. I don't see how that breaks any laws.'

'Fighting them breaks the law, Bob, as you well know. We haven't checked them yet but I expect your little video collection makes for interesting viewing.'

'Has my lawyer arrived?' Woollard asked, ignoring Bevan's observation.

'He's on his way,' Bevan replied. 'Face facts, Bob, you are going down. In flames.'

'We'll see about that won't we?' Woollard smiled.

'There are ways to make this better for yourself.' Bevan leaned forward. 'Let's just talk man to man for a second. Once your lawyer gets here things get official and nasty. I won't be able to make you any sort of offer.'

'I'm listening,' Woollard said suspiciously.

'Tell me about the man who killed Leonard Shaw: this George Norlington.'

'I don't know him,' Woollard said in exasperation. 'He was Gwynne's mate not mine.'

'If you help us on this, I might be able to drop

one or two of the charges. You are in a lot of trouble, Bob. Forensic found blood splashes on the floor of your barn. Splashes that you tried to conceal. That's conspiracy. Naughty, naughty. If you help us we would take that into consideration. Maybe you'd just be left with the dog-related violations.' Bevan knew that such an eventuality was highly unlikely.

'That's very generous Inspector Bevan but as I don't know the bloke, there's not much I can tell you.'

Bevan slid a photofit of Bartholomew Garrod across the table that separated them. 'Is this a good likeness of him?'

Woollard looked down at the picture. 'His face was fuller. He looked older in the flesh.'

'Grey hair?'

'I suppose so. I only saw the guy for twenty minutes or so. He was big – like a fighter gone to seed. He must be fifty plus. I expect he was formidable when he was younger.'

'What about his dog?' Bevan asked. 'Gwynne said that he had a Tosa. That's unusual.'

'Very,' Woollard sniffed.

'Did you ask him about it, Bob? I can't believe that you would fight one of your dogs without knowing a bit about its opponent's previous.'

Woollard scratched the back of his head in

thought. He had responsibilities. He could not risk a prison term: not a long one in any case. Cooperation was his only option. He would give them a little taster for now.

'He said that he'd owned the dog for a couple of years.'

'Where did he get it?'

'Essex. Clacton I think.'

'From a breeder?'

'No. I don't think so. He said that he'd won the dog in a fight. He said something about putting the owner in hospital. That's all I know about the bloke. Like I said, he was Gwynne's monkey, not mine.'

Bevan wrote the information in his notebook. It was something.

37.

At ten o'clock that evening, Bartholomew Garrod stood in the smoky kitchen of Craxten Fen Psychiatric Hospital chopping onions. He carefully trimmed them into tiny chunks, as small as he could make them. He knew that exposing the maximum surface area of the onion was the way to enhance its taste most effectively.

The facilities were proving barely adequate for

his purposes and his initial enthusiasm for the location was waning. The lack of light was problematic: Garrod kept bashing his legs against the unfamiliar cabinets and corners. The single saucepan he had uncovered was old and battered and his camping stove laughably minuscule. Still, it would have to do until he could collect his own, more appropriate cooking tools.

Garrod liked to eat late. Appetite had not yet overtaken him. He had some work to do first and a phone call to make.

There were busy times ahead. He had arranged an appointment at Delaney's Animal Feed Suppliers outside Meldreth. He was committed to a full week's work at the abattoir and he still had some further preparatory work on the pit he had dug out for Alison Dexter.

It was good to be busy.

38.

Underwood could not face returning to his cramped little flat on the outskirts of New Bolden. Instead he stayed in the office. Dexter left at 10.45 p.m. He wrote the time in his notebook but felt no pleasure. Her attitude towards him was increasingly acidic. Underwood wanted to express his affection: make her aware of his concern. Dexter had refused to move into secure accommodation, preferring to remain in her flat. To Underwood, that seemed like the height of folly.

He decided that he could help her best by working the hunt for Bartholomew Garrod as vigorously as possible. Harrison's four o'clock press conference had been well attended. By the following morning, the photofit impression of Garrod would be on the front pages of most local newspapers and perhaps one or two nationals: just as it had seven years previously. That thought disturbed Underwood. This was clearly an individual with intellectual ability. Britain was a small country: it was hard for a man like Garrod to disappear. Where could he have gone for seven years? It was impossible for him to have owned a property and the records compiled by Leyton CID showed no other evidence of family properties. Had Garrod rented a room or a flat? Again, it seemed unusual. Landlords required proof of identity now: bank account details and personal references. Garrod's bank accounts had been frozen by the Metropolitan Police in 1996. Renting was expensive; it made you conspicuous, too. Living rough was the obvious option: camping out or squatting in some broken down outbuilding.

And yet, Garrod had rented a room at the Dog

and Feathers for over a month.

He opened the 'Primal Cut' case file that he had retrieved from Dexter's office after she had left. He began to look for any details that might suggest an explanation for Garrod's disappearance after his brother's death. Was there something that McInally and Dexter had missed?

Instinctively, Underwood turned directly to the appendices that contained background on the Garrod family. He started by reading the profile of Bartholomew Garrod's mother:

May Garrod (nee Shildon). Born Dalston, London 2nd July 1920. Married Cornelius Garrod at Leyton Registry Office on 13th December 1940. Brother Sgt Eric Shildon (RER) killed in action France 1940. May Garrod pronounced dead at St Bartholomew's Hospital London in March 1975 (stroke).

Underwood mused at the tragedy of a life reduced to four lines of text. He noted with only passing interest that the hospital shared the same name as the target of his manhunt: he knew that many male babies were named Bartholomew in the East End after the hospital in which they were born. He wondered what 'RER' denoted. It referred to Sgt Shildon. If it was a military term the final 'R' could mean 'regiment'. Was it the Royal East London Regiment? Underwood wondered if such a thing existed. He turned to his computer and found the Commonwealth War Graves Commission website. Underwood's great grandfather had been killed in the Great War so he was familiar with the Commission's activities. He entered Shildon's details into the search engine and pressed 'enter'. The following appeared on his screen:

Surname	Rank	Service	Date of Death	Age	Regiment	Nationality
Shildon E	Sgt	781692	28 May 1940	28	Royal Essex Regiment	United Kingdom

So 'RER' was the Royal Essex Regiment. Underwood left the War Graves Commission website and ran a general search for the history of the Royal Essex Regiment. Eventually he found the official regimental website and opened a paragraph of text that recorded the regimental history. He read that the Regiment had been raised and based in Colchester; that it had fought with distinction in both World Wars.

Underwood stopped himself going any further. His mind, as always, was flying off at useless tangents. Fascinating though the history of the Royal Essex Regiment undoubtedly was, he needed to stay focused. He switched off his Internet connection and returned to the brief biographical profile of Cornelius Garrod in the 'Primal Cut' case file. He drank some cold coffee to focus his mind.

Cornelius Garrod was born in Leyton, London on 11th February 1919. He married May Shildon at Leyton Registry Office on 13th December 1940. Garrod served as a private in the Royal Fusiliers 1939–46 (North Africa & Burma). He was arrested for drunk and disorderly behaviour on 3rd January 1950, in Wanstead, London but was released without charge. He bought 398 Norlington Road, Leyton in November 1950. An application for planning permission on that property was registered with Leyton Council in December 1950. Garrod was arrested again for drunkenness on 4th August 1960, in Great Oakley. Cornelius Garrod was pronounced dead at St Bartholomew's Hospital London in March 1975 (heart attack).

Underwood scratched his head in mild confusion. There was little in the family histories of the Garrods and the Shildons that excited his interest. True, there were some similarities: both were East London families; both Eric Shildon and Cornelius Garrod had fought in World War Two. Were the two men friends? Underwood wondered if that was how Cornelius Garrod had met May Shildon: had Eric Shildon introduced his friend to his sister?

There wasn't much else. Cornelius Garrod had

been arrested drunk on two separate occasions but there was nothing unusual in that. Or was there? Underwood looked again at Cornelius Garrod's history:

Arrested drunk 3rd January 1950, Wanstead, London… Arrested drunk 4th August 1960, Great Oakley.

Underwood frowned. Great Oakley was not in London. Great Oakley was in Essex. He opened his top drawer and pulled out his street atlases: he had three for Cambridgeshire, two for Suffolk and two for Essex. The east Essex street atlas gave him what he was after: Great Oakley was on the Essex coast about five miles south-west of Harwich and about ten miles east of Colchester. Earlier that evening, Mike Bevan had told Underwood that Garrod had won his Tosa dog in a fight in Clacton-on-Sea. Clacton was about ten miles due south of Great Oakley.

Underwood's mind was beginning to accelerate. There was a family connection with a particular part of Essex. He consulted his map. Three separate pieces of information spread over fifty years had created the three points of a triangle: from Colchester in the west to Harwich in the north down to Clacton in the south. In the middle was Great Oakley. Why? Why the link to Essex? Underwood mused. Eric Shildon had been based in

Colchester. He would have known the area. Did he buy a house there? It seemed unlikely on a service salary. Underwood looked at the arrest record of Cornelius Garrod, this time concentrating on the date: August 1960.

'Jesus Christ,' Underwood whispered to himself as realisation dawned. Cornelius Garrod had been on holiday in the area: on holiday with his family most likely. What if Shildon had bought a plot of land, a chalet or a caravan on the coast? After his death in 1940, perhaps ownership passed to his sister. May Shildon was married to Cornelius Garrod.

Underwood knew that there were several large caravan sites in the area. There were dozens spread between Clacton, Frinton and up as far as Harwich. Out of season, on the deserted sites, Bartholomew Garrod would have been virtually anonymous. In season, when the camps filled with pensioners and screaming kids, perhaps he moved out of the area. Perhaps he stayed in bed and breakfast accommodation elsewhere.

'And now that we've made him leave his rented bedsit,' Underwood extrapolated, 'maybe he has been forced back into his caravan.'

He wrote down the key strands of his logic on a piece of paper. He wanted Dexter to be in no doubt as to the strength of this revelation:

HYPOTHESIS: Garrod family has connections to East Essex. (Eric Shildon based in Colchester, Cornelius Garrod arrested in Great Oakley 1960, Bartholomew Garrod obtained his fighting dog in Clacton two years ago.) My suggestion is that the family owned a land plot, a static caravan or a chalet on one of the sites along the Essex coast. Given that they have been visiting the area since at least 1960, it must be located on one of the older sites.

ACTION: We need to contact the management offices of all the campsites on the Essex coast. We should concentrate our efforts on those sites that have been in existence since before 1960. It is possible that the caravan is still registered in the name Shildon. I believe that the caravan was originally bought by Eric Shildon. When he was killed in 1940, it is reasonable to assume that the caravan passed into the ownership of his sister, May Shildon, Bartholomew Garrod's mother.

There was a plausible logic underpinning Underwood's thought process. Having organised it into words, he felt that his theory was worth exploring. He hoped that Dexter would agree. Her mind appeared to have been scrambled slightly. Underwood had watched her kiss Kelsi Hensy. The notion that Dexter was a lesbian had upset him. And yet, he knew that Dexter had had relationships with men in the past. He hoped that she was merely exploring alternative options: seeking physical excitement in the same way that her mind sought intellectual arousal.

Underwood believed that their two minds were similar: perhaps more similar than Alison Dexter would appreciate. True, her ability to prioritise and assimilate information was far superior to his but they both had minds that craved stimulus. Underwood had realised, in his more honest moments, that his approach to life was also one of seeking stimuli. Police work had given him variety. He knew that when such a mind became bored with itself, strange outcomes could ensue. It could tear itself apart, sink into addiction or submerge its identity in someone else. He hoped that Dexter's relationship with Kelsi Hensy could be explained in these terms.

Underwood wondered if Garrod had been following Dexter. Perhaps the way to catch Garrod would be to put an unmarked car on her tail when she wasn't in the office. However, if he had been tailing her why hadn't he made his move already? Underwood thought of his own past: of the time when he had confronted his ex-wife's lover and almost beaten him to death. His mind that night had been a terrible mess. Underwood's abiding memory was not of wanting to kill the man but to hurt him, to torment him.

He looked at the picture of Bartholomew Garrod that he had distributed to uniformed officers across the county. If Garrod had been following Dexter already, Underwood thought, what could he have learned?

'Everything that I know about her,' he concluded, *'where she works, where she shops, where she exercises, the people that she is close to.'*

Underwood's thoughts ground to a shuddering halt.

'If I wanted to hurt Alison Dexter,' Underwood thought, *'I would go for the people that she cared for. Let her live with the agony of loss. The agony that I've suffered.'*

Bartholomew Garrod had lost his brother. Who could the man take from Alison Dexter in return? Suddenly realising the awful possibility that his ideas had created, Underwood grabbed his coat and hurried downstairs and out into the cold night air.

It took him ten minutes through deserted streets to arrive at Farleigh Mews, the home of Kelsi Hensy. Underwood waited in his car, uncertain how to proceed. If Dexter was there and she saw him, his career at New Bolden CID would effectively be over. Wind blew against the car. The weather forecast had warned of gales. Underwood looked along the row of houses: all the lights were off. It was 2.00 a.m. There was no sign of anybody else: just the wind rushing at the trees.

Movement. Underwood looked out across the small stone courtyard. Kelsi Hensy's front door had blown open. There was nobody in sight.

With a terrible sense of foreboding, Underwood unbuckled his seat belt.

39.

Thursday, 17th October 2002

Alison Dexter lay in bed on the irritating cusp of consciousness. She was confident her flat was secure: the front door was double-bolted, her burglar alarm had been activated in all zones other than her bedroom. She had also placed a carving knife under her pillow. However, her nerves had beaten her. Bartholomew Garrod had haunted her for years. Now he was near, she could almost sense his presence. Underwood had betrayed her too. Perhaps she had been mistaken to allow him back into New Bolden CID after his breakdown. Pity had overwhelmed her better judgement. Besides, if she was being honest, she had always felt a peculiar affection for the man. His powers as a detective had waned. There was no doubt about that in Dexter's mind. Underwood's intuitive leaps had once surprised and inspired her. Until, of course, they had started to go wrong.

Now, it seemed the man's grip on sanity had finally faltered. He was fumbling at her life as surely as if he was pulling at her bra strap. Alison Dexter was confounded by the men in her life: her father had deserted her as a child, her ex-lover Mark Willis had betrayed and brutalised her. Now even John Underwood, the emotional Titanic she had hauled up from the depths of despair, was fingering at the edges of her sanity. Dexter knew she was the common denominator in all these disastrous equations. However, explanations eluded her.

Her night with Kelsi Hensy had liberated her from this mindset. Abandoning fear and prejudice had been a gloriously savage pleasure. And yet, somehow, she had managed to alienate Kelsi too. Dexter wondered if that situation was retrievable or if – like Underwood – it had already sunk beneath the waves. Perhaps there was some kind of infection in her DNA: some pre-programmed propensity for emotional disaster. Or was she an emotional hollow: a vacuum that people momentarily filled before draining away? It could be that she was just unlucky. Dexter wanted the chance to be born again. To have the slate of pain wiped clean – to emerge screaming into the light again with a host of possible futures before her. Alternatively, she wished she had never existed.

It was after three o'clock in the morning when her phone rang.

She contemplated ignoring it. Self-indulgence battled briefly with professionalism. As always, professionalism won.

'Hello,' she said quietly into the mouthpiece.

There was no immediate reply. Dexter could hear muffled traffic noise, someone fumbling at the other end of the line. The line went dead. Dexter sat up in bed. Alert suddenly. The phone rang again.

'Hello,' she said, more loudly this time.

'You know who this is?' Bartholomew Garrod asked.

Dexter felt fear squeeze at her heart.

'What do you want?' she replied, her mind racing. Her mobile phone was on her bedside table. She reached across and grabbed it.

'I want you. You know that. You know I've been coming for you.'

Dexter hesitated. She put her mobile back down on the table. The professional inside her saw an opportunity.

'How did you get my number?' she asked.

'Wouldn't you like to know,' Garrod replied. 'I

know everything about you dearie. Sorry to call so late but I've been getting my dinner ready.'

Dexter tried to contain her fear. *Concentrate.*

'I know a lot about you too, Mr Garrod. You shouldn't have come back. We're closer to you than you realise.' Dexter hoped the lie would unsettle him.

'There's something I want you to hear,' Garrod said without rising to the bait, 'something I recorded.'

'I'm not interested, Garrod.' Dexter was straining her ears, hunting for some giveaway noise in the background; something that would locate Garrod. A police or ambulance siren would have been useful.

'I think you will be.' Five miles away, in a telephone box in the centre of New Bolden, Bartholomew Garrod held the Dictaphone that he had stolen to the mouthpiece of the payphone and pressed play.

Dexter could hear a crackling white noise like the fuzz between radio stations. Then she heard voices, a deep guttural male voice that she presumed was Garrod's.

'...Wake up you fucking bitch...' grunted Garrod's voice on the Dictaphone.

A woman moaning in pain.

'I said wake up you bitch...' Garrod continued.

'Who are you...get out of my house...I won't...get off me...'

Screaming.

Dexter's mind raced. Had Garrod set her up? Was he using this tape to distract her as he broke into her flat? If he knew her phone number, maybe he knew her address. How could he have discovered her number?

'...tell me your name...you bitch or I will cut you again...'

Sobbing.

'...Kelsi...Hensy,' said the terrified voice.

Dexter's world inverted as the awful realisation struck at her.

'What do you say?...Say what I told you...'

There were sounds of scuffling punctuated by a terrible scream.

'Help me...' Kelsi Hensy shouted in pain and desperation.

'What have you done?' Dexter shouted into the phone. 'What have you done you fucking bastard?'

Garrod turned off the Dictaphone. 'I followed her home. Knocked her unconscious. Made myself comfortable. Found this little Dictaphone gizmo sitting on her coffee table and decided to make you a present. Amazing sound quality, isn't it? I bet you feel like you were there. Well, don't worry, you'll enjoy Old Bart's magic soon enough for yourself. Do you understand how it works now? My brother's dead because of you and now your little lezzie friend is dead too. Rest assured she didn't die a lezzie though. Old Bart made sure of that. You most probably heard me sticking it in her on the tape.'

Dexter slammed the phone down. She dressed, grabbed her keys and left her flat.

By 3.40 a.m., the moment that Alison Dexter's Mondeo screamed to a halt outside Farleigh Mews, a Scene of Crime team had already arrived and blocked the entrance to the cul-de-sac. Dexter ran across the road, tears of fury and despair blurring her vision. Underwood stepped from the chaotic scene to grab her.

'You can't go in there, Alison!' he shouted at her.

'Get your hands off me,' she screamed, flailing at him.

'There's nothing you can do,' he replied, tightening his grip as she started to slip away from him. 'She's dead.'

'No!' Dexter struggled furiously as Underwood dragged her from the bemused SOCO team.

'She's dead, Alison. You can't see her as she is. There's a team in there helping her now. Don't be an idiot.'

Dexter could feel her strength draining from her. The horror of the moment overwhelmed her. As Underwood felt her body weakening, his grip changed from restraint to support. She hung uselessly in his arms.

'I'm sorry,' he said quietly. 'I'm so sorry.'

That was the last thing that Dexter remembered as consciousness left her.

At that moment, in his kitchen at Craxten Fen, Bartholomew Garrod celebrated his triumph with a late supper. Once he was happy that the onions were sizzling properly, Garrod added the pieces of chuck steak and kidney that he had cut from Kelsi Hensy. He had underestimated the woman. She had fought him violently, scratching at his right eye with her nails as he had pushed backwards through her front door. Now it had swollen horribly to the point that Garrod could hardly see out of it. Eventually he had knocked her down though and Old Bart had had his way.

He had lifted up her skirt: she wore white panties under her tights. Garrod fondly remembered a rush of sexuality. It had been a long time.

Breaking off from his happy reminiscences, Garrod added Worcester sauce to his saucepan. He stirred in ketchup for flavour then added salt and pepper seasoning. Once he was confident that the concoction was ready, he poured it into one of his Tupperware containers and chewed thoughtfully on Kelsi Hensy.

DRESSING THE MEAT

40.

Burma
January 1945

The moisture hung in the air. You could cut it, step through it as if it were a delicate curtain. The curtain clung to you though, encumbered and eventually exhausted you. It weighed on you like the terror of ambush: the terror of a sniper's bullet or what awaited you in the Japanese prisoner of war camps. The platoon had read the stories. The oral history of atrocity was infectious. They knew about the Banka island massacre of twenty female Australian nurses. Those stories were compelling. They drove the platoon forward and sharpened its senses on their sweep through dense jungle outside Tilin.

The Hurricane from 258 squadron had been on a reconnaissance swoop. It had gone down just after midnight the previous evening somewhere in the patrol area. There was little chance of finding the pilot alive as the area was still designated hostile. They had penetrated deep into occupied territory.

They had learned about the jungle, begun to use the terrain to their advantage; they had learned to move soundlessly. And to listen.

The abiding concern of 'A' Company, 4th Battalion, Royal Fusiliers, was to stay alive. The jungle was waiting to kill them as the war stumbled into its final phase. They had heard about the Russian advances across eastern Europe and the Allied penetrations along the German border. The war was nearly over. It would be a stupid time to get shot. Or infected. The jungle sheltered swarms of black flies, leeches and furious, ferocious insects. Typhus and cholera, dysentery and malaria consumed ten times as many men as combat. Two million men creeping terrified ankle deep in mud, cut by razor sharp elephant grass, wracked by terrible disease. A dirty, sweaty, parasite-ridden, stinking, forgotten war.

Sergeant Ian Rae refused to let such thoughts cloud his judgement. He was a veteran of the vicious fighting at Sahak and Frontier Hill. He had learned that caution, professionalism and cold blooded brutality were his way home. He edged his small platoon forward along the edge of what might once have been a track. Rae guessed that it had been eroded in the monsoon season that had persisted well into the previous October. The pathway had disintegrated into sliding filth on one side. It looked useless and was almost impassable.

He paused, crouching in heavy foliage, sweat streaming down his back. His patrol consisted of twenty-four men: two dozen individuals thrown into danger to find one downed fighter pilot. The mathematics of war seemed absurd to him. He looked back along the line of British soldiers that had halted behind him. Rae gestured Corporal Gendall to join him at the front of the column.

'What's up, Sarge?' Gendall asked. Rae noticed the breathlessness of his favourite corporal. The jungle gnawed at you from within and without.

'Have you any idea where we are?' Rae replied hoarsely, fumbling for his pocket map of the operations zone. 'All the bastard tracks are washed away.'

Gendall pulled out his own map and compass. 'We are in hostile territory, that's for sure. North is that way, roughly in the direction of the ridge to the left. Say we've covered one click in the last two hours. I'd say we were about here.' He pointed a muddy index finger at his map. 'The middle of fucking nowhere.'

Rae looked at the dense foliage ahead of them. 'We must be at the edge of the search zone. This is a waste of time. We couldn't find Windsor Castle in this. I am not pushing the lads into that for some stupid bloody Hurricane pilot who got his wings *with his first pair of long trousers.' Rae felt frustration surging inside him. This was a ridiculous place for him to be.*

'What do you want to do?' Gendall asked. 'We can't sit here.'

Rae's conscience was chewing at him. He decided on a compromise. 'OK, let's tie this thing up. I want two squads: four men in each to sweep left and right of our current position. Say five minutes out then double-time it back. Ten-yard spread. The rest of the patrol will hold here. Tell the boys to stay sharp. It's bloody quiet out here.'

Gendall nodded. 'I was just thinking the same thing. Maybe we've scared all the wildlife off. This isn't the most discreet of patrols.'

'Let's get this sweep done and get the fuck out of here. My feet are itching like bloody murder.'

Gendall scurried back to the lines and selected eight men. Privates Hawkins, O'Malley, Palmer and Gregory took the left sweep. Gendall himself led Lance Corporal Hillen, Private Baines and Private Cornelius Garrod down the treacherous slope that fell away into a gully, right of the patrol's position.

Rae watched them sink into the undergrowth, infuriated by the unscratchable itching trench foot inside his right boot.

41.
Friday, 18th October 2002

Bartholomew Garrod had agreed to work a late shift at the abattoir. The money was slightly better and he liked the fact that the buildings were less congested with people. That gave him the freedom to explore his taste for off-cuts of meat. He knew that he was taking risks. He had emerged from anonymous security to find Alison Dexter. Garrod suspected that time was against him. He would have to move quickly.

Garrod had rerun the day of Ray's arrest a thousand times in his head. Somehow little Alison Dexter had linked them to the death of Brian Patterson, the Smithfield porter whose liver had been salty with cirrhosis. He had read the lurid details of the case in the newspapers after the event but the woman's method had eluded him. Garrod had reassured himself that the fault was Ray's not his own. However, he had a nagging doubt that Alison Dexter was a formidable opponent.

Six years previously, Garrod had witnessed his brother's death. He had located Alison Dexter's home in East London (at considerable effort and expense) in anticipation of a sumptuous revenge. Then, as he had fantasised in hiding about the smell of her cooking flesh and begun to prepare a marinade, she had disappeared. Tentative enquiries revealed nothing: Alison Dexter had vanished like spit from a frying pan. Garrod could have looked harder but every favour called in, every trip from Essex back to London was a terrible risk. His next mistake was to assume that she had remained in London. Garrod scanned the *Evening Standard* and other London newspapers for six years trying to locate the woman that had killed his brother.

Then, in June 2002, a miracle had occurred. In the musty, peeling claustrophobia of his temporary accommodation, as he lay projecting his despair as bloody pictures onto the darkness, a tired part of his mind began to register a female voice crackling out a local news report from his ancient radio set:

'Cambridgeshire Police today confirmed that former City trader Max Fallon will not stand trial for murder. Fallon, formerly a director of London Investment Bank Fogle & Moore, was arrested last month in connection with the murder of his colleague Elizabeth Koplinsky. Fallon has been judged unfit to stand trial and has been sectioned under the Mental Health Act. Inspector Alison Dexter of Cambridgeshire Police refused to comment on the decision.'

The report lasted no more than twenty seconds but it hit Bartholomew Garrod like a lightning bolt.

He became convinced that some beautiful Providence was at work. A throwaway fragment of information floated into the midnight ether by a sloppy radio journalist had given him hope. It meant that his meandering, shallow existence had been re-imbued with purpose. It meant that he could finally avenge his brother's unnecessary death. And for Alison Dexter it meant pain: savage, prolonged pain.

Seeking her out would be dangerous but he would have surprise on his side. The temptation of gnawing on her loins was too exciting to resist. Garrod had always been a creature of impulse: a man of reckless, passionate decision. However, this time he knew that he would have to be very careful indeed. In preparation, he had begun to make regular visits to Cambridgeshire. Discreet inquiries had led him quickly to the anonymous town of New Bolden: uniquely forgettable with its unsightly litters of starter homes, pubescent mothers and cluttered car parks.

And suddenly there she was, climbing out of a squad car by New Bolden police station, climbing out of his darkest fantasies: rare, lean and accessible.

Delaney's Animal Feed Suppliers stunk out the neighbouring village of Skreen. It was a kind of sickly sweet, dry smell that hung perpetually in the air. It reminded Garrod of breakfast cereal.

He parked his van in front of a giant aluminium shed. Security cameras peered down on him. He hadn't anticipated that. He wished he'd put his hat on.

Garrod found a broken down looking girl in the reception office and smiled his best, stained smile. She was drinking coffee from a mug that said 'England 5. Germany 1.'

'I called yesterday. I have an appointment with Mr Delaney for 8.30 this morning,' he said politely.

'Are you Mr Francis?' she asked in a watery, expressionless slur.

'The very same.' Garrod couldn't see any worthwhile cuts of meat on her. At best, she was dripping.

'He said you should meet him round the back. He's doing the inventory in storage. Over there,' she pointed, 'behind the double doors.'

Garrod turned out of the office and crossed a stone courtyard. His stomach rumbled. Either the smell of cereal was making him hungry or Kelsi Hensy's kidney did not agree with him.

Terry Delaney saw him coming.

'You Francis?' he called out as Garrod's huge bulk approached him.

'That's right.'

'You're a bit early but we've got your order ready

here. You want 200 litres of molasses right?'

'Yes.'

'Pigs?'

'What?'

'You fattening pigs?' Delaney asked as he led Garrod around the metal side of his storage shed. 'I warn you. It makes them shit like there's no tomorrow. I mean a pig is a shitting machine anyway. Disgusting animals. People say they're intelligent but what sort of intelligence lives up to its ankles in shit? Sixteen million pigs are slaughtered in Britain every year so they can't be that bleeding intelligent. This stuff has laxative qualities I'm told. But it's top of the range.'

'It's for my boss,' Garrod replied blankly. 'He's the farmer. I'm just the driver.'

Delaney nodded. 'It's decent stuff. You know, it tastes a bit like honey.'

Garrod nodded: he had been counting on that.

He and Garrod arrived in front of five large black tins, each about a yard in diameter and height. 'Iranian sugar cane molasses. This is unsulphured, no chemicals. The real McCoy.' Delaney pulled a large screwdriver from his jacket pocket and prised the lid off one of the tins.

Garrod peered inside at the thick syrup. It was dark brown and viscous.

Delaney dipped his finger into the tin and sucked

off the syrup. 'Try some, mate. It's tasty. It might be pig food but it's sweet as a nut. I could kill a million diabetics with this.'

Garrod used his right index finger to sample the molasses; it was certainly sweet. There was a raw quality to it though: a rough sweetness. Perfect.

'This is too good for pigs, mate,' he said with a smile.

'Forty-seven pounds per tin – that's including VAT – five tins makes two hundred and thirty-five quid,' Delaney replied.

'Discount for cash?'

'Funny man!' Delaney grinned. 'It don't work that way no more.'

'Shame,' Garrod sniffed. 'The world's changing.'

'It's called progress. I'll get some of the boys to help you load up your van.'

'No. I'll do it. It's no problem.'

Delaney shrugged. 'Your funeral mate. Money?'

Garrod handed over a roll of banknotes that Delaney eagerly counted. He looked at the huge tins of syrup and wondered if he had bought enough.

'I'll get you a receipt.' Delaney walked off to the reception office.

Garrod crouched down and heaved the first of the giant tins up onto his chest.

42.

Alison Dexter had folded her pain into self-annihilation.

Kelsi Hensy was dead and she was responsible. She had abandoned caution and paid a terrible price. Drawing other people into her world had always been disastrous. It was better to be alone: better still to not exist at all. And yet, as she sat listening to Marty Farrell describing the crime scene to John Underwood, Dexter realised that her thought process, destructive though it was, still ran down rails of logic. It was an unsettling realisation. Learning that Kelsi Hensy had been murdered had overwhelmed her. Now she sat inside the shell of herself wondering at her logic. Was she really so hard, so untouchable that even the brutalisation of her friend could not derail her mind? Dexter found that – a few hours after the event – she was functional. The knowledge was terrifying. She had always assumed logical thought was a skill; an ability that you honed; the cutting edge of a diverse mind. Now she saw her mistake. In its entirety, her mind was logic. No creativity, no spontaneity, no vulnerability. Just electrical, mathematical logic. It was not a personality that she wished to be trapped in.

Logic also sought to apportion blame. Dexter

thought of her runaway father, her twisted ex-boyfriend, the career that demanded straight-line thinking, the fumbling fool that John Underwood had become to her. However, logic's straight lines kept bringing her back to where she started: a little girl in a lonely place.

'The blood spray against the TV screen and south wall is evidence that she was killed in the front room. Heavy-duty knife. She had damage to her hands too. There was hair and blood under her fingernails. Put up a hell of a fight I'd say. She was raped before he killed her. There are traces of semen on the carpet and on the girl. Judging from the temperature of the body, I estimate that she was killed late on Wednesday night: maybe between eleven and midnight. The mutilations were *post-mortem*. Flesh removed from the thighs and some organs were taken out. Do you want to hear the details?' Farrell asked Underwood.

Underwood shook his head. He knew that Kelsi Hensy's kidneys, liver and a portion of her guts had been removed. Pathologist Roger Leach had told him as much after examining the body earlier that morning. He didn't want Dexter to know how her friend had been desecrated. Although he knew that her mind could paint terrible pictures on its own.

'I know about the body,' Underwood eventually replied. 'Tell me about the rest of the house.'

'Blood traces have been trodden into the kitchen and up the stairs. A number of drawers have been emptied. It suggests he went looking for something after he murdered the girl.' Farrell rubbed his chin to focus his mind. 'He's a pretty cool customer this Garrod bloke, isn't he? After what he'd just done, you'd think he'd hightail it out of there as quickly as possible.'

'He was looking for something,' Underwood hypothesised. 'But what?'

Dexter found her colleague's question irritating, even through the bars of her cage. 'My address and phone number,' she said quietly. 'He called me, didn't he? There's nowhere else he could have got them. Marty, we're about done here. There'll be a meeting on this soon. I'll want you to be there.'

'No problem,' he said, rising from his seat. 'We'll get the report up to you as quickly as we can.'

Dexter managed a thin smile. 'I know you will. John, can you stay here for a moment. Shut the door on the way out, Marty,' she instructed.

With Farrell out of the way, Dexter looked Underwood directly in the eye.

'Despatch says that you called the team in last night,' she observed. 'How did you know to go to Kelsi Hensy's house?'

Underwood was twisting in the wind. This was the question that he had feared. 'Alison, I'll be honest with you, since Garrod turned up I've been concerned about you. I've been staying a bit closer to you than perhaps I should have.'

'You're a bad liar, John,' she shook her head. 'Try again.'

'It's true. I followed you there the other night. I realised that this Hensy woman was a friend of yours. I thought that Garrod might try to get to you through her. You don't put your head above the battlements much. There was a risk that he might go for her.'

'You've been stalking me: following me about. Writing down my movements in a notebook like some wanking train spotter.' Dexter's despair was mutating into cold fury. 'Give me one good reason why I shouldn't kick your arse down those stairs.'

'I was right,' said Underwood quietly, too ashamed to look at her.

'What else have you interfered with? I imagine you've been through my desk. Not much there though. Have you been hanging around in my garden, taking pictures of me filling a kettle? Watching me get undressed?'

Underwood said nothing: she was uncannily close to the truth.

'What do you think the Super would think? It's only because of me that he agreed to have you back here at all. This is how you repay me? You're supposed to be running an investigation not following me about. People are dead and you are pissing around.' Dexter felt tears behind her eyes: she kept them there.

'I have been running an investigation,' Underwood responded, his wounds bleeding inside. 'I suspected Garrod would go for anyone that you were close to. She was the obvious person. I just wish I'd thought of it sooner.'

There was so much Underwood wanted to tell her, to explain his misdemeanours. Restraint defeated self-interest.

'We do have an investigation. One: we have been running PNC checks on the list of possible names that you drew up. It takes time to follow those up. Two: I have been rereading the "Primal Cut" file and I think there might be a family connection with Essex. It's possible that Garrod might own a static caravan or a beach chalet under another name – possibly Shildon.'

Dexter shook her head in disbelief. 'And that's it? Garrod is carving people up on our manor and your best idea is that he might own a fucking caravan in Essex! For Christ's sake!' Dexter slammed her clenched fist on her desk. 'It's not very promising, Sherlock.'

Underwood felt anger rising through the cloud of his love for Alison Dexter.

'And what exactly have you done?' he asked bitterly. 'You know more about this guy than anyone. I've read his file. You wrote it, Alison! What have you done? What tangible progress have you made?'

She stared back at him.

'I'll remind you,' Underwood continued. 'None. You stormed into a witness interview with Gwynne and thereby almost certainly rendered that interview inadmissible. You seem to forget that Garrod is here for you. So what do you do? Arrange for protection, leave the area, set a trap? No. You start a relationship with a stranger and place her life in jeopardy. She is now dead. So don't try your Metropolitan Police "what exactly have you done?" sarcasm on me. The only tangible contribution you have made to this case is lying on a metal table in the basement with her guts in a bag.'

Dexter shook her head. 'You are unbelievable. You are trying to make me feel guilty?'

'If the cap fits,' Underwood suggested.

'Essex, you say?' came the unexpected reply.

'I'm sorry?' Underwood's heart was racing with frustration.

'You say there's a connection with Essex?'

'Possibly. Garrod won his dog at Clacton. His father was arrested drunk a few miles up the road in 1950. It's tenuous but – as I said – I wondered if there might be some sort of family home in the area.'

Dexter nodded, 'I want you to go out there. Spend a few days in Essex. Trawl a few campsites.'

'Me?'

'It's your idea, isn't it? I doubt Sauerwine or Harrison would come up with anything as fucking wafer thin as that.'

'You just want me out of the way,' Underwood responded.

'Go to Essex, go to Butlins or Frinton or wherever you want to. Play out your little theory. Just get out of my sight.'

'What will you do?'

'I'm going to do what you should have done already: figure out how Bartholomew Garrod is earning money and where he is living. I'm going to second a couple of Armed Response coppers from Huntingdon too. If I see you here before the end of the week, they'll use you for target practice.'

Underwood felt the sadness and the cancer in his blood weighing heavily on him. 'I'm not your enemy. Far from it. You are very important to me.'

Dexter heard the words and felt them sting. 'Just go away, John. Just go away.'

Outside rain stretched out in puddles on the grey stone of the station car park. It was a hard, dark little world. Loneliness is our enemy and our refuge. We are shadows on the acid water: distorted and unable to evaporate. One chance: one haemorrhage of days and every day an erosion of our ability to face the next. Thrashing in sinking mud we scramble and tear at each other: sinking together. Rain fell on the shadows of Cambridgeshire: loudly on some, softly on others. Underwood scarcely heard the rain as he left the main entrance of the station and headed for his car, unable to disentangle love from self-pity and frustration. To Alison Dexter, sitting head in hands in her lonely office, the rain battered at her window as blood pounded in the delicate vessels of her mind. She had always seen life as a maze: a progress through logical possibilities, building direction from alternatives, a learning game. Now she could see nowhere out of the nightmare world she had created for herself.

43.

Underwood did not drive east to Essex. He drove south to London.

It was exhausting. In heavy rain he had struggled to see the road in front of him. It had been a depressing experience: a miserable drive to a miserable place. The Care Home was in

Leytonstone: in the thrashing darkness it looked like some terrible asylum of the damned.

'You look tired,' said the man in room seven.

'It's a long drive.'

'M11?'

'Nightmare.'

'I appreciate you coming down. I really do.'

'It's not a problem.'

'You haven't said anything?'

'Of course not.'

'That's good of you. Is she well?'

Hesitation. 'She's been better. It's been a terrible week.'

'She's not been hurt?'

'No, nothing like that. Pressure. It's a tough job. Worse for a woman.'

'Did you bring any pictures?'

'One or two. It's getting harder I'm afraid. She knows I've been following her.'

The pictures were dark, shadowy, taken from a distance.

A nurse brought up two cups of tea. They drank them in silence.

44.

Saturday, 19th October 2002

For one of the few times in his life, Bartholomew
Garrod felt embarrassed. The abattoir manager,
Robert Sandway, had asked him to give a
presentation to the Saturday shift meat cutters on
butchery techniques and flesh types. Now as he
stood in front of twenty of his work mates, in a
small office next to the cutting floor, he felt his
heart racing.

'Right gentlemen,' Sandway began, 'first of all,
thank you for staying late. I'll make sure that you
all get an extra hour of pay.'

'Double time boss?' a voice asked from the back
of the room.

'Time and a half, you cheeky sod. You're not
working are you?' Sandway shot back with a smile.
'Now as some of you know, old George here
worked as a master butcher. He's been cutting meat
for thirty years, he knows his stuff and you lot
should listen to him. We've been getting sloppy
recently. As you know, I had to let Damian go for
clumsiness on the cutting floor. We have to abide by
very strict Health and Safety rules these days
because of E. coli, BSE and all that. It's also worth
remembering that the margins in this business are

very thin. We waste too much product. I've asked George here to talk to you about cutting techniques and about some of the by-products from the animals we cut.'

Garrod tried to organise the information in his mind. He wondered how to condense thirty years' experience into a few sentences. 'Well you all know the basic beef cuts – sirloin, rump, chucks, brisket, sloat and so on – so I won't go over them. Part of the problem here is the equipment we use. Modern knives and the electronic saws are just not the same quality as they used to be. The tempering is bad in some. Now, you hit a hard piece of bone and that knife could slide into organs and infect the meat. That's what Damo was doing. He was sliding his knife into the stomachs of them cows. There are four sorts of shit in there that ruin the meat.'

Sandway nodded. 'Cutting knives are delicate instruments. But that makes the art of the cutter even more important these days. Accuracy is the key.'

'Keep your knives razor sharp,' Garrod added. 'Bluntness encourages waste. Now I was always taught that you could tell a slovenly cutler from the amount in his fat drawer. You can also tell from the old meat ratios. You lot don't use them no more – they're a bit old-fashioned I suppose – but when I ran my own butchers those ratios were the difference between profit and loss.'

'What are you talking about, George?' asked Vince Grub, a young cutter with chronic acne. 'I cut the basic cuts: primals, whatever. I just do what I've been taught.'

Garrod found the ignorance disturbing. His experience on the cutting floor where hundreds of animals were sliced up each day had been a frustration. The meat men at Smithfield would have been horrified by the wastage in this abattoir. He had worked out some statistics earlier that afternoon to prove his point. 'I've been watching the way we cut pig meat. I reckon that on leg cuts alone we could be losing five to ten per cent of the good meat. Multiply that out by the number of pigs we cut here and you are talking thousands of pounds in wastage.'

Sandway was nodding his agreement. 'Absolutely. Good practice is the key here. This is about money as well as Health and Safety. Watch George cutting. Learn from him. Don't be snotty about it. We have to be professional. This is a business. We don't have a God-given right to exist. There are much bigger abattoirs out there with stronger economies of scale. We need to maximise our efficiency to stay competitive. If that means we go back to old-fashioned ratios and equipment, so be it. George here is an important information source. I want you to use him.'

Garrod's mind was drifting away. His thoughts focused on Alison Dexter. Kelsi Hensy had been of a slightly heavier build than Dexter. Say one hundred and fifty pounds. He had removed about seven and a half pounds of flesh from each leg: fifteen pounds in all. So that made the ratio of leg meat to carcass weight about a tenth. Dexter was lean. He estimated that she weighed about ten pounds less. One tenth of one hundred and forty amounted to fourteen pounds of leg meat. Slightly less, but Garrod knew that preparation was the key.

45.

The interview room was just as uncomfortable and claustrophobic as Woollard had remembered it. This time it was more crowded. DI Mike Bevan sat opposite him reading from a file. Woollard's lawyer, Anthony Dearing, was speaking to DI Alison Dexter: the smallest person in the room but the only one that he felt intimidated by.

'My client has been extremely helpful so far,' Dearing said to Bevan. 'He has been subject to harassment, to a house search and verbal bullying from police officers. We request that you particularise the allegations and charge my client or release him this evening.'

Bevan nodded. 'I agree. Mr Woollard, Inspector Dexter and I have decided that your suspected involvement in the murder of Leonard Shaw...'

'For which you have no proof,' Dearing interjected.

'For which we have traces of Shaw's blood in your client's outhouse and a witness who says that the murder took place on Mr Woollard's premises with Mr Woollard watching,' Dexter replied harshly.

Dearing was undeterred. 'By witness, I take it you mean Keith Gwynne: a convicted thief, drunkard and con man?'

Bevan was determined not to allow Dexter to sidetrack his case again. 'As I was saying, we have decided to treat the investigation into Mr Shaw's death and your client's alleged dog fighting offences separately.'

'Carry on.' Dearing began to write notes in his leather-bound folder.

'Specifically: we will be charging Mr Woollard with a series of breaches of the 1911 Protection of Animals Act, the Dangerous Dogs Act of 1991, the 1973 Breeding of Dogs Act, the 1991 Breeding of Dogs Act and the 1999 Breeding and Sale of Dogs Act.' Bevan looked for a response in Woollard's dead eyes: he saw none.

Dearing peered at Bevan over his half-moon glasses. 'Which breaches specifically?'

'There are several. I'll give you the highlights.' Bevan looked down at his file. '1911 Protection of Animals Act: Mr Woollard has breached Sections 1A, B, and C. In particular, Section A states that to "overload, torture, infuriate or terrify any animal" is an offence.

'Section C states that to "cause, procure or assist at the fighting or baiting of any animal...or act or assist in the management of any premises for the purpose of fighting or baiting any animal" is an offence punishable by a maximum of six months' imprisonment and a level 5 fine.'

'We have explained to you that Mr Woollard has never arranged or participated in dog fighting,' Dearing replied.

'I am aware of that, yes.' Bevan continued. 'We will also be charging Mr Woollard with contraventions of the 1991 Dangerous Dogs Act. Section 1 of this act identifies species of dog including the pit bull terrier and the Japanese Tosa and states that to "breed, sell, exchange or make a gift" of such dogs is an offence. Both types of animal were found on Mr Woollard's premises. This offence is also punishable with a maximum six-month prison sentence and a level 5 fine.'

'Those dogs never leave Mr Woollard's farm and

are always muzzled around people,' Dearing said.

'Irrelevant.' Bevan turned the page. 'The 1973 Breeding of Dogs Act specifies that "no person shall keep a breeding establishment for dogs except under the authority of a licence." Mr Woollard has no such licence. That is an offence punishable by a maximum three-month prison term or a level 4 fine. Furthermore the 1991 Breeding of Dogs Act makes it an offence "to obstruct or delay any person in exercise of powers of entry or inspection". Mr Woollard did precisely that when we visited his premises.'

Dearing said nothing as his pen scratched furiously onto his file paper.

'Finally,' Bevan continued, 'the 1999 Breeding and Sale of Dogs Act places a number of restrictions on the commercial sale of dogs. We believe that Mr Woollard has breached at least two provisions of this Act. The maximum sentence is either three months' imprisonment or a level 4 fine. That's it.' Bevan sat back in his chair.

Dearing finished writing. 'You have been busy Inspector Bevan. We will of course challenge these charges.'

'That's your prerogative.'

'On the other matter,' Dearing continued, 'the death of Mr Shaw. I understand that charges have not yet been levelled.'

'Not yet,' Dexter replied, 'but we are investigating charges of conspiracy and obstruction of justice.'

'My client has already given you information relating to that matter – without my presence, I might add.' Dearing had encountered Dexter before. He disliked her commonplace accent and her acidic manner. 'He claims that Inspector Bevan made him some kind of unsolicited offer of leniency in return for information.'

'No official offer has been made,' Dexter said sharply, 'and if your client is in possession of information regarding the death of Leonard Shaw that he is withholding, that, in itself, is an offence.'

Woollard was beginning to see the impossibility of his position and decided that desperate times required desperate measures. 'Look, when I met this Norlington guy or Garrod – whatever his fucking name is – he said that he'd won his dog in a fight in Clacton.'

'You told me that already,' Bevan responded.

'You'll have to do better,' Dexter added.

'I asked him if he knew a bloke called Jack Whiteside. He's a dog man – well known in Essex and Cambridgeshire. Or he was anyway. Jack was killed a couple of years ago. He was from Maldon.'

'How was he killed?' Dexter asked.

'His throat was cut. It was in the papers. Look it

up. When I said that Jack had been murdered the guy insisted he didn't know him. I didn't think anything of it at the time. It seems a bit weird now because he must have heard of Jack if he's fought dogs in that part of the world.'

Dexter thought of Underwood. She wondered if the link he had made between Garrod and Essex was as tenuous as she had originally thought.

She became aware of Woollard staring at her.

'So?' he asked, 'can we talk about a deal?'

She looked at him. 'No deal on the dog charges. They stand. The Essex business is a separate matter. I'll discuss it after we have checked out this Whiteside story.'

She left Bevan to formally charge Woollard on the cruelty charges he had previously outlined.

46.

Driving in the rain through some of the less visually stimulating parts of Essex gave Underwood's mind an opportunity to wander.

Six months earlier he had begun a missing person's hunt for Alison Dexter's father. She had not seen Gary Dexter since she was a child. Underwood placed that loss at the centre of her intellectual spider's web.

Initially he had drawn a blank. He had authorised Police National Computer checks on Gary Dexter and found nothing. Underwood knew that Alison had grown up in Leyton and Walthamstow. He knew that she had lived with her mother. He also knew from conversations with her that her father had disappeared some time in 1978.

Underwood knew that Alison Dexter had tried half-heartedly to locate her father a couple of years previously. One night, in the deserted CID office he had rifled through her desk drawers. He found a blank PNC check and a photograph of a baby that he presumed was Alison with a man that he presumed to be Gary Dexter. The man was sitting on the bonnet of a car with the baby in his arms. On the back of the photograph was a comment and a date – 'Gary and Alison on Daddy's new Car September 1969'.

Then, sitting alone in the glass office that smelt faintly of her, as the station clock had crawled around past three in the morning, Underwood had experienced a minor revelation. On the photograph of Alison and Gary Dexter was a partial car licence plate. Gary Dexter was perched on the front of his car; his leg obscured some but not all of the registration plate:

'J__16__'

Underwood remembered that the old licence

plates had two letters then a number in those blocked spaces followed by a year suffix letter. He also remembered that the two missing letters were the code of the local registration office. So 'NB', for example, denoted a registration issued by the New Bolden registration office.

If he had a complete registration, he might be able to locate the original dealership. DVLA records – if they went back that far – might also give an address that the car was registered to. Certainly they would give the original owner's details. Underwood wondered if Gary Dexter had been the original owner of that car. It did say 'Daddy's new car' on the photograph after all. He had written out the licence plate again:

'J__16__'

If, he reasoned, the car was new in September 1969, he would be able to identify the last letter. He had searched carefully on the Internet and eventually discovered that the year suffix for new cars registered between August 1969 and July 1970 had been 'H'.

'J__16_H'

The next step would be to identify the two missing letters. An hour of research produced good news and bad news. The second and third letters on the suffix-style plates denoted the original registration office. That was the good news. The bad news was that Underwood had no idea where the original registration office was. If he did, he would have had an almost complete registration number. He had called DVLA in Swansea early the following morning and had them fax over a list of registration office identity codes from the 1960s.

He then remembered that the car was a Ford Cortina. In the 1960s, the Ford production plant in Dagenham was at the peak of its output. That increased the likelihood that the car was originally registered in London.

To his dismay, he discovered that there were eight codes listed for the North London registration office near Stanmore. It seemed hopeless. Or did it? A single double letter combination was obscured on the plate as was a single number. If the combination was one of the London prefix codes, then there could only be a limited number of possibilities.

He had tried an example. Say Gary Dexter's car had originally been registered in London with the identity prefix 'LK'. That would give Dexter's plate as:

'JLK 16_H'

That would mean that the final plate could only be one of nine possible combinations. If there were eight North London prefix codes and nine numerical suffixes that meant that there were only seventy-two potential registrations for Gary

Dexter's car. Underwood had written them all out painstakingly on a piece of A4 paper then sent his finding by fax to a contact at the DVLA offices in Swansea. A fax came back the following afternoon. The key section was the second paragraph:

'A Ford Cortina was registered on 16th September 1969 to Gary Dexter of 44a Churchill Terrace, Dagenham, London. Records show that Mr Dexter sold this car to a Mr Niraj Patel of Flat 19, Twyford House, Seven Sisters Road, Tottenham on 3rd January 1974. Subsequent to this, there is no evidence of any cars registered to Mr G Dexter of 44a Churchill Terrace, Dagenham. It should be noted that registration was computerised in the 1980s and many earlier records were either not transposed or lost.'

He had made a start. He had found an address to work with in addition to a name.

His next move had been to contact the Public Records Office and the Inland Revenue. If Gary Dexter had died, a death certificate would have been filed at the PRO. Alternatively, if he was still alive, he was almost certainly either paying taxes or receiving a pension. Underwood was confident that Inland Revenue records might provide him with a new opening.

He had been half-correct. After an irritating

week of silence, the Inland Revenue Service had contacted Underwood and informed him that they did have a record of a Gary Dexter at the said address, then at two subsequent London addresses. They also provided information on two companies that Gary Dexter worked for: Ford Motors at Dagenham and then at a garage called 'Jowseys' in Wanstead, London. Unfortunately for Underwood, they had no record of Gary Dexter since November 1994 when he had left Jowseys and a rented address in Wanstead. Since then, there had been no tax or National Insurance payments in his name. Gary Dexter had either vanished or died. However, there was no death certificate filed at the PRO.

Underwood now had an address in Wanstead to look into: 9 Grove Gardens, Gosling Road. However, the last record of Gary Dexter at that address was eight years out of date. On a Tuesday, using up a day of his annual leave, Underwood had driven down to Wanstead himself.

Grove Gardens was a small cul-de-sac. The houses were tiny bungalows. Some had football-related graffiti on the walls. Underwood knocked on the door of number nine to find that the house was now occupied by an old lady called Maud. She had never heard of Gary Dexter. Disappointed, Underwood tried a similar approach with the other houses in Grove Gardens. Those people who answered their doors were similarly unhelpful. Returning to his car, Underwood had felt a terrible sense of frustration.

He sat behind the wheel of his car and stared out into the grey skies above East London. He was over eight years behind Gary Dexter. For some reason, the man had disappeared off the face of the earth in 1994. How could that have happened? Underwood wondered. If he were dead then a certificate would have been filed somewhere. If he had been imprisoned, then Gary Dexter would have appeared on the Police National Computer check that he had authorised.

Irritated and on the verge of giving up hope, Underwood had eventually headed to the London Borough of Redbridge Library in Sprat Hall Road, Wanstead.

Underwood flashed his police identification card on arrival and requested back copies of the local newspapers: the Ilford Leader *and the* Wanstead and Woodford Guardian. *The librarian, Elizabeth, had shown him to an archive room where back copies of the paper were kept on microfilm.*

'The Wanstead Guardian *has its own website,' she had told him. 'But they don't keep papers from before 2001 online.'*

And so, Underwood settled himself down for an

afternoon's research. He found the microfilm viewer a cumbersome, annoying piece of equipment. He started with a September 1994 edition of the Ilford Leader *and began to wind his way through local history. Hours slid away.*

The silence of the library began to chew at his conscience. What would Alison think if she knew what he was doing? Underwood could not imagine that she would be pleased. The reality was that his motives were muddled and contradictory. He was becoming an increasingly peripheral shape in the crystalline lattice of logic that was Alison Dexter's mind. She was a conundrum to him: a seemingly straightforward person whose abilities constantly surprised and humbled him. Was this the riddle at the heart of Alison Dexter – the memory of a man who had deserted her?

The complete quiet of the room was terrifying. Underwood knew that silence was dangerous to him. Stripping away the white noise in his mind left him only with the sound of his own emptiness. Underwood was trying to fill that emptiness now.

He wondered desperately at his madness.

Time was passing. Underwood found himself staring at a microfilm copy of the Ilford Leader *from November 1994. A headline looked back at him through the viewer.*

'MAN DIES IN HORROR CRASH'

Underwood wiped his eyes and tried to concentrate. His breakdown a couple of years previously had left his ability to focus in tatters.

Concentrate.

'MAN DIES IN HORROR CRASH'

A man from Walthamstow died in a tragic car accident on Lea Bridge road. Another local man was seriously injured. Oliver Donovan's Vauxhall Nova hit a lamppost on Lea Bridge Road at about 10.30 p.m. on Friday night.

His passenger, Mr Gary Dexter, 58, of Grove Gardens, Wanstead, had to be cut from the wreckage by the rescue services. He was taken to Whipps Cross Hospital and is said to be in a stable but critical condition.

The causes of the accident have not yet been established. The Lea Bridge road is a notorious accident black spot. There is no suggestion that the driver had been drinking. Police are appealing for witnesses to this incident.

Sweat ran into Underwood's eyes. There it was. Gary Dexter had been in a car accident in November 1994. He had survived at least in the short term. There would be records of his treatment at Whipps Cross Hospital. Underwood was unsure of the legal position with regard to accessing patient medical records. He suspected that he would need a court order.

Underwood found a telephone number for the switchboard at Whipps Cross Hospital, Leytonstone. He called on his mobile. After a long delay while he was connected with the relevant department, Underwood was finally put through to Susan Bruce, the Medical Records Manager. He requested a meeting and, after much persuasion, she eventually agreed to see him at five-thirty that afternoon.

Susan Bruce's office was much tidier than Underwood had expected. He had imagined a frantic chaos of paperwork and aggression. Her manner on the phone had been curt to say the least: very much the no nonsense young NHS executive. As it happened, the office was extremely well appointed with a brand new flat screen computer, a stylish posture chair and some tasteful prints of King's College Cambridge on the wall.

After a minute of exchanging pleasantries, Underwood decided that, under different circumstances, he might rather like Susan Bruce. She was assertive, obviously intelligent and frank. Qualities he admired.

And lacked.

'I have an unusual request,' Underwood said as she sat down behind her desk.

'Go on.'

'At New Bolden CID we are currently conducting a murder investigation. Time is a factor. A name has cropped up. Someone we are trying to locate was treated here for serious injuries in November 1994 after a car accident. I need to see his medical record.'

Susan Bruce shook her head. 'That's not possible. The police have no automatic right of access to clinical information.'

'Yes, I thought that might be the case.'

'This trust has a duty to protect the confidentiality of its patients. I'm sure you understand that.'

'Absolutely.'

'Do you have a subpoena?'

'No, I don't. The person in question is not a suspect. We merely wish to question him.'

'Why do you need to see his medical records then?'

'I was hoping to find his current whereabouts.'

'Mr Underwood, you can't just charge in here and demand to see private clinical records. There are procedures. The police may only compel an NHS Trust to hand over such records after *the receipt of a court order.'*

'Is it possible to make an exception?' Underwood pleaded.

'No. Exceptional disclosures can only be made to a court on receipt of a subpoena or to a coroner on receipt of a written request.'

'If I had a fax from a coroner requesting information from a patient's clinical records, could you provide it to me?'

'No. I could provide it to the coroner in question.' Susan Bruce seemed to be running out of patience with Underwood.

'Is there somewhere I could make a phone call in private?' Underwood asked.

'Try the office next door. Mr Underwood, I'm very busy…'

'I understand. Give me two minutes.'

Underwood walked into the adjacent office and closed the connecting door. He found Roger Leach's phone number on his mobile and called.

'Leach.'

'Roger, it's John Underwood.'

'Why are you whispering? I can hardly hear you old chap,' Leach said.

'What's the name of your mate at the district coroner's office?'

'Chris Ball.'

'Can you call him and ask him to fax a request

for clinical record information to Whipps Cross Hospital in London?'

'Why, may I ask?'

'I need access to someone's medical records. It's for a case. The Medical Records Officer at Whipps Cross won't let me.'

'Quite right too. You should know better.'

'I wouldn't ask unless it was urgent. All I need is an address.'

'I dare say.'

'Come on Roger,' Underwood urged. *'The woman here says she can release the information if she gets a fax from a coroner's office.'*

'Yes, but she'll only tell the coroner, not you.'

'I thought you could find out from him and tell me.'

'God help us,' Leach exhaled loudly. *'I'll see what I can do.'*

'I appreciate it.'

'I'll call you back.'

Underwood waited impatiently. His mobile rang five minutes later. It was Leach.

'OK. He'll do it. Give me the patient's name and the fax number of the hospital.'

'The name is Gary Dexter. He was admitted in November 1994 after a serious road crash.'

'Dexter? Is he a relation of our esteemed leader?'

'No,' Underwood lied, *'it's a common name.'* He

walked back into Susan Bruce's office and asked her for her fax number.

The fax from the Cambridge District Coroner's Office came through fifteen minutes later. Susan Bruce entered Gary Dexter's name into her computer and printed his details.

'You realise that I can't give you this information, Inspector,' she said. 'It goes directly back on the fax to the coroner.'

'I appreciate everything you've done,' Underwood gabbled back at her. 'You have been a huge help to our enquiry.'

Back inside his car a few minutes later, Underwood awaited the call from Leach. It came shortly before 6.45 p.m.

'OK John, do you have a pen and paper?'

'Go ahead.'

'Gary Dexter, formerly of 9 Grove Gardens, Wanstead. Admitted 9th November 1994 after road traffic accident. Discharged six months later to Beech View Care Centre, Wilding Road, Leytonstone, London. That's all there is.'

'That's brilliant, Roger. I owe you one.'

'You owe me several. Don't put me in a position like that again. Procedures exist for good reasons, John: to protect patients and to protect you. You could have got us all in serious trouble pissing about like that.'

Underwood clicked off his phone and drove the short distance through rush hour traffic to Leytonstone.

The Beech View Care Centre was located in a quiet residential street. Underwood parked on the road outside. A nurse sat at the reception desk in the entrance hall of the old building. She smiled.

'Can I help?' she asked.

'Hello. I'm John Underwood. I'm a police officer.' He showed her his identification card which she checked carefully. 'I have an enquiry about someone who was a patient here about eight years ago. Can I speak to whoever's in charge?'

'The consultant won't be back until the morning. What was the name of the patient?'

'Gary Dexter.'

'Oh. Mr Dexter is in room seven on the first floor.'

'I'm sorry?'

'Gary Dexter is in room seven on the first floor.'

'He's still here?' Underwood was stunned.

'He doesn't have any choice, Inspector,' the nurse continued. 'I'm Hannah. Would you like me to take you up?'

'What's wrong with him?'

'He's been paralysed since the accident.'

'For eight years?'

'Forever, I'm afraid. His neck was broken. I've

*been here for two years. You're the first person
that's visited him. He's got no living family
apparently.'*

Hannah stepped out from behind the reception
desk.

'I'll take you up.'

Six months on from that day of uncomfortable
revelations in East London, as rain spilled across his
car windscreen and the grey sprawl of the North
Sea stretched ahead of him, Underwood wondered
if he could find the strength to carry on.

47.

Henry Braun left the Admiral pub at 11.30 p.m.
The pub was located at the centre of a large sprawl
of council housing south-west of Peterborough
town centre. A young couple were having sex
against the wall of the pub. Normally, Braun would
have lit a cigarette and watched. However, tonight
he was in no mood for jollities. Rain spread across
the road in front of him. Braun folded up the collar
of his jacket as he began to walk home. His
thoughts – only partially stewed by export lager –
focused on his brother. Nicholas had been given a
sentence of twelve years. Already, his brother
looked like a man broken by prison life. Henry

Braun's anger was mitigated only by the realisation that he had only narrowly escaped prosecution himself.

He had visited Nicholas that afternoon in Bunden Prison, a dismal, grey sprawl in the Fens north of Cambridge. Nicholas had cried behind the glass that divided them. The sight had shocked him. His brother was broken. Twelve years seemed like a lifetime.

He tried not to let the memory upset him. Henry knew he had a job to do. He had moved into Nicholas Braun's house in Gorton Row, Peterborough a couple of days previously. Ostensibly, this was to keep a close watch on Nicholas's wife, Janice. He had already screwed her once that afternoon. As she had sat eating crisps in front of a chat show, he had dragged her onto the floor and pumped her next to the electric fire. Janice hadn't taken her eyes off the television once. It had just made him pump harder. Henry didn't feel any guilt. Nicholas had asked him to make sure that his wife was being taken care of. Henry knew it was always best to keep it in the family.

As he turned into Gorton Row, Henry Braun became aware that a man was following him. Unafraid, grasping the kitchen knife that he always carried in his jacket pocket, he turned suddenly and confronted his pursuer.

'Is there a problem mate?' Henry snarled at the huge shape of Bartholomew Garrod.

'Are you Henry Braun?' came the reply.

'What if I am?' Henry took a half step back: the size of the man before him was instantly sobering.

'I have a business proposition for you,' Garrod replied.

'That's nice of you,' Henry said sarcastically, 'but seeing as I don't know you, seeing as you do business by following people about in the dark, you'll forgive me if I tell you to sod off.'

'I saw your brother on television,' Garrod said. 'He was treated badly I hear.'

'What is this?' Braun snapped angrily, 'are you a copper? Because if you are, you can tell DI bleeding Dexter that her time will come soon enough.'

Garrod's smile appeared under the yellow fuzz of a streetlight. 'That's exactly what I wanted to talk with you about.'

Braun watched him closely. 'Who are you?'

'Call me George. Can we go inside?'

'What makes you think I live here?'

'I heard on the news that your family live on Gorton Row. I've been waiting for you.'

'What sort of business proposition are you offering?'

'I'll tell you inside.'

Henry considered for a moment. 'Wait a minute.

Did you write a note to my brother? He mentioned someone called George had written some cryptic fucking message to him.'

'I did write to him.'

Braun decided to take a chance. 'It's over here: number eleven.'

The house was tiny. Its narrow entrance hall made Garrod look even more enormous. Braun led him into the sparse little living room and flicked on the light.

For the first time he could see Garrod's features clearly. 'Do I know you?' he asked between puffs on his cigarette. 'You look familiar.'

'We haven't met.' Garrod sat in what had been Nicholas Braun's favourite armchair. 'I watched your brother's case on the television. I read about it too. I collect newspapers. There was an interesting story in there today about a Mr Woollard. The police are prosecuting him for dog fighting offences. He's an old acquaintance of mine.'

'Why are you so interested in my brother?'

'I'm not really. I'm more interested in the policewoman who put him away.'

Henry Braun looked at Garrod carefully. The man was huge, with arms at least twice the thickness of his own. His face was pitted and scarred from years of violence. Braun recognised the hallmarks of a serious player.

'DI Dexter,' Braun said eventually, 'fucking bitch. What about her?'

'I have a personal issue to resolve with her,' Garrod said. 'I thought you might like to be involved.'

'What makes you think that?'

'She put your brother away. You just called her a "fucking bitch".'

'She is a fucking bitch. But I don't want to go to prison for her.'

'I had a brother once too,' Garrod observed. 'She killed him. He had mental problems. She scared him. Turned up at our shop with about twenty coppers. Well, poor old Ray wouldn't have known what was happening. He used to get scared by the television sometimes. He ran out into the street. He was trying to get away you see. A car hit him. I saw it. I heard his bones snap. Alison Dexter took my brother's life and now she's done the same to yours.'

Henry Braun hesitated. He remembered Nicholas, broken and pathetic, dead behind prison glass.

Sensing success, Garrod continued, 'My brother was my best friend. Our Dad was mean you see. He was fucked up by the war. Saw terrible things. He was a drinker and used to knock me about. It never bothered me really. I had Ray you see. Once my Dad was gone, Ray sort of became my son. She took him away from me. Now, it's time for payback.'

'Where do I fit into all this?' Braun asked, intrigued.

'I need some help. I'll give you the details if you're interested.'

'What's in it for me?'

'Satisfaction.'

'What do you mean?'

'Once we've got her, I'll let you watch.'

'Watch what?'

Garrod smiled. 'She's got a big surprise coming. I thought you'd enjoy it.'

'You're going to grab her?'

'And a lot more besides.'

Braun scratched the back of his neck thoughtfully. 'I don't know mate. I hardly know you. This is serious shit.'

'She's quite pretty, I suppose,' Garrod said quietly. 'If you like that sort of thing.'

'What do you mean?'

'Once we've got her, I could give you half an hour alone with her I suppose. Your brother might like to see some photographs.'

'You're mad.' Braun found the idea richly tempting but common sense still lingered. 'Killing a copper is a seriously bad idea. We'll have every uniform in the country after us.'

'They'll assume that I did her by myself. Why would they think you'd be involved? They've been after me for years and haven't got close yet.'

Braun hovered uncertainly, the risks were huge but the reward was too exciting to ignore.

'I don't know.'

'Think about your brother.'

Braun stared back at the giant shape sprawled in his brother's armchair. The man's confidence was infectious.

'What's your plan then?' he asked eventually.

Two hours later, Garrod returned to Craxten Fen Psychiatric Hospital. Despite the rain, he went straight out onto the back lawn to the edge of the pit he had now completed. He carefully lined the walls with yellow plastic refuse bags that he had stolen from the abattoir and covered the hole with a wooden table top that he had found inside the hospital. The pit was roughly square: three feet across and about four feet deep. One of the walls was sloped at about a forty-five degree angle.

Ghosts of the insane watched him from a hundred black windows.

He would have to make a trip soon. Most of his equipment was elsewhere. He had agreed to work all day Sunday at the abattoir. He was then due to make a meat delivery to the market in Cambridge on Monday morning.

However, once he had completed that, he would have time to head east.

48.

Sunday, 20ᵗʰ October 2002

At 5.00 a.m. the following morning, Alison Dexter left room 212 of the Holiday Inn Hotel, Cambridge and drove the relatively short distance up to New Bolden. She had checked in the previous evening as a precautionary measure. The murder of Kelsi Hensy showed that Garrod could get to her. That he could intervene in her life with devastating effect. She had underestimated the man seven years previously and was not going to repeat the mistake. She knew that men like Garrod were pure, animal predators. He would seek out patterns in her life, look for choke points, moments when she was vulnerable. It was time to get smart.

Garrod would eventually locate her flat in New Bolden. She knew that. He had found her home in London once before. Her flat was now being watched round the clock by a police observation team. Dexter knew that Garrod wasn't daft. She had tried to locate the other choke points in her daily routine: weaknesses that he might already have observed. She decided that she would vary the time that she arrived and left New Bolden police headquarters. She had swapped her blue Mondeo for a Volkswagen hire car. Dexter had even decided not to use any of the cash points or food shops in New Bolden town centre: animals were most vulnerable when they went to the water to drink.

From now on, if she left the office on police business, she would always be accompanied. An Armed Response Unit had been drafted in to New Bolden CID from the County Police Headquarters at Huntingdon. When they finally located Garrod, she would not be taking any risks.

At ten a.m., the incident room at police headquarters had become crowded with CID officers and police sergeants that Dexter had seconded from the uniform division. She got proceedings underway with a briskness that belied the turmoil within.

'OK everybody. Sorry to get you all in on a Sunday. Let's get started. As you know, a woman called Kelsi Hensy was murdered last week. This meeting is to discuss that and to update everybody on the manhunt for Bartholomew Garrod.'

She was amazed by her own coldness: *'a woman called Kelsi Hensy'*.

Forensic pathologist Roger Leach took over. 'We have DNA matched samples of blood and semen on the victim Kelsi Hensy to Bartholomew Garrod. There is no doubt that he murdered her.'

'How was she killed, sir?' asked DC Sauerwine.

'Her throat was cut: expertly, as it happens,' Leach replied. He was conscious of Alison Dexter's presence to his right. He chose his words carefully. 'Death would have been fairly quick. Although there are clear signs of a struggle: defence wounds to Hensy's hands and wrists plus samples of Garrod's blood and skin beneath her fingernails. She fought him. After death, he removed some of her internal organs. I'll spare you the details.'

'Fucking bastard,' said DS Harrison, 'sick, fucking bastard.'

'Inspector Dexter,' asked DC Sauerwine, 'did the Garrods sexually molest any of their victims in London? I don't remember anything in the file.'

'There was no obvious sexual molestation of any of the London victims. As far as we know, there was only one female victim – a librarian. But nothing sexual was ever suggested.'

'Weird then, that he should rape this Hensy woman,' Sauerwine thought out loud, 'it's a break with his modus operandi. Do you think he's losing control? Sometimes these nutcases start out all organised but then get more demented as they go along.'

Dexter tried to crawl out from the sinking mud of terrible images. Garrod's rape of Kelsi Hensy was a message to her. She knew that. 'I doubt it's significant. He is an opportunist. The chance was there and he took it. Let's clarify exactly what we are doing. Harrison, any luck on the list of names that we put together: the potential aliases?'

Harrison shook his head. 'Nothing concrete. There are so many possible matches that it's taking hours to check each one out. We need to narrow the search criteria if that line of enquiry is going to work.'

Dexter nodded. 'Any ideas?' she asked the floor.

Sauerwine raised his hand. 'I'm confused about two things ma'am: where he's living and how he's financing himself.'

'We have a possible lead on the question of his accommodation. I have sent DI Underwood to pursue a family link with Essex. It may be that Garrod owned or owns some sort of prefabricated accommodation there. On the question of how he's financing himself, I am open to suggestions.'

Roger Leach though for a moment. 'Is it too stupid to suggest that he might be working as a butcher somewhere?'

Dexter shrugged. 'It's not stupid at all. He is a qualified master butcher. It seems pretty obvious that he loves his job.'

Harrison was unconvinced. 'He's not that daft, Guv. This guy has evaded capture for all this time. I can't believe he's done that by bagging sausages for old ladies. For all we know, he's still earning money from prize fighting. Maybe he's going to matches in neighbouring counties, places we don't know about. Our intelligence on that kind of stuff is pretty limited even after this Woollard arrest.'

The name of Woollard stirred DI Mike Bevan from his musings on the mutilation of Kelsi Hensy.

'On that subject,' he said, 'most of you now know that we will be prosecuting Woollard for various animal cruelty offences. Trial is set for Peterborough Crown Court. Preliminary hearing will be next week. Court Notices have gone out. There was a piece in yesterday's *Clarion* about it.'

Harrison laughed. 'I saw it: "Police Charge Local Farmer". There was a classic picture of Woollard looking hard done by.'

Dexter nodded. 'Thanks to everyone who helped on that case. For your information, Woollard did mention a possible link between Garrod and a murder in Essex a couple of years ago. I'll be checking that today.'

In his mind, Leach was still exploring the notion

that Garrod might still be working in the meat trade. 'Returning to the point in hand,' he said, 'I don't think that we should discount the idea that Garrod is still employed in some aspect of butchery.'

Dexter turned to him. 'Explain,' she said.

'Well, I have read the case file that you, Inspector Dexter, prepared on the so called "Primal Cut" murders back in London,' Leach continued. 'The manner in which Garrod mutilated his victims was directly conditioned by the knowledge of anatomy that he had gleaned as master butcher. Indeed, as you know, that's why those crimes were called the "Primal Cut" murders. The Garrods were removing cuts of flesh that resembled common prime meat cuts.'

'You are saying he's a one-dimensional personality,' Dexter inferred. 'That he can't do anything else.'

'I'm saying that his knowledge, his expertise, is very narrowly based,' Leach continued. 'Our passions consume us. A historian sees everything in terms of its relationship with the past. A priest sees everything in the universe as a justification for his own belief system. A policeman sees everything in terms of the law. If Garrod is so consumed by his passion for meat that he will butcher people as he would butcher cattle, then it stands to reason that he might still be butchering cattle as he butchers people.'

Harrison was beginning to see the point. 'We do what we have to. Then we do what we enjoy.'

'Right.'

Sauerwine frowned. 'I'm not sure about this. It seems a big assumption to make. This guy is pretty smart. Working in the meat trade would make him visible.'

Leach turned to Dexter. 'He removed Kelsi Hensy's kidneys and liver with impressive precision. I think he enjoys his work too much to turn his back on it.'

His argument seemed persuasive to Dexter. She had learned from previous manhunts that sometimes assumptions and leaps of intuition could pay off.

'OK,' she said, 'Harrison, you were looking for a way to narrow down the name search. Let's start by calling meat retailers, butchers, slaughterhouses, knacker men. Run your list of names and the photofit past them. Start with Cambridgeshire, then fan out into Essex and other neighbouring counties if nothing turns up.'

'Will do,' Harrison nodded.

'This guy is a menace. He is slippery and will keep killing people until we get him. Catching him is our single priority for now,' Dexter said sharply.

'We do have one advantage Inspector,' Leach mused.

'What's that?'

'You.'

'I'm sorry?'

'He is here because of you. He will stay close to you. That makes him vulnerable.'

Dexter considered this point for a moment. Leach had a way of stating the obvious that she found irritatingly useful. 'I agree. This bastard has it in for me and my people. That probably means he's closer than we realise. I have taken precautions. So should each of you. Don't follow up leads alone. Check you're not being followed. Avoid patterns and repetition in your daily routine. If we make it hard for him, he's more likely to make a mistake.'

Her comments created a ripple of anxiety through the department. Bartholomew Garrod had become everybody's problem.

49.

Burma 1945

The patrol had pushed deep into the gully. Moisture silently slid from the leaves. The ground was mushy underfoot: it squelched unavoidably as they advanced. Corporal Pete Gendall tried not to think about this or the wet heat in his boots. He had an unnerving sense that something was terribly wrong.

The jungle had become very quiet. His four-man patrol had separated from the main body of his infantry company to undertake one final sweep for a downed Hurricane pilot. The soldiers with him were nervous. He could see their fingers tensed on the triggers of their rifles.

They were making slow progress. The bush was dense, almost impenetrable, and every step towards Japanese lines increased the likelihood of a surprise attack. Now the jungle was terribly quiet. He suddenly gestured his men to stop with a clenched fist. He could smell something, something unnatural. It reminded him of his father's garage at home: a kind of oily, greasy, mechanical smell.

There was a small clearing unfolding ahead of them. They could hear voices. Gendall's men immediately fanned out to his right and left as he signalled enemy contact. The patrol crawled on their bellies through the mud and insects to obtain a viewpoint.

Through the steaming jungle and the vibration of his pounding heart, Gendall could make out the twisted wreckage of a British fighter plane at the base of a tree: its red, white and blue roundels were unmistakeable. More worryingly, he counted six Japanese soldiers standing and sitting amongst the wreckage. Three of them were sitting on a fallen branch eating stew from a cooking pot.

Gendall gestured Private Hillen to join him. Hillen was the only man on the patrol with a machine gun. He came from Sunderland and hated to be called 'Geordie'.

'Geordie,' whispered Gendall once the private had joined him, 'how many do you see?'

'Six, Corp,' Hillen replied. 'They're a bit fucking casual.'

Gendall nodded. 'We must have penetrated further than we thought. No sign of the pilot.'

'What do you want to do? Head back and get the platoon?'

Gendall shook his head. 'Too difficult. They'll hear us. We can handle this. When I give the signal I want you to pop the two guys standing by the plane. I'll get their mate over there.'

Gendall turned to his right and pointed towards the three Japanese soldiers sitting eating. Privates Garrod and Baines nodded and took aim with their rifles.

In the centre of the clearing, Ryoushin Osuka, infantry private first class, stirred meat in his steaming cooking pot.

'Hayaku onegai shimasu!' his friend Kanji urged him to cook faster. The hunger was tearing them apart.

'Chotto matte!' Osuka replied irritably. Wait a moment.

Osuka ladled the boiled meat into the cupped hands of Kanji and Kariudo. It burned them slightly but they were past caring. They ate hungrily, pushing the meat into their mouths.

Osuka felt a sense of satisfaction. To serve his friends was an honour despite their ignominious surroundings.

'Karai?' he asked quietly. Too salty?

'Oishii!' Kanji replied. Delicious.

Osuka nodded, pleased that he had helped his friends. 'Kanji' meant 'soul mate'. In the heat and horror of the Burmese jungle, that was precisely what he had become.

At that moment, Osuka heard two loud cracks ahead of him. Before his eyes, Kanji's jaw exploded in a haze of blood and splintered bone. Kariudo fell backwards, a black hole in the centre of his forehead. He could hear shouting from his officer, suddenly silenced by the staccato cracks of a British Bren-gun. Osuka grabbed his rifle and fell to the floor, his eyes hunting for targets in the undergrowth. Machine gun fire spat bullets into the mud ahead of him. He returned shots into the jungle but could see nothing: the British soldiers had become harder to fight. They had learned from the mistakes of 1941 and 1942.

Two hundred yards away, the main body of the British platoon heard the gunfire resounding up from the gully. Sergeant Rae ordered the remainder of his force into action, leading them slipping and sliding down into the undergrowth himself.

Osuka tried to marshal his thoughts. He had not been hit. He had a small amount of cover behind the branch that he and his friends had been sitting on. He called out to the other men in his squad but heard no replies. They had been stupid to sit in such an exposed position. His officer was an idiot. However, the British army were supposed to be fifteen miles from this location. Perhaps things were not going as well as they had been led to believe. Something thudded into the mud beside him. Osuka turned his head and spotted the grenade a split second before it went off.

After the explosion, the jungle fell silent again. The smoke of discharged weapons hung in the air. Gendall's men advanced cautiously into the clearing, Hillen's Bren-gun ranging over the Japanese corpses in case one moved suddenly or tried to run.

'We got 'em, Corporal,' Baines said cheerily. 'I nailed my yellow bastard right between the eyes.'

'Look for the pilot,' Gendall ordered, peering down on the now headless remains of Ryoushin Osuka. He heard footsteps behind him and swung his gun in the direction of Sergeant Rae and the rest of his platoon.

'Secure the area,' Rae ordered. 'We move out in five minutes.'

Gendall waved Rae over. 'Looks like an advance patrol. Six men. One officer over there by the plane; four privates and one private first class here. Single stripe on the arm see.'

Rae nodded. 'This is our plane.' He pointed to the squadron code on the Hurricane's fuselage. 'I doubt the pilot got out of here alive.'

'There's blood in the cockpit Sarge,' Hillen called out. 'No sign of our man though.'

'Where is the silly bugger?' Gendall asked.

'We need to get out of here,' Rae said. 'Let's record the coordinates of this place, salvage any paperwork from the cockpit and double-time it out of here before the rest of the Imperial Army turn up.'

'Sergeant Rae! Corporal Gendall!' a voice screamed from behind the wrecked plane. The two men turned and ran in the direction of the shouting.

Behind the mangled Hurricane, partially obscured by foliage, hung the remains of Squadron Leader Nigel Wilde. His body had been stripped and strung up against a tree, his hands tied together above his head.

'Jesus Christ,' Rae muttered. 'Those fucking bastards.'

The body had six portions of flesh removed: one from each arm and two from the thigh and calf muscle of each leg.

'What the bloody hell have they done?' Gendall

asked, transfixed by the horror in front of him.

Rae shook his head. 'You remember that story we heard about those Aussie engineers.'

Gendall stared at him. 'You are joking me? You mean they carved this poor bastard up and ate him?'

'They were eating when we popped them, weren't they?'

'Three of them were.'

'There you go. I've heard it's a kind of mark of honour. You eat your enemy if he proves his valour. The Japs think the Burmese are animals. But we are prime flesh, I suppose.'

'I think I'm going to puke,' Gendall span away and retched violently onto the mud.

Rae turned to the infantryman who had discovered Wilde's remains.

'Cut him down, son. Do it now before the rest of the lads get back here.'

'Will do, Sarge,' came the immediate reply.

Rae led Gendall away from the corpse and back to the centre of the clearing.

With great care and no small amount of fascination, Private Cornelius Garrod pulled out his army knife and cut the remains of Squadron Leader Nigel Wilde to the jungle floor. After he had done so, he pulled a small camera from his pack and took a picture.

WISDOM AND INDUSTRY

50.

Monday, 21st October 2002

At 6.30 a.m., Bartholomew Garrod finished loading meat cuts into the back of the Sandway abattoir van. It was heavy work and his hands felt the chill. Garrod had always admired the energy and enthusiasm of the meat workers at Smithfield when he had worked in London. Dead meat is cold. The chill of death passed from the meat into his fingers. Health and Safety rules suggested that he should be wearing gloves. However, nobody was watching and most of the blood under his fingernails was bovine.

Having filled the small van in as organised a manner as was possible, Garrod walked across the abattoir forecourt to the site office. Robert Sandway was completing the necessary paperwork for the delivery. He looked up as the Portakabin sagged under Garrod's weight.

'Ah! George,' Sandway said with a smile, 'here is the invoice for the meat. Make sure Chissel signs it before you leave. He's a slippery little sod.'

He handed over two pieces of paper that he had just stapled together.

'Will do, Mr Sandway,' Garrod replied.

'There's a map on the back. Do you know Cambridge?'

'Vaguely.'

'Follow signs for the city centre. You can't really miss the market square. The one-way system is a bit of a pig but you shouldn't have any difficulties. Call me if you get stuck. There's a mobile phone in the glove box of the van. The office number is pre-programmed in.'

'No problem, Mr Sandway.'

'George, I really appreciate you stepping in like this.'

'I don't mind.'

'You look very tired. I think you've been working too hard.'

'I feel fine.'

'I have a proposition for you.' Sandway sat back down in his chair. 'How would you feel about becoming a supervisor? Chief of the cutting-floor, something like that?'

Garrod was uncertain how to react. He had tried hard to be ordinary in his job and yet he had clearly attracted too much attention. 'I appreciate that, Mr Sandway. It's good to know that your work is recognised.'

'George, the way you handled the boys on the cutting floor during your presentation the other day was impressive. They are a difficult crowd but they listen to you. Whatever impression that the boys give to the contrary, they respect expertise.'

'Experience is worth more than certificates, sir,' Garrod agreed.

'I couldn't agree more. Look, I've only been running this place for a few years. It was my father's business really. He started out as a master butcher.'

'Mine too.'

'I am still very green in some ways. It would be useful for me to have someone with your wisdom helping out in a managerial capacity.'

Garrod couldn't help but like Robert Sandway. He despised arrogance. Humility was the first step towards earning his respect. 'I'd be happy to help out,' he replied.

'Excellent,' Sandway smiled. 'There will obviously be a big pay increase. Shall we shall say twenty thousand a year before tax?'

'That's very generous, Mr Sandway.'

'Not at all. That's the best I can offer you without bankrupting myself. The margins in this business are paper thin.'

'That's why we have to cut accurately,' Garrod agreed. 'As I was telling the boys.'

'Quite.' Sandway reached inside his desk

drawer and pulled out a piece of paper.

'Have a look at this,' he handed it over to Garrod. 'It's the job specification for Floor Supervisor.'

'I'll read it after the drop off this morning.' Garrod folded the paper and placed it in the pocket of his overalls.

'If you do agree to take the job,' Sandway continued, 'we would need to put you on the payroll.'

'I'm sorry?'

'Well, at the moment we pay you cash in hand. That's not really appropriate for someone in a management position. I realise that you have had tax problems before but as you will be earning a regular income, surely you can come to some arrangement with the Inland Revenue?'

Garrod felt a stab of disappointment. This would be problematic. 'I'd have to think about it, Mr Sandway. Those bastards just won't leave me alone.'

'Think about it, George. You must be approaching retirement. This is an opportunity to put away a bit of a pension. Sort your affairs out.'

'I'll let you know by the end of the day, Mr Sandway.'

Food for thought.

* * *

Ten minutes later Garrod was driving south, through Sawtry and Craxton, then down towards Cambridge. His mind tried to work through ways in which he could take on the job of supervisor without exposing his fraudulent identity. He had always taken pride in his work. Even when he cut people he had always endeavoured to do so with the precision and attention to efficiency ratios that a master butcher depended upon. This was his trade. For years he had lived a marginal existence, hiding his true identity, earning money through prize fighting and theft. He had crushed his true ability and with it his self-esteem. Again, his mind came to focus upon Alison Dexter. His life had become a game of snakes and ladders. Whenever he seemed to be climbing upwards, his thoughts slipped on her and he tumbled back down into obsession and fury. She would soon pay for that. With Henry Braun's assistance, he would dismantle her piece by piece. He had already stripped away her secret sexuality with the murder and consumption of Kelsi Hensy. He hoped that he had also infected her mind with the guilt that had dogged him since the death of his brother. Soon he would consume the rest of her.

There. It had happened again. Garrod had allowed his mind to wander from the issue of his promotion and fall into the pit occupied by Alison Dexter.

The van rolled on through the misty fens. Moisture settled on the windscreen. Garrod flicked on the wipers. It helped him to focus. The reality was that he could not allow himself to be placed on the payroll at Sandways. His false identity would be immediately exposed. It was a terrible frustration. Robert Sandway had shown a level of trust and faith in his abilities that had unsettled Garrod. For the first time in years, he had begun to feel a sense of pride in himself. Quite simply, he did not want to let Robert Sandway down.

Garrod was slowed down by traffic on the outskirts of Cambridge. He wound his way through the ancient city at a snail's pace, eventually crawling into the market square from Sidney Street. The Chissels' stall was one of the front row pitches directly opposite the Senate House. Garrod drew up in front of it. He leaned across the passenger seat and wound down the window to speak to two men, one in his late forties constructing the scaffolding frame of their stall, the other in his late teens sitting on a plastic chair and eating a sandwich.

'Steve Chissel?' Garrod called out.

The older man looked up. 'That's me.'

'I'm from Sandway's,' Garrod announced.

Chissel walked around to the back of the van where Garrod joined him.

'No Ozzie today?' Chissel asked as Garrod

unlocked the back door of his van.

'He's sick this week.'

'Who are you?'

'I'm George.'

'Right, George. Let's get all this out and onto the stall.'

Garrod looked over to the teenager sitting behind the stall. Chissel read his mind.

'Don't expect any help from Jack. My son has a severe dose of "teenager".'

Garrod and Chissel began to unload the meat cuts and arrange them on the stall.

'These look different,' Chissel observed as he looked over a set of twenty pork chops.

Garrod smiled. 'We're just cutting them properly now. Are you complaining?'

Chissel shrugged. 'I won't complain until he starts putting the prices up. You know how it works.'

Jack Chissel was now cooking rashers of bacon on a gas camping stove. The smell was making Garrod hungry.

'Do you always cook breakfast out here?' he asked Steve, trying to ignore his rumbling stomach.

'He does,' Steve sniffed. 'I prefer the real McCoy myself. As soon as we're unloaded, I'm off to grab a breakfast burger from the greasy spoon up there. Did you bring the dog meat?'

'Yeah. There's fifty bags in the smaller box.'

'What, entrails and stuff?'

'Exactly.'

'It's a right little earner that, you know. Don't tell Sandway but it's one of our big sellers.'

'I can imagine.'

It took the two men about ten minutes to complete their task.

'Right,' Chissel looked around him, 'we're done.'

Garrod handed him the invoice for the meat as Sandway had requested.

Chissel tapped his jacket pockets. 'Do you know what? I haven't got a pen.'

Garrod smiled and handed him a biro. Chissel looked slightly deflated. He signed on the dotted line.

'Pleasure doing business with you,' Garrod said as he took the invoice back and stuffed it into his overall pocket.

'Likewise.' Chissel turned to his son, now in the middle of eating a bacon sandwich. 'Right, Fatso, I'm off to get my breakfast.'

'Don't call me that,' Jack replied between acne-bordered mouthfuls.

'Just mind the stall, Porky.' Chissel grinned at Garrod. 'He's got an appetite on him that one. Nice to meet you, George. Will I see you next week?'

'Probably not.'

'Never mind. Give my best to Sandway.'

Chissel slapped Garrod on the arm as he wandered off through the market in search of his burger. Garrod slammed the van doors shut and locked them.

'Don't mind my dad,' Jack called out, after wiping the fat from his lips.

'Eh?'

'He's always talking. He won't shut up.'

Garrod nodded. 'How was your breakfast?'

'Nice. Well nice,' Jack replied. 'Are you from London?'

'How did you know that?' Garrod tensed slightly.

'I'm good with accents. You've got a well strong London accent.'

'I'm from the East End originally,' Garrod responded.

'Wicked. I bet it's more fun in London than up here.'

'I wouldn't say that. There's good and bad everywhere.'

'This place is a dump.'

Garrod chuckled to himself. 'London's no picnic, sonny.'

'At least there are things to do. This place is a morgue. Fucking students and slags with shopping bags. Bores the shit out of me.'

Garrod looked at the cold beauty of the Senate House, the perpendicular reaches of King's College Chapel. 'It's prettier here,' he said.

'I suppose so,' said Jack sadly.

Garrod felt a stab of pity for the lonely teenager shivering in the bitter East Anglian morning. He remembered helping his own father, Con Garrod, on the freezing cold morning meat run to Smithfield forty years previously.

'Here.' Garrod walked up to the stall and picked up one of the dog meat bags that he had recently deposited there. 'You should have a real cockney breakfast.'

'What do you mean?'

Garrod untied the bag and tipped the contents into Jack's small frying pan. 'These are pig entrails: pancreas, a bit of intestine, sweetbreads. When I was back in London, I used to eat this every day.'

Jack peered at the strange collection of giblets that was sizzling in his pan. 'But dog meat's bad, isn't it?'

'Not at all. Personally, I prefer this stuff. You get a much stronger taste from the organs than from muscle. After the war, you see, cockney women like my old mum couldn't afford to eat the best cuts of meat,' Garrod used Jack's fork to prod the frying entrails about in the pan, 'so we used to eat this instead.'

Intrigued now, Jack leaned forward. 'How do you eat it?'

'You get a slice of bread and spread the meats on it, fold it over and eat it like a sandwich.'

Jack reached into his rucksack and withdrew a loaf of bread. He proffered a slice up to Garrod who promptly slid pieces of the cooked meat onto the bread.

'There you go,' he said after a moment, 'tell me what you think.'

Jack Chissel took a nervous bite of the bread then chewed on it thoughtfully. He swallowed his first mouthful of cockney cooking.

'It's really tasty actually,' he said with an edge of surprise to his voice.

'Told you. It's called 'Pig's Fry'.'

'Thanks mate.'

Garrod left Jack Chissel chewing happily in the cold morning air. The market clock banged as he drove out of the square. At roughly the same time, a few hundred yards away, Alison Dexter drove her hire car out of the car park of the Holiday Inn. She had overslept in the comfort of her hotel room and was late for work. Ten minutes later she found herself caught in a traffic jam on the ring road.

Bartholomew Garrod's Sandway Abattoir van was caught in the same jam a few hundred yards ahead.

Both were oblivious to each other's proximity.

Stand still for long enough and you'll eventually see everybody that you ever knew.

Better to keep moving.

51.

Underwood was determinedly mobile. He was on the A133 heading out from Colchester towards Clacton. His hypothesis based upon admittedly shaky assumptions was that the Garrod family had connections to East Essex. Cornelius Garrod had been arrested in Great Oakley in Essex in 1960. Bartholomew Garrod had, according to Keith Gwynne, obtained his fighting dog in Clacton. These two locations were about ten miles from each other on the east Essex coast. Underwood's theory was that Garrod was using a caravan or beach chalet on one of the sites in the area as a base. However, testing the theory was proving difficult. He had searched through Sunday without success.

There were numerous caravan sites in the region: too many for him to check on his own. And yet, here he was. Excommunicated to Clacton by DI Alison Dexter. He wondered what it was about her that prompted such extremes of emotion.

He consoled himself with the knowledge that he

was engaged in a race. They had to find Garrod before Garrod found and isolated Dexter. Underwood sensed that Garrod must have already formulated a plan. The man had already got close enough to Dexter to strike out and yet he had chosen not to. He had raped and murdered Kelsi Hensy.

Underwood considered the alternatives as he turned south-east of Clacton towards the first site on his list: Sea Breezes Holiday Centre was just outside Jaywick. He didn't hold out much hope for this site. It had originally been constructed in early 1960. Eric Shildon had died in 1940. However, it was possible that Garrod might have changed site at some point. It was also the most southerly point on his route: somewhere to start. He pulled up in the car park at the front of the site. Out of season, it was a desolate place. Wind tumbled in brutally from the North Sea. Underwood turned off the engine.

He tried to decipher motive in the madness. Garrod murdered people. Garrod ate people. Dexter identified the Garrods. Ray Garrod was killed. Garrod wanted revenge.

Underwood's eyes ached in their sockets. He really needed glasses for driving now. Wasting away from the inside out, Underwood felt his age. The cancer that he suspected inside him was gaining. He stared out at the bleak campsite: its white and blue caravans huddled together on Essex's most sterile of promontories. It seemed that he was already in purgatory.

Killing her is not enough. Garrod wants to humiliate her. Do to her what she did to him. Destroy the person closest to her. Marginalise and isolate her. Consume her.

The Garrods cannibalised their victims. Underwood wondered what drove such perversity. How had something so unnatural become a commonplace to them? Did being surrounded by mutilation, blood and flesh desensitise the Garrods? Perhaps carving animal meat became a mundane chore to them and they had sought stimulation elsewhere. Perhaps they wanted to consume and reduce their victims to base matter. Or was it something else? Underwood liked to flip ideas over: heads on one side inevitably revealed tails on the other. Was Bartholomew Garrod honouring his victims? Stripping them of attributes that he desired in himself. Filling the void in his heart with other people. Underwood understood that position well. Had he not also stripped elements from Alison Dexter's life – her movements, her picture, her father – to fill the darkness in his mind? He had cannibalised her personality out of love not hatred. Did Garrod want to do the same to her body?

How would he want to eat her?

Underwood forced the ideas out of his head. He knew he had an ability to slide down into the whirlpool of human monstrosity. His terrible imagination had nearly consumed him before as surely as the cancer that was eating him alive.

He sensed a migraine building behind his eyes. Suddenly Underwood was aware of his surroundings again, the dismal little campsite, the thundering North Sea gale at his window. Someone was looking at him through the windows of the site office. He unbuckled his seat belt.

52.

Alison Dexter was reading the case file on the death of Jack Whiteside. Essex Police had couriered the documents to her that morning. She flicked through the written text to the photographs of Whiteside's body. It was badly decomposed after what the post-mortem report described as 'prolonged immersion in water'. However, the cut across the throat was still visible. The victim had not been mutilated in any other way. Dexter could not be certain that this was the work of Garrod. Certainly the killing blow was similar but every one of the 'Primal Cut' murders and Garrod's recent attacks had involved removal of internal organs or flesh from the victim.

Kelsi Hensy's taste in my mouth; in his mouth.

Dexter tried to push away the guilt welling up inside her. She had to be tough now. Otherwise the case and her sanity would undoubtedly fall apart. There was a knock at the door of her office. Joe Harrison stood at her door.

'Guv, do you have a moment?' he asked.

Dexter nodded, grateful to be lifted out of herself. 'Come in. Have a seat.'

'I've been putting together a list of names: slaughterhouses, abattoirs, knacker men. There are a whole load of butchers too but I guessed they'd be less of a priority.'

'I agree,' Dexter smiled faintly. 'He's not stupid enough to be selling pies. How many names?'

'There's about a dozen in Cambridgeshire if you exclude the butchers' shops. How do you want me to play it?'

'Split the list with Sauerwine. Take a plod each and go and check out each location. If you find him, call in straight away. You won't be able to take him out otherwise. We've got two ARU coppers downstairs scratching their arses. Bringing him down is their job. All we have to do is find the bastard.'

'I understand.' Harrison stood and headed for the door.

'Joe,' Dexter called after him.

'Guv?'

'Be careful. No more corpses on this one.'

Harrison smiled, 'First sight we get, I'm calling the cavalry.'

'Do that.'

'What about you?'

'I'm going to check out this Whiteside business. Then I want to talk to Bevan about the Woollard hearing. Whether he wants me there or not.'

'Fair enough.'

Dexter turned back to the case file on Jack Whiteside. She read quietly to herself, hoping that the text would keep Kelsi Hensy from the spaces of her mind.

The victim was identified to be Jack Edward Whiteside, 50, of 28 Woodham Crescent, Maldon, Essex. Occupation lorry driver. Whiteside was reported missing by his wife on 17th January 1999. Whiteside is known to have frequented the Albion public house in West Mersea. Two witnesses confirmed that he was at the pub on the evening of 16th January. He left at closing time. This is the last recorded sighting of Whiteside alive.

Dexter did not know Essex particularly well. The names were unfamiliar but she did not have the energy to check them on a map. The more she read about this case, the more she began to think that it had nothing to do with Garrod. She turned to the introductory pages to the post-mortem report.

The body of the victim was discovered on 6ᵗʰ February 2000, in shallow water at Bramble Creek, Bull's Ooze, Essex. The remains were found by Mr Cyril Delvis (local resident – details appended) while walking his dog in the area. Post-mortem examination took place at Colchester Infirmary on 7ᵗʰ February. Chief Medical Examiner Dr Ramsey Holland identified cause of death as blood loss following knife slash to the throat. Foul play.

Dexter picked up her police telephone directory and located Dr Holland's number. He answered the call immediately.

'Holland.'

'Dr Holland, my name is Alison Dexter. I am head of New Bolden CID in Cambridgeshire.'

'I've heard of you. You work with Roger Leach.'

'On occasion.'

'We meet at conferences occasionally. To what do I owe the honour of a call from the famous Inspector Dexter?'

'Doctor, in 2000 you did a post-mortem on a Mr Jack Whiteside: a murder victim. Do you remember it?'

'I do actually. It was a particularly messy job. The body had been rotting in the sea for best part of a month. Accurate forensic analysis was impossible. Knife wound to the throat. Case was never closed as far as I know.'

'It wasn't. Can you tell me? Was there anything unusual about the body? Any dismemberment or mutilation?'

'Nothing as I recall. If there was it would be in the report.'

'Could you hazard a guess about the kind of knife that was used?'

'Not really,' Holland replied, 'the wound was degraded by water immersion. A knife certainly and most likely a fairly hefty one. I don't think it was serrated but I'd have to check my notes.'

'Butcher's knife?'

'Possibly. I couldn't really be sure.'

They exchanged some more niceties about Roger Leach before Dexter hung up. She had drawn a blank. She wondered if Underwood had made better progress on the Essex connection than her.

53.

Henry Braun had started the day badly. He awoke with a terrible headache. This he treated with a can of Special Brew from the store he kept under the stairs. He had not yet adjusted to sleeping in his brother's bed. It bulged and nagged into his back.

Janice Braun had left for work earlier. He had watched his brother's wife dress for work through half closed eyes. She was skinny. Nick had told him that sex with his wife was like shagging a skeleton. Having now tried it himself, Henry understood that description.

He flicked through some of Nick's porn mags while he ate his cornflakes and relieved himself rapidly afterwards. He remembered that a bloke called Dunthorne he had known at school used to roll up porn mags and shag them for a laugh. That memory made him grin as he eventually dispensed himself over the photo of Lucy, twenty-two, from Newcastle. Henry Braun saw sexuality as an infection: an irresistible compulsion. His brother had not been able to control it. It wasn't Nick's fault, Henry reminded himself; sometimes the plague consumes you and corrupts your every conscious thought. Henry could keep the disease under control, if he kept it in the palm of his hand: at least until he met up again with DI Alison Dexter.

His new associate George had given him a clear set of instructions the previous evening. Henry had written them out on a piece of notepaper. His natural suspicion of strangers had initially made him reject the notion. However, as George had spoken in more detail about his plans, Henry had found himself listening in stunned awe. He was terrified, absorbed and very excited at what lay in store.

At 10.30 a.m., he fried himself an egg, which he ate with toast and ketchup. In an hour or so, he would call Peterborough Crown Court to get the listings for the coming week.

54.

Garrod returned to Sandway's abattoir nursing a changed mind. The long drive back from Cambridge had given him an opportunity to reconsider the prospect of promotion. It was simply unworkable. He had been marginalised from normal society. It was therefore impossible for him to be re-integrated. Besides, he knew that if he accepted Robert Sandway's offer, he would inevitably bring aggravation down upon his employer's head. That was not a prospect that appealed to him. Sandway had treated him with respect. He would give his boss the same courtesy.

Garrod found Robert Sandway on the cutting floor scribbling notes onto his clipboard.

'Ah! George!' Sandway exclaimed, 'just the man. I've been thinking. The set up of the floor is all wrong.'

'Excuse me?'

'The cutters are standing too close together. We are probably in violation of COHSE rules. There's a risk that the guys could cut each other. Look how close they are standing.'

Garrod looked out across the cutting floor. The dangling pig carcasses bled with a beautiful, dark predictability. He felt a twinge of sadness.

'Mr Sandway, I'm going to have to say no to your offer.'

'Why, George? You seemed so keen earlier.'

'It wouldn't be right, sir. I've been thinking about moving on.'

'Don't be hasty, George.' Sandway seemed genuinely upset. 'I would hate to lose you. Is it because of your tax problems?'

'Partly.' Garrod found it hard to look the man in the eye.

'Forget the promotion then. Stay as you were.'

'Mr Sandway, you've been very good to me. I appreciate everything you've done. But I've been having a few personal problems recently and I'm finding it hard to do my job properly. It wouldn't be fair on you if I stayed.'

'That's rubbish, George. I want you to stay. You've saved me a fortune already.'

'I've made up my mind, sir.'

Exasperated, Sandway stared up at Garrod. He

could see in Garrod's black eyes that there was no room for compromise.

'How long will you stay?' Sandway asked eventually.

'I thought I'd leave at the end of today,' Garrod responded.

Sandway nodded. 'Come and say goodbye before you go.'

Garrod watched him leave. The noise of the cutting room suddenly became an annoyance to him. He walked across the floor and into the locker room where he kept his own knives safely locked away. He removed them from locker number sixteen, checking first that none had been taken. His knives were the source of much comment on the cutting floor. They looked old-fashioned but he kept them in pristine condition. They were razor sharp, with tempered steel blades that seemed to slide effortlessly through meat as if it were butter. Garrod disliked many of the lighter modern knives as they tended to slip in his heavy hands. He wanted his rendering of Alison Dexter to be perfect.

However, he still lacked a couple of vital items. The honey pit was dug out and waterproofed in the lawn at Craxten Fen Hospital. His vast supply of molasses was stacked in a hospital storage shed. All that he required were his cooking pans and spices from the static caravan. He also remembered that he had a pair of handcuffs secreted there too, courtesy of a prostitute he had used once in Southend. It would take him about two hours to drive there cross-country. He decided to leave at three. That would give him time to finish up properly and say goodbye to Mr Sandway.

55.

Henry Braun waited anxiously for the phone to connect. He knew he was doing nothing illegal but his heart pounded with guilty intent.

'Court Centre,' said a female voice at the other end of the phone.

'I have an enquiry about court listing for this week,' Braun said crisply in his most polite voice.

'One moment please.' The line went silent as his call was redirected. Henry Braun tried to remain calm.

'Court office. Can I help you?' said a different female voice.

'Hello,' Braun coughed nervously, 'I have an enquiry about the court timetable for next week.'

'Have you looked at the website?'

'I don't have access to the Internet,' he replied. That was true at least.

'OK. The court lists for the forthcoming week are

printed every Friday and displayed on the notice boards next to the main entrance to the Court Centre.'

'Ah,' Braun looked at the scrawled notes that George had left for him, 'I can't get into Peterborough to check I'm afraid. It's a specific case. A relative of mine is on trial soon. I wanted to come along and give him moral support.'

'What's his name?'

Braun checked his notes. 'Woollard. First name Bob.'

'One moment please.'

'Thank you.'

About a minute passed.

'OK. We have Crown versus Robert Woollard scheduled for 9 a.m. on Wednesday.'

Braun tried not to let excitement surge in his reply. 'That's him. Thank you very much.'

'If you need directions on how to find us, look…'

Braun had hung up.

56.

DS Joe Harrison spent that afternoon trawling around some of the more dismal locations in Cambridgeshire. As Dexter had instructed, he had split the list of meat processing plants, abattoirs and knacker men with DC Sauerwine. The seven sites on his own target list were scattered across the north and east of the county. Sauerwine was covering the south and the west. By mid-afternoon, he was beginning to consider it a fruitless mission. Moreover, the sight of cows being quietly herded into slaughter pens at Smith's Meat Processing near Ely had been an unsettling experience.

Both he and Sauerwine were working off the list of names that DI Dexter had previously prepared:

	Claude	Albert	Francis	George
George	George	George	George	NO
Morley	Morley	Morley	Morley	Morley
Claude	NO	Claude	Claude	Claude
Murchison	Murchison	Murchison	Murchison	Murchison
Albert	Albert	NO	Albert	Albert
Tyndall	Tyndall	Tyndall	Tyndall	Tyndall
Francis	Francis	Francis	NO	Francis
Cavendish	Cavendish	Cavendish	Cavendish	Cavendish
Norlington	Norlington	Norlington	Norlington	Norlington

The list had been based on streets in the Leyton area of London where the Garrods had lived. In addition, Harrison and Sauerwine both carried two A4 pictures of Garrod: a picture from the 'Primal Cut' case file and a more recent photofit impression based upon Keith Gwynne's evidence. Harrison had been assigned PC Brooke as his assistant for the day. Brooke was an expert on Tottenham Hotspur Football Club and little else.

'Of course, in those days, we had a proper team. The famous five across midfield: Hoddle, Waddle, Allen, Hodge and Ardiles. That was a right team. We played the Tottenham way. King Clive scored forty-nine goals that season.'

'Is that a fact?' Harrison asked wearily as he turned left past a road sign that said 'Sawtry 10'.

'On the ground. Pass and move. Pass and move. We were the most attractive team in Europe then,' Brooke burbled on.

'So what happened?' Harrison replied stifling a yawn.

'No strategy. We bought Lineker and sold Waddle. What's the point of that?'

'Seems a bit daft.'

'It was catastrophic, Sarge. Then El Tel comes in. All right he bought us Gascoigne, fair dos, but he also got Paul Stewart. What was that about? Since when did a club like Tottenham need to buy players from Man City? Meanwhile of course, those red bastards at Highbury are winning league titles and FA Cups left, right and centre. I threw a snowball at Tony Adams once while he was putting petrol in his motor. Hit him on the back of the head. Fucking hilarious. He was well pissed off.'

Harrison's car phone rang. DC Sauerwine's

voice spoke through the speaker.

'Are you as fed up as I am?' he asked.

Harrison grinned. 'I've had more productive afternoons.'

'Well, I'm done on my list now,' Sauerwine continued.

'Anything?'

'Not a sausage. Well, actually, I've seen hundreds of fucking sausages. But there is no sign of our man.'

'Likewise. I've got Brookey with me. We have two more stops to make.'

'Where are you now?'

'Heading for somewhere called Sawtry.'

Sauerwine laughed. 'Good luck. Sawtry makes New Bolden look like Monte Carlo.'

'Bit quiet is it?'

'Last stop before the underworld.'

'I get you.'

PC Brooke leaned unnecessarily towards the speakers. 'You all right "Sauers"?'

'I'm good thanks, Andy,' Sauerwine replied. Harrison could hear the smile in his voice. 'You be nice to the Detective Sergeant. None of your Spurs stories. He's a Gooner you know.'

Brooke was horrified. 'You're joking me?'

Harrison kept his eyes fixed on the road ahead trying not to grin.

'I'm heading back to the station, Sarge,' Sauerwine continued, 'this is a waste of time.'

'I'm inclined to agree.' Harrison clicked his mobile phone off. PC Brooke was staring at him.

'I'm sorry, Guv. I didn't know you was Arsenal,' he spluttered.

'Don't worry about it.' Harrison couldn't resist a jibe. 'You want to hear a joke?'

Brooke nodded, relieved: 'Go on.'

Harrison nodded, 'OK. The Spurs manager is doing his weekly shopping on Tottenham High Road, when he sees this old lady. She's got these three massive bags of shopping and she's really struggling. Right?'

'Right.'

'So he goes up to her and he says, "Can you manage, love?" And the old girl says, "Piss off! You got yourself into this mess, don't ask me to sort it out…!"'

Brooke looked blank. 'That's not funny, Sarge. Not funny at all.'

Harrison accelerated the squad car along the road that led eventually into Sawtry village, then out again into open countryside.

57.

Bartholomew Garrod rattled east in his own transit van. He had said goodbye to Robert Sandway an hour or so previously. Now he was on his way out of Cambridgeshire to complete his preparations for Alison Dexter. Sandway had shaken his hand with genuine affection and thanked him 'for all his wisdom and industry'.

Wisdom and industry.

Garrod liked that description of his contribution to life at the abattoir. He had almost cried at the time. His life had not been cluttered with appreciative comments. His customers back in London, hard East End women with hawk eyes and suspicious minds, had usually criticised his prices or his ungenerous cuts of meat. Men had paid money to watch him fight other men: mindless, savage violence. Ray Garrod had demanded constant attention but given little back in return.

Wisdom and industry.

Bartholomew Garrod allowed himself to fantasise as he crossed the border from Cambridgeshire to Essex. He imagined a small butcher's shop in an English country village: Hampshire or Cornwall possibly. He imagined being a local character: conversing with his customers, helping them to select the best cuts, the primal cuts, of meat. He imagined a small garden out back where Ray could sit quietly in the sunshine. There would be a plaque above the entrance to his shop. It would say 'Wisdom and Industry'.

Rain splattered across the windscreen of his van: car headlights smeared into droplets of water. Garrod tightened his grip on the steering wheel.

He imagined carving Alison Dexter's naked body.

58.

The silence was distracting. It made her uneasy. It suggested an ominous inertia. Alison Dexter felt imprisoned in the office. She was under strict instructions not to leave the building unaccompanied. The Chief Superintendent had been insistent on that point. The CID floor was fairly deserted. Most of her team were out chasing ghosts. She was beginning to suspect that Bartholomew Garrod would elude her again. The man had extraordinary resilience. Even now, when he was virtually on her doorstep, she had no clear idea of how to catch him. She thought of Underwood and debated briefly whether she should call him. She decided instead to reread the case file on the murder of Jack Whiteside.

At 5.30 p.m. her telephone rang. It was DS Harrison.

'Guv, I think we might have something,' he said quietly.

'I'm listening.'

'I'm up with PC Brooke at Sandway's abattoir in Sawtry. Do you know it?'

'Never heard of it.'

'North Cambridgeshire, west of Ely. I'm with the owner, one Robert Sandway. He says a man fitting Garrod's description has been working here.'

'Does he have an address?' Dexter was already pulling on her jacket.

'Afraid not.'

'I'm on my way. Stay with him.'

Dexter stopped at the Desk Sergeant before she left. He assigned her a motorcycle escort for the drive up to Sawtry. It made her feel ridiculous.

At roughly the same time, Underwood was heading north along the Essex coast towards Harwich. He could scarcely remember a more depressing day in his life although there were many contenders for that particular title. He had visited nine utterly barren, wind-blasted campsites; seen what felt like a million static caravans and mobile homes; spoken to several dead-eyed site managers, trawled through lists of meaningless names and discovered absolutely nothing.

The surroundings weren't helping either. He knew that Essex was among the country's most ancient counties. However, this desolate stretch of land and its muddy, featureless coast made him wonder why the Saxons and Angles had bothered staying. To battle across the North Sea in a wooden boat only to end up stranded in an Essex swamp seemed to him an utterly futile exercise. It also amazed him that so many people would choose to take holidays there. Underwood found English seaside towns horrific: amusement arcades, dog shit, candyfloss and paedophiles. Perhaps modern Anglo-Saxons felt impelled to head east: to push their mud huts and caravans as close to their ancestral home land as possible; to tow their plundered tat in aluminium boxes. Or perhaps they were lemmings, driven by the banality of their existence to throw themselves into the sea.

He had one more campsite to visit. 'The Regency' was three miles outside Great Oakley.

DI Alison Dexter sat in the prefabricated office that Bartholomew Garrod had left a few hours previously. Robert Sandway sat in front of her, wringing his hands uncomfortably.

'You must understand, Inspector,' Sandway said,

'I had no idea that this man was a fugitive.'

Dexter was not impressed. 'You are certain that this "George Francis" is the man on our photofit?'

'Yes,' Sandway looked at the picture again, 'his face is rounder than this. Heavier. He is fatter than this image suggests but I'm certain it's him.'

Dexter sighed. 'Do you ever watch the news, Mr Sandway? Or read the papers? This man is a wanted murderer.'

'Look, he came to me wanting a job. He seemed a decent chap. As it happens, he was about the most effective worker that I've ever employed.'

'This job,' Dexter asked, 'where was it advertised?'

'*Cambridge Evening News*. I have a copy somewhere.'

'Give it to my sergeant when you find it.' Dexter frowned at her notes. 'I can't believe that you employed a man with no references and no permanent address.'

'Inspector, it was a labouring job. Lifting carcasses onto lorries. He told me that he had tax problems and was prepared to work for low pay, cash in hand. This business is dying on its arse. It's my job to run things as efficiently as possible. As it happens, this "George Francis" person had already suggested a number of improvements to the way that we operate. I offered him a promotion. He turned it down and left.'

'Have you any idea where he was living?'

Sandway shook his head. 'I'm sorry. He was always on time though, even on the early shifts. So I would guess he had to be local.'

'Transport,' Dexter asked, 'what was he driving?'

'Ah! A transit van. I remember that. It was an old one: white. I don't remember the registration but I think it started with an "S".'

DS Harrison had been listening to the exchange. 'You have CCTV cameras on the site. They would almost certainly have picked up his registration plate. We will need to take the security tapes.'

Sandway scratched the top of his head thoughtfully. 'That won't be possible. You see, the cameras are dummies. They don't work. The idea was to deter rather than record. Security systems are bloody expensive for operations of this size. We have a burglar alarm but the cameras are duff. Sorry.'

Dexter shut her notebook. 'This is pretty fucking dismal to be honest, Mr Sandway. You have not shown due diligence with your employees and as a result this man has evaded us again.'

'I trusted him. He seemed to like me. As I said, I had no reason to disbelieve him.'

Harrison intervened. 'You said he liked you? What makes you think that?'

'His manner, the things he said. I don't know. We spoke very frankly to each other about the business. I respected his honesty and he respected mine.'

Dexter didn't understand what Harrison had been driving at. 'What's in your mind, Joe?'

Harrison looked back at her. 'I was just thinking. Nothing I've heard about this guy suggests that he forms friendships easily. If Garrod feels he has a relationship with Mr Sandway, it's not inconceivable that he might come back.'

It was plausible. In the absence of any other ideas, Dexter realised that it might be worth pursuing.

'Mr Sandway, I'll do a deal with you. We will need to do a search of your premises tonight. We will be out of here with minimum fuss and aggravation to yourself on one condition. If this "George Francis" calls you, turns up here or makes any other form of contact, you call us at once.'

'Absolutely,' Sandway agreed, 'no problem.'

Dexter asked Harrison to join her outside. It was bitterly cold in the forecourt of the abattoir. Dexter pulled her jacket tight around her.

'As I see it,' she said, 'we've got two options.'

'What do you mean?' Harrison answered.

'We expand from this point, do house to house in all the surrounding villages.'

'Option two?'

'We sit tight. If we get very high profile we might scare him off. I think your point was a valid one. If he runs out of cash he may well contact Sandway again.'

'And Garrod won't know we've been here, if we get out quickly.'

Dexter had made up her mind. 'I think if we flood the area with plods, he'll disappear. Let's be low key. We have an advantage over him now.'

'A trap,' Harrison clarified. 'We also know he's driving a transit with an "S" registration. I'll alert traffic to be on the lookout.'

'I'm going to head back. Will you wrap it up here?'

'No problem.' Harrison turned and headed back up the steps into Sandway's Portakabin. Dexter signalled to her escort that it was time to leave.

59.

Underwood was sitting in the site manager's office of 'The Regency' campsite on the Essex coast. A small electric heater pumped warmth into the draughty little room. There were back editions of the *Sunday Sport* spread across the manager's desk. Underwood wondered if he'd intruded on a moment of personal enrichment.

'The plot register gives the names of the caravan owners,' said Melvin Stour, 'Site Director', according to his badge.

'How far do the lists go back?' Underwood asked. 'I'm looking for a plot that was purchased before 1960.'

'That makes it easier.' Stour opened the bottom drawer of his filing cabinet. 'We've got over a thousand static homes on this site. We're one of the bigger facilities. But there's only a few that have been here that long. My Dad bought the place back in 1959 but he kept all the existing documents. Many of our plots stay with the same family for years.'

'I'm looking for a plot bought in the name of Shildon or Garrod,' Underwood explained.

'We don't normally get any excitement out of season. In the summer there's the girls to look at. You wouldn't believe some of the things I've seen. Shocking.' Stour placed two files on the desk in front of Underwood. 'Here you go. These are the pre-1960 lists.'

Underwood began to scan the pages of plot numbers and purchasers. It took him about three minutes to realise that there was neither a Shildon nor a Garrod listed. Disappointment welled inside him.

'Do you have any records from before 1940?' Underwood asked.

'No. Sorry mate. We've got no records before then.'

Underwood rubbed his eyes in exhaustion. It had been a long day scraping around at the bottom of the geographical barrel. 'Can I see the current register then?' he asked, 'this year's list of residents?'

Stour returned obligingly to his filing cabinet. Underwood checked his mobile phone for messages:

'No Network Coverage' stared back at him.

For the thousandth time that day, he cursed the desolate Essex coast.

Alison Dexter had returned to her office. She wanted to tear out the tight ball of frustration in her stomach. They had missed Garrod leaving Sandway's by a couple of hours. She wondered if her own leaden-footed approach to the case since the murder of Kelsi Hensy made her culpable. It was true that they had made relatively little progress apart from the identification of Garrod at the abattoir. Now he had gone. They were always a step behind. She needed to get ahead.

She returned to the Jack Whiteside case file. Something about it had been troubling her: the kind of unease that floats inexplicably but persistently at the back of your mind. She flicked back through the pages that she had read earlier that day:

The body of the victim was discovered on 6th February 2000, in shallow water at Bramble Creek, Bull's Ooze, Essex. The remains were found by Mr Cyril Delvis (local resident – details appended) while walking his dog in the area.

She turned to the back of the file, found Cyril Delvis's contact information and called his home number.

'Hello?' said a male voice softened by age.

'Mr Delvis?'

'Speaking.'

'My name is Alison Dexter. I work for Cambridgeshire Police.'

'Oh! Hello! What's happened?'

'Nothing. Don't worry. I am investigating the death of a Mr Jack Whiteside. I understand that it was you that found the body back in February 2000.'

'Yes. You had me worried there for a moment!' Delvis chuckled down the phone. 'What would you like to know?'

'Was there anything unusual about the body? Anything missing? Any items in the water or on the beach nearby? Anything that you didn't mention to the police at the time?'

'Nothing I'm afraid,' Delvis replied. 'I was walking out by Bull's Ooze with my dog. I was on the footpath. Well, Reggie – that's my dog – he stopped to do his business and I had a moment to look at the water. That's when I saw it.'

'Mr Whiteside?'

'Yeah. He was floating face down in the water. I never did see his face. I double-timed it over to the Great Oakley sewage works and got a foreman there to phone the old Bill.'

Dexter absorbed this information. It seemed innocuous enough. There was clearly no point in...

'Where did you say?' she snapped suddenly.

'It was on Bull's Ooze, near the Great Oakley sewage works.'

'Yes.' Dexter tried to organise her thoughts. 'Thank you.'

She slammed her phone down and fumbled amongst the paper on her desk for the 'Primal Cut' case file that she had meticulously crafted seven years previously. On page ten she found what she was looking for:

'*Cornelius Garrod. Born Leyton, London 11th February 1919... Arrested drunk 4th August 1960, Great Oakley.*'

Dexter immediately reached for her mobile and called Underwood's number. Her former boss's assumptions had not been as shaky as she had believed.

'The number you have called is unavailable. Please try later,' said the computerised voice of the telephone company.

'Fuck!'

Dexter retrieved her East Essex Road Atlas from her drawer and thumbed through to the page on Great Oakley. She saw two villages: Little Oakley and Great Oakley connected by the Harwich Road. To the right she saw Bramble Island and next to it Bull's Ooze and the sewage works. She could even see the footpath where Delvis had been walking his dog. Further along, pressed up against the coast at Dugmore Creek, about half a mile from the sewage works, she saw the small caravan symbol that denoted a campsite.

She tried unsuccessfully to contact John Underwood again. Then she called Essex police headquarters at Colchester.

Underwood now had the 2001–2002 register of caravan owners on his lap. Stour was babbling happily.

'Of course,' he said, 'when all those little slags come up during the season, they don't hang about here. Oh no. They want the action, don't they? The bright lights. Party time. Clacton and Harwich – that's where they want to go. Come crashing back in here at four in the morning. Banging my door down because they've lost their keys.'

'Is that a fact?' Underwood asked distractedly.

'Gospel.' Stour was warming to his theme. 'And the men they bring back with them! Squaddies, pikeys, spades you name it. It's a disgrace. I'd love to sling them all out but I've got to make a profit somehow.'

Underwood had given up. There was no 'Shildon' or 'Garrod' listed; not even a 'Norlington'. He flipped back to page one of the file. He was about to hand it back to Stour when something caught his eye: the first name on the list in fact.

'What do you know about this Mr Bartholomew?' he asked Stour, pointing at the file.

'Don't see him much. Older chap. Big fella.'

Underwood pulled the photofit of Garrod from his back pocket and unfolded it.

'Is that him?' he asked quietly.

Stour looked hard at the image. 'Not sure. My bloke is much heavier than this.'

'Is he around now?' Underwood asked.

'No. I haven't seen him for weeks. Months maybe.'

Underwood was beginning to feel a surge of adrenalin. 'Did I hear you say something just now about keeping spare keys?'

* * *

Alison Dexter exchanged a series of calls with the duty officer at Colchester CID. The result of this exchange was that one CID officer and two squad cars were despatched from Colchester to the campsite north-east of Great Oakley. Colchester despatch estimated that the journey would take approximately twenty-five minutes.

Again, she failed to get through to Underwood's mobile.

Oblivious to all this, Underwood was at that moment picking his way through the dark spaces between caravans on The Regency site. The only thing that overrode his nervousness was the appalling stench in the air.

'What is that fucking smell?' he muttered to himself as the aroma of distant shit arrested him again.

He eventually found Plot Eleven: the static caravan belonging to Mr Bartholomew. Immediately, Underwood began to sense success. The caravan was of an old-fashioned and basic construction. It might once have been silver but Underwood's torch beam now only revealed flaking grey metal. The curtains were drawn and the door padlocked. He knocked firmly. There was no reply.

Underwood fumbled for the spare key that Stour had given him a minute or two previously. His hands were freezing cold. He looked around: the caravan was only a few hundred yards from the dark expanse of water that reached from Great Oakley round to Harwich then out into the North Sea. Underwood could see the lights of a container ship crawling into Harwich. The padlock clicked. Underwood removed it and pulled the door open. Edgy now, he shone his torch inside.

Nothing obviously horrific snarled back at him. The inside was basically furnished. The torchlight picked out a small stove and a black and white television. There were some clothes on the bed next to a book called *A History of the British Empire*. Underwood opened it at a bookmarked page. It concerned the story of HMS *Boyd* and the unfortunate fate of its crew who drowned in honey pits then were eaten by cannibals.

Underwood placed the book back on the bed and decided to search the vehicle properly. He pulled open the drawers of the mini-kitchen. There were some ancient knives and forks, some plates and a truly dismal collection of crockery. In the cupboard under the plastic sink, Underwood found a more impressive collection of saucepans and skillets. On the nearby work surface, Underwood found a small but very sharp cheese knife. Carefully, he picked it up and dropped it into a small plastic evidence bag. If he could find no other concrete evidence that the caravan was indeed Garrod's, he would send the knife to be fingerprinted by Marty Farrell at New Bolden.

He moved into the living space, inspecting the clothes on the bed. They certainly belonged to a large man but the pockets were all empty. Underwood sat on the bed, uncertain how to proceed. His foot bumped a bedside cupboard. He knelt on the floor of the caravan and shone his torch into the small cupboard space. There were some old newspapers stuffed in there, mostly London editions, an old black and white photo of something that Underwood couldn't quite make out and what looked like a jar of jam. There were breadcrumbs on the carpet next to the bed. Whoever Mr Bartholomew was, he clearly liked to eat sandwiches in bed.

He stood and carried the photo and the jam jar to the kitchen work surface. On closer inspection the photograph appeared to be of some kind of mangled body. It was old though: its image was barely visible. On the back, someone had written '1945'. Underwood then unscrewed the glass jar and discovered that it wasn't jam at all: it was honey. Moreover, there were three other empty honey jars on the work surface. Garrod clearly had a sweet tooth.

The thought rushed up at him. Underwood suddenly imagined Alison Dexter spread out naked on a bed in front of him. He imagined honey dripping slowly onto her stomach. He imagined licking the glaze from her flesh.

How would he want to eat her?

Underwood remembered the crew of the *Boyd*.

He would want her to be sweet.

He placed the photo into an evidence bag and pocketed it. Immediate contact with Dexter was essential. The caravan would need to be properly searched by a forensic team. Or even observed in case anyone returned to it. Either way, he had to move quickly. He climbed down from the caravan and padlocked the door behind him, the cold metal clinging momentarily to his skin. Satisfied that the door was secured, Underwood turned.

Bartholomew Garrod stood directly in front of him.

'Who the fuck are you?' he asked.

Underwood's mind raced. He was backed against the caravan. Garrod was too close, barring his way.

'I'm John from the Regency office,' he spluttered, trying not to let his rising terror betray him. 'We got a call. The door of your caravan was open. We were worried someone had broken in.'

Garrod stared quietly. This man was afraid. 'You're lying,' he said. 'What do you want?'

'Nothing,' Underwood replied. 'Why don't we go back up to the site office and I'll give you a claim form and a new padlock.'

Garrod had fought too many bare knuckles not to understand the nature of fear. He was debating what to do when Underwood's mobile phone rang. For a second, Underwood thought his heart had stopped.

'Aren't you going to answer it then?' Garrod asked advancing on Underwood.

'It's probably the wife checking up on me,' Underwood said.

'Answer it,' Garrod instructed. 'Now.'

Underwood could smell Garrod's breath now. The man was huge. He knew he would have no chance if Garrod went for him. He pulled his mobile from his pocket and answered.

'Hello.'

'John, it's Alison. Where are you?'

'I'm at the campsite, sweetheart,' Underwood replied with mock levity, his eyes never leaving Garrod's. 'We got a call about a possible break in.'

There was a silence as Dexter absorbed the significance of Underwood's unusual tone.

'Are you at Great Oakley?' she asked.

'That's right,' Underwood responded, 'with a customer.'

Garrod's right hand slammed into Underwood's solar plexus, throwing him gasping for air against the side of the caravan. He snatched the mobile from Underwood's hand and read the caller identification on the LCD display: 'Dexter'. He lifted the phone to his ear.

'Hello dearie,' he said, 'it's your old friend.'

Dexter's blood chilled at Garrod's voice.

'I'll be seeing you soon.'

Garrod dropped the phone to the floor and smashed a giant fist into Underwood's face breaking his nose and spraying blood against the tin wall of the caravan. Underwood's head cracked against the stone footing of the caravan as he fell unconscious to the ground.

Garrod felt for a pulse or signs of life but found none. He sensed that he had little time. He would bag up the body and sink it into the creek as he had done with the body of Jack Whiteside three years earlier. However, first he wanted to retrieve his pans and other personal items from the caravan.

Alison Dexter sat stunned in the silence of her office. She knew that John Underwood had to be dead.

60.

Henry Braun returned to Gorton Row from Tesco with all the provisions that he required for Wednesday's festivities. He had bought a bottle of champagne in anticipation of success, a six-pack of

Special Brew to build an atmosphere and a Polaroid camera to record the details of Alison Dexter's debasement for his brother and for posterity. He could hardly wait. In the cigarette-smoke haze of Nick's living room, Janice Braun stared at a documentary about properties in Spain. Henry resisted the urge to fuck her again. He would keep the infection to himself until Wednesday when it would surge out of him like poisoned blood.

61.

Garrod lifted John Underwood's body into a strong, yellow refuse sack. He added a heavy chunk of stone paving that he had pulled up from the pathway. He placed that sack inside another and tied it tightly at the top. Having loaded Underwood into his van, Garrod then drove down a dirt track to the disused jetty south of the Great Oakley sewage works. He pulled the heavy bundle from the back of his transit van, slung it over his shoulder and marched to the end of the small pier. It jutted out about twenty yards into the black waters of Oakley Creek.

He did not delay. In the distance, Garrod thought he could hear the wail of a police siren. He took an almighty swing and hurled the weighted sack into the water. Gratifyingly, it sank immediately. The sirens were getting louder. Garrod climbed back into his van and drove, with his lights off, south until he hit the track that led to Old Moze Hall. He immediately turned right past the hall itself and onto the Harwich Road.

Underwood hovered at the edge of consciousness. He was aware of cold, of a sinking sensation and that he was short of air. Pain burned across the front of his face. He couldn't move. Disorientated. Was he dead? A terrible sadness surged behind his eyes. He had died without saying goodbye.

His mind was falling in on itself. So this was how it was to be: falling into the cold of eternity. Images flickered at him: Alison Dexter, the monstrous shape of Bartholomew Garrod. There were pains in his head, radiating throbbing pains. Underwood had thought himself reconciled to death. He had previously resigned himself to comfortable decay in the strangulating arms of cancer. Now death had immediacy, a cold plummeting immediacy.

He began to panic. He could feel the plastic walls of his incarceration. He tried to kick out but couldn't. Gagging now, air deserting him. His hands were beneath him. Terror. Underwood saw in the moment of his suffocation that he was terrified of dying. He desperately tried to move his hands.

He scrabbled vainly at the dense plastic that encapsulated him. Where was he? He thrashed vainly at the plastic sacks in a frightened, instinctive panic to be reborn, to be forgiven, to be alive.

Then his right hand touched the cheese knife in his pocket. The sinking had stopped. The bags had come to rest. Underwood began to sense what had happened to him. Time was short. His breaths were becoming more rapid, more panicky as oxygen disappeared from the refuse sacks that imprisoned him. He fumbled in his pocket for the knife, cursing the evidence bag that he had placed it in. Finally, he could feel its sharp, cold edge between his fingers. He lunged as best he could for the walls of his entombment. The knife pierced a hole, Underwood tried to drag it downwards. Freezing water tore into the bags.

In a second, his air had gone. He thrust frantically with the knife, tearing and ripping the plastic shells around him. His lungs were burning. Underwood tried to drive with his legs but the plastic held him. He waved the knife blindly above him; his strength fading into the silent chill of the water.

He pushed again and suddenly he was free. Underwood drove upwards as powerfully as his weakened body would allow. His chest, desperate for air, contracted involuntarily. He drew silty water into his lungs. Panicking and in agony his head finally broke the surface of the water after nearly two minutes' immersion. He gasped and choked, coughing the filthy water from his body. His eyes tried to focus on the jetty. It was about ten yards away. He kicked hard until his arms grabbed and hung onto the wooden leg of the little pier.

He was alive. Underwood gripped the wooden beam with all his remaining strength as he tried to understand what had happened to him. Water lapped at the sides of his face. It stank of shit. His broken nose raged angrily at him. Underwood didn't care. He could hear sirens; police sirens and they were nearby. The lights of another container ship slid across the distant water. He hung in the darkness and stared, as if hypnotised.

He had chosen to live. Despite all his petty-minded, self-destructive bullshit, all the mental agonies he had imposed on himself and others, when the moment of choice had come, he had chosen life. In the freezing, black waters of the North Sea on Monday 21st October 2002, John Underwood had wanted to survive.

As his breath and strength returned, Underwood looked up and around him. There was no sign of Garrod. When he was confident enough to move, Underwood let go of the wooden beam, turned and swam for the shore.

Bartholomew Garrod drove west on the A133 towards Colchester and eventually picked up the A604, the road that would take him back to Cambridgeshire. He was careful to keep within the speed limits. He knew that there would be traffic police about and he did not want to attract attention. He twiddled the tuning dial on his radio seeking out an old tune to keep him company. He tuned noisily through thumping house music and the news before he found a Sinatra tune he could tap along to. There was a bar of chocolate in his pocket that he had bought at a service station earlier. He unwrapped it with one hand as he drove. It was delicious. Bartholomew Garrod had always possessed a sweet tooth. Alison Dexter would find that out soon enough.

His dishes clattered in the back of his van as Garrod chewed happily.

62.

At 9.53 p.m. that night, Dexter crashed through the entrance of the Accident and Emergency wing of Colchester Hospital. She showed her police ID at reception and was ushered into the recovery ward. John Underwood was sitting upright in a hospital bed, his busted nose distorting his facial features.

'Jesus Christ, John!' Dexter exclaimed. 'Are you all right?'

Underwood wanted to smile but smiling hurt. 'I'm fine. It feels like a lorry reversed into my face but otherwise I'm in good nick.'

'What happened?' There was genuine concern in Dexter's eyes as she sat next to him. Underwood was pleased to see that. Another emotion floated in their green depths too. Was it relief?

'I found his caravan. He found me.'

'You are lucky to be alive.'

'He knocked me out. Then I woke up in a dustbin bag at the bottom of Oakley Creek.'

'Bloody hell,' Dexter said.

'Yes.' Underwood saw shock in her eyes now. 'That was an interesting experience. Not quite the end to the evening that I'd envisaged.'

Dexter sat back in her chair. 'This is my fault, John. I should never have sent you down there on your own.'

'Don't be silly. It was my idea.'

Dexter smiled and for a moment her frustration and irritation at the man's former misconduct melted away. She could tell he was genuinely pleased to see her.

The moment passed: business as usual. Underwood saw the change in her expression.

'You want to know about the caravan, don't you?' he asked.

Dexter made a non-committal shrug of her shoulders. 'It's up to you. If you feel up to it.'

'There's not a whole lot to tell.' Underwood shifted uncomfortably. 'It's very plain. I didn't find anything significant. But I think Garrod has a taste for honey.'

'Honey?'

Underwood hesitated, he could not find the correct form of words. 'There were four honey jars in the caravan.'

'How does that help?'

Underwood did not want to impart the awful image that had formed in his mind. 'Look for places where he can buy honey: lots of it. I'll explain properly when I get out of here.'

'What, farm shops? Apiaries? That sort of thing?'

'Yes.' Underwood tried to banish the image from his mind: the pain helped.

'Was there anything about me?' Dexter asked quietly.

'Not that I could see. I wasn't in there for long. Is the caravan being checked by Essex plods?'

'As we speak,' Dexter replied. 'Do you think we spooked him? Getting that close I mean. You clearly took him by surprise.'

'You know the man better than me,' Underwood responded, trying not to imagine her sexually, the taste of her dipped in honey. 'What do you think?'

'He came back for me. I doubt he'll disappear until he's got me.'

'Don't talk like that,' Underwood remonstrated. 'We are catching up on this bastard. He's too big and ugly to vanish completely.'

'Did he look like the photofit?'

'He's heavier. The face is much rounder. He looks older too. We need to work up a new image for publication. I'll organise it.'

'You need to rest,' Dexter advised.

'I'm fine. Apart from the unbearable, fucking agony where my nose used to be.'

Dexter smiled. 'We found where he was working – an abattoir in Sawtry.'

'He's left already?'

'How did you know that?'

'You spoke in the past tense.'

'You are a pedantic wanker. He left there earlier today. We've pulled out. There's apparently a chance he might go back. The owner is under strict instructions to keep us posted.'

'He won't go back,' Underwood said quietly. 'He's no fool. The key to catching this guy is figuring out where he is based now.'

'That's always been the problem. We found the caravan though.'

'The site manager said that Garrod hadn't been back there for weeks, months even. Where has he been hiding since he left that squat at the Dog and Feathers?'

'Any ideas?'

'Missing persons, derelict accommodation,' Underwood said.

'What do you mean?'

'Check if anyone has been reported missing in the Sawtry area.'

'What's in your mind?'

'If he's been working in that part of the world, it stands to reason he has been living nearby. He would want to spend as little time on the roads as possible. There's speed cameras and traffic plods to contend with. Besides, I don't think that he can live the life he wants to live out of a van.'

'Why do you say that?'

'I think he might need a garden. Somewhere sheltered.'

'What for?'

Underwood did not want to tell her. The fate that awaited her if Garrod remained undetected was better left unanticipated. 'Privacy,' he said eventually.

Dexter looked at him, unconvinced. 'You can do better than that,' she suggested.

Underwood decided to change the subject. 'The

most important thing is you. What precautions are you taking?'

Dexter sighed, 'I can't do much more short of wearing a bloody suit of armour. I've moved out of the flat into a hotel.'

'Not in New Bolden?'

'No. Why?'

'He would probably have anticipated that.'

'I'm in Cambridge at the Holiday Inn. It's very secure.'

'Good.'

'I'm staying in the office mostly. We have two ARU officers based there. I never go out unaccompanied.'

'Are you varying your routine? You know, different routes to work, different times of day?'

'And a different car.'

Underwood nodded. 'That's good, Dex. Avoid repetition and patterns of behaviour. If he decides to have a crack at you, it will be at a bottleneck. Somewhere he knows you will have to visit: supermarket, cash point, hotel car park, crime scene even.'

'I know. I'm being very careful.'

Underwood felt he had to say something else.

'Alison, I owe you an apology. For the things that happened. I'm very sorry about that. I'm very sorry about Kelsi Hensy too. I can't imagine how that has made you feel.'

Dexter found it hard to look him in the eye.

'It's all right. You know me, hard as nails.'

'There is sometimes motive in madness, Alison. Even mine.' Underwood had so much that he wanted to tell her: the dilemma was whether he could bear to hurt her even more.

'What are you talking about?' She rubbed her eyes dry. 'Don't talk to me in fucking riddles. Why do men always churn out such bullshit?'

Underwood decided to seize the opportunity. 'OK. Listen to me then. You are not alone. I know I have intruded into your life more than I should have. That's because I want to be part of it. Alison, I am smart enough to realise that you have no special interest in me. I accept that. But I know that we could be good friends too.'

Dexter stood up. 'I think I better go now.'

Underwood felt his guts twist in the pain of separation. 'It's not just me,' he blurted out as she turned to leave, 'people care about you.'

Dexter stopped. 'People? What people? What are you talking about?'

The moment had come. Underwood's dilemma burned in him. Should he tell her? His motives were questionable. Did he really have her best interests at heart? Gary Dexter lay with a smashed spinal column in a whitewashed room in Leytonstone. How could that information possibly help his only daughter to move forward? It was just as likely to destroy her hope as to strengthen it. Does love demand the revelation of truth or the concealment of it? Underwood's instinct was that love could not exist in ignorance. However, his insecurity told him otherwise.

'Nothing,' he eventually muttered to his immediate shame, 'ignore me.'

63.

Tuesday, 22nd October 2002

Bartholomew Garrod was in a thoughtful mood. He had dug out a small pit that he had lined with plastic. Inside, he planned to soak the bitterness out of Alison Dexter's flesh. The bitterness he had seen her use to sour the mind of his brother in 1995; the bitterness that had driven Ray under the wheels of a police car. He was going to marinade it out of her. The conundrum was how to keep her alive long enough for the marinade to work.

Garrod had decided that he wanted her to be alive when he started to render the meat. Besides, he knew that Henry Braun would want a living body more than a dead one. A primitive form of breathing apparatus would clearly be necessary.

Garrod found a hose-pipe dumped amongst the rubbish underneath Craxten Fen Psychiatric Hospital's water tower. He sawed off a yard-long section. It was crude and success would depend on Dexter being conscious when he sank her into the honey pit. That might present logistical problems that he had not anticipated. It would clearly be easier to glaze the flesh after she was dead. However, Garrod wanted her conscious. He wanted her to feel the sweetness soaking into her. He wanted her to feel the sticky terror absorbing her.

Recruiting Henry Braun had been risky. However, the man was simple-minded. Given clear instructions and an irresistible sexual motive, he was confident that Braun would deliver. Besides, an extra pair of hands had proved useful to him in the past. Garrod sensed that time was running short. The previous night's discovery of a police officer at his caravan had unnerved him. For the second time in his career, Alison Dexter appeared to have stolen a march on him. Her capacity for surprise made her a worthy opponent. Consuming her would undoubtedly strengthen him.

He had considered a number of different recipes: choosing was part of the fun. A glaze seasoned with Dijon mustard and cloves appealed to him. Garrod considered how he could score the meat to ensure the juices were properly absorbed. He also favoured slow cooking to tenderise the meat.

His father liked slow cooking. Cornelius Garrod had taught him the basic skills of butchery. He had learned about cutting techniques; about the identification of glands; the history of the trade; weights and ratios.

'Into which regions do the hind limb glands of a pig drain?' Cornelius Garrod asked.

Bartholomew showed his father the areas on the diagram of a pig they had laid in front of them.

'Good. Now what are the chief points of a Romney Marsh sheep?'

Garrod lay in front of the glowing fireplace in his makeshift kitchen, drifting in and out of sleep. His father's ripe east London accent reached out from his memory.

'Explain how you would kill and dress a sheep.'

'Where would you locate the superficial inguinal glands?'

'Explain the process for making beef sausage in a mincer.'

'Identify the primal cuts of home-killed beef.'

'Animals have a structure. People have a structure. You can disassemble a cow or a man, the same way you can strip a gun or a motorbike. Every bit does something useful and every bit has a use to the butcher: muscle, glands, brain, even blood. You

can make pies out of blood, Bartholomew. A good butcher will waste as little as possible. Wasted product means wasted money. Of course, we need meat to live. There's no disgrace in that. It is an honourable thing to eat an animal. You should respect what you eat. Nature makes us that way. Pigs will eat each other given half a chance. There's nothing immoral in meat. It's just an asset the same as a piece of wood or a glass of water. We consume the asset.

'Now, when I was in the jungle, during the war, people lived by different rules. The Japanese were proud fighters. Scared the shit out of us. But they were honourable in a funny way. You know, we found a camp once and the Japs had eaten a British pilot. Can you believe it? Stripped and ate the bugger. They wouldn't eat the Burmese or the Indians. Oh no. That's because they had no respect for them. They didn't respect us after Singapore – what a cock up that was – but they grew to respect us. They saw we were just as mean, just as ruthless as they were. They ate that Hurricane pilot because they respected us. They wanted to be as strong and as powerful as we were. I've got a picture of him here. Look at this, Bartholomew.'

Bartholomew Garrod opened his eyes. He had forgotten about his photograph. He must have left it behind in the caravan. It would be impossible to retrieve it now. He cursed his stupidity. The last link between him and the bygone age of brutality and honour had disappeared.

All that remained now was the brutality.

64.

Underwood discharged himself from the hospital at 3 p.m. and headed home to his little flat on the outskirts of New Bolden. He was in considerable pain but he had an uneasy sense of urgency in his veins. His exchange with Dexter the previous evening had given him a sleepless night, in spite of several powerful tranquillisers. In the hot, half-light of the hospital ward in the small hours of the morning, Underwood had resolved the dilemma. He needed to change his clothes, take a significant amount of Nurofen then head south: to London.

Throughout the afternoon, Dexter and Harrison scoured missing persons reports for the area. They began by looking at Sawtry. When that proved fruitless they expanded the search area to cover the entire county. There were forty-three persons recorded as missing in the county over the previous month.

'This is going to take time,' Harrison observed.

'Frankly, Guv, I can't see it working.'

Dexter agreed. 'We should probably roll the dice anyway. Get the last known addresses for as many names on the list as you can. Remember that he would want a house with a garage and a garden.'

'Garden?'

'According to Underwood, he wants a garden,' Dexter explained. 'We should also draw up a list of derelict factories, disused RAF bases, that kind of thing. The Council probably have all that stuff on record.'

'How do you feel about us putting some plods in plain clothes and sending them up to Sandway's abattoir? At least then we'd have some faces on the ground if this bastard turns up again. I'm not sure I trust that Sandway geezer.'

'Can we spare the bodies?' Dexter asked.

'Not really. We are stretched pretty thin. It might be an idea though. Especially since we've found his caravan. He'll need clothes, food maybe. Sandway is probably his best bet if he hasn't disappeared altogether.'

'OK. You persuaded me.'

'What else is there?' Harrison asked.

'Underwood had some mad idea about honey. Where could you buy it in bulk?'

'Dunno. Supermarkets I suppose, bee keepers.'

'He thinks Garrod has a hard on for honey.'

'I'll check it out.'

'Other than that,' Dexter observed, 'we have bugger all.'

'It could be worse,' Harrison replied. 'A lot worse.'

Dexter thought of Underwood's smashed face. She thought of herself.

'Point taken,' she said quietly.

DI Mike Bevan entered the office.

'I'm sorry to disturb you guys. Alison, I need to speak with you about tomorrow.'

Dexter nodded. 'Are you all set?'

'Pretty much,' Bevan answered. 'Woollard is still unrepentant and not admitting much, but I'm confident that we'll get a conviction or two.'

'Once this Garrod business is done, we'll have Woollard for conspiracy to pervert justice as well,' Dexter added. 'He must be looking at a serious stretch.'

'Let's hope so,' Bevan said. 'I think you should be there. At least for the first session in case there are any procedural issues or questions about the liaison between my office and yours.'

Dexter was prepared for that. 'I agree. As I'm the Senior CID Officer here, I should probably come along.'

'You can chuck oranges at Woollard from the gallery,' Harrison interjected with a grin.

'Sharpened fifty pence pieces would do more damage,' Dexter replied, appreciating the joke.

Bevan smiled. 'I'll see you there.'

Once he had gone, Dexter and Harrison began to draft a statement for a police press conference the following morning.

65.

Wednesday, 23rd October 2002

The evidence presented against Woollard was compelling. Sitting in the public gallery above Court B of the Peterborough Court Centre, Alison Dexter couldn't see any way in which Woollard would escape the charges. She had been pleased to see that the jury was mainly female. She suspected that their sensitivity to animal cruelty crimes would be sharper.

The Counsel for the Crown put forward a series of powerful arguments against Woollard. The defendant was, he said, 'a notorious, nefarious individual'. He was someone 'well known both to Cambridgeshire Police and Cambridgeshire criminals'. The momentum of the case had begun to build. The Crown outlined the chronology of events up to and including the illegal dog fights that had taken place at Swanscombe Farm the previous month. Photographs, taken by Mike Bevan, were submitted as Prosecution Exhibits A, B and C. These showed various cars arriving at the farm on the night in question. The Crown then informed the Court that under the authority of a warrant, New Bolden Police had searched Swanscombe Farm. The results, he said, were compelling: illegal dog breeding, forensic evidence of prize fighting, documentation relating to the importation of dangerous dogs.

The case, according to the Prosecution, was utterly irrefutable. Woollard had committed a series of offences under UK laws governing animal welfare. Dexter was pleased that the Counsel listed the specific pieces of legislation for the jury. The very names seemed to condemn Woollard even more.

'Lest we underestimate the gravity of Mr Woollard's offences, I would like to reiterate exactly which laws we believe that the defendant has broken. These are the 1911 Protection of Animals Act, the 1973 Breeding of Dogs Act, the Dangerous Dogs Act of 1991, the second Breeding of Dogs Act – also 1991 – and the 1999 Breeding and Sale of Dogs Act.'

The silence of a crowded courtroom had always been a source of awe for Alison Dexter. It was part of the job that she enjoyed immensely.

'The Prosecution's case will show that these multiple offences were not accidental. Mr Woollard has systematically ignored and subverted this country's animal welfare legislation for a number of years. The result of this has been the imposition of untold suffering on several animals which are banned in the UK. Let the Court note that Mr Woollard has no exceptional licences granted for the possession and breeding of these animals nor had he ever applied for such licences. The Court should also note that he was deliberately obstructive during the official police search of his premises.'

Woollard stared impassively into space as the offences were listed and the central tenets of the Prosecution's case outlined. The Court adjourned for lunch at 12.30 p.m.

At roughly the same time, Underwood met DS Harrison on the stairs leading up to New Bolden CID.

'Joe, what's new?'

'Bloody hell!' Harrison exclaimed. 'You look like you've gone ten rounds with George Foreman.'

Underwood was not amused. 'This bastard is bigger than George Foreman. Trust me.'

'It's good to see you in any case,' Harrison said.

'Thanks. Is DI Dexter upstairs?' he asked.

'No. She's up at Peterborough for the Woollard hearing. She'll be in this afternoon.'

'I'll see her then.'

Underwood swiped his ID card through the computer lock on the entrance to the CID floor and wandered in. Sure enough, Dexter's office was empty. He noted with interest that she had locked the glass door. His desk was its usual chaotic sprawl of paper and files. He fetched himself a coffee from the machine; its plastic heat burned his tongue.

Bartholomew Garrod had proved himself a formidable opponent. Underwood's face bore witness to the man's physical strength. Their inability to capture him demonstrated his resilience. Underwood believed that part of Garrod's advantage was his age. Mature adults were less likely to act impulsively. In his experience, the easiest criminals to catch had been those hamstrung by youthful impetuosity. Violent offenders in their twenties or thirties tended to be driven more by emotion: anger or lust most commonly. Garrod's wisdom had prevented him from lunging at Alison Dexter in a way that would expose his location or master plan.

Underwood knew that the only person who would have studied Dexter's life and routine more avidly than Garrod was himself. After all, had he not recorded her personal information in a notebook? Had he not skulked in Kelsi Hensy's garden and watched her private life unfold in front of him? His thought process was gathering momentum. Undoubtedly, Garrod would try to seize Dexter at some point. But where? How?

Underwood gulped coffee as it began to cool in his hand. He put himself in Garrod's position. If he had wanted to abduct Dexter, he would want the choke points. There were certain places that she had to go: home for example, into the station for work. Underwood knew where Dexter liked to shop. He knew which entrance to the building she used. He knew details about Alison Dexter's personal life that no one else on the planet was aware of. That thought had previously empowered him. Now it made him feel rather seedy.

If he planned to grab Dexter, he would do it early in the morning or late at night. She liked to be in the office early in the morning. He could predict with some confidence when her alarm woke her, when she got into her car, which roads she would take to work. Underwood knew that Thursday was rubbish collection day in Dexter's street. That meant that at some point on Wednesday nights she would put her rubbish sacks out in front of her flat for collection the following morning. She always did that between ten and ten-thirty p.m. That was a choke point. He would grab her then.

And yet, that didn't help. Underwood realised that the flaw in his assessment was that it was based on an overload of information. He had built a level of knowledge of data relating to Alison Dexter that Garrod could not possibly match. Garrod would have to make the same assessment based upon much less information. He would look for the fixed points in Dexter's life. Where would her shadow stretch at particular times of the day? The fixed points were her home address and her place of work. Now, Underwood knew that Dexter had recently vacated her flat and moved to the Holiday Inn, Cambridge. Even if Garrod had located her flat, she wasn't there anymore.

That left one fixed point. Garrod knew that Dexter came to work at New Bolden CID every day. Could he snatch her in the car park – early in the morning or in the evening as she left? It was the most obvious place. Too obvious. The car park was always being used. The station was manned round the clock. The risk of grabbing her at the station was enormous, Underwood realised. Now, of course, she had a motorcycle escort whenever she left the station. That would make it hard for Garrod to follow her without being noticed; harder still to snatch her successfully.

Underwood drummed his fingers on the surface of his desktop. What was that old Sherlock Holmes quote? 'Once you eliminate the impossible only the truth remains' or something like that? Underwood's mind had eliminated the impossible. What was left?

Alison Dexter was a CID officer. What do CID officers do? Where do they go? They go to work, they go to crime scenes; they do press conferences like the one Harrison was giving.

They go to court.

Dexter was at Peterborough Crown Court. Underwood tried to focus. Could Garrod have anticipated her presence there? Surely not. Most of their cases were tried in Cambridge. Woollard was only being tried elsewhere because his farm fell within the orbit of Peterborough magistrates. The only other case that they had tried there recently was the prosecution of Nicholas Braun – another Peterborough resident. Underwood remembered watching Alison Dexter's uncomfortable TV interview on the front steps of the Court Centre.

A cold panic enveloped him: for a split second, he was struggling, thrashing underwater, desperately reaching for the light.

Then he was on his feet and shouting for assistance.

* * *

Alison Dexter met up with her new motorcycle escort at the entrance to the Peterborough Court Centre.

'You all right, Jamie?'

PC James Kemp nodded. 'We off then, Ma'am?'

'Yes. This case is a done deal,' she replied.

'Despatch said that you're parked in Draper Street.'

Dexter always parked in Draper Street whenever she came to Peterborough. 'That's right. I'll wait for you at the T-junction.'

The two separated as Dexter headed left to cross the main road and Kemp jogged down to his motorbike. Henry Braun, collar turned up and wearing a Yankees baseball cap, watched them split up from the relative obscurity of a shop doorway. Realising his moment had arrived, he closed his hand around the steel crowbar in his pocket and advanced on PC Jamie Kemp. Dexter dodged through traffic on the main road, feeling in her jacket pocket for the keys to her new Volkswagen.

'Morning cunt,' Braun said to PC Kemp a hundred yards away.

'What did you say?' Kemp shot back.

'I said "morning cunt",' said Braun with a smile. 'While you were poncing about on your bike yesterday, I was shagging your missus. I just wanted you to know that.'

Kemp left his keys in the ignition of his bike and

advanced on Braun. He could see DI Dexter turn right into Draper Street and disappear from his view. There was still a little time.

'Do we have a problem here, mate?' he asked.

'Only you, dickhead,' Braun spat back.

Kemp had heard enough. He reached for the radio microphone on his jacket and clicked 'transmit'. 'Despatch, this is Mobile Seven. Request assistance at Peterborough Court Centre...'

Before Kemp could finish his sentence, Braun swung his crowbar in a vicious arc across the front of Kemp's face. Blood and fragments of teeth flew through the air. Kemp staggered back and fell to the ground. Stunned passers by stopped and stared in shock at the bizarre scene that was unfolding in front of them. Determined to press home his advantage, Braun stepped up to Kemp and booted him hard twice in the side of the head. Satisfied that his victim was unlikely to get up in a hurry, Braun pushed over Kemp's police motorcycle and ran away from the crime scene as fast as he could.

Oblivious to this commotion, Alison Dexter walked the short distance down Draper Street to her Volkswagen. The narrow road was a useful parking spot in a busy town centre. It was especially convenient for the Court House; no more than a two minute walk. Today the road was busier though. Two transit vans were parked either side of her. The first had 'Excelsior Parcel Service' stamped in navy blue print on its side panel. She stepped in front of it and onto the road so she could access the driver's side of her car. As she stopped to open the door, she felt a sudden wrench of pain as powerful fingers closed around her mouth and dragged her backwards.

She screamed and lashed out frantically, throwing a clenched fist back into the face of the man she knew was Bartholomew Garrod.

'You'll have to do better than that,' Garrod snarled at her. Dexter felt his saliva drip on to her neck. She struggled desperately as he hauled her down the road towards his van. Now he had a huge arm around her neck and one around her waist. Trapped in a powerful bear hug, Dexter gasped for breath, wriggling and twisting violently in a panic-stricken attempt to break away. She knew that Kemp's motorcycle would appear at the top of Draper Street at any moment. All she had to do was to hang on for as long as she could.

They were at the back of the van now. Its doors were open. Dexter tried to wedge a foot against the bumper to prevent Garrod from pushing her inside. It worked for a couple of seconds, but the man was far too strong. Without breaking his grip, using the expertise of a professional prize fighter he turned Dexter around in his arms like a corkscrew in a wine bottle

'You're going to pay,' he said softly. 'Long and hard.'

Dexter tried to swing a punch in his groin, to no avail.

'Slow and messy,' he continued.

Panicking now, Dexter frantically thrashed at her assailant, screaming for assistance.

'Night, night,' said Garrod with a smile before slamming a vicious head butt against Dexter's forehead. She slumped in his arms, her head bleeding above her right eye and lolling back uselessly. He dumped her into the back of his van and tied her hands behind her back with a length of rope that he had stolen from Sandway's abattoir. This done, he rolled her onto her back. A dark stream of blood ran from the wound on her forehead; Garrod leaned forward and licked it.

It was as he had suspected.

Bitter.

He slammed the double doors of his transit van shut. His stomach was rumbling. Henry Braun had clearly done his job properly. Garrod was pleased that the risk had paid off. He drove up to the T-junction at the top of Draper Street. As he waited for a space in the traffic, Garrod could see a crowd had gathered at the entrance to the Court Centre. He hoped that Braun had not lingered at the scene. Despite the apparent success of their enterprise,

Garrod had a nagging feeling that the involvement of Braun might rebound uncomfortably on him. For now though, he was happy. He turned into the flow of traffic that had slowed to view the commotion at the court house and accelerated away from the chaos; his prize unconscious in the rear of his van.

66.

Twenty minutes later Underwood stood outside the Court House himself, furious at the slowness of his own mind. Jamie Kemp lay in the back of a nearby ambulance. A small group of onlookers still hung about hoping for something morbid to shock their minds out of senselessness. DS Harrison joined Underwood.

'Her car's over there, sir,' Harrison told him. 'The driver door is unlocked.'

Underwood understood the implication of Harrison's words. 'It looks like he's got her then. What the bloody hell happened here, Joe? Who clocked Kemp? Garrod can't have been in two places at the same time.'

'I agree. It looks like he's got someone helping him.' Harrison wracked his mind for possible explanations. 'Someone from London maybe: an old acquaintance. Or maybe somebody he met on the fighting circuit up here.'

'What do the witnesses say?' Underwood asked.

'Man in a baseball cap whacked Kemp in the face. He was about six feet apparently but no one saw his face. Nobody saw Dexter being taken but then Draper Street over there is out of sight from here. They wouldn't have seen anything. This was a classic bit of diversion. Divert attention and isolate Dexter. Some planning went into this.'

'We need road blocks on all the major routes out of here,' Underwood instructed, although he knew it was probably too late. 'Right now.'

'It'll take a bit of time, sir,' Harrison advised.

'Get on it,' Underwood snapped.

He had failed her. Garrod had Dexter. There was little he could do now. The man could be anywhere. He had evaded capture for years and had now secured his primary objective. Underwood suspected the man would disappear altogether. Leave the country or at least sink into distant anonymity. His heart sank. The miserable little scene that surrounded him drove him deeper. Rain was beginning to stain the concrete, making it smell. The spinning blue lights of the ambulance threw odd shadows along the ground; the pasty-faced locals peered back at him for stimulation, the dismal line of shops and advertisements grinned stupidly across the road. Traffic rumbled past.

An ambulance man approached Underwood.

'Inspector, we should get him to the hospital now. He still hasn't regained consciousness. We need to get him under a scanner.'

Underwood nodded; he had been hoping that Kemp would come round and provide a description of his assailant. His hopes were being snuffed out like candles after a funeral.

'I understand,' he said. 'If he wakes up and starts talking, let us know.'

'Will do.'

A moment or two later the siren on the ambulance started up as it pulled away from the crime scene. Underwood realised that, in all probability, he would never see Alison Dexter again. He would have to explain her death to her father: Gary Dexter smashed and paralysed on an east London bed. How could he do that? How could he sever the man's only remaining link with sanity?

Underwood tried not to dwell on that possibility.

Rain began to shiver at his neck. He found himself looking up at the CCTV security camera above the Discount HiFi Store. It pointed directly back at him.

Something drove him suddenly towards it.

67.

Bartholomew Garrod pulled up in front of Craxten Fen Psychiatric Hospital. The rain was falling more heavily now. It drummed against the roof of his van and tickled coldly at his neck when he climbed outside. Garrod didn't mind the rain. He found it energising.

It had taken him an eternity to reach this moment, this glorious moment. He wasn't sure how to feel. His emotions were awash: charged with sexuality, boiling with vengeance. He wrenched open the back doors of his van. Alison Dexter still lay unconscious within. Garrod rubbed his chin thoughtfully. He was struggling to resist temptation: the desire to debase her there and then. She was completely at his mercy and the realisation almost overwhelmed him.

However, he resisted. He wanted her awake when he started work. And he wanted her sweet. He leaned forward, hauling her upwards with his immense strength and slinging her limp frame over his right shoulder. As he carried her through the gap he had created in the steel fencing and then towards the rear of the building, he could not stop himself feeling for the key cuts: tenderloin, silverside, brisket. Eventually, he placed Alison Dexter on the floor of the special kitchen he had created for her.

Garrod had instructed Henry Braun to come up to Sawtry at midnight. By then the immediate furore over Dexter's abduction would have begun to settle back into the slow crawl of procedure. Being pursued by the British police was, Garrod felt, like being chased by a glacier.

Garrod knew that eventually the glacier would probably consume him. Eventually, he would get sloppy or some squirt in a uniform would spot him in a crowd. He was resigned to that eventuality. Only Alison Dexter had jumped ahead of the creeping, ponderous juggernaut of investigation. She had somehow made the connection between the Garrods and the death of Brian Patterson in 1995. Somehow, the police had located his caravan in Essex. That made her unusual and dangerous: worthy of consumption.

He stripped her to her knickers. They were made of black cotton and the label said they came from Marks and Spencer. He crushed the desire to peer inside. Her flesh was tight, wiry. She would undoubtedly yield less meat than Kelsi Hensy. However, her skin was entirely free of blemishes. Garrod kneeled and rolled her limp body from one side to the other. There wasn't a single mole or imperfection. He had never seen such perfectly smooth skin. Eventually, he found some faded scars around her wrists but they were barely visible.

Garrod felt his erection harden as he touched her, his giant hands moving across her body, enjoying his moment of triumph. It took considerable will power to return to the task of food preparation.

The rain began to slow outside. Garrod was satisfied that he could begin. He tied Dexter's wrists in front of her and bound her ankles tightly with rope. He stretched masking tape across her mouth. Satisfied that she would be unable to move when she came around, Garrod left the kitchen. One by one, he removed the giant tins of molasses that he had bought from Delaney's and rolled them out of the storage shed where he had secured them. The overgrown back lawn of the hospital squelched underfoot. Garrod uncovered the honey pit and checked for water infiltration. He was pleased to see that the lining of plastic sacks had worked. The pit would not leak in either direction.

The rain had stopped. He levered off the lid of the first tin, enjoying the sugary smell that it released into the air. Carefully, he emptied its contents into the pit. The thick, viscous fluid glooped pleasantly. He repeated the exercise with each of the other containers. The pit filled. As he had calculated, the molasses did not quite brim to the top of the hole. There would clearly be some displacement once its contents had been added.

Once the pit was complete, he covered it and returned to the kitchen.

Alison Dexter was still lying where he had left her. Now Garrod focused on the issue of respiration. He ripped the masking tape from her mouth. She groaned slightly as he did so. She was coming round. That suited him. He wanted her to be conscious in the pit. He picked up the plastic tube he had fashioned and inserted it into Alison Dexter's mouth. He then secured it in position by wrapping masking tape around and around her head. Once he was confident that the pipe would not slip, he stuffed cotton wool in each of her nostrils and completed the seal with the remainder of his tape. Her body shuddered for a second or two. Then, happily, he heard the rasp of her breath resonating through the hose-pipe. Garrod was delighted with his handiwork. The bottom half of her face was entirely blocked with tape and the breathing apparatus was functioning effectively. It looked as though someone had taped a giant cigar into her mouth. Grinning at the image, Garrod allowed himself a moment of contemplation. He spread some jam onto a slice of bread and munched away the immediacy of his appetite.

Maybe he would take off her knickers after all.

This done, Garrod decided that it was time to put her in the marinade. He picked her up in his powerful arms and carried her outside. He would have to be careful now. Her position in the pit would be vital. Garrod had deliberately sloped one of the pit walls to support her body after immersion. One end of the hose-pipe obviously needed exposure to the air. As delicately as his huge hands would allow, Garrod manoeuvred Dexter's naked body onto her back and slid her feet-first into the molasses. The dark fluid began to engulf her, crawling up her legs in an inexorable sticky tide. Garrod allowed Dexter's body to fall back slightly, her back against the sloping wall of the pit, her face and breathing tube pointing upwards. As her feet touched the bottom of the pit, Garrod reached into the thick, syrupy liquid and felt for her knees. He bent them and drew them up in front of her. Dexter's body slid further into the molasses until her breasts, shoulders and eventually her entire head was subsumed. Garrod felt her body come to rest against the walls and floor of the pit. He held the top of the hose-pipe in his hand. He could still hear her breathing. Molasses brimmed over the lips of the pit and onto the exposed soil around it.

Garrod used his free hand to haul the wooden tabletop along the ground to cover the hole again. He wedged the top of the pipe between the edge of the cover and the wall of the pit. Delicately, he let go. The tube pointed directly upwards into the air. She was breathing. Confident that it would not slip immediately, Garrod walked to the water tower, returning with one of the heavy sacks of refuse that had been dumped there. He laid it on the tabletop, weighting it against any movement from below. The pit was secure. He drove a wooden stake into the soil next to the pit and immobilised the breathing tube with a string tie.

He sat back on the wet ground. His work was complete. He was sweating. Garrod was beginning to tire more easily. He hoped that he wasn't ill. However, such things did not bother him. The first and second stages of his plan were complete: he had snatched Alison Dexter and placed her securely in his honey pit. As long as she didn't try to move too suddenly or violently, or swallow her tongue, he was confident that she would survive immersion.

He was marinating the bitch.

Ray would have enjoyed watching. Garrod could almost imagine his brother jumping up in excitement at his shoulder, shouting encouragement. Anticipating his dinner with childish enthusiasm. The idea was suddenly painful to him. Ray wasn't there and the person responsible was soaking in syrup a few yards away.

Garrod stood and headed back into the kitchen.

He looked at the resources at his disposal: onions, peppers and oils were not a problem. He had his knives and had also retrieved his pans from the caravan after dealing with the rogue copper that had arrived there. He wondered how best to render the meat. There would be steaks, some breast meat and sausages too. He had noticed that Alison Dexter had pretty feet. It had reminded him of a dish his father had cooked for him as a child. You boiled a cow's heel with carrots and some seasoning then cooled it into a jelly.

Jellied cow's heel: a real taste of London.

Garrod rooted through a shopping bag for some mint or parsley.

68.

Alison Dexter opened her eyes suddenly. They immediately stung terribly. The pain was insistent as if it was glued to her face.

Glue.

She tried to orientate herself. Her breathing became more rapid, and panicky. Her nose was blocked, her head forced backwards. Something was rammed into her mouth. Shallow, rasping breaths. Tightness across her face. Hard ground against her back.

Glue.

Cold glue was all around her; sucking at her, penetrating her. Pain seared against her tongue. Gasping for air. She was unable to move properly. Her head was forced backwards, upwards. She was breathing through a tube. It was some kind of snorkel.

Dexter tried to move her tongue away from the pipe that was jammed against it. She sucked desperately for air.

Where was she? Her wrists were tied. Her legs were drawn up in front of her, knees together. She could move them slightly. Dexter tried to lift her head. The pipe scraped against the inside of her mouth. She tasted blood.

Buried alive.

The awful thought exploded in her mind. Garrod had buried her alive. Had he cut her? She tried to assess her body. She twitched as many muscles as she could. Everything still seemed functional. Was she underwater? Dexter had the strange sense of her legs almost floating. Her arms met with gluey resistance as she tried to move them. With her feet and shoulders she felt out the limits of her confinement. Blood ran into the back of her throat. She tried to swallow it away.

Had he left her? Had Garrod sunk her into some swamp or cesspit? Feeding her with oxygen until the tube was blocked or sunk into the mud? The thought terrified her. She tried again to lift her head. Something pressed down heavily upon it. Hard ground pressed through the plastic underneath her into the small of her back. The pain was growing. She had pins and needles tingling in her feet.

Movement was impossible. Dexter tried desperately to think through her situation. To apply logic to the horrible suspension in which she now found herself. Rotting into glue was a thought that terrified her: better he came back and finished her off. At least then, she would go down fighting. The idea of being left to suck frantically at life until the will deserted you was almost too hideous for her to contemplate.

Then she realised that she was naked. The disgust she felt at the idea that Garrod had stripped or molested her while she was unconscious was quickly outweighed by another possibility: the possibility that he had stripped her for another reason. Dexter tried to think of explanations as she squirmed against the slippery walls of her captivity.

Then she remembered Underwood's strange suggestion that Garrod had a taste for honey.

She was being glazed.

69.

Underwood was sitting in Dexter's office at New Bolden CID. His initial despair had been replaced with a grim resolve. He would kill Bartholomew Garrod himself. He would dedicate his life to hunting the man down and discharging a shotgun cartridge into his face. Underwood tried hard not to think of what Garrod might, at that moment, be doing to Alison Dexter. Perhaps Garrod would not kill her immediately. The man had waited years to find Dexter, surely he would want to relish his victory. Maybe there was still time before she died. Underwood wondered if that was a good or a bad thing for Alison Dexter.

Harrison joined him in the office.

'Sorry it's taken so long, Guv. We had to put the CCTV tapes onto VHS format. Our equipment is so fucking slow. I've seen most of the footage. It's not great,' he said bitterly.

Underwood unlocked the TV and video cabinet that Dexter kept in her office. 'That's OK. Let's slam it in and see what it caught.'

Harrison inserted the video and pressed play. After a brief moment, a black and white image of the road in front of Peterborough Court Centre appeared before them.

'Right,' Harrison said, 'we've wound the tape to

start about a minute before the attack on Kemp. That's his motorbike to the far left of the shot.'

People and traffic criss-crossed in front of the camera. Underwood leaned forward. The footage was of poor quality. He instinctively sensed that the exercise would be futile.

Harrison pointed at the TV screen. 'There's Dexter and Kemp heading down the steps.' He pressed pause on the VCR and the image froze. 'Now look at the bottom of the picture. This guy in the jacket and baseball cap is Kemp's assailant.'

'OK.' Underwood could see the individual in question.

Harrison restarted the video. The man in the baseball cap crossed through the traffic almost immediately that Dexter and Kemp split up and headed in opposite directions. Dexter disappeared out of the right of the shot. Underwood wondered if he would ever see her again. He refocused on Kemp, now standing at his motorcycle.

'Now,' Harrison explained, 'baseball cap man confronts Kemp at his motorcycle. Unfortunately we can't see their faces or hear the exchange.'

Underwood watched the images unfold in front of him. He tensed as he saw the baseball cap man suddenly swing something viciously into Kemp's face. Kemp reeled backwards. His assailant continued the assault.

'Kemp gets a boot in the head for his trouble here,' Harrison murmured, 'then our boy does a runner.'

On the screen, the baseball cap man turned back towards the camera and ran across the road.

'There,' Underwood said, 'stop it there.'

Harrison obliged. The grainy image of Kemp's mysterious attacker appeared in front of them. It was a poor shot. The camera was too far away. The man's features were too indistinct.

Underwood peered at the picture. 'Who are you, you bastard?'

Harrison said it for him. 'It could be anyone, Guv. The picture is shit.'

Underwood could feel despair rising again in his throat. 'Can we get a still from the video? One of the forensic boys must be able to blow up this image, clean it up a bit possibly.'

'I'll take the tape downstairs,' Harrison agreed. 'They should be able to work something up.'

He hurried from the office a moment later. Underwood tried hard to understand the footage he had just seen. It was clearly a coordinated attack. Kemp had been liquidated to isolate Dexter. That clearly took a degree of organisation. Underwood found the notion confusing. It was not Garrod's typical modus operandi to involve others. Serial murderers worked alone. That was one of the basic characteristics of the beast.

Underwood opened Dexter's 'Primal Cut' case file. He flicked through the neatly typed pages, wincing at some of the pictures that the then DS Alison Dexter had seen fit to include. He realised quickly that Garrod had been unusual: atypical in terms of his assaults. Forensic evidence from the 'Primal Cut' murders had also implicated Raymond Garrod. Bartholomew had clearly been the organisational force behind the killings but he had not worked alone. The Garrod brothers had murdered and eaten their victims together. Underwood sensed that the two men must have had a terrifically strong bond. That kind of closeness was impossible to replicate. However, he had just seen photographic evidence that the abduction of Alison Dexter involved two men. Who would Garrod entrust with such a vital responsibility? It had to be somebody he could trust implicitly; somebody that he could exert control over; somebody with a vested interest in the successful completion of the project.

His mind ran up against an impenetrable wall. Trying to understand the motives of madmen had driven him distracted in the past; rendered him unable to function effectively in normal society. Underwood's mind was supple and flexible. He had the ability to squeeze it into the empty shapes made by madness. Unfortunately, those shapes left imprints. Sometimes, the distortions caused his logical mind to founder: like traffic slowing to observe an accident. He realised that his understanding of Bartholomew Garrod was limited. His investigation, without the clarity and insight of Alison Dexter, was in danger of breaking down altogether. He looked up at the clock. It was 5 p.m. Underwood feared that time was running out.

70.

Henry Braun had spent the afternoon in a state of heightened excitement. Firstly, he had driven directly from the Peterborough Court Centre to visit his brother Nick at Bunden Prison outside Cambridge. Although he feared that their conversation might be taped, Henry could not resist hinting to his brother about his impending enterprise.

'I've got a bird lined up tonight,' he whispered to his brother through the glass that separated them.

'Is that supposed to cheer me up?' asked Nicholas Braun bitterly. 'Because it don't.'

'It will cheer you up.' Henry desperately wanted to tell his brother about his part in the abduction of Alison Dexter. He managed to restrain himself. 'It's someone you know.'

'Who?'

'Your least favourite bitch,' Henry said with a wink.

Nicholas Braun thought his brother had gone mad. 'What are you talking about? Don't come here if you're going to talk shit.'

'Listen you twat,' Henry muttered, 'let's just say I will be putting a few things to rights on your behalf. Remember you told me about that bloke who wrote to you? George Francis. Me and him have worked something out.'

Nicholas shrugged. 'Whatever mate. I don't know what you're on about.'

'I'll bring you some pictures. Then you'll see what I mean.'

'I can't wait,' said Nicholas Braun without emotion, his mind flashing between irritation with his brother and the look on the face of his final victim when she realised what was about to happen to her. Prison gave you time to dwell on happy reminiscences.

'You'll just have to trust me, Nick,' Henry advised. 'You won't be disappointed.'

'Unless you are going to spring me out of here or bring me the head of that dyke copper on a silver platter, I can't see how you can avoid disappointing me.'

Henry Braun winked at his brother.

Nicholas frowned until the penny finally dropped.

Once he had returned home to Gorton Row, Henry Braun had found that time passed too slowly. Garrod had specified a location near Craxten Fen and a time to be there. However, during the drag of an unemployed Wednesday afternoon when boredom and sex soak through men's tired minds like honey, he became irritable and fidgety. He consoled himself with two cans of Special Brew and a bacon sandwich. Janice Braun watched him with her usual mixture of contempt and awe. She wanted to hate her brother-in-law but the pills wouldn't let her. They just made her sleepy and desensitised.

The clock crawled at a snail's pace. Henry Braun had a shower at 6.30 p.m. The infection was surging inside him: virulent with hatred and fizzy with beer.

71.

DS Harrison found Underwood staring out of the window of Alison Dexter's office as if he was looking into the black depths of his own failure.

'Guv. We have the still picture.'

Underwood turned without speaking and took the A4 sized photograph from Harrison.

'The boys tried to clean the image up but it's not

much better really,' Harrison continued.

Underwood nodded. They could at least now see some of the man's features. It was impossible to tell his hair colour but the picture was good enough that somebody might recognise it. There was something familiar about it.

'Let's circulate it,' Underwood said. 'Try to get it on the regional TV news. Get copies for the uniform monkeys and all our people. We'll make some posters up then distribute them all over town.'

Underwood looked again at the photograph. 'Does he look familiar to you? I'm sure I've seen this face before.'

Harrison looked harder at the picture. 'I don't know. I did have one thought on the way up but it won't help.'

'What thought?' Underwood asked.

'It won't help, Guv,' Harrison insisted.

'Tell me,' Underwood requested, 'we've got nothing else.'

Harrison shrugged. 'Give me the picture.'

Underwood placed the photograph on the desk in front of him.

Harrison placed his left hand over the white baseball cap so that only the face of Kemp's attacker was visible. 'Forget the hat, who does that remind you of?'

'Nobody. What's in your mind, Joe?'

'I think that looks like Nicholas Braun.'

'The rapist?' Underwood looked again at the photograph. 'But he's banged up.'

'I told you it was a waste of time.'

Underwood peered at the image on the desk before him. The more he looked, the more the face began to resemble the dark, mean features of Nicholas Braun. He tried to make them into something else, some other face that he could fix and identify. The shapes moved in front him. He was infuriated with himself and the cruel absurdity of his universe. Garrod was most likely – at that very moment – tearing up Alison Dexter for the sake of his lost brother. The best Underwood could do in response was to gawp at a photograph.

Lost brother.

'Oh fucking hell, Joe,' he said as realisation dawned brightly and painfully in his mind. 'Get me Nicholas Braun's case file.'

72.

It was eleven p.m. She had been marinating for over eight hours. She was still alive. Garrod had finished chopping onions and peppers. He left them in a covered dish ready for frying. He had opened two bottles of red wine to breathe. His preparations were almost complete. His cutting knives were aligned on the kitchen table, his cooking pans were greased, the table laid for dinner. There was one major job remaining. Garrod went outside and scrambled around in the back of his van for the meat hook that he had stolen from Sandway's abattoir. He found three appropriately sized screws in a hospital storage cupboard and returned to the kitchen. He stood on a chair and drilled into the top of the kitchen doorframe. It took him about ten minutes to fix the meat hook securely to the frame. She would hang from the hook and bleed into the washing up bowl beneath it. He hoped that the wood was strong enough to hold her weight.

73.

At the same time, Underwood and Harrison sat in an unmarked police car opposite the terraced houses of Gorton Row in Peterborough.

'The Brauns lived in the end terrace,' Harrison pointed out. 'What a shit tip this street is.'

Underwood stared through the windscreen. The house had no front garden and he doubted whether there was any privacy at the back. Moreover, there was no sign of a transit van fitting the description of Garrod's vehicle previously given to them by

Robert Sandway. It didn't look very promising. Harrison's radio buzzed.

'Sergeant, we have eyes on the suspect,' said DI Lisa Armstrong, one of the two Armed Response Officers seconded from Huntingdon. They had both been ordered to approach Braun's premises from the rear. They were clearly in position.

'What do you see?' Harrison asked.

A crackle and fizz of radio white noise filled the car.

'Male suspect and female sitting in living room. TV on. No one else visible,' Armstrong replied.

Underwood felt energy and hope draining from his body. Perhaps his hunch about Henry Braun had been wrong. Harrison was thinking similar thoughts.

'What do you want to do, Guv?' he asked quietly. 'You want us to go in?'

Underwood couldn't bring himself to answer. They had no grounds for entry other than a grainy CCTV photo image that, in truth, might have been anybody.

'Fuck!' Underwood slammed his hands against the steering wheel in frustration.

The radio crackled again. 'Male suspect standing. Suspect moving to front of the house. We have lost visual contact.'

Underwood looked up as the front of 11 Gorton

Row opened. Henry Braun walked out of his brother's house into the cold Cambridgeshire air.

'He's on the move,' said Harrison quietly.

Braun unlocked his battered white Ford Sierra and climbed inside. His headlights suddenly filled the street ahead of them. The car began to pull away. Underwood made an instant decision. He started his own car and, without turning on his headlights, pulled out into the street behind the Sierra. Harrison called in this information to the ARU team.

'ARU1 we are on the move. Get yourselves mobile. Suspect is heading south on Muldon Street. Looks like he's heading out of town. We are in pursuit. Head south and we will advise further.'

'Will do,' Armstrong replied, gesturing for her partner DS Murphy to join her.

Underwood hung back as far as he dared from the Sierra as it picked up speed in the outer limits of Peterborough then raced south-east towards Cambridge. He allowed another car to overtake him, obscuring him from Braun's rear view mirror. The Sierra was cutting through the dark at eighty miles per hour.

'He's in a big hurry,' Harrison observed.

Underwood nodded. 'Advise the ARU to head for Cambridge.'

His eyes fixed unwaveringly on the road ahead.

* * *

Garrod was ready. It was almost time to start cooking. He opened the back door and headed out into the darkness. His excitement was intense. Other than two slices of bread and jam, he had hardly eaten all day. He had deliberately worked up a ferocious appetite. The breathing tube still poked up from the honey pit. Garrod heaved the sack of concrete away from the pit and lifted the tabletop. In the moonlight the molasses appeared jet-black. He reached down into the cold syrupy pool and slid his right arm under Alison Dexter's legs. She wriggled in shock, trying forlornly to squirm away from him. He slid his left arm underneath her back and hauled her naked body up from the pit. Molasses slid from her skin onto the ground, smearing against his shirt. Dexter writhed and twisted in his arms, gasping at her breathing tube, trying to open her eyes through the sugary glue that had enclosed them. It was like trying to hold an eel but he managed.

Braun's Sierra turned right at a country crossroads. Harrison looked at his map.

'Looks like Craxten or Sawtry, Guv,' he observed. 'You think he's meeting Garrod at the abattoir?'

'Unlikely,' Underwood replied. 'My bet is on a private address. High fences. Nice and quiet.'

The ARU unit was apparently about five minutes behind them. Underwood began to wonder what his move would be when they arrived. If Braun met up with Garrod, he would have to intervene as quickly as possible. However, Underwood's previous encounter with Garrod had demonstrated that he would be unable to do much to stop the man. Unless he could cause some sort of distraction, delay the process until the ARU turned up. A signpost saying 'Craxten 2' flashed by on their left. He needed a plan quickly.

Henry Braun was too excited to consider checking his mirrors. The prospect of what lay in store was filling his imagination. Once he'd passed the village of Craxten, Braun slowed until the narrow track that led to the hospital appeared on his left. He drove slowly down the overgrown lane until the massive, desolate sprawl of Craxten Fen Psychiatric Hospital loomed ahead of him. He drew up at the gap in the steel fence that Garrod had described to him and then fumbled his possessions – camera, KY jelly, towel – into a rucksack.

Alison Dexter's eyes were open. She lay in a puddle of molasses on the kitchen floor. Her hands cuffed in front of her, her feet tied at the ankle. Bartholomew Garrod moved around in front of her, illuminated by the flickering half light of three paraffin lamps, dropping chopped vegetables into a frying pan. Dexter knew exactly what fate awaited her. She remembered the photographs from the 'Primal Cut' case file. She remembered the contents of the Garrods' refrigerator. She hoped that consciousness would fail her quickly. Garrod had removed the tubing from her mouth and most of the masking tape: she could at least now breathe through her nose although her mouth was sealed shut.

Garrod crouched down in front of her.

'Hello there,' he said through a giant yellow smile, 'you've woken up in time for dinner. Ain't that sweet?'

She tried to move away from him but his hands stretched under her armpits and dragged her up from the ground. Dexter now knew pure terror. Naked, glazed and unable to defend herself, she tried to make herself as limp and awkward as possible. Garrod struggled, one handed, to raise her arms in the air. She slipped and flopped and resisted as effectively as she could. However, eventually he lifted her handcuffs up to the meat hook that he had fixed into the doorframe and she dangled there, utterly helpless. Then, in her darkest most shame-filled moment, she heard footsteps in the adjoining corridor.

Garrod moved past her as she screamed soundlessly into her gag and walked into the doorway. He recognised the dark outline of Henry Braun.

'You're a bit early,' said Garrod as he admitted his guest.

'Couldn't wait,' said Braun with a grin. 'We all set?'

'Yes,' Garrod replied. 'She's in here.'

They walked through. 'Went off all right then?'

'Like a dream. You've had no contact from the police?' Garrod asked.

Henry Braun wasn't listening. He was standing, transfixed by the sight of Alison Dexter hanging naked in the doorway, glaze dripping from her body. Her eyes, for an instant pleading and hopeful, seemed to die as she recognised Braun and finally understood the horror of what awaited her.

'What's all that stuff all over her?' Braun whispered, riveted by the shocking image in front of him.

'Molasses. It's a kind of sugar syrup. Make her taste sweeter.' Garrod was enjoying the obvious awe he had engendered in Braun. Perhaps the man could be useful to him again in future. They had both lost their brothers. That created a bond of tragedy between the two of them.

Braun reached into his rucksack and pulled out a

Polaroid camera. He began taking pictures, placing each on Garrod's kitchen table as it was spat out of the camera.

'These are for my brother, bitch,' Braun whispered in Dexter's ear. He bent down in front of her and licked molasses from her stomach in a vertical line up to her neck. Dexter tensed and tried to wrench herself free of the meat hook. 'When I've finished, you'll wish you'd put me away, not him.'

Garrod poured some red wine into his frying pan. It sizzled happily.

Underwood's car pulled up outside the derelict hospital.

'There it is,' Harrison said pointing at the white Sierra parked ahead of them.

'Thank Christ for that,' Underwood muttered. They had momentarily lost contact with the car a minute or two previously. When Braun had turned off the main road, the police car had overshot the approach road. Underwood had feared the worst. Now they were back in the game.

'What is this place?' he asked.

Harrison used a torch to locate their current position on a map. 'Craxten Fen Psychiatric Hospital.'

'You are kidding me?' Underwood stared out at the huge building with considerable trepidation: madness lived inside.

'What's your plan?' Harrison asked.

'Where is the ARU?'

'At the crossroads. Five minutes maybe seven. You think we should wait?'

Underwood heard himself make a decision from within the shell of his fear.

'No. I think we should go in. My problem is I have no idea what to do when we get in there.'

Unarmed, he did not fancy his chances against Bartholomew Garrod. But then, Alison Dexter could be inside that building somewhere. If he was too late to help her, he knew he would never forgive himself.

'I'm going up there for a look,' he said. 'Stay here and direct the ARU. Call for back up, an ambulance, the SAS, whatever's available.'

'Will do.'

Underwood withdrew a torch from the glove compartment and climbed out of the car. He headed nervously towards the hospital, clambering through the break in the fence line just as Braun had done a minute or two previously. Underwood ducked down low against the stone wall of the east wing and moved as quickly as he could through the darkness. The front door was padlocked. He headed around the side of the building, passing gingerly through the maze of discarded machinery and below the looming silhouette of the water tower.

Underwood could smell cooking. He prayed to whatever God that still listened to him for help.

Inside, Bartholomew Garrod was almost ready. He lifted his frying pan from the heat of his cooking stove and placed it to one side. He picked up his favourite cutting knife and turned towards Alison Dexter. Braun had finished taking photo-graphs and was in the process of taking off his trousers. He saw Garrod approaching with a knife.

'Jesus Christ, George!' he exclaimed. 'What are you going to do with that?'

'I'm going to start with some silverside, then maybe move on to some rump fillet,' Garrod replied. 'Get out of the way. I've waited a long time for this.'

Braun stood with his trousers around his ankles, barring Garrod's way. 'Hang on, mate. I thought I was going to slip her one before you did your business with her. I'm not doing this for charity you know. We had an arrangement.'

'Do you think I'd eat anything after you'd been crawling all over it?' Garrod spat back. 'Get out of my way, sonny. I'll take what I want and you can shag whatever's left.'

Garrod moved quickly: he flung Braun against

the kitchen wall and now stood in front of Dexter, his knife gleaming. 'And now, dearie, you know what's coming next, don't you?'

Dexter's eyes followed the point of the knife as it moved gently down her body. 'Silverside is one of my favourite cuts. It's that bit of your inner thigh just under your arse.' He used his foot to slide a washing up bowl underneath her.

John Underwood was standing at the door.

Braun saw him first. 'Who the fuck is this bloke?' he asked Garrod as he pulled his jeans back up to his waist.

Garrod turned to face the man he had battered and left for dead in the North Sea.

'He's a copper, you stupid bastard,' Garrod shouted back. 'They followed you.' Furious at his partner's idiocy, Garrod turned and plunged his cutting knife straight into Braun's solar plexus. Stunned, Braun staggered backwards gasping for air, flailing hopelessly before tripping in his half-pulled up trousers and falling to the kitchen floor.

Underwood stepped into the kitchen. 'Bartholomew Garrod, you have the right to remain silent.' Underwood's warning sounded pathetic but he could see Dexter was still alive and he had to play for time. 'I should warn you that anything you say might be used against you.'

Garrod laughed. 'Come on then, arrest me. I'll

rip your fucking head off. You should have stayed at the bottom of the North Sea. I'll have your tongue out for that.'

Underwood exchanged a glance with Dexter. Her eyes were either pleading with him to help or warning him to run away. 'The place is surrounded. There are armed police outside. Give yourself up now. Don't end up like that idiot brother of yours.'

Cold hatred flickered in Garrod's eyes. 'What did you say?'

'You had some simple-minded oaf in tow in London. But you let him down, didn't you? You left him to take the rap while you did a runner. Real fraternal love that is. I bet you still have nightmares about leaving him behind. You see, I know all about you Bartholomew. This little mess you've created isn't going to bring him back.'

'What can you possibly know about me?'

'I know about the photo.' Underwood said pulling the picture he had found in Garrod's caravan from his pocket. 'Is that what got you started? Daddy's photo collection?'

Garrod saw his photo in Underwood's hand. 'Give it to me,' he said, 'give me the picture and I won't kill you.'

Underwood shook his head. 'It doesn't work like that.' He backed up, stepping out of the kitchen door and into the corridor. Garrod followed him out. Underwood took a cigarette lighter from his pocket.

Dexter tried to strain her eyes into the darkness beyond the kitchen to see what was happening. She hoped sincerely that Underwood had a plan. His words had a very empty ring to them. She hung uselessly in the air and watched Henry Braun's life pump away in front of her.

Underwood continued backing up. They were both outside now, on the lawn next to the back entrance to the kitchen corridor. Garrod looked from side to side. There were no other policemen to be seen. Once again this idiotic copper had made the mistake of facing him alone.

'Give yourself up Bartholomew,' Underwood said.

'Don't be silly,' Garrod snarled, bearing down on him. 'I'm having too much fun.'

'You must be even thicker than your brother then,' Underwood laughed. 'I thought he was the family freak.' He suddenly sparked the flint on his cigarette lighter: it flamed brightly. Underwood set fire to Garrod's photograph and held it up as it burned.

Furious and seeing an opportunity, Garrod lunged forward and slammed both hands into Underwood's chest. The speed and ferocity of the attack sent Underwood staggering off balance, stumbling backwards into the honey pit. Molasses welled around him, Garrod was above him in an instant: his monstrous hands forcing Underwood's head down into the deep pool of brown syrup. Underwood thrashed helplessly and tried desperately not to breathe in the mess that was engulfing him.

'You see,' Garrod said, 'the problem with dumb animals is that they get slaughtered. It's the law of nature. It's not their fault and we shouldn't even pity them. They are meant to be slaughtered from the very moment that they're born.'

Underwood was on the verge of losing consciousness. He was fading, he had nothing to respond to Garrod's huge strength and superior position. He went limp in the hope that Garrod might let go. He didn't. Underwood's broken nose pressed agonisingly against the hard plastic lining of the honey pit. He knew that he only had seconds remaining.

Harrison had directed the ARU team through the fencing and towards the hospital. Armstrong pushed on down the alley at the side of the east wing, her Glock pistol pointed directly in front of her. Harrison and Murphy – the other armed officer – ran a flanking manoeuvre around the west side of the hospital.

Armstrong rounded the side of the building first and, through the darkness, saw the huge bulk of Bartholomew Garrod hunched over the pit in the centre of the lawn.

'Cambridge police!' she shouted. 'Stand up and put your hands above your head!'

Garrod released his grip on Underwood and turned to face the source of the voice. For the first time that night, he began to sense that events were sliding away from him. He started to walk towards the voice. Behind him, an exhausted John Underwood hauled himself out of the pit trying, agonisingly, to catch his breath.

'Stand still or I will shoot!' Armstrong warned him. Garrod was closing on her rapidly. She levelled her gun and fired. The shot cracked out, echoing across the huge still space of Craxten Fen. The bullet smashed into Garrod's right shoulder. The impact made him stagger sideways but, to Armstrong's horror and surprise, the man kept coming at her. The second shot hit him in the stomach a split second before he crashed into her and drove her hard into the hospital wall snapping a number of her ribs.

Armstrong's Glock fell to the ground. Garrod, wounded but still functional, flung the broken ARU officer down and turned back towards the kitchen. He could hear other voices approaching through the darkness. Other policemen would soon be on him. He was not afraid to die: only of dying unavenged. He staggered back to the kitchen corridor, blood oozing from the two bullet wounds. Seeing this, Underwood got uneasily to his feet.

Garrod lurched past Alison Dexter and fell against his kitchen table, his feet sliding in the pool of blood made by Braun's terrible chest wound. He clattered amongst his tools until he found an appropriately long cutting knife. Gutting her would have to suffice. His strength was ebbing away rapidly, the room starting to swim around him. He steadied himself and turned towards Alison Dexter.

John Underwood stood between them, Lisa Armstrong's Glock pistol aimed squarely at the centre of Garrod's forehead.

'Put the knife down,' Underwood said. 'It's over Bartholomew.'

Garrod half heard the words. The room was spinning: pain wracked his body at every heartbeat. He could smell onions cooking and hear Ray shouting at him:

'Ah ate some bit of him, Bollamew!'

Alison Dexter hung a few feet away from him. Garrod decided to take her with him; drag her into the honey pit for eternity; he would chew at her soul instead of her body.

He lunged forwards.

Underwood fired the Glock directly into the centre of Garrod's forehead. Garrod's head snapped back and the prize fighter fell to the ground. Underwood stepped over him and fired another shot into the fallen man's head. Garrod's body spasmed at the impact. Then he fired again; power and satisfaction surged through the weapon. Underwood stared at the animal he had put to the ground.

'Guv! That's enough!' Harrison shouted as he and Murphy charged through the back door, 'enough!'

Underwood let his grip relax and the Glock pistol fell to the floor.

Harrison reached up and unhooked Dexter's hands from the meat hook; she slumped exhausted into his arms.

Underwood studied the holes he had put in Garrod's head. Inexplicably, he started to laugh.

REDEMPTION

74.

Monday, 28th October 2002

Bob Woollard stood as Judge Arthur Barnard addressed the foreman of the jury. Barnard had a rich, deep tone to his voice that made DI Mike Bevan imagine that the God of Justice himself had come to Peterborough.

'How do you find the defendant Mr Robert Woollard on the charge of "overloading, infuriating and terrifying" animals under Section A of the 1991 Protection of Animals Act?'

The foreman, a physics teacher from Newmarket, cleared his throat. 'Guilty.'

'On charge two, that the defendant Mr Robert Woollard "caused, procured or assisted in the fighting of animals and managed premises for that purpose", do you find him guilty or not guilty?'

'Guilty, your worship.'

'Guilty, your honour,' the judge corrected him with the ghost of a smile lurking on his lips.

Woollard was also found guilty of four additional charges relating to the breeding and sale of illegal dogs. After a brief deliberation, Judge Barnard sentenced him to a minimum of three years' imprisonment: the maximum permitted by the existing legislation. In the Public Gallery, DI Mike Bevan punched a clenched fist into the palm of his hand.

Bevan looked across the courtroom at Woollard, keen to try and read the man's reaction. The sentence would send a message out into the dog fighting community that none of them was untouchable. Hopefully, it would disrupt the Cambridgeshire circuit enough to jeopardise its existence altogether. There was also the comforting thought that Woollard would soon be facing separate charges of conspiracy to pervert the course of justice relating to the murder of Leonard Shaw.

As Woollard was led away, he looked up at the gallery and impassively met Bevan's gaze.

The policeman allowed himself a smile.

75.

Sandway's abattoir struggled to continue its normal business. Since the capture of Bartholomew Garrod, a number of police officers had visited the processing plant and conducted interviews with

Robert Sandway and his employees. The unwanted publicity had been damaging. The Ministry had scheduled a full-scale inspection. Preparation for this was disrupting his normal operating procedures. He could not afford such distractions. Time in his business was undoubtedly money and he had no desire to see his narrow profit margins crushed any further.

Sandway was still a minor player in the industry. Economies of scale were loaded against him. Over nine hundred million animals are slaughtered annually in Britain. Only seventy thousand of them were rendered at his plant in 2001. His business was always peripheral; its margins wafer thin, its survival dependent on a narrow base of local buyers and a shallow stream of cash flows. Now Sandway could almost feel the ministry pithing stick scratching at his brain.

Only ruthless efficiency and attention to the regulatory framework could keep his business alive. Ironically, nobody had made those points more strongly than the man he now knew as Bartholomew Garrod.

76.

Tuesday, 29th October 2002

At her suggestion, DI Alison Dexter met John Underwood for lunch in Cambridge. She was sitting at the vulnerable table next to the darts board of the Cross Keys on Lensfield Road. He found her mood difficult to read. The burning intelligence in her eyes seemed, for once, to be clouded with something else. Underwood sensed it was vulnerability. Or shame. Either way, she looked half-pleased to see him. This, at least, was progress. He chewed thoughtfully on a steak and kidney pie as she talked business.

'McInally called me at the hotel,' she said crisply. 'He said that you'd been in touch.'

'I knew that he'd be concerned about you,' Underwood replied.

'I appreciate it,' Dexter said quietly.

'How much longer will you stay at the hotel?' Underwood asked. 'It's safe to come home now.'

'I know. It just doesn't feel right yet.'

For the millionth time, her cold beauty drove an ice pick through his heart.

'Everything is chugging along at the office anyway,' Underwood volunteered eventually. 'Harrison and I are tying up the Leonard Shaw case.

We've certainly got enough to have Woollard and that hairy little bollock Keith Gwynne for conspiracy.'

'What have they done with Garrod's body?' Dexter asked.

'Leach has been handling the post-mortem. Frankly, my opinion is that they should have incinerated the bastard immediately but there is apparently a question of procedure. Some concern has been expressed at a high level about the way I handled the matter.'

'How do you mean?'

Underwood took a sip of lemonade and pretended it was gin. 'The Chief Super is unhappy that I shot Garrod three times. Unnecessary force he reckons. Given my psychiatric record, I can understand his concern.'

'What a load of shit!' Dexter snorted. 'I'd have done the same thing. I will speak to the Chief Super on your behalf.'

'You don't owe me anything,' Underwood replied.

'Let's not talk about that, John,' Dexter said, trying to bury the contempt she felt for Underwood's clandestine observation of her private life with the knowledge that without him she would undoubtedly be dead. 'If you can assure me that stuff is all behind you, I am happy to give you the benefit of the doubt. John, since Julia left, you have had a terrible time of it. I can accept that your behaviour towards me is simply a product of that.'

Underwood struggled to find a form of words that would express his true emotions without confounding his position. 'I feel a degree of responsibility towards you.'

'I don't need anyone to take responsibility for me.'

There was an edge to her voice now that unsettled him. Underwood knew that he had pushed Alison Dexter to the limits of her patience.

'Can I ask you a question?' Dexter asked him.

'Go ahead.'

She looked uncomfortable, the memory of her humiliation pressing at the front of her brain. 'How many people know about what happened?'

'Only Harrison and myself know the full story,' Underwood said. 'I wrote the full report.'

'I don't want people gossiping about me,' Dexter said quietly. 'About the way you found me.'

'I understand that.' Underwood could see the shame in her eyes. It was upsetting.

'I don't want to become a dirty story for canteen coppers.'

'My report is very sparse on that kind of detail. I stated that you were unconscious and tied up when we arrived. As I see it, beyond that you played no part in the proceedings.'

'What happened to the camera that Braun was using?' Dexter asked anxiously. 'He took pictures of me.'

'How angry would you be if I told you that I destroyed evidence from a crime scene?' Underwood asked with a faint smile.

'You destroyed it?' Dexter asked suspiciously.

Underwood nodded. On the night of Garrod's death, he had taken Henry Braun's camera and Polaroid exposures from the kitchen floor at Craxten Fen Psychiatric Hospital. The camera had not been mentioned in his report. For a dark, sinking moment he had thought of keeping the pictures for himself. Then, disgusted by his own perversity, he had burned them and smashed up the camera. Somehow, he needed to scorch that particular infection from his mind.

'I burned everything,' he told her. 'The whole lot.'

She looked hard into his eyes, seeking out some flicker of deceit, some hint that he was trying to fool her. She saw nothing.

'Thank you,' she said simply.

Underwood looked out of the window. 'It's stopped raining. Shall we go for a walk?'

Traffic splashed noisily up Trumpington Street.

Underwood led Dexter down a side alley next to St Peter's Terrace that led to the back of Peterhouse Deer Park. It was Underwood's favourite college garden. Gravel crunched beneath them on the pathway.

'Are we allowed in here?' Dexter asked. 'I can't cope with some stroppy college porter throwing me off the premises.'

'If they do, tell them we'll come back with a warrant.'

They walked for a moment or two in silence. Birds squawked on the nearby Cam. The white bulk of the Fitzwilliam Museum loomed to their right. Underwood felt the pain nagging again in his chest. It drove him on.

'Alison, your friendship is important to me,' he said eventually. 'I feel terrible that I've jeopardised that.'

'We can be friends, John,' Dexter said. 'I can accept that.'

Underwood nodded. He still had a single card to play. However, raising the stakes was dangerous. He faced losing everything.

'I took another liberty,' he said. 'When I spoke to McInally earlier in the week, I said that we'd have lunch with him.'

'When?'

'Tomorrow. I know it's short notice but he's desperate to see you and since you're on leave, I thought you might be glad of the company.'

Dexter thought about the last two weeks: the worst of her life. She thought of the shame she felt at the death of Kelsi Hensy, the fury she had focused on John Underwood, the terror she had felt as she hung naked in front of Henry Braun and Bartholomew Garrod. She was emotionally exhausted. But she was also tired of being alone.

'Where are we meeting him?' she asked.

'London,' Underwood said briskly. 'I'll pick you up from the hotel. I thought you might appreciate getting out of Cambridgeshire for an afternoon.'

'Fair enough,' Dexter nodded. 'It'll be good to see the old sod.'

As they approached the side of the old college, the crumbling stonework of its thirteenth-century hall loomed in front of them. Underwood had found their conversation unsatisfying. He had pushed Dexter as far as he dared. She had assured him of friendship and that at least was a cause of optimism. Was it enough?

Dexter turned and looked back across the gardens that they had just traversed. There was colour in her face, a blush of pink on her pale cheeks wrought by the cold Cambridgeshire air. 'It's beautiful here,' she said softly.

Maybe that was enough.

* * *

Underwood left her in King's Parade and headed for his car up on the third level of the Lion Yard car park. He drove south through the narrow crowded streets of the city towards Addenbrookes Hospital. He had cancelled his two previous appointments to see the oncology consultant. Fear and resignation had previously stopped Underwood from seeking treatment for the pain that was growing inside him. In the depths of his despair, he had seen the coming darkness as a blessed relief. Perhaps it would also be an opportunity to revenge himself upon the wife that had deserted him and the woman he had fallen in love with. Why then bother to seek diagnosis and treatment? Underwood had reasoned that his fear of dying was less than his fear of living on in desolation.

Now he had two reasons to stay alive. The first was his memory – all too vivid – of scrambling for freedom and air at the bottom of Oakley Creek. Death had stared him directly in the eye then and Underwood had blinked first. He remembered his desperate, writhing struggle to survive. His instinct had been to fight death not to passively accept his fate.

Secondly, his conversation with Alison Dexter that afternoon had given him a small measure of hope. She had – at least – assured him that there was a possibility of them remaining friends. That was something. The prospect of sharing lunches with Alison Dexter, of basking in the light of her fierce intelligence, of watching her skin blush red in the cold air were all powerful incentives to survive.

Or were they? Underwood pulled up in a space near the main entrance of Addenbrookes Hospital. The immediacy of his situation unnerved him. He found his resolve faltering. His friendship with Dexter had been one of the factors that characterised his current state of affairs. Was her friendship – friendship from a distance – an adequate reason to stay alive? He suddenly doubted it. There is no emotion more debilitating than unrequited love. Underwood doubted that he could play the thwarted, melancholy hero of a tortuous courtly love poem. The ghosts of the future were gathering around him. He sensed his future self, wracked with cancer and loneliness, standing at the entrance to the hospital remembering the moment that he currently occupied. Nature had given him a way out: a way to shuffle into the darkness with dignity. He had the option of a comfortable death. Now, faced again with a straight choice, Underwood lapsed into indecision.

The car clock told him it was 3.04 p.m. He was already late for his appointment.

Underwood's mind tried desperately to understand itself.

* * *

Alison Dexter walked through Cambridge town centre feeling strength and self-confidence slowly seeping back into her flesh. She had always found Cambridge a peculiar place. It always seemed so open and bleak: beautiful in its desolation. She thought King's College Chapel was the most dramatically desolate building she had ever seen: a construction desperately trying to outreach its own ugliness and touch beauty.

She had touched beauty. Kelsi Hensy had been beautiful. In the heat of their passion, Dexter had momentarily outreached her mental ugliness; exceeded the ordinariness of existence. And yet, the ghosts of her past had desecrated that beauty. She headed up King's Parade towards the market square. Was she wrong to blame herself? Had Bartholomew Garrod merely been the manifestation of all the ugliness within her? He was a remnant of the life she had tried to run away from. Undoubtedly, the man was a monster but Dexter kept coming back to the same conclusion. If Kelsi Hensy had never met her, she would still be alive. That made the disaster hers alone. It was a responsibility she would have to accept and carry with her.

The market square teemed with people. Students, townies and tourists perused the stalls. Dexter found herself drifting through the crowd. The energy and chatter, movement and laughter, reminded her that chaotically and painfully, mundane and beautiful, life goes on. Garrod was dead. The memory of her capture and humiliation would live with her but memories were manageable. Even Underwood was now showing flashes of sanity that were almost endearing.

Almost.

She was in front of a meat stall. The sight of dead flesh made her immediately want to wretch. Dexter was about to walk away when she saw the teenage boy sitting at the side of the stool eating a sandwich. She stared at him. Something was unsettling her.

'Can I help you, love?' Jack Chissel asked. As he spoke a piece of pig kidney fell out of his mouth and on to his apron.

'What are you eating?' she asked.

'It's called 'Pig's Fry', darling,' came the greasy response. 'You want some?'

The market swam around her; the noise receded and then welled up into a terrible scream. Dexter felt Garrod's presence suddenly at the front of her mind; his hands pulling her guts from her stomach, his teeth tearing the flesh from her bones; the grease of her body smeared on his lips; the machinery of her body stripped and dismantled; the monstrousness of the world she had chosen to inhabit.

She suddenly, inexplicably, missed John Underwood.

77.

Wednesday, 30th October 2002

Underwood collected Alison Dexter from the Cambridge Holiday Inn, and headed towards the M11 just outside Cambridge. He drove them south towards London, eventually leaving the motorway at junction four. The grey complexities of London unwound around them. Dexter began to recognise the roads as they drove through Wanstead towards Leyton.

They met DCI Paddy McInally at Leyton CID. He drove them down to the Blind Beggar on the Mile End Road. Underwood found McInally excellent company. The man's profoundly filthy sense of humour had him laughing into his pint glass. Dexter seemed to be enjoying herself too. Underwood noticed that her voice and manner had changed slightly. Maybe it was the presence of her former boss, more likely it was the effect of being in London. The city had an energy, a tension that Cambridgeshire lacked. Dexter was back in her natural habitat.

McInally took an enormous swig of London Pride beer and launched into another joke.

'Here's one for you, Dexy,' he spluttered. 'There's this poof in the back of a squad car, right?'

Dexter rolled her eyes. 'Right,' she said with mock weariness.

McInally grinned. 'So the copper asks him "Have you ever been picked up by the fuzz before?" And the poof says, "no but I've been swung around by me bollocks."'

He laughed uproariously.

'Isn't that called a "Hampstead Handshake?"' Dexter replied.

Underwood listened enviously to the exchange between his two colleagues. He had rarely enjoyed any banter with Dexter. There was a warmth between her and McInally that he could never hope to replicate. Now Garrod was out of the picture, Underwood feared the worst. McInally seemed to anticipate his concern.

'Look, I have an ulterior motive for bringing you down here today, Dexy. I mentioned it to John on the phone the other night.'

'I knew that if you were buying there had to be a catch,' Dexter shot back. 'Let's have it then.'

McInally looked over at Underwood who was staring intently into his pint glass. 'An opening has come up here in Leyton.'

'What sort of opening?' Dexter asked suspiciously.

'I'm taking early retirement,' McInally continued. 'That means there's a DCI job going.

You've got local knowledge. I could recommend that you replace me.'

Underwood shifted uncomfortably in his chair. He tried to smile but could not look Dexter in the eye. He knew this was coming but it still made his guts churn horribly.

'I don't know,' Dexter responded. 'It's a huge job.'

'You're going to get upped sooner or later,' McInally said. 'This could be the opportunity. You're a London girl, you even know some of the villains we deal with. I can't think of anybody better.'

The ground opened up in front of Underwood. His saw the long, twisting slide to Hell.

'Besides, you've got the energy, Dexy,' McInally continued. 'I've let things sink a little bit over the last year or two. This department needs a pocket battleship.'

Dexter watched Underwood's expression carefully. The man was staring at the carpet now. Only his drumming fingers betrayed his inner turmoil.

'I don't know, Paddy,' Dexter said. 'I'd have to think about it, but thank you.'

'Don't thank me, thank old Johnny boy here.'

Dexter's shock was profound. 'This was your idea?' she asked Underwood.

'I know you've been unhappy,' Underwood replied. 'When Paddy told me he was thinking of packing it in, I thought of you.'

Dexter was unsure whether to be angry or grateful at Underwood's latest intervention in her life. The prospect of returning to London was an alluring one. She had always found Cambridgeshire desperately empty: at least, until recently. There was an obvious logic to her replacing McInally. She was his protégée but she had been away from the area long enough to be apolitical. That would make her an attractive candidate. It was tempting. In London she could rebuild an infrastructure to support her. Why then was she not jumping all over McInally's offer?

An hour later McInally said goodbye to Underwood and Dexter outside Leyton police station. Dexter promised to call him the following day with a response. Underwood began to weave his way through London traffic.

'So that was your idea then, John?' Dexter said eventually.

He nodded. Despair was eating at his soul.

'You would be happy for me to leave?'

'I wouldn't be happy at all,' he said. 'But that's not really the point is it?'

'The point is that you are prepared for me to leave,' Dexter said.

'You are a London girl, Alison. Always will be.'

'You know something, John. You are the only person that calls me Alison.'

'I'm sorry.'

'I didn't mean that,' Dexter corrected him. 'You heard McInally back there. To him I'm always "Dexy" or even "Sexy Dexy" for God's sake. The people in the office all call me "Dexter", "Guv" or worse. Kelsi Hensy called me "Ali". I'm tired of people reshaping me into a form that makes me manageable, palatable to them.'

'I don't see your point.' Underwood frowned.

'My name is Alison,' she said. 'But only two people have ever called me that. You're one of them.'

Underwood's emotions tore at him. Dexter was speaking in code. She still was oblivious to the fact that he had discovered and befriended her father: the man that she hadn't seen for over twenty years was lying in a hospital bed not two miles from their current location. Had she suffered enough? Could he bear to inflict more pain on the woman he loved? He saw no answer to his dilemma on the chaotic London streets or the patterns of dirt on his windscreen.

'Do you ever think about him? Your dad, I mean?' he asked tentatively.

'Sometimes. My memory of him is vague though. I try not to dwell on it. If he was interested in me he'd have stayed in touch.'

Underwood turned towards Leytonstone.

'What if he thought it was in your best interests that he stay away?' he said.

'I'd say that the only person who should decide my best interests is me.'

'Supposing he was a criminal,' Underwood speculated, 'an armed robber or something. Getting in contact with you might damage your career. If he loved you he might stay out of the picture.'

'Unlikely,' Dexter mused. 'In any case, I did a Police Records Check on him a few years ago and it turned up nothing.'

There was no emotion in her voice to help him. Underwood tried to consider his options. His instincts told him that Alison Dexter would accept McInally's offer and return to Leyton CID. If that happened, then his last tenuous grip on her life would be torn away. It suddenly occurred to him that the decision was not his to make. In his experience, Alison Dexter's cold logic rarely let her down. His duty, as her friend, was simply to present her with all the available information. If he truly loved her, he would have to trust her to use that information properly. Only she could judge her interests. He would have to let go.

Underwood turned into Leytonstone High Road.

'You've got a bit lost,' Dexter observed, recognising some local landmarks. 'Take a right at the next lights.'

Underwood's heart raced. 'Alison, I need to make a stop. It's only a few minutes out of our way.'

'A stop where?' she asked, unable to fathom what possible connection Underwood could have with Leytonstone.

'Trust me,' he said without looking at her.

Underwood followed a black cab to the traffic lights. He turned left instead of right then crossed the next two sets of roundabouts. A few moments later he pulled up outside the Beech View Care Centre in Wilding Road.

'What's this place then?' Dexter asked, peering through the passenger window.

Underwood wondered for a moment how to answer. 'I want you to know that whatever happens, whether you stay in New Bolden or go back to London, you are not alone.'

'What are you talking about?'

Underwood climbed out of the car and walked towards the building. Leaves swirled on the ground. The cold, dry London wind scraped at his throat. Dexter joined him at the front entrance to the building.

'John, what is going on?'

Underwood didn't reply. He pushed open the door to the Beech View Care Centre and stepped inside. Hannah looked up from the reception desk.

'Good afternoon, Mr Underwood,' she said brightly, 'nice to see you again.'

'You too, Hannah,' Underwood said. 'Is it all right if we go up?'

'No problem. He's awake. He's listening to one of those football phone-ins on the radio.'

'Thank you.'

Underwood headed up the stairs with Alison Dexter snapping at his heels.

'John, are you going to give me a straight answer or not?' she asked irritably. 'You are beginning to freak me out. I though that we'd decided to be straight with each other.'

'You are a very suspicious person. You have to be more trusting.'

'Oh! That's rich coming from you,' she snorted. 'You are the most cynical old sod I've ever met.'

They arrived at the first floor landing. Underwood led her to room seven. He turned to face her lowering his voice to a whisper as he spoke.

'You need to be strong, Alison.'

'What are you talking about?'

Underwood pushed open the door. The room was small and square with whitewashed walls. An old man lay on a bed in the centre of the room.

Alison Dexter found herself looking into a pair of familiar green eyes.

'Hello, Alison,' said Gary Dexter softly.

Dexter found herself standing in stunned silence inside the little bedroom. The radio babbled. The pale, tired face in front of her concealed a person that she recognised. Slowly her mind broke down and reformed the man's features into those of the father she barely knew.

'I always said you'd turn out to be a right heartbreaker,' he said.

Unable to respond, conscious of tears building behind her eyes, Alison Dexter turned to John Underwood for an explanation.

But he had gone.

78.

Outside, Leytonstone was laughing at him. People pushed past him on the pavement as he walked. Minutes slipped into oblivion. He wondered at the monstrosity he had become. Bartholomew Garrod had physically consumed his victims, assimilated their primal cuts into his own being. Was he any different? He had tried to absorb Alison Dexter's life, her very personality, the essence of her being into himself. Love is the ultimate act of consumption. There were dark holes in his soul that he had desperately hoped she would fill. He had wanted to feel her strength, intelligence and fire within him as if they would burn away the cancers that dwelled there.

In the cold hard reality of that East London evening, Underwood could see the folly of his actions. Redemption was uniquely personal. His unrequited love, his failed consumption of Alison Dexter, had merely debased him further: it created more questions than it answered. Now it seemed that she would leave him altogether and return to the city that had fashioned her. Terrible though that prospect was to him, it did resolve the equation that had been infecting his thought processes. If she left his life there would truly be nothing in it worth clinging onto. That thought came not as a dark revelation but as a relief.

An hour passed. Underwood found himself back in Wilding Road. He tried to find consolation in the concrete rolling beneath him. At least her memories of him would be positive. At least he had shown the courage to let her go. In the darkest moments of the decay that lay ahead of him he could find some solace in that act of selflessness. It might be the only redemption he could hope for.

Alison Dexter was waiting for him by his car. He could see she had been crying. Her face was streaked and exhausted. Underwood felt a surge of shame as he sensed her pain and shock. He stood directly in front of her unable to find any words. It was obvious to him that he had said and done enough.

Without speaking, Alison Dexter suddenly enfolded her arms around him. Underwood was uncertain how to react. He stood awkwardly as she hung onto him in the quiet desolation of the roadside. He began to feel the warmth of her body streaming into him, filling the dark spaces, cauterising the cancers inside. Perhaps he could find sustenance in a friendship. Perhaps it could feed him with the will to fight.

And perhaps, in the months of adjustment and renewal that lay ahead, Alison Dexter might even begin to find some small comfort in him.

For John Underwood, that was the most encouraging thought of all.